*No Matter What*

**Cara Bastone** is a full-time writer who lives and writes in Brooklyn with her husband, son and an almost-golden doodle. Her goal with her work is to find the swoon in ordinary love stories. She's been a fan of the romance genre since she found a grocery bag filled with her grandmother's old Harlequin Romance books when she was in high school. She's a fangirl for pretzel sticks, long walks through Prospect Park, and love stories featuring men who aren't hobbled by their own masculinity.

To find out more, visit **carabastone.com** or follow Cara on X and Instagram @**carabastone**.

*By Cara Bastone*

Ready or Not
Promise Me Sunshine
No Matter What

*Love Lines Series*
Call Me Maybe
Sweet Talk
Seatmate

# Praise for Cara Bastone's rom-coms!

'Cara Bastone handles grief with an unflinchingly tender touch, reminding us that life goes on and love never dies. This story is tucked inside my heart for good'
**Jessica Joyce, *USA Today* bestselling author**

'Flawlessly crafted and deeply emotional, *Promise Me Sunshine* grabbed hold of my heart from the very first page and didn't let go. I was laughing, sobbing, and everything in between. The story left me breathless and stayed with me long after I reached The End'
**Amy Ewing, *New York Times* bestselling author**

'Bastone delivers on this truly heartwarming, funny, and real story. Come for the dog bar, stay for the special, slow-burn romcom'
**Abby Jimenez, *New York Times* bestselling author**

'*Ready or Not* is the very definition of the perfect slow burn, friends-to-lovers romance. Cara Bastone's voice is wholly unique and sparkles with effervescence and joy. I savored every page'
**KJ Dell'Antonia, *New York Times* bestselling author**

'An absolute treasure of a book! Cara Bastone gives readers a gift, and pays humanity a compliment, with this warmly witty, profoundly tender story of a love that makes the world bigger and better. One of the most emotionally satisfying romances I've read in years'
**Joanna Lowell**

'A wholehearted meditation on all kinds of love, this novel is pure joy'
**Annabel Monaghan**

'With loads of humor, lovable characters, and a first kiss that will leave you flushed and breathless, *Ready or Not* is a delightfully romantic story that celebrates modern love and the excitement of the unexpected. Readers will adore Cara Bastone's joyful, swoony novel!'
**Amy Poeppel**

'Cara Bastone is one of the most talented writers in the romance genre today. With her signature blend of heart, humor, and honesty, Cara's books remind you that the best stories begin and end with hope'
**Lyssa Kay Adams**

# No Matter What

Cara Bastone

Copyright © Cara Bastone 2026

The right of Cara Bastone to be identified as the Author of the Work has been
asserted by her in accordance with the Copyright, Designs and Patents Act 1988.

Published in agreement with The Dial Press
An imprint of Penguin Random House
A division of Penguin Random House LLC

First published in the UK in 2026 by Headline Eternal
An imprint of Headline Publishing Group Limited

This paperback edition published in 2026

1

Apart from any use permitted under UK copyright law, this publication may
only be reproduced, stored, or transmitted, in any form, or by any means,
with prior permission in writing of the publishers or, in the case of
reprographic production, in accordance with the terms of licences
issued by the Copyright Licensing Agency.

All characters in this publication are fictitious and any resemblance
to real persons, living or dead, is purely coincidental.

Cataloguing in Publication Data is available from the British Library

Paperback ISBN 978 1 0354 2741 3

Offset in 11/14.4pt GoudyOlSt BT by Six Red Marbles UK, Thetford, Norfolk

Printed and bound in Great Britain by Clays Ltd, Elcograf S.p.A.

Headline's policy is to use papers that are natural, renewable and recyclable
products and made from wood grown in well-managed forests and other
controlled sources. The logging and manufacturing processes are expected
to conform to the environmental regulations of the country of origin.

Headline Publishing Group Limited
An Hachette UK Company
Carmelite House
50 Victoria Embankment
London EC4Y 0DZ

The authorised representative in the EEA is Hachette Ireland,
8 Castlecourt Centre, Dublin 15, D15 XTP3, Ireland (email: info@hbgi.ie)

www.headlineeternal.com
www.headline.co.uk
www.hachette.co.uk

*For my mom and dad, who always answer the phone,
and who never seem to tire of reminding me that I am resilient.*

*And for San Telmo, which gave me something
to draw when I needed it the most.*

Drawing is the clarification of thought.
—HENRI MATISSE

In earlier times I used to draw the thing seen;
now I see the thing drawn.
—BRIDGET RILEY

Draw Antonio, draw Antonio.
Draw, and don't waste time.
—MICHELANGELO

# No Matter What

# One

*Is now a* good time to mention that my husband has been leaving me in increments (first the far side of the bed, then the guest room, and now, apparently, his own apartment) and I'm not taking it well?

**Lease start date August 15.**

Join me here, in my kitchen, with a glass of wine that's somehow found its way into my trembling hand, staring at this sheaf of paper I've just discovered, that my husband has pinned to the kitchen counter with a twenty-eight-ounce can of diced tomatoes.

So.

He's moving out.

What the fuck do we do with this? If you're like me, you might be asking yourself this very question.

Well, what the fuck *do* I do with it?

I set my wine down.

The fact that he's chosen a twenty-eight-ounce can of diced tomatoes to pin that lease to the counter suddenly feels a bit like a gauntlet.

Because, when my world is crumbling, I feed people.

Actually, when my world is gorgeous and peachy and shining with the light of a thousand Instagram filters, I feed people.

Can you guess the pattern?

I feed people!

He could have chosen a twelve-ounce can. He could have left it on the counter with nothing holding it in place.

He could have not *left* the lease out *at all* and relayed this information with *words* and *eye contact*, but no, who am I kidding, this is Vin we're talking about here.

Twenty-eight ounces? Game on.

I take the can and leave the lease. I don my second-favorite striped apron. The one that makes me feel like Queen Martha Stewart. I've never diced onions into neater squares. Never once peeled garlic with such speed. When they hit the hot oil in the pot, they sear with such a satisfying hiss I grin like the devil.

And now. For the fun part. I grab the diced tomatoes off the counter. The lease immediately skates a foot to the side in the breeze from our kitchen window. Every crank of the opener feels like cracking open the door to a room I'm not permitted to enter. The can pops open and I feel I've done something almost naughty. I'm supposed to be crying over these tomatoes, right?

Surely not simmering them.

I watch until they bubble on the stove.

Holding the immersion blender in one hand, I rev it in the air, yes, like that one murderer with the chain saw in those movies I've never actually seen. And then the sauce gets it. I'm turning those tomatoes to velvet in that pot. My hand slips on the immersion blender and tomato sauce paints a zebra stripe across the counter. And the lease.

A splash of red across the death certificate.

I season and simmer and stir. When the scent grows heady and rich and layered, when there's nothing left to do but clean up the kitchen, when the wine is gone but the tremble in my hand is not, I pick up the lease from the counter and fasten it to the fridge door like all of our to-do lists. Step one: get a divorce. Step two: buy mushrooms.

There's the unmistakable scrunch of keys in our apartment door. I reach out and swipe the stripe of sauce off the lease with one finger. It leaves a stain behind.

Vin steps into our apartment. I turn to him, just a normal woman in an apron.

He's got an intensely determined, did-she-see-it-yet look on his face. He's breathing hard. His endlessly green eyes dart from the empty kitchen counter to the fridge door and then to my face.

I lick the sauce off my finger.

"Sauce is on the stove if you're hungry."

One hand on the doorknob still, he looks again from the lease to me. I wait, interminably, for him to say anything.

And then he turns, and he walks back out, closing the door behind him, like he'd never even been there.

She was pretty.

She had a flower on her sweater. I don't know what kind. Not a real one. Part of the fabric. Actually it might have just been a shirt. Not a sweater. Why am I so bad at this?

She was pretty. Her smile. Her mouth. But mostly her eyes. When she smiled. Dark eyes. Friendly. That's what I remember. About the first time I ever saw her.

Imagine there's a world in which you just happen to know the address of the apartment your husband is moving into on August fifteenth. Imagine that address is Nine Five Four East 12th Street, apartment 9J.

And look, you're you. You're not me, but I suppose some of you, in your version of this imaginary world, *don't* Google Maps that apartment building and imagine him arriving there, after work, with those tired eyes he gets, and some of you, probably, would be like, *Screw him!* and fair, that's fair, but *I* might be kind of, sort of, dropping a pin on this location with cold, stiff fingers.

And that's that! Mystery solved, okay? Now I know where it is and I don't have to wonder about it anymore.

I *am* wondering who in God's name is going to drop my compost off at the drop-off point on Sunday mornings. Because one of the best parts of forming a partnership with someone is divvying up all the crap you didn't want to do in the first place.

And now he wants to undivvy? We already divvied! You can't take back a divvy!

I'm saved from myself—and this moment, and getting lost in a perpetual loop of trying to make the word *divvy* sound like an actual word again (do I have bad taste or would that make a really cute baby name? [for someone else's baby, of course])— by a text from my erratic but brilliant custom framing guy.

*Frame is ready. Leaving for Montreaux in half an hour. You can get it next week if you can't make it.*

His name is, I kid you not, St. Michel, and he does extremely fine, shockingly cheap work but his shop does not keep regular hours and occasionally he'll keep your project hostage for a year. And I definitely need this framed portrait now. It's Vin's mother's birthday gift, and her birthday is in two days.

*On my way!*

I turn off the heat, put a lid on the sauce, shove my feet into running shoes (because I'll need them), and jog out the door. I skid from one bus to another and then sprint the last two blocks to the shop. I'm forty feet away when I see him step out onto the sidewalk with a rolly bag.

"St. Michel! I'm here!"

He turns, his silver hair hidden under a beanie even though it's seventy degrees outside. I make it to his side and sag against the bricks of his building, panting, melting, trying very hard not to puke on his, surely, cobbled shoes.

"Darling," he says with a frown. "What is this look?"

Look, I'm not high-fashion, but normally I can throw a silhouette together. I'm on the shorter side, with dark hair I keep in bangs straight down to my eyebrows and a pair of, admittedly, gigantic glasses. I have—if not style—*a* style. And let's just say it doesn't normally include bike shorts, knee socks, a sweatshirt, running shoes, and my hair in a pile on my head.

"Well, I didn't have much warning before I left the house!" I have my hands on my hips and a scowl on my face. St. Michel responds positively to light derision.

"Right, right. Your project. Let's go." He keys us into his darkened shop and we walk straight back to the work area. It smells like freshly sawn wood and polyurethane. He doesn't bother flipping on the lights.

He hands me a brown paper package, eleven by fourteen, and when my fingers close around it, they start to tingle.

"Open, open!" he demands. "I have a flight."

Normally I'd be peeling back the tape and inspecting his work. The first time I ever did this was to make sure I'd gotten what I'd paid for. Every time since then has simply been to make him preen with compliments because his work is just *that* good. But now, the weight of the frame in my hands, I'm suddenly remembering which photo he's framed and I just can't do it. I can't look at that right now.

"I don't want to make you late!" I say instead, and head back out through the shop. "What's in Montreaux?" I ask as he relocks the shop and drags his bag to the curb, his hand already in the air for a cab.

"Montreaux," he responds, as if I'm absurd for even asking.

"Just going to sightsee?"

A cab pulls up and St. Michel walks around to the back and pulls open the trunk. He tosses his bag in and turns to look at me, hands on his hips. "What is going on with you?" His eyes are narrowed.

I don't usually make small talk in knee socks while I wait to wave goodbye to him on the street.

It's possible I'm coming off a little wrecked.

And he's just such a *handsome* older man. With his one silver tooth and vintage peacoat. I once ran into him on a Tuesday morning drinking an aperitif at an outdoor café and eating oysters. On a Tuesday morning! He's a man of the world with a sharp and realistic view on life, and maybe that's why I clutch the package to my chest and say my worst fear.

"My husband is moving out. I think I might be getting a divorce."

My eyes fill and he disappears into a blur of light and color.

Something cold touches my face and then again. I dash my tears away and realize that a light drizzle has started up.

The cabdriver calls something terse out the passenger-side window and St. Michel waves a dismissive hand toward him. And then he's there, right in front of me. He puts one finger under my chin, a light, friendly touch.

"Darling," he says.

I'm rapt.

He's about to say something medicinal and necessary, I can feel it.

"Divorce is *fine*."

"Oh . . ."

And then he kisses me brusquely on the cheek and waves his hand over his head as he walks back to the cab and slides away down the street.

"Okay," I say to myself. "So . . ."

The bus stop is two blocks away and the brown paper around my package is already starting to dampen from the drizzle.

*Mad dash home!* is the logical train of thought, probably.

But . . . here's the thing about having memorized the address of the apartment that your husband is moving into on August fifteenth . . . here's the thing about having put it into Google Maps . . . and having pinned it on the map . . . it beats like a blinking cursor on the map in your head.

Which is what is happening to me. Right this very second.

The rain is increasing from a drizzle to a more insistent pitter-patter, enough that I see a drip form at the end of my bangs. This package is not going to survive if I keep standing on the curb in front of St. Michel's shop.

I can't keep standing still. I have to move.

So I shove the package under my sweatshirt as best I can and start to run. In the direction of the bus stop, and home. Within moments my socks and shoes are soaked. It's dumping rain now, and a buffet of wind tosses a sheet of water onto me from the side. There's the bus stop at the end of the block!

Here it is!

There it goes!

I keep running right on past.

In front of me, cars slice a gigantic puddle in half. The light changes, I jump the puddle, scamper across the street, there's rain down my back. This is such a bad idea that the universe is attempting to stop me in my tracks with bodily discomfort. But I've chosen belligerence. I press on.

There's a yellow awning up ahead and I sprint.

I make it there and huddle up onto the single stair, out of the worst of the downpour.

Nine Five Four. The enormous metal numbers leer down at me.

It's a brick building, this new address of Vin's. I can't see, because the rain has turned the world gray and opaque, but I bet there are flowers on the windowsills. Probably someone upstairs plays grand piano with their window open on the sunny days. There is probably a band of plucky and precocious children who knock on the doors of their neighbors to deliver the kugel their mothers have just made too much of.

This is clearly the most charming apartment building in all five boroughs and I hate it.

I'm just about finished cursing it, about to drag my soggy ass back into the pouring rain, when the foggy glass door behind me comes open an inch and shunts me back onto the street, out of the cover of the awning.

"Honey, come in! Come in!" a voice says behind me.

There's rain sliding down the back of my neck, wetting my eyelashes, dripping off my ears.

Come in? As in enter the premises? Of Nine Five Four? Unthinkable.

"Come in!" she says again, and this time she grips my wrist and tugs. All my aforementioned belligerence washes away into meek obedience. Maybe I'm too soaked? Maybe she's just the right amount of bossy? I stumble through the door and gasp with relief when I step into a warm, dry hallway. The door slams shut behind me.

"Are you Miri?" she asks.

I wipe at my glasses and turn to see my savior. She's got big brown eyes and a long gray braid spiraled into a crown on her head. She's wearing a cashmere sweater set and New Balance sneakers.

"Oh. No, I'm Roz."

"Ah. Well. We're waiting on Miri." She cracks the door and sticks her head out, peering through the torrential rain. She ducks back in and shrugs. "They sent me to wait here for participants but with this rain . . . We always lose a few on the first day anyhow. People sign up but don't end up showing. Come on, then."

Her voice is so full of authority that I almost take a step after her. "Sorry, I . . . I'm not signed up." I actually don't know what this is. Isn't this an apartment building?

She stops and beckons me. "It's raining. At least come sit. I think there are towels in the classroom."

As I follow her down the hallway (hardwood floors and a mop bucket off to one side, a cheerily flickering line of lights along the wall, rows of doors with nameplates instead of numbers), I see that this is a mixed-use building. We pass a dermatologist's office, a therapist, a door that just says MR. GREG in all caps, and then, finally, on to the only open doorway in the hallway.

She disappears through and I peek in after her. It's bright and merry in there. Ten or so people chatting and milling. Ah. I see. It's a figure drawing class. They're setting up their easels in a circle, sharpening pencils, flipping gigantic sheets of paper to the clean side. In the middle of the circle is a midtwenties man with spiky black hair and a terry-cloth robe to his knees. He's sitting on a wooden platform, leaning on his palms and yawning hugely.

"Miri? Hi, I'm Daniel. The instructor," a man says from next to me in the doorway. He's middle-aged, trim brown beard and friendly eyes, just an inch or two taller than I am.

"No. This is Roz," calls the older woman as she digs through a big set of drawers in the corner. "I'm calling Miri as a no-show."

The man smiles fondly at her. "Esther is our registrar."

"Ah."

Esther pads back to me, hand towel in tow. "Here you go, love."

After a moment's consideration, I pull the packaged frame out from under my sweatshirt, which makes both Esther and the man laugh in surprise. Then I gratefully take the towel and scrunch at my hair, wipe off my soaking wet legs.

"If you wanted to stay and warm up," Daniel the instructor says, "you could take the class. We're not at capacity, you know."

"Oh." I'm completely befuddled by this suggestion.

Doesn't he know that I haven't picked up a pencil to draw since middle school? Doesn't he see that I'm soaking wet and need to go home and change into my fuzzy slippers? And most importantly, that I'm only here because I'm creeping on my husband's new address and under no circumstances was I actually supposed to *enter* this building?

He's looking at me expectantly and all I've said is "Oh."

I try again. "Um . . ."

I attempt to summon all that sauce-making ferocity from earlier this evening. Unfortunately, I'm only coming up with the sort of exhaustion you get when you realize you might be about to start your entire life from scratch.

His eyebrows rise in a friendly way. "Lots of beginners in the class."

"Right."

"'Scuse me," says a deep voice at my back.

I jump to the side and a man who, I shit you not, looks exactly like Aladdin, is grinning, dripping wet, peering down at me from under a raincoat.

"Sorry!"

"No worries." He gives me a lingering, seashell-white smile; he has friendly eyes and floppy black hair. As he walks past me, he pulls his hood down and I get a whiff of his scent. He smells like Louis Vuitton's rich Gen Z grandson.

"Lauro!"

"Laur-*oh*!"

"It's my man."

The class has perked up immensely at this man's presence and he makes his rounds, bussing cheeks, giving daps, and finally, one enormous hug to the model, who doesn't seem to mind embracing a sopping wet raincoat.

"So, Roz." Daniel checks his watch and then looks down at my feet, neatly lined up in the hallway, while my head peeks around the doorway. "In or out. Class is about to start and we keep the door closed during session out of respect for our model."

"I'm not signed up . . ." I say again, uselessly, as if it will stop time and prevent any sort of decision from needing to be made. I could just drip on this doorstep into infinity, enjoying the vibes and risking nothing.

"First one's free." He winks but then jolts as Esther pops up from nowhere.

"No, it's not," she says. "But if you decide to sign up you can pay later."

"I don't have any supplies . . ."

"We have plenty extra lying around," Daniel insists.

"I'm soaking wet . . ."

"Live with it?" he suggests, and I laugh.

It looks so warm and bright in there. The people, each very different from the next, seem to know one another well. The air is rich with charcoal and wax and paper. This is how some people spend an early Friday evening in June.

Esther fans every imaginable shade of colored pencils in front of me. "Pick a color," she says sternly.

Sometimes, someone tells you to do something and you just do it. Which is how I find myself with a forest-green colored pencil in my hand and a pad of paper on my lap. Daniel's gone to find an easel for me, so I'm sitting on a free stool and trying not to draw attention to myself. Even though I'm soaking wet and wearing knee socks and the only person not chatting freely with someone else.

Glancing up at the model in the robe (peeling a banana and still doing some pre-class chitchat), I figure I better quickly check and see if there is some sort of prodigious hidden talent I'm about to unearth. Perhaps the universe has plunked me on this wobbly stool for a reason.

But, yeah, just as I thought. No. No, I'm not secretly amazing at drawing. The model, wiry and vivacious in real life, is reduced to a lumpy, squat little alienoid on my paper.

What am I even doing here?

"Oh. That's wonderful." I startle and turn to see Daniel, easel in hand, peering at my paper. "So, I see you already have an established drawing practice!" he says.

"Absolutely not," I say.

He laughs and then studies my drawing again. "Well, then you're just naturally talented."

Either he's seeing something I'm not or he's a hell of a salesman. I narrow my eyes. "Are we looking at the same blob?"

He laughs. "No, seriously. Most newbies drawing the figure . . . they just try to copy exactly what they're seeing and put it down on the page. But look, what you're doing with Alan . . . you're building him part by part. Constructing him. As an *idea*, not a likeness. Not easy to do with a stubby colored pencil. Very cool." He gives me a double thumbs-up. Someone calls his name and he leaves me there with the empty easel and a possibly terrible drawing on my lap.

My toe hits one wet corner of the packaged frame resting on the floor and the paper wrinkles accusingly. I wince and gather it up, clutching it against my chest.

What would it be like to have the chutzpah to just start a new life? To be someone who goes to drawing class on Friday nights with a roomful of strangers? What would it be like to be brave enough to even *wonder* about life without Vin?

I don't find the answer.

Because I want my old life back, not a new hobby. Because I've failed at marriage and I don't know if I can handle being bad at one more thing.

I'm on my feet and meeting Daniel at the door to the classroom, where he's about to close it up and start class.

"I really have to go," I whisper.

"Sure," Daniel says easily. "In that case . . ." He gestures for me to step out into the hallway. At the last second, he pokes his head back out into the hall and catches my eye. "I'm closing this, but door's always open. I mean, again, not literally, because like I said we keep it closed during class. But if you want to come back. Come back. Okay. Get home safe."

And then the door is closed in my face and the light dims accordingly.

I walk back down the hallway toward the rain. Because the framed photo is beating like a heart on its last few pumps. Because I really don't think I can try something new when everything old in my life is dying.

I waited a week before I asked Raff about her. No, wait, I should tell about the night I first saw her. But we weren't together yet. So maybe that part doesn't matter. Whatever. I waited a week. That's probably what she would say was the important part.

(What do you think is the most important part?)

I really, honestly, don't know how to tell this story. It's supposed to be the story of how we met, right? That's the assignment.

(Start at the beginning.)

Which beginning? She's my wife. The story of who I am to her, the story of what kind of husband I am, all that starts decades before I even met her.

(Start anywhere!)

(Just start!)

(There's no wrong answer!)

Okay. Anywhere. Okay. Well. Have you ever met someone for the first time and it seems like you've already known them for a really long time?

I spent a week trying to figure out where I knew her from.

And then I figured it out.

(Where?)

(Where was it?)

Nowhere. I didn't know her from anywhere. I just . . . I just recognized her. Remember that sweater I talked about before? The one I couldn't describe? Flower or whatever? Well, she walked in, wearing that sweater, and her hair and that smile and I just . . . recognized her. That's the best I can describe it.

I saw her and thought, *Here comes my wife.*

# Two

*For the record*, I'm not a total loser.

I, for instance, have places to go and people to see.

Or rather, I have one person to see and one place to go with that particular person.

It's the next night after I found Vin's lease, I haven't seen him since he walked out of our apartment, and having plans with someone who wants me around feels a bit, oh, *vitally important* right now.

Luckily, I've already received the very common *You're doing what I tell you to do tonight* text from my best friend, Raffi.

Raffi is the sort of person who can take an unbothered shit in a public restroom. When he wants to fuck someone, he asks, nicely, if he can. Generally the answer is a yes. He's messier than he is handsome, more colorful than he is stylish, and wears mittens instead of gloves in the wintertime.

Our friendship is laughter-forward with top notes of *Project Runway* and Bruce Springsteen. Base notes of showing up for one another on our darkest days. Which we've both, unfortunately, had a lot of this year.

He's lived in this new apartment for two months now, but I'm still not used to the fact that he doesn't live in my guest bedroom anymore. It feels weird to have to knock on a front door to access my best friend. He's supposed to just already be sitting at my kitchen table.

I knock and hear him throwing the locks from the other

side. I'm already calling to him. "Hurry up, hurry up, I have to pee! Oh—"

I cut off because it's not Raffi who's opened the door. It's my husband.

Okay, one more thing to know about Raffi:

He's Vin's little brother.

Which is how I met Vin.

So. Yeah. *That's* a thing.

"Hi," he of the green eyes says to me. He's also fled our marital home and come to Raffi's.

"Hi?" I reply, because what is anyone supposed to say in this awful situation?

The moment stretches and he scratches the back of his neck. "I was just gonna go. I know you two have plans."

"Oh. Okay."

"You, uh, have to pee?" He's stepping aside from the door, beckoning me in.

I can hear Raff loudly singing a Madonna B side while water splats onto the shower floor. The bathroom is clearly occupied. "I'll wait."

"Okay."

I still haven't entered Raff's apartment. "I put your mother's birthday gift on your bed." *Which you'd know if you'd come home last night. Which you didn't.*

"Oh." He doesn't even ask what it is.

"I got a portrait framed for her. I picked it up yesterday."

"From St. Michel?"

"Yeah."

There's a long pause. He's looking at the floor, then glancing up at me. His eyes are green fire. "Did you check it?"

Since when does he care if I check St. Michel's work? "I'm sure it's fine."

His gaze drops. "Right."

I can't help it. My eyes narrow and something hot and ugly licks to life in my insides. That was *not* a thank-you. For organizing and executing his mother's gift, in time for him to drive it up for her birthday tomorrow, no less.

"*You* can check it, if you want." *If you're so worried about it, dickhead* is what I definitely don't say.

"Okay."

I can't help it. I *have* to ask. "What are you going to tell her?"

"Who?"

"Your mom."

"What am I going to tell her about what?"

What other topic could I possibly be addressing right now? "About us."

"What about us."

I'm going to either scream or burst into tears. Why is he making me say this out loud?

"That you're *moving out*."

My blood is firework-fizzling with adrenaline, everything is fuzzy around the edges. Almost nothing could have hurt me more than this emergency exit strategy, this I'm-getting-out-of-here-without-even-a-word.

His nostrils flare and his lips purse. Looking into Vin's eyes used to give me the same sense of safety that tucking blankets up to my chin does. I used to call him Vinny Green Eyes. But now, with his new beard obscuring the bottom half of his face, he looks like a different man. His eyes are suddenly so fierce upon me that it physically hurts to hold eye contact.

Luckily, he rips his eyeline away and slowly scrubs his hands over his face, beard and all.

"I'm not going to tell her that," he says low.

"Yeah. I guess that makes sense considering you didn't even bother to tell *me*."

His face just sort of shuts down. I'm fatiguing him already.

Throughout our marriage, interactions between us have often had this sort of pacing:

Long pause . . . Finally Vin says something.

I immediately reply!

Long pause . . .

This pattern repeats into infinity.

He lets out a long breath (after the requisite long pause). "And what am I supposed to say?"

"I don't know, Vin. *Words* might have been nice."

His mouth opens, then closes. His lips purse again and his eyes pinch closed. He's got both hands laced over the top of his head. He tries to speak but falters again. Tries again. "Roz . . . Nothing . . . has been the same since the accident—"

I can't help it. It's a defensive thing. My hands fly up and cover my eyes. "Can you *not* bring up the accident without a warning? *Please?*"

I hate the word *accident*. It has a certain slicing ring to it that makes me instantly queasy. The rest of his sentence slips in through the wound of hearing that word when I didn't expect it. *Nothing has been the same* . . . Yeah. No shit.

"I can't do this," he mutters. His hands drop down and he crowds the doorway, trying to get past me into the hallway, but I don't cede ground.

"So you're just—" My voice gives way. "You're just leaving."

"No. I mean I *literally* can't do *this*." He points at his heart and then at mine.

By which I think he means deal with me in any capacity.

"Wow."

This feeling in my gut? It's like if someone threw you a surprise party but for bad news. "Eight years, Vin. Eight years and you're just *done* without even a word."

There's a snap in his gaze. A pulse of fury. At me. An emotion so strong it gusts off him. When he speaks, his voice is low and strung as tight as a cello. "Roz. *If you think*—"

"You're here!" Raff is slamming out of the bathroom with a little purple towel cinched around his waist. "Sorry, sorry! Lemme just get dressed and I'll be ready!"

And then he's locked in his bedroom and Vin and I are locked in silence, breathing hard and looking anywhere but at each other.

"There are two months until the lease starts," Vin says tightly.

"Oh, great. Wonderful. Should be a really comfortable living situation until then." I thought our permafrost was bad before this? I can only imagine how the next two months are going to feel. Like getting slowly crushed to death by a glacier, probably.

His eyes are closed again. He's so frustrated he's practically vibrating. He takes a long, slow breath. Seconds tick past. "Do you want me to move in with Raffi in the meantime?"

Obviously I'm handing him knives here, but I didn't, actually, expect him to stab me with them. I make a sound that I hope registers as disgust, and not as mortal pain. "*No*. No, I don't even want you to tell Raffi this is happening."

His eyes search mine until I look away. I can feel his questions, but he doesn't ask them. "Okay. Fine. We won't tell Raffi."

"Yet."

"And I'll stay in the guest room."

"Great." He's been there since Raff moved out anyways.

Raffi is going to be coming out any second and if he sees us in this standoff, he's going to know something is terribly wrong without us having to tell him.

I finally step aside, my arms tightly crossed against my

chest. I point toward the hallway with my chin. "If you're leaving, then . . ." *Do it now.*

His eyes drop. "I'll go."

And just like that, we're sliding past one another in a tight doorway. We don't touch, our hearts pass within an inch.

And that, friends, is what a conversation with my husband is like!

Okay, okay, so maybe I haven't been a total peach this year either.

Those first few weeks after the accident . . .

A snapshot: Me awake at four A.M. in sweatpants I haven't changed in two days. I'm on the couch in the living room so I don't wake up Vin, who is sleeping fitfully anyways. The lights are off even though I know I should just give in and turn them on and read, because who am I fooling? I'm not going to sleep. Then there's a noise, it's Vin. He's up and stumbling out of our room. Shoot. He woke up and I wasn't there. He's come to find me. But he hasn't. He doesn't notice me on the couch. He goes straight for the industrial-sized bottle of ibuprofen on the kitchen counter. He takes the medicine and drinks straight from the faucet, rests against the counter with his eyes closed, goes back to bed.

And then I'm awake before sunrise, sweating and aggravated, clinging two-handedly to a cup of coffee that does nothing but make me nervous. Check the schedule for doctor's appointments, phone calls with our lawyers, and errands (usually to the pharmacy) that need to be done. Make breakfast. And then the fun stuff. Changing Raffi's bandages, administering pain meds. He was badly concussed from the accident and had to have major surgery on his dominant arm, so . . . in addition to housing him in our guest room I was also helping him get dressed and wash his hair and eat. I was the only one of the three of us who wasn't injured enough to have to take leave from work, but I took it anyways just so they'd have someone there to put meals on the table and count NSAIDs. Vin's injuries were technically less severe than Raffi's—he hadn't needed surgery—but he still needed everything else. Pain meds, bandage changing, and PT so he could get used to how to move his body with a fourteen-inch scar down his back.

Then the months after the accident . . .

A snapshot: Vin's back at work, so a lot of the time it's just me and Raffi. Raffi's still on leave. Four times a week we head to PT, where he spends time practicing how to pick up a pencil and squeezing stress balls for strength. He gets so frustrated that sometimes he screams into our couch pillows when he gets home. I've learned how to (metaphorically) tap-dance. Anything and everything to keep Raff buoyant. Movie marathons, online shopping, tea parties, at-home pedicures, literally anything he wants to eat. When he goes to sleep, I go to sleep, utterly exhausted. Most nights, I only know Vin's finally home from work when the sheets tug against me as he's crawling into bed.

Then two months ago . . .

A snapshot: We're all back at work now. Raffi's doing so much better. Taking life by the horns again. Correspondingly (now that I'm not the one driving his ship) I'm starting to buckle. I spend more and more time in my bed, Raff spends more and more time wheedling me out into the world with cronuts and trips to the Museum of Ice Cream. We spend one weekend moving him into his new apartment. When we get back home, Vin sits on the couch, completely wiped. "Well," he says with a shrug. And that about sums it up. It's just the two of us again. The silence from Raff's recently vacated room is excruciating. The silence in our bed that night is even more excruciating. We barely sleep. Our house feels wrong without

Raff. Our house feels wrong with just the two of us. It's suddenly extremely clear that we have nothing to say to one another if Raff isn't there, ricocheting our words back and forth. I sleep on the farthest edge of the bed I possibly can and wake up with no covers. Vin's already gone to work. I don't see him until dinnertime. He asks me a question about our electricity bill and then goes to bed. This goes on for two days.

On the third day, I'm reading in bed and Vin is standing next to it. He picks up his pillow.

"I'm just gonna . . ." he says, and points behind him, toward the guest room.

He sleeps there that night. And he never comes back.

When Raff emerges from his bedroom, Vin is gone and I'm safely ensconced in the tiny kitchen. I've decided to hide the tremble in my heart by slicing the baguette laid out on the counter. I have the general idea to just do an impression of myself tonight. That should disguise the wreckage, right?

"Smells great!" Raff calls as he tosses his towel into the bathroom.

"Why do you sound surprised? Didn't you make it? And go hang up your towel, you mongrel."

He pops into the bathroom and back out. "You're the one who made dinner."

"Me?"

"Vin brought it over. I just boiled the pasta."

I set down the bread knife and eye the stove. There's pasta in a colander and . . . a pot of something that does, indeed, smell delicious. My blood's gone cold.

Raffi's voice fades out behind me and my steps echo. I approach the stove, reach out a hand, lift the lid, and—dammit! The lid is hot and I jostle the pot trying to get my hand free. A mini tsunami of Divorce Tomato Sauce douses me from boobs to hips.

"Are you all right?" Raff is at my side, eyes wide, handing me paper towels.

I close my eyes and let out a long breath. "Fine."

When I open my eyes, my white T-shirt and jean shorts are still ruined. I look like I belong in an episode of *CSI*.

As I stand there, covered in sauce, my resolve wobbles. I almost tell Raff everything. He's my best friend and I need him. But then those recent, injured months rear up within me again. I've gotten it reversed. Really, I'm *his* best friend and he needs *me*. My first instincts were right. If I tell him that Vin is moving out, he's going to break.

"You have anything I can change into?" I ask.

"Sure. Go get cleaned up. I'll grab it." His eyes are still wide.

I don't think I'm nailing this impression of myself.

I rinse my clothes in his bathroom sink and he passes in a folded-up pair of light green sweatpants and a sweatshirt. I freeze, arms halfway through sleeves and head buried in cloth. Because this sweatshirt smells like Vin. I would bet my life savings that he's recently worn these clothes.

I finish getting dressed and then look at myself in the mirror. Cozy, mussed, swimming in cloth, smelling like my husband: I've been here before. Many times. But in happier circumstances.

"Did Vin wear these?" I ask Raff (in my normal voice, thank you very much) as I reemerge.

His brow comes down. "Those are his."

I look down at the clothes again. Spring green, hope green, I bet his eyes sparkle like a fucking disaster in this color. I do not recognize these clothes.

"He brought them over to wear when he slept here last night," Raff says, with the slight tang of *duh* in his voice.

"Right." I eye the rest of the treacherous sauce on the stove. It bubbles in the pot like a potion.

I shouldn't care. It would be so much easier if I just didn't care. But . . .

"Did—" I clear my throat. "Did he eat before he left?"

"Nah. He said he wasn't hungry."

I watch the sauce bubble. He couldn't bring himself to eat it. But he eats literally anything I cook. I guess not anymore.

I stand here in his clothes from yesterday. Because he slept here. Clothes I don't recognize.

*I'll go.*

"I'm actually—" I clear my throat again. "I'm actually not very hungry either."

"Are you sure? Big night ahead of us." He's serving himself an obscenely large bowl.

"Wait, really? Oh no. It's not funtivities, is it?"

Raffi has recently become obsessed with Groupon. Which sort of makes sense. He's extremely excitable. He'd be the one leading the standing ovation at the octogenarian choir concert, et cetera. And now he's become very excited about dragging me around New York to experience all our city has to offer (on a budget).

In the last two months we've already gotten dubious pedicures in the East Village ($14.50 apiece), fed the budgies at the Bronx Zoo (8 bucks apiece and patently terrifying), and gone to see bad stand-up (25 dollars apiece and Raff went home with one of the comics).

So why am I doing all of these terrible activities? Am I really just that supportive of a pal?

No.

I'm doing it because where else do I really have to be? Home? Obviously not.

At this point, if Raffi used a Groupon for us to get our leg hair tweezed off hair by hair, I'd go with him. Just to spend time with someone with a teaspoon of affection for me. Just to get the hell out of my silent apartment.

Which is why, an hour later, I have an enormous goblet of wine in one hand and a paintbrush in the other.

"Excuse me. Are we supposed to be painting what the instructor is painting? Or is this, like, free-form?"

Raffi and I turn to the woman who has just addressed us. She's looking worriedly between her painting and ours. Hers looks very similar to the instructor's, who is, in fact, providing a step-by-step of how to turn a white canvas into a non-ironic sunset over a titanium ocean. "I just wanted to make sure I hadn't misunderstood," the woman further prompts.

If she's looking to our work for guidance, I can see why she's worried.

I've decided that sunsets are a little too on the nose for me and, perhaps with that drawing class in mind, have embarked, instead, on an all-blue portrait of Raff's profile. He looks like Cookie Monster.

Raff, to his credit, has done a sunset. He's just added a sinking oil tanker. As I watch, he beaches a whale in the sand.

"You're doing great," I assure the woman. "We're just absurd."

"Speak for yourself!" Raffi insists, taking an enormous gulp of wine and then painting blue blobby tears dripping out of the whale's eyes. "I'm painting for my life over here."

It's a joke, and the woman laughs. I, on the other hand, don't laugh. Because also it's not a joke.

He *is* painting for his life. Just like he jogs for his life every morning and showers for his life before work. Just like he got a pedicure for his life and let birds attack his hands at the Bronx Zoo, for his life.

Those tears Raff is painting onto the whale may look comically juvenile, but, look, it's been an epically shit year for us. He does anything he can to keep moving forward.

Raff empties the rest of his bottle of wine into his glass, nearly overflowing it. "It's missing something," he muses about his painting. "It needs a touch more emotional impact."

"More emotional impact? You've already harpooned a whale!"

"Oh!" He has an epiphany. "I know! The whale needs a buddy." He quickly paints in another whale, tiny in the distance. Trapped in its own life in the water, unable to get to its loved one dying on the beach.

"This is supposed to be *fun*," I gripe at him. Not humiliating. I'm not supposed to get misty in public over a whale painted so badly it looks like a wool sock.

"Is it?" he asks. He turns to me with a quizzical expression in place.

"Quit it!" I scold him. He's convinced I've got an ocean of tears dammed up on the inside. A dying whale sinking to the bottom of my gut. He's certain that I'm just one bad painting away from baring my soul and finally getting over this terrible year.

Well, he's in for a surprise when he finds out Vin's leaving me.

I turn my eye back to my own painting of Raff. Well, it's not really a painting. It's more like a drawing that happens to be with a paintbrush. But still . . .

"I'm building him, huh? Part by part . . ." I'm remembering what Daniel the drawing teacher said about my bad drawing of the model.

"What'd you say?" Raff asks.

"Nothing. Just this thing that someone said to me . . ." I almost don't tell him. But I'm straining under the pressure of all the things I'm not saying to Raff. So, "I wandered into this figure drawing class yesterday."

He immediately perks up. "Really! So cool!"

"The instructor actually seemed to like my drawing. He said something about how instead of trying to draw a likeness of the model, I was putting him together on the paper. Piece by piece."

"That fits."

"What do you mean?"

He shrugs. "I mean . . . that's what you do. You're not trying to make anything look pretty. You're trying to fit it all together. So it works."

I chew on this.

"Are you gonna go back to the art class? I think you should!" Raff insists. Nothing would make him happier than me embarking on a journey of personal growth.

The instructor comes over to look at Raff's whales, and he turns his attention to charming the pants off her (likely literally, as there's a fifty-fifty chance she goes home with him tonight, if history is any indicator), so I take an unobserved second to lift my paintbrush again. There's a big patch of white in the bottom corner. I decide to fill it with another blue Raff, smaller this time. I catch him gesticulating, a familiar posture. The thing I paint doesn't look like a human, exactly, and certainly not a specific human. But there's something there, a slant of line, that does, in fact, call Raff to mind.

The paint is somehow both blobby and too thin. Unwieldy.

I don't think I'm doing myself any favors with jumping headfirst into painting. On a whim (or maybe with Daniel's voice still in my head), I reach into the art supplies basket and just grab a Sharpie.

I try one more Raff, this one in marker and almost microscopic in order to fit in the white space. As I draw him, I spike up his hair, give him all ten fingers.

It's not a likeness. But it is Raff. The idea of him, at least. Constructed and alive, on the page.

For the first time since I found that lease, I realize my brain is calm, my thoughts are quiet. I take a long breath and it washes down all the way to my toes.

Ugh. It's annoying when your friends actually know what's good for you. I'd rather rot in my own despair.

It's time to leave now. The instructor, I realize, is actually all dolled up. A glossy black blowout and cat-eye makeup. She's shooing us out of the classroom, I'm assuming she has a big date with someone she thinks might be her whole future. Or maybe she just wants to get laid. Either way, class is over and once again my possibilities are limited. The world is narrowing in again. She pushes us out onto the street. We're halfway down the block when I realize I left my painting behind.

It's fitting really, that I managed to capture someone I love, ensconce them safely on a canvas, and then I leave it behind by accident. I want the dim, tipsy classroom back. I don't want to be out here, in reality, in a world where I don't even know where my husband is.

I'm not . . . I didn't write anything down today. Is that okay?
(Go, baby, go!)

Okay. I'll try to do this, like, free-form, then. Okay. So, I'm sure it's weird to be happy on a bad day. Has that happened to any of you before?

(What do you mean?)

I mean... okay, well, I can't think of other examples, so I'll just tell you what I'm talking about. It was back when I was first dating Roz.

(Roz again!)

(This guy is obsessed.)

(OMG shut up, let him talk, I die every time he talks about her.)

So, we'd been together about two months. And I'd never met anyone like her. Also... I'd never been treated like that before. Like... a princess?

(Yes!)

(Every man deserves to get treated like a princess!)

(Say more, baby!)

Ha. Yeah. Well, it's true. Roz is the sort of person that if you see a commercial for a certain food and you say, oh, that looks good, then tomorrow night she'll have made it from scratch for you. She would walk past a store and see a sweatshirt she thought would look good with my eyes and then bring it home for me. Just, like, on a Wednesday. It didn't have to be my birthday or anything... Let's see... She came with me to wait in line at the DMV.

(That's love, right there!)

(Keeper!)

Right? I went from doing everything. For myself, for my mom, for my brother. Then suddenly I had someone using a magnifying glass and tweezers to pull a splinter out of the bottom of my foot. Wait... where was I? I lost my train of thought.

(Bad day!)

(The topic is Bad Day!)

Oh, yeah. Thanks. Anyways, it was early days, and happy as I was with her, I was starting to worry a little bit. I guess . . . I guess I was thinking I was kind of useless in comparison to her? Like deadweight? Well, then I got laid off. I'd been working for a home renovation crew and getting really good at it, but hard times, yadda yadda, I'd been the newest hire, I was the first to go. So, I have this new girlfriend, who I already feel like is out of my league. And she's so thoughtful and feeding me and clothing me and . . . I'm about to show up for our date and tell her that I'm unemployed now. I just thought . . . there's a chance this is it. There's a chance she's going to count all the tally marks and realize there just aren't enough. So, as I'm walking, I'm looking in the shop windows, thinking, should I buy her a sweater that would match her eyes? Then I'm passing a grocery store and I'm thinking, which foods did she mention liking and could I ever cook them? But I don't really land on anything and before I know it, I'm already to her apartment, where we are meeting for our date.

Usually, when she'd open the door, she'd be, you know, with the makeup and the hair and the outfit. And if we were staying in, there'd be something for dinner. I'm making it sound like I was expecting her to do all that, which I really wasn't, I swear. It just was a fact. That was what she did. But this night, she had, like, sweats on. And she was standing there like this.

(HA)

So, I asked, I said, are you sick?

(HAHAHAHAHA)

(OH NOOOOOOO)

Yes, well, I can see that all of you know that that is always the wrong thing to ask someone. And that was the first time she ever called me a butthead. The first of very, very many. "No, you butthead," she said. "I'm just grumpy."

She gets these days, maybe three or four times a year, when she's just grumpy and there's nothing she can do about it and she just has to wait it out. But . . . it made me happy. Because even on that day. Like, if that day had a title, up until that moment, it would just have been "Vin Is a Failure." But then I realized that the title could change. I could change it to "Vin Has an Opportunity." So I came into her house, popped popcorn, and then picked her up and tucked us into the couch and put on the TV and waited for her to not be grumpy. And it took like eight seconds. And then she was turning toward me and playing with the buttons on my shirt . . . And then she was telling me about her day . . . And then she was laughing with me . . . And then she was sitting up and deciding she was hungry for a slice of pizza . . . And then she was dragging me off the couch to a pizza shop a few blocks away . . . She was still in sweats, by the way, with her hair like, wild, and that was the night I learned that she really, usually, tries to look totally put together, but then sometimes she just doesn't give a shit at all, which I've always really dug . . . But anyways, she said, what are you smiling about? And I realized while we were eating pizza that I had this huge grin on my face, even though I'd had such a bad day up until an hour ago. "You were grumpy, but I cheered you up," I told her. And then I told her I lost my job. And . . . yeah. That's Roz kind of in a nutshell, I think. There weren't tally marks, not really. My whole life, it's always been about . . . what can I bring to the table? What can I offer? But even when I thought I didn't have anything to offer her . . . I was still the right, I don't know, recipe. For her. It was just that . . . we fit. We. The two of us. It wasn't about stats. My job or my skills or anything you could ever list out on a piece a paper. And . . . that was the first time that had ever happened for me. And sitting there, jobless, I still felt useful to her.

(It was in the intangibles!)

Yes. Thank you. Exactly. What she really liked about me . . . it was in these little moments you can't tally. On the couch, cheering her up. And that made me feel . . . she made me feel . . . perfect. Perfect on a Bad Day. Perfect without even having to try. That would be the actual title of that day. If I had to go back and name it. I've learned . . . the hard way . . . that you don't get very many of those days. Where everything is perfect without trying. I've learned that trying . . . is maybe all you can do? Even if I used to get it right without having to think about it. But that's . . . that's not . . . we were talking about me being perfect on that one bad day. Oh, and she didn't mind that I got laid off. I mean, she felt bad, but she didn't think I was a loser. A couple weeks later, she told me I should move in with her to save on rent. So I could afford to go to technical college. And that's the story of how I became an electrician. Or . . . something. All right. That's it. That's it for tonight. Next time I'll write it down.

# Three

*It's not exactly* a coincidence that next Friday, when Vin gets home from work—blank expression in place—I've got my ass in the air and two oven mitts in the oven.

Look, I'm not an incredible cook.

In the kitchen I have one indelible skill, really. Resourcefulness.

I was raised a staunch middle-class New Yorker. Sing it with me now: wasting food is a sin! (Said my mother as she put a spoon in a leftover can of pinto beans when I complained of being hungry after dinner.)

Not many people take their formative-childhood-inflicted neuroses and turn them into careers (or maybe they do, IDK) but I sure did!

I'm a recipe creator and food distribution coordinator with Harvest NYC, a food rescue org. Basically, we dispatch teams of volunteers to race around the city, rescuing the excess food from farmer's markets and restaurants and grocery stores. Then I'm sent this week's list of what we've rescued and I rush to put together something edible out of the mishmash. So that when people come to pick up their free boxes of rescued produce, they have some vague guideline on what the heck they could make out of bok choy, damaged jars of peanut butter, garlic, and romaine. (A *very* festive salad, in case you were wondering.)

All this is to say that cooking is my zone of competence. You need dinner on the table, I'm putting dinner on the table.

Which is why this current tableau is not a coincidence. Vin closes the front door and I turn toward him, holding a frittata framed in pink-and-green-striped fabric. (The apron matches the mitts.)

I feel like a stick-figure wife someone might have as a bumper sticker on their Subaru.

But, look, as much as cooking is my zone of competence, it's also my zone of confidence. And I really needed to feel confident tonight.

Because this morning I received one of the worst texts that someone can ever send. From Vin: *Are you going to be home tonight? I have something to tell you.*

*I have something to tell you* via text message should be illegal. Seriously. You should have to, at least, show up in front of a judge, in your Sunday best, and explain yourself for sending a text like that.

He sent it in the moments after I heard him leave for work, and it ruined my entire day. Not that it's been a great week so far. Vin leaves before I get up, returns home after I've locked myself in the room at night.

But tonight we're both here. I've got a frittata and he's got drywall dust on his clothes.

"Smells good," he murmurs, toeing off his work boots.

I blink at him. Well, look at us. It's like a night from happier times got airdropped into the present moment.

This is excruciating.

I all but slam the frittata down on the counter. "Just tell me!"

He jolts, assessing me with wide eyes. But says nothing.

"Seriously, Vin! You have something ominous and terrible

to tell me and I'm all ears. I've been all ears the entire day. So tell me already!"

"Oh. It's not ominous. Or terrible. I don't think. Just. Maybe. Complicated?"

I've got two hands on my hips and I'm eyeing him with the intensity of a high-speed train. I know that if I interrupt now, it'll only derail him further, but everything in me wants to scream the word SPEAK.

He walks to our dinner table, pulls out a chair for me. I pole-vault into it and fold my hands. SPEAK.

He pulls out a chair for himself, but then takes stock of his dusty work clothes and instead stands behind it, bracing himself on his elbows. His eyes are down.

"It's . . ." His eyes come up. "About the accident."

I take a deep breath. My mind already racing through every possible combination of unknowns he's about to make known. "Okay . . ."

"I've been thinking . . . everything got fractured . . . nothing's been easy since . . ."

I'm pinning the insides of my lips closed with my teeth. I want so badly to hurry him along. Waiting for him to say what he's really here to say is excruciating.

"There have just been a lot of bad days this year," he says finally. "And I thought . . . maybe if I went back . . . to that day . . ."

"Back?" I ask, certain I'm not hearing him right. My voice is scraping out of me. "To that day?"

"I . . . I found the other guy . . . The guy who was with us . . ."

*"Are you serious?"*

He nods and his eyes settle, for a moment, on my right collarbone, where there's a vertical scar hidden underneath my shirt. Even after he looks away I know he's seeing it in his mind's eye. I know because I'm seeing *his* scar, long and not-so-thin, down the left side of his back.

"I guess the paramedics had put all our stuff in one box and brought it to the hospital," he says. "Someone . . . I guess . . . got confused and stuffed his ID into my wallet."

"You've . . . you've known his name this whole time?"

"No." He shakes his head. "I didn't realize it was in there. I just found it. I googled him . . . he works in Brooklyn . . . Lives there too."

I'm gripping my elbows so hard it makes my fingers ache to release them. "Is he . . . okay?"

"I don't know. I think so. When I googled him, an event website for his kid's birthday party popped up. So. Yeah. I don't know. Looks like he's got family."

"Are you . . . are you going to contact him?"

"Look," he says in a low voice. "I think so . . . And I know . . . things between you and me . . . but the anniversary is coming up and—"

He cuts off when my eyes fill and I slam my hands over my face.

Of course the accident was going to have an anniversary. It was always going to have an anniversary. It just hadn't occurred to me that I would be marking it while Vin packed his things to leave.

*Don't you feel like someone's just tossed you out of a plane, Vin? Isn't there a knife in your gut? Aren't you already homesick for me?*

If he was, how could I even tell? His beard is a brick wall between him and the world. No light gets through.

"Why?" I finally ask in a low, shaky voice. "Why open all this up again? Raff is only *just* better—"

I cut off because I notice his hands have tightened around the back of the chair where he's leaning. "I'm not—I can't—"

He straightens up and jams his hands in his pockets. His eyes are closed. "Roz. This part of my life . . . This whole chapter . . . I need it to be over."

*Which part. Which chapter.*

I think I'm going to be sick.

"It can't go on like this anymore," he continues. "I thought . . . maybe meeting him . . . could bring some closure. Maybe *then* I could start new. Without the bad shit. Put it all behind me. Put *everything* behind me."

Well, I'm not sure if I am part of the bad shit he is referring to, but I certainly fall into the category of *everything.*

I—and I hate that this is true because I would love nothing more than to be cool and calm and cold right now—am stricken.

The worst part is that I get it. The worst fucking year of his life took place in this apartment that used to be our beloved home. And he lived it right alongside me, who used to be his beloved wife. We've been shredded into pieces and he can't put himself back together here. He's basically telling me that he wants to go off and live. And what can I say? *No, Vin. Stay and suffer.*

I say the only word I can force out through my burning throat. "Okay."

There's a long silence. And then, "Do . . ."

I wait for as long as humanly possible for him to finish that sentence, but he can't, or won't. I only realize I've been holding my breath when it all gets exhaled on a huge whoosh.

His eyes snap to my face, stumbling over the tears, hot and thin, sliding down my cheeks. I dash them away and can't believe my fingertips don't come away red.

"Roz—" His hands come out of his pockets, freeze, and then slide immediately back into his pockets. He straightens up.

There was a time when, if I was crying, it was always directly into Vin's shirt. His arms around me at the first hint of a sniffle. Back when he used to join me in the shower without a second thought. Back when he'd zip my coat up to my chin on a chilly day because it made him warmer to see me warm. Back when he'd sit me up on the kitchen counter to kiss me hello when he got home from work.

But now? Now he's brushing drywall dust from his shirt and frowning. He's clearing gravel from his voice, stepping toward me and then—God—directly past me. "I should shower," he mumbles. "I'll be right back."

Thank goodness he's gone because for a minute or two, I just completely crumble. *Till death do us part.* Or, rather, *till bad stuff happens and then he can't even be in the same room with me when I cry do us part.*

I turn, taking a few deep breaths, and realize the oven is still on. I turn it off, quickly put away a few dishes from the drying rack, and then the laundry basket at the edge of the living room catches my eye.

It's all my laundry, except for the green sweatpants and hoodie of Vin's that I wore home from Raff's last weekend. He's still in the shower, so now is as good a time as any. I force myself to move forward, get this task done.

Even though it means walking into the guest bedroom. Which used to be Raff's room. But of course, before it was ever a guest bedroom it was actually *my* bedroom.

So I should probably explain about the apartment. And in particular, I should probably explain how the hell two middle-class New Yorkers afford a two-bedroom in the West Village.

Let me tell you a little tale.

Once there was a girl (me) aged fourteen, growing up in Bay Ridge. And one day, the girl's mother came into her room while she was working on an English paper and said the following: "You're moving in with Aunt Therese."

Aunt Therese is actually Great-Aunt Therese. A rich old bat who wore fur to the grocery store, could make Tony Soprano cry, and taught me how to cook at knifepoint.

You see, Aunt Therese was the proud occupant of a rent-controlled apartment (you know you're a true New Yorker when those words turn you on) and had been since her mother literally gave birth to her in the main bedroom. Here's the thing about rent-controlled apartments: the lease has to be bequeathed to someone who already lives there in order to stay rent-controlled.

My mother, ever the penny-pincher—and certain Aunt Therese was going to croak any moment—couldn't stand to see it go. So she sent me, unwillingly, to go inherit the lease.

Aunt Therese took me in with many a grumble. But she then proceeded to feed me gorgeously homemade meals every night and dropped a water balloon filled with olive oil on my first boyfriend's head from our fifth-floor apartment as he was walking out after dumping me.

For quite a while, Aunt Therese refused to kick the bucket, probably just to spite my mother. We were pretty happy roommates until I was twenty-eight, when Aunt Therese decided she'd rather die without me sobbing into her hair and moved into an assisted living facility, and then, a few months later, hospice, and two weeks after that, the family plot on Long Island. She donated every single penny of her money to the youth center on the corner that she always used to complain played music too loud and left me a note saying people should make their own futures and not inherit them.

Once I finally got the gumption to move my things from the little bedroom to the big bedroom, I opened up her ancient (read: antique) set of drawers and found a string of pearls rolling around in there. There was a Post-it note stuck to them in her handwriting: *for you, my heart.*

I was determined—*determined*—to pull an Aunt Therese and grow old on my own in this apartment. Eventually choosing some darling young foundling to leave the apartment (and the pearls) to.

But then I met Vin.

And I was seized with the desire to share my life and space and bed and blah, blah, blah. We've all been there with a beautiful man who knows how to swing a hammer.

Anyways, we fell in graphic, heart-stopping love, made sincere proclamations about eternity, tried (three or four times a week) to turn our bodies into one thing . . . and on the weekends Vin did things like grout and caulk and varnish our charmingly decrepit apartment.

I did things like find old curtains at the Housing Works on Broadway and take them home and turn them into throw pillows.

Our apartment was a home. And then our apartment was Raffi's home too.

And soon, apparently, I'll live here alone once again.

Anyways. Over there is the main bedroom. Then, yes, here is the guest bedroom. Vin's room. The door between is the bathroom (where Vin is currently scrubbing the day, and our conversation, off himself). And then there, obviously, the living room and kitchen are one big space. But how about those gigantic windows, huh? And the hardwood floors? Vin wasn't sure about emerald green for the living room, but once I hung up those paintings (that St. Michel framed), he finally agreed it was nice. I think, really, at the end of the day, I'd just like to live inside a patchwork quilt. And my decorating aesthetic obviously reflects that.

The clawfoot tub leaks if you take a bath, by the way.

But enough of memory lane. I walk into the guest room with Vin's folded clothes in my hand. His scent is all around me. His words are all around me. The anniversary is coming up and I can't even hear the word *accident* without shivering. Meanwhile, Vin wants to go to Brooklyn and meet the guy who . . . the other guy who was injured. Who was there with us that day. Rode the ambulances.

No.

I stare at his closet, filled with new clothes. A step into a new life.

*I need this to be over,* he said. His old life, he meant.

The truth hits me.

Vin and I are going in different directions. No, that's not quite it. Vin is moving on and I'm standing still.

I dash tears out of my eyes. I don't want to stand still. I don't want to be stuck here any more than he does.

The shower shuts off and I jolt. I can't let him find me in his room, crying over his laundry. In fact, I can't let him find me at all.

I skitter out of his room and into mine. I'm applying makeup with a vengeance (and a shaky hand). I quickly change my clothes and grab my purse. Before I think twice I've got one hand on our front door knob.

I'm going to do things too. I'm going to move on too. I'm going to sprint in a direction just like him. I'm out the door.

There's a dim gold sunset on the horizon; the rest of the world is a gray drizzling rain. The bus is crowded and late.

Brakes, the doors open, fresh night air, the sidewalks are glistening orange under the streetlamps and slippery.

And then I'm back in the hallway of Nine Five Four, passing MR. GREG's door.

The figure drawing class is probably almost over by now.

I'm not sure what I'm expecting. Maybe Daniel packing up a messenger bag and clicking the light off for the night, me catching him at the last second to share a private word.

But instead, the door to the art room bangs open and people come streaming out.

"Fifteen-minute break, people!" Daniel shouts from inside the room. Apparently this class is a lot longer than I thought it would be. "And I *mean* fifteen minutes. You're locked out if you're late. Oh, and don't bring any halal from the cart back with you! It makes the model hungry."

The class participants are stretching and chatting as they make their way past me out into the night.

The guy Lauro stops cold in front of me. "Oh, look. Knee Socks is back."

His smile is charmingly poisonous. He looks like he'd feel so good he'd hurt.

"Who?" Daniel pokes his head out the door. "Oh! Roz! You made it."

"Yes." The words are so sharp I almost don't believe them. "I made it."

Daniel lays a gentle hand on Lauro's shoulder and firmly foists him down the hallway. Then he steps back and sweeps a hand through the door of the classroom.

"Welcome."

# Four

*Hopefully I look* cool enough this time to wipe those knee socks from the record. I've got a smoky eye you can't even see behind my bangs and glasses. I'm in vintage Kaliko trousers I found at Buffalo Exchange, a handsewn button-down Raff bought me for my birthday last year, and what I've chronically (and ironically) referred to as my "art school boots." Yes, they are combat boots and yes, it almost always gets a laugh.

My goal here is to effortlessly convey *yeah, I draw* vibes. Essentially this is Halloween and I'm winning the costume contest.

I think.

Everyone but me and one other student is out enjoying the fifteen-minute break.

The other student doesn't look up when I walk over to the easel next to hers.

"Hi. I'm Roz."

She's looking through a drawing pad of what I assume are her drawings, though I can't see any of them. She glances up with bright eyes that don't quite focus on me. "Hi. I'm Em."

And then she returns to her drawing pad, not a word more.

I'm not getting shy or unfriendly vibes, more that she's in the middle of a massively important thought.

"Can I sit here?" I ask (it's the last time I'll interrupt her, I swear).

"Yes." This time she doesn't even look up.

I immediately sit down in the chair next to hers, surreptitiously glancing her way. She's got a severe face. Pale skin. Big, hooked nose, thin lips, square jaw, inset eyes, and eyebrows so pale they're almost invisible. Her strawberry blond hair is wavy, parted down the middle, and braided down her back. She's got overalls over a tight black T-shirt. On the back of her chair is a coat that looks like it was sewn out of an old patchwork quilt.

She's the most interesting type of attractive. The is-she-or-isn't-she type. The way some fashion models are. Every feature turned up to 11, she'd be the girl next door if you happened to live next to a crash-landed spaceship.

I notice her easel is a very different height than mine, so I quickly fiddle around and match hers. I put my blank white drawing pad up and then examine my brand-new pencil bag (stopped at the art supply store on my way here).

The door bangs open and in gallops an extremely long-legged youth in wildly short cutoff jeans and a cropped turquoise football jersey that simply reads *Sports!* They have shiny, dark brown skin and a mega-wattage smile, grinning from across the circle of easels.

"Hi! Oh, you were here for a minute last week, right?"

"Yes! I'm Roz."

"You can call me Penny. Hey, heads up, Daniel's probably not going to let you sit there."

"Oh. Okay." I stand and scramble all my things up into my arms. I glance at the student sitting beside me, still leafing through her drawings and seemingly oblivious to me and Penny. "Why? Where should I sit?"

"Anywhere but where you sat last week is Daniel's rule."

Ah.

Apparently I've GPS'd back to the exact stool I'd sat on before without even noticing. How robustly loser-ish.

As I skitter to a different seat, my "art school boots" start pinching my toes.

Penny is humming and doing something at the big aluminum wash sink in the corner of the room, so I just sit my ass down and start resharpening my pencils.

Daniel returns next, a thermos of tea steaming between his hands.

He gives me a little wave from his desk.

I expect him to say something. Maybe, you know, offer me some foolproof affirmation that will make me feel energized and resilient. Instead, his eyes track over to the other students.

Em finally looks up. "Daniel," she calls to him, not warmly but not blandly either. "What's the deal with the perspective on this one?"

He joins her at her easel and they jump into a discussion that has the effortlessly tumbling rhythm of a conversation they never stop having, but pick up again whenever they see each other.

The other students start to return to the classroom. They are youngish and oldish. Brown skin, pale skin, tan skin, braids, blowouts, coiled curls in a structured halo. A small gold cross framed against chest hair. The Star of David tumbles out of a ruby-red V-neck when its wearer bends to dig through a messenger bag. A PB&J is taken down in three bites by one student (Lauro—in a mesh short-sleeve that shows his nips). A bento box lunch pail is carefully opened by another student and a line of gorgeous kimbap revealed. I smell a delicate tendril of rosewater from one direction and the vague fug of body odor from the other direction.

This classroom is a true New York City People Salad.

This is why I absolutely love living here. It makes the world feel so big. Everywhere you turn there are people living their lives differently.

How expansive.

*Right,* I remind myself. *Roz, no one gives a shit about your combat boots but you. They're here to draw and eat kimbap.*

Daniel makes his way to the classroom door and glances at his watch. Almost start time.

At the last moment, Esther bustles through the door holding the hand of a seven- or eight-year-old boy with a Messi jersey on and a mulish expression on his face.

Daniel sighs, belabored. "Esther . . ."

She purses her lips at him. "My neighbor who usually watches him is currently passing a gallstone. That's why we're late and that's why he's here."

The little boy shrinks as he looks at Daniel's face. "Abuela," he hisses. "You said it was okay."

"It's okay, Fabi," Daniel reassures the kid. "I just have to clear it with the model."

Oh! The model! I eagerly watch as Daniel approaches a short, square man in basketball shorts. He's the one wearing the small gold cross. They converse in an easy way and then Daniel returns to Esther. There's an alcove to the classroom, where a bunch of extra easels are set up and I see, in the far back, there's a beanbag chair. Esther gets Fabi set up with an iPad and headphones and then comes back out, dusting her hands. She grins and waves when she sees me.

I grin and wave back but I'm also wondering what the big deal is about bringing a kid to a drawing class—

*Oh. Right.*

The model hops up onto the wooden modeling platform in the middle of the circle of easels, strips off his shirt, and drops his basketball shorts. Stark raving naked.

Right.

*Because this is a figure drawing class, Roz. Where you draw models in the nude.*

I knew this going in. Still, it can't be denied, conceptual dick is very different from literal dick.

I glance around and, as I'm the only one with eyes wide enough to show the perfect globes of my eyeballs, I take it that everyone else is completely comfortable with this reality.

And it's not that I'm not comfortable.

It's just I'm married. So the only dick I ever see in person is Vin's and—stop thinking about Vin's dick!—that hasn't actually happened in almost a year, so I'm just, you know, scrambling to put everything in its right place, if you will!

"We'll start with five two-minute poses. Thank you, Pavel!" Daniel calls to the model, who, still completely naked, does some beepy beeps on a stopwatch, sets it down, then spreads his feet wide and puts both hands on his head, eyes tipped to the ceiling.

I take quick stock and see that every other member of the class has busily begun to draw. I gape and turn to look at Daniel, who is slowly circumnavigating the classroom, arms crossed, eyes bouncing from easel to easel as he passes.

I'd assumed the class would come with some instruction. Where Daniel might tell us, you know, *how to draw.*

Or maybe a lecture? One where I'd be spared for a week from the burning humiliation of drawing something stupid in front of other people?

I never imagined—ah! He's getting closer! I'm sweating.

The stopwatch beeps. I've already completely missed the first pose. Pavel bends down, resets the watch and then drops to a sit, legs crossed at the ankle, hands planted, face tipped, again, to the ceiling.

And now Daniel is beside me. He smiles.

"Stand," he whispers to me.

I immediately comply. Half the class are sitting and half are standing, so I don't think I was doing anything wrong, but I take the suggestion like the lifeline it is.

He quicky adjusts my easel about a foot higher than I would have thought it needed to be. He leans forward again.

"Now, draw."

Again, with the gaping.

*That's it?*

He laughs at my expression, then leans toward my squeaky-clean drawing pad. He pulls a colored pencil the rich rose of sun-baked terra-cotta from behind his ear and makes a fierce, elegant slash across the top of the paper. And then, for good measure, some nonthreatening curlicues down the side.

"Seriously," he says in a low voice. "Just draw."

He moves on to the next student and I eye the marks he's made. No longer blank white and staring at me, the paper is affected, altered. Anything I add will now be just that: *adding* to what he's already laid down.

I release a breath.

The timer beeps. Instead of drawing the model's new pose, I just make some squiggles, like Daniel did. Then some big lines. Then some coloring book shading. As the two-minute poses pass, I just doodle, getting used to putting marks down. I try all my different kinds of pencils.

I glance at Pavel. *Just draw, just draw.* He's got a towel laid out and he's lounging belly down, his chin on his hands. I involuntarily time-travel back to a very memorable time when Vin lay, naked, face down on our bedroom floor. We'd been quarreling in the shower about water temperature and he'd finally acquiesced to letting me boil him alive with my desired setting. He'd overheated and basically crawled out, collapsing in a heap. I'd collapsed in a heap, too. With laughter. Over the top of him. He'd refused to get up until I brought him ice wrapped in a dish towel. See . . . that . . . that I could picture drawing. I know the exact curve of Vin's lower spine. The exact angle of armpit to elbow.

*I wish I had a photo of that moment.*

The thought comes out of nowhere and my heart puckers like it's been sucking on a lemon. I don't mean a nude photo of Vin . . . I mean a photo of . . . how it felt to live that moment.

Of course, no such photo exists, or could ever exist. But still, the memory trembles, crystal clear in my brain, like a Technicolor pearl of dew at the end of a blade of grass. My hand moves of its own accord, the pencil touches the paper and it jolts me.

"Last pose," Daniel calls. "All good, Pavel?"

Pavel nods, sets the timer, and we're gifted with a new pose. Right! Class! I'm here for a reason. It's time. I need to attempt to draw the model. No more faking it.

Pavel is sitting down and facing me, leaning back on one hand, resting one elbow on his other bent knee. He's looking out the window over my head, at the top of the classroom.

Okay.

Okay, so.

Drawing. Right.

I put pencil to paper. Everyone else is producing the sort of sweeping scritcha-scratches that can only mean masterpiece. I've flipped to a new, accusatorily blank page. It's judging me. *This is all you've got?*

I press the tip of my pencil to the middle of the page and study Pavel. I study his *face*. Thank you very much. (His dick, by the way, just happens to be flopped against his leg. So casual. Business casual. A total yawn. It couldn't care less about me. It has its own purpose in life and will not be judged. I immediately resolve to be much more like this model's dick.)

Anyways. Drawing.

I guess . . . I'll start . . . with the nose? Why did I start with the nose? Oh, my gosh, no, has anyone else ever realized how phallic a nose can be? Oh, get a life, Roz! You're in a fine arts class intended to better yourself! You're surrounded by sophisticates! (Presumably.) Quick! Draw ears! That'll help.

I get the right one down in a wrinkly crescent moon and the timer dings halfway through the left.

I'm aghast. Horrified.

I lift my traitorous pencil.

"Huh, you went straight for the genitalia, huh?"

Says a woman who introduces herself to me as Cindy. She's standing behind me now, leaning over my shoulder, studying my unintentionally obscene drawing.

"Awesome," she says, and seems to mean it. "Most newbies avoid the crotch area altogether. Way to dive in."

She gives me a thumbs-up that I couldn't return if it saved my life. My hands creep up over my face.

"I didn't. I swear." I'm terrified the model overheard her. Or anyone has heard her.

So much for cool and sophisticated. One round with a model and now I'm the class pervert.

I scramble to turn the page on my incriminating drawing but unfortunately there's a crowd gathering behind me.

"I love newbie day," says someone.

"I should have drawn a stick figure," I lament. At least I'd have my dignity.

"Roz!" says Daniel, weaving through the crowd to get to me. "This is so wonderful. Can I discuss your drawing with the class?"

*"Ohmygodwhy."*

Everyone laughs, but it's friendly and indulgent. I get the sudden feeling that almost all of them have survived a very similar gauntlet.

"Your drawing brings up a concept I'd love to lecture on."

I glance at the crowd and am greeted by multiple open and expectant faces.

Esther switches her glasses from distance to readers. A redheaded, middle-aged man named Reggie pulls out a notebook and pen. Apparently Daniel's lectures are a prized part of this class. It becomes clear to me that there is only one path forward. Yup. The only thing to do here is own it.

I sigh and step back.

Daniel gestures for the class to scrunch in so they can see. He lifts the terra-cotta pencil from behind his ear again and, to my surprise, as he talks, he draws directly on my drawing.

"What Roz has highlighted with this drawing is the seemingly accidental, but wholly repeatable, *organic rhythms*."

Around my scratchy, double-lined drawing he fluidly, gorgeously adds a cranium, eyes, a neck, a mouth, shoulders. With elegant, sweeping lines, he's just given my little drawing a home.

And then below it, he does a reproduction of my original lines. The nose and ears I'd hacked my way through. Only, this time he draws legs and hips and thighs around them. Turning those lines, yes, into a crotch area. "See, here, as we've discussed countless times, a body has a rhythm. It correlates to itself. Parts of it look like other parts of it." He's in the zone like an athlete as his arm sweeps and retracts. "There is inherent curve. Ratio that is repeatable. Meaningful. If this drawing were a poem, I'd say that Roz found a *refrain*. And she used it here, in this stanza." He goes back up to my original drawing and adds an elegant set of eyelashes and a smattering of freckles that call forth the model so readily it raises the hairs on my arm. "And it can be found again in this stanza." He refers to the crotch he's drawn and gives it a torso, connecting shoulders and clavicle to the drawing of the face above, joining them to be one Pavel. He uses the posed elbow on the knee as a place marker and skips gracefully down the page, riding on a shin, to draw one-through-ten perfectly askance toes.

He steps back and eyes the whole thing. "There's an honesty in what Roz drew that speaks of trueness. Could we immediately decipher which body part this was? Perhaps not. But there is a big, logical, recognizable honesty in it that rings *true*. Roz drew a body part. *This is a real body of a real person!* Her lines tell us."

He starts to draw again in the upper left corner of the paper. "It's the opposite of this."

He's drawn a stick figure.

"A stick figure is instantly recognizable, sure. But *never* honest."

# Five

"*I'm an artiste!*" I say with a twirl of my barstool. Raffi has met me for a drink the night after art class and I am *still* riding. a. high. "Seriously. Don't let your fears get the best of you. Try something new, kids. Take life by the horns!"

"This is heady stuff," he says to me, eyeing my general manic-ness.

"Maybe I really *have* been a heretofore untapped genius."

"Draw a cat." He's slid a bar napkin and pen toward me.

I accidentally tear the napkin with the pen and then draw what looks like a potato with an oddly pirate-ish flair. "There."

"Wow. I think I just found my next tattoo."

"Okay, okay, so maybe I'm not an *artiste*. Maybe it's not the drawing part. It's just the trying-something-I-was-scared-of part." As soon as I've said it, I feel a little deflated. Because the drawing part was really cool. Especially what Daniel had to say about it. I'm about to try to explain the stick figure thing when I take my first really good look at Raff since I got here. "Hey, are you all right?"

As soon as I ask, he crumples forward onto the bar. "I'm terrible. I ran into Marine at Dirtbag."

"Oh, Raff." I put a hand between his shoulder blades. "Did you get the number 7 or the number 9?" Dirtbag is our favorite sandwich joint in the city and I can only hope it isn't forever sullied for him by the unexpected appearance of his ex.

"I panicked and got the number 4!"

"The number 4 is good!"

"*She* seemed good."

"I'm sorry." I rub his back a little more. Marine is the only nice person that Raffi has ever dated. She never picked on him or manipulated him, she thought he was funny and hot, and she liked spending time with me and Vin. But Raff got a little too obsessed with a personal trainer he met in a bar in Queens (as he's known to do) and Marine just got fed up. When she dumped him, she told him she didn't want to be with someone who made her nervous all the time. She wanted to be with someone who was happy with what he had.

This was two years ago and Raff's missed her ever since.

"She looked cute, too," he grumps, taking a big swig of beer. "She was wearing a sweater that made me want to go camping with her."

I get a tingly feeling on the back of my neck and spin on my stool, only to find Lauro eyeing me from a booth in the corner. I *might* have picked this bar because I happened to hear Lauro talking about it at class last night, so it's not a *total* shocker to have run into him. I wave and he grins. Then he lifts one of his feet out the side of the booth and gestures vigorously. He's mouthing words at me and I'm pretty sure it's *Where are your knee socks?*

I give him a friendly thumbs-down and a smile and then spin back to Raff.

"Do you know that guy? Jesus *Christ*, he's hot. Do you think *I* could pull off a mesh shirt?"

"Yes, and . . . actually, yes. I think chest hair and mesh would be a good look for you. He's in my art class."

He's still looking over my shoulder toward Lauro. "Well, break me off a piece of that Kit Kat bar."

"I had my suspicions but now that I know you're this attracted to him I'm positive he's a fuckboy."

"Who cares? Fuckboys are fun."

"Raff." I lay a hand on his arm. He's lonely and we both know it. His fuckboy proclivities are not helping. He flips his hand up to give my hand a squeeze and when he does I get a clear view of the long, meaty scar down his left forearm. There are pinpricks dotting along either side of the main scar from the stitches. "Hey, it's looking good!"

He cocks his head to one side. "You think?"

"Oh, definitely," Lauro says as he cozies up to the bar beside me. "Scars are hot. Fancy seeing you here, Roz. Tequila soda, please. Can I buy you two a drink?"

The bartender waits and I make eye contact with Raff and shrug.

"Pale ale for me," he says.

"I'll have what she's having," I say, with a point at Lauro, which makes him laugh.

"So. Pretty gnarly scar," Lauro says, with the sort of conversational rudeness that extremely hot and charismatic people get to use at will. "How'd you get it?"

"Shattered my arm in an accident about a year ago," Raff replies easily, like he didn't almost lose the hand. Like he, Vin, and I didn't almost die. He lifts the hand and does a few stiffly crooked extensions with his fingers. "She ain't pretty, but she'll do."

"I think functional *is* pretty," Lauro says, and it might be the first genuine thing I've heard him say. He leans into me. "Hey, did you tell him about your epic discovery in class yesterday?"

I laugh and lift my face toward the heavens, grateful for the round of drinks the bartender has just delivered. "I left that part out, actually."

"Oh, come on." Lauro is grinning like a tiger.

"Okay, *fine*. Raff—oh, Lauro, this is Raffi by the way—

anyways, Raff, I may have inadvertently discovered that all noses bear a passing resemblance to penises."

Raff stares at me blankly for a half second and then his jaw absolutely drops.

Lauro leans back and howls with laughter.

"Roz. Roz. *Roz*. Did you just make it so that I can never look another person in the face without accidentally thinking of penises? Did you just *ruin* faces for me forever?" Raffi demands.

"By that logic she just ruined penises for you, too," Lauro says, still grinning.

"No." Raffi is shaking his head aggressively. "*Nothing* could ever ruin penises for me."

"A man after my own heart," Lauro replies with his chronically flirtatious grin.

Lauro's hand grazes my shoulder as he reaches for his drink and I straighten up. That prickly feeling is back, only this time I feel as if someone is staring at me with the fire of a thousand suns. I turn and quickly scan the room. No one is looking my way except for . . . oh.

I jolt when I realize that it's Vin standing at the door of the bar, having just come in.

I've suddenly got cymbals where my heart just was. I haven't seen him since I bolted from our apartment last night. I'm assuming he got out of the shower and turned into a human question mark when he saw that I was gone. I'm aware that we live together and that at some point we would be seeing one another again. But still, I did not expect him to be here. "Did you invite Vin?" I ask Raff, hopefully nonchalantly.

But it's not exactly easy to be nonchalant when a man is cutting through a crowd like a great white shark.

"He texted me earlier to see if we were hanging out and I invited him. You made it!" Raffi says as Vin reaches us. He's leaning backwards into Vin's arms and reaching up to pat his cheek.

Vin texted Raff to ask if he and I were hanging out? Is he checking up on my whereabouts?

"Meet our new friend, Lauro," Raff says. "This is my brother, Vin."

Vin shakes Lauro's hand, then leans against me in order to ask the bartender for a Guinness.

"I only have it in the can," she says, clearly, loudly, in the queen's English.

"Hm?" Vin says, then uses his shoulder to get in between Lauro and me so that he can lean on the bar and talk to the bartender.

Lauro raises his eyebrows and moves around to Raff's other side, happily squeezing in next to him. Vin finishes ordering his drink and then straightens up. If this were a year ago, he'd have put a hand on the back of my neck and sucked on my bottom lip to say hello. If this were a year ago, he'd have put me on his lap on this barstool and whispered things in my ear while Raff entertained Lauro.

But it's today. So he just stands behind me. "Hi," he says next to my ear, not quite a whisper.

"Hi."

He's not touching me, but he's not *not* touching me either. He must be six or eight inches back but I can feel him. He reaches past me, to my drink, and I catch the quick breeze of his familiar deodorant. Even though we're in shambles I could still, unfortunately, live in this man's armpit. I would really rather he stood behind Raff. I want him where I can see him.

Lauro's gaze is bouncing between the three of us. I can

practically read the ticker tape behind his eyes. *Which one of these brothers is she fucking?*

Neither, if we're being honest, but I don't care to satisfy his curiosity.

Vin puts my drink back and clears his throat.

Raff and Lauro have, for some reason, decided to swap drinks and are now arguing over whether the bartender looks like Tilda Swinton or Timothée Chalamet.

Vin leans against me again and I suck in a breath, but he's just reaching over for a bar napkin. "Why'd you draw a cat?" he asks me, studying the napkin.

"How'd you know I drew that?" I ask, amazed. "And more importantly, how could you tell it was a cat?"

His face quirks. Or I think it does. Hard to tell behind the beard. "I know what your drawings look like, Roz."

Now I turn to face him fully. My knees press his legs and he takes a step back. "What have you ever seen me draw?" I demand.

His chin drops. "Grandma Vittoria."

"Ohhhhhh." How could I have forgotten this? This was the (almost) worst thing ever! Right after Vin and I eloped, Vin's grandmother flew in from Italy, mostly to admonish us for not having a big Catholic wedding, from what I could tell. But I was new to the family, desperate for brownie points, and took it upon myself to befriend bitter, bitter Vittoria. Who doesn't speak English. Also, I don't speak Italian. Thus . . . a week and a half of the most torturous game of charades ever played. Complete with reems of shoddy drawings. Done by yours truly. Truly genius stuff. Like it would be time for lunch so I'd draw a picture of a pickle with an arrow next to it.

Vin collected the drawings and (affectionately) laughed until he had tears in his eyes, poring over all of them every night in bed. I'd find those damn drawings under my pillow the next day.

"Also, you draw on the grocery list," he says.

"Oh. Right." I would call those doodles more than drawings, but sure. Sometimes I draw a little tomato next to the word *tomato*.

You'd think this would be a catalog of my failures as an artist, but actually, the fact that Vin could identify a drawing done by me, because he's seen so many of my drawings, makes me feel way more *yeah, I draw* than those damn art school boots.

"How in the *what*?" I hear Lauro say, so I swivel back toward the boys.

"What?" I ask.

Lauro is studying Raff inquisitively, his eyes narrowed.

"We just had a little competition to see who could get the bartender's number," Raff says innocently, sipping Lauro's former drink.

I can't help but laugh. I already know who won. Lauro just fell for the oldest trick in the book. "Oh, don't let the Jimmy Buffett shirt fool you," I tell him. "Raff is *lethal* when he wants to be."

"I've never lost that game in my life," Lauro says with a frown down at his mesh-covered nips. "The headlights are on and everything."

"Don't feel bad. Lebowski over here always wins," Vin says.

"We all have our little gifts," Raff says. "And I have the number of a *very* handsome woman."

Lauro checks his phone. "Look, I'm about to meet some friends for bowling in Queens . . ." He lets it hang there for a moment, looking between the three of us.

"I'm too old to go to a different borough at midnight," I say.

"I'll come," Raff says easily.

"Oh, great!" Lauro says. He seems genuinely glad for Raffi's company.

Raff gives hugs, Lauro gives pounds, and then they're out the door together.

"Is he going to break Raff's heart?" Vin asks, watching them go.

"Your guess is as good as mine."

My drink is sweating and watered-down now.

"So . . ." he says quietly, his eyes on his beer. "Tequila?"

Ah. He wants to know why I wasn't drinking my usual glass of house red. Tequila is extremely unusual for me. Pretty much reserved for that one time that Vin, Raff, and I went to Atlantic City together.

I shrug. "Lauro ordered one and it sounded good."

". . . Is it?" he asks.

"Is it what?" I'm confused.

". . . Is it good?"

My brow comes down. I can tell what he's really asking me, but if he wants to ask, he's gonna have to ask. "I mean. It's new. Different."

"Right." His eyes are on his beer again.

"So . . ." I can't help but fish. "Sorry Raffi just bailed on your plans."

"Oh." He's frowning down, avoiding my gaze. "It wasn't really *plans* with Raff. I . . . knew you were going to be here."

My stomach swoops on an updraft. He can be frustratingly evasive, yes. He can also be very, very blunt.

My mouth has gone dry.

"You were gone last night," he says.

*Ask me where I went.* My heart is pitter-pattering.

"I figured . . . our conversation . . ."

Now my stomach plummets. Oh, right. He hasn't tracked

me down because he wanted to see me. He's tracked me down because he wants to finish what we started last night.

I'm sure my face betrays the dismay I wish weren't threading through me but he's not looking at me anyways. He's looking for answers in his beer glass. He's lifting it to his lips, and then a Great Dane of a man bumps Vin's shoulder on the way past.

"Sorry, dude!" he says with a friendly wave, his eyes popping out of his head when he sees that Vin's beer has just upended itself onto my shirt. Which is now basically translucent. My blue lace bra waves hello to Vin and anyone else who cares to look.

He immediately bands an arm around my shoulders and pulls me into his chest, covering me. I'm stiff with the shock of his arms suddenly around me.

"Bathrooms are back there," the bartender says with a point.

Vin quickly swims me along through the crowd and then we're in a beautiful single-stall bathroom with a silvered-blue mirror and a wingback chair in the corner. It's spooky-sexy in here. Like a Victorian powder room where the duke ravishes the maid he's not supposed to have fallen for. Or the other way around.

Vin is cranking paper towels like he's trying to qualify for the Olympics. And then he's there. Blocking out the world and pressing the paper towels to my stomach and chest. I can see his broad back reflected in the mirror.

His hands are huge and firm and gentle and the wet fabric lightly abrades my skin. This bra doesn't hide a damn thing and his movements get a little less businesslike when he sees the points forming under his hands. His breath washes over my face, his eyes are doing that thousand-suns thing again, and I look anywhere but at him.

We've been here so many times. I'm dizzy with the déjà vu of it. Vin's shoulder close enough to bite. The only difference? All those times were borne on the back of our wedding vows. Our forever. Our till death.

But this, wet clothes, his hands firm on my hips—he's leaning back on the sink, trying to read me—this is borne on the back of that lease. His emergency exit. I get the reverse of déjà vu. I've *never* had this feeling with Vin before. Like I'm standing in wet clothes with a stranger in a cold room.

His hands are still on my hips. There's an infinitesimal press, him moving me slightly closer. Muscle memory, probably, from a time when he'd have already been unbuttoning my jeans.

Time passes between us like a veil. For a moment I glimpse a different Vin. Like there are two of him.

The one I married and the one I've been living with for the last year.

He must read something in my expression because his hands fall back to his sides.

A thought occurs: *I wonder if there are two of me, too.*

"Roz—"

"It's fine. Really. I just wanna go home." I push past him and back out into the bar. I've got cash in my hand, but I'm not fast enough because Vin's already leaving some next to our half-full drinks. And then he's falling into step beside me. I can feel his eyes on the side of my face. It isn't until the noise of the bar cuts out with the closed door that I realize exactly how close this bar is to my art class, to the dreaded Nine Five Four. Just around the corner from Vin's residence in less than eight weeks. I wonder if he's thinking about it. Imagining his new spot. I wonder if it's furnished. Oh, God. I wonder if he's going to ask to take half of our furniture with him when he goes.

Also he doesn't know I'm in an art class in that very residence, and still will be after his move-in date. Also he doesn't know I'm in an art class at *all*. With Lauro. Who he probably thinks is just some guy Raffi picked up at the bar.

I'm itchy with nerves. I'm looking at a negative of my normal life, where everything has changed to the opposite of the color it used to be. Everything, and I mean everything, feels like a lie.

I suddenly hate this neighborhood. And I hate that bar. With all the brass and the sexy lighting. I bet people get laid courtesy of that bar all the time. What a reprehensible neighborhood bar. Where all the soon-to-be-divorced newly arrived tenants can go and mingle. They should have neighborhood confessional booths instead of bars. This city is going to shit.

"Oh, shit, we'll miss the bus." We both start running, and we do, indeed, miss it.

"Long way from Sal's," he says eventually, after a long while, after our breathing has evened out again and we're waiting for the next bus. Sal's is the bar that is exactly an eight-minute walk between our house and Raff's. What he means is, why the hell did me and Raff meet for a drink on the Lower East Side?

I shrug.

He opens his mouth, obviously about to say something. But then he just . . . doesn't.

So we don't say anything at all while we wait for the bus. Or while we board the bus or while we sit and watch the city pass by.

So look, I know that we obviously—painfully—are not on the same wavelength anymore. I know that we are at the furthest possible point from in sync with one another. But I know Vin. And I can feel him turning over and over whatever it is he didn't say.

He waits until I've got keys in our apartment door, about to let us inside. He's behind me, hands in his pockets. I bet he recognizes his very last chance. Once we're inside, I'll be behind my bedroom door faster than he can blink.

"Roz," he says, in the same tone that he used in the bathroom at the bar.

"Yeah?" I'm pausing. *Ask me about this Lauro guy. Ask me why I was on the Lower East Side. Ask me what I did tonight.*

". . . I'm sorry," he says. About the shirt? About leaving me?

"I know."

And then I push through the door.

Tonight I'm going from paper.

(Overachiever!)

You told me to write them down before I read them aloud! Can't win with you dorks.

(Finally he's starting to get a little sassy!)

Okay, here I go, it's called The Cat Doesn't Come Back.

(Cat story!) (We got a cat story, people!) (Ring the cat bell!)

What's the cat bell? Oh, my God. You actually have a bell you ring when someone tells a cat story?

(You got a lot to learn, kid.) (We get a lot of cat stories around here.)

All right. Well. The Cat Doesn't Come Back.

I rescued a cat when I was about ten years old. And I really mean rescued. It was stuck on a third-floor windowsill of an apartment building in my neighborhood in Marine Park. I climbed up on a fire escape, knocked on the kitchen window of the unit, had the grandma who lived there let me in and walk through (she made me take my shoes off), open the window, and get the cat.

I'd never had a cat and didn't know a lot about them. But I knew when they didn't like you they'd claw and bite, so I expected to get the hell scratched out of me while I brought it back down to the street. But the cat was actually really sweet to me. She just kind of curled up in my arms and started purring with her eyes closed.

I actually recognized her too. She was cute, but sort of weird-looking for a cat. Really big, ragged ears, splotchy brown fur, and one of her pupils was super dilated. I knew where she lived. In this dodgy bodega my mother and brother and I avoided because of the crowd of guys that stayed in there all day. I was pretty sure they kept her there as a mouser.

Anyhow, she was sweet to me and I could tell she was in bad shape. Up close, her ears were ragged because she'd been fighting, or attacked or something, and one of them looked infected. So I walked straight to a vet that I knew of, where we'd taken my brother's pet parakeet when it had a virus.

Turns out, the dilated-pupil thing was something she just needed medicine for, it happens to a lot of street cats, I guess. And they put her on antibiotics for the ear, and cleaned her up, and by the time I left, with her in my arms, still purring, I had a new pet cat. And there was a bill that was about to be mailed to my mother's house that was so high I knew that when she got it I was going to get smacked with a wooden spoon. But it was worth it. Because the cat was purring.

Anyways. My mother actually really liked the cat and honestly, it's not a bad idea to have a mouser in Brooklyn.

(What was her name?)

Oh. Well. My brother named her. It was, uh, Puma. Puma Thurman.

(YESSS.) (Couldn't love it more!)

(What about the parakeet?)

Oh, the parakeet? His name was Rick. He'd died the year before. We'd gotten him from our cousin when she moved to California. He was super old when he died. Anyways, my mom liked the cat and so did Raff. My brother. And me? I really liked the cat. She slept on my bed, played with a feather on a string that I made for her. She ate high-quality cat food I bought for her with my pocket money, and she got to lick the extra tuna from the can when my mom made tuna sandwiches. It was a good life.

One day, when I got home from school, though, she wasn't there.

(Oh no. The title of the story wasn't ironic!)

Yeah. Well, I looked everywhere, but she'd escaped somehow. So I went looking for her in the neighborhood. And I found her in the bad news bodega. The guys there were mad at me for taking her, but she was wearing a collar now, so they didn't give me too much trouble. And she seemed happy to see me, in that cat way. I took her home.

A few weeks later, the same thing happened again. And again. And again. We never did figure out how she was getting out of the house. But every time it had been a few hours since we'd seen her, it would be time to go down the street to the bodega and get her again.

I didn't get it. She had tuna from the can and a warm bed at my house. And me.

At the bodega she had to hide under the chip display so she wouldn't get stepped on and a bowl of dry food they kept on the sidewalk that she had to fight other cats for. She never fought me when I brought her home. In fact, she'd twine around my legs whenever she saw me. Purr when I picked her up.

It was Raff who had the idea. "Let's see if she'll come back on her own," he suggested. So the next time she disappeared, I didn't go get her from the store. I waited all through the night. And the next morning. And then I couldn't wait anymore. And I went down to the store and got her. Maybe if I'd waited long enough, I'd have gotten to learn that the cat comes back. But also, maybe I'd have learned that the cat comes back . . . to the bodega. But not to me. And I didn't want to learn that.

So what did I learn? I learned that she would leave, again and again.

But I also learned that if I went and got her, I got to have her.

So, what's worse? Having a cat that leaves you? Or having no cat at all?

Thank you.

(Woot woot!) (Okay, Vin!) (Damn good cat story, Vinny!)

# Six

*I wonder who* the first person to ever say *Life goes on* was. What an asshole. Well, regardless, they're right. And so even though my beer-stained shirt leers at me from where it hangs on my closet door, even though Vin's closed door leers at me from across the apartment, even though my apartment leers at me from across town, I do, in fact, sit at my desk, at work, ignoring all the leering. Because yes, life goes on.

When Vin and I first got together and combined lives, I used to bring home the bacon. I was the head cook at one of The New School cafeterias and it was a seriously good job. But I hated the waste. We were told to overestimate on our ordering and our prep, because it's a private college and the worst thing management could imagine was running out of pesto penne on a Wednesday. The result? Trash cans full of pesto penne in the alley on Thursday morning. There are all sorts of regulations about what you can and can't re-serve, and I'd come home every night after work with tears in my eyes over the waste.

So, when he graduated electrical school five years ago and got hired on as an electrician at Mauricio Electrics, he told me *he'd* bring home the bacon for a while and I quit at The New School. Now I spend about twenty-five hours a week at Harvest NYC's office, spread across a few different days.

For an org that does such cool work, Harvest NYC is

housed in a very sad office building in East Harlem. If it weren't for my coworkers with purple hair and big smiles and loud voices and tats and their bikes parked in their cubicles and their rescue-produce salads in the fridge, this could be any other boring old company selling business cards to other boring companies. But it's not! It's a 501(c)(3) that is doing honest-to-goodness God's work.

"Sweetie, Kitchen B is open today, if you want to do some testing," Cherise, my boss, says with an air-kiss as she whisks past me.

"What's going on in A?" I call after her.

"All the 101s got moved to Tuesdays!" And she's gone, around the corner.

I peek into Kitchen A, on my way past, because I love to watch Deb, the resident nutrition educator, teach. She's got a no-nonsense sensibility and was born to feed people. Seriously. She once put a hot dog in my mouth when I was in the middle of saying something.

Today must be the New Moms Nutrition class. There are strollers and car seats next to rows of students taking notes, and Deb is at the front burners lecturing and effortlessly flipping pancakes while she balances someone else's baby on her hip.

Like I said, it's God's work.

I sneak back out to my desk. And now for the part of my job I could really take or leave: the volunteer coordinator part. Once a week (tomorrow), I lead an orientation for any new volunteers. It's generally very sparsely attended (except for the first two weeks of January when everyone remembers that they do, indeed, want to go to heaven). But today, I'm here to make the volunteer schedule. Which is basically a game of Jenga played on an Excel sheet. I send Jaylen to the Union Square farmer's market on Wednesday but then have to figure out how Warren will get the produce from there to the Bronx in time for the soup kitchen to use it. Et cetera, et cetera. I've never once planned a week with zero hiccups. Everyone knows that this part of my job could very well be done by AI, but no one mentions it because I do fine enough, don't bill for extra hours if I make a mistake, and we're all just trying to keep bread on the table.

After I work through the schedule, I decide I need a pick-me-up and head into Kitchen B. Which is old and shabby compared to Kitchen A, but it's clean. And honestly it's better to work in the least flashy and outfitted settings possible, because the recipes we're trying to create should be able to be replicated in anyone's kitchen. Not a chef's kitchen.

I like to keep my "make something from nothing" skills sharp by practicing here as well as at home. And there are about five hundred old cookbooks here. So once or twice a week, I use the kitchens to pad my recipe-creation skill set. Basically, I open the Kitchen B fridge, see what we have on hand, and then search the cookbooks for ideas.

It's like food Mad Libs: make this stromboli with (insert vine vegetable here) and a can of (insert canned vegetable here).

Because of a crate of rescued lasagna noodles (originally thrown out due to inaccurately printed labels), I've spent the last few weeks working on different varieties of lasagna. I'm trying to figure out how to replace the cheese (which can be expensive) with beans (which are generally cheaper and in people's pantries already) and have it not turn into a dried-out, tasteless mush. I've yet to succeed. I make it in these tiny casserole dishes and choke it down for lunch.

Which is exactly what I do today. Someday we'll get to the end of this enormous store of lasagna noodles.

Grandma Vittoria would kick my ass if she ever heard I was making lasagna with beans and no cheese.

I'm crouched down, watching my latest attempt bubble through the oven window, when my cell rings in my back pocket.

I've still got my eye on the lasagna and it's Raff's ringtone, so I answer without looking. "Yello."

"Hey."

But it's not Raff's voice. It's Vin.

And then I remember that I changed Vin's ringtone to match Raff's back when Raff was living with us, so that it was more like "call from home." Only it's clearly been a very long time since Vin called me because I didn't even remember that. He's usually more of a one-word texter.

"Roz? You there?"

"Oh. Yeah. Hi. What's up?"

"I just . . . you're not home."

I blink. "Are *you* home?" It's a Tuesday afternoon. Vin usually works a very reliable eight-to-five workday.

"Yeah. Are you . . ."

"I'm at Harvest. I'm working today."

"Right. Okay."

I get that we haven't really run into each other in a few days and he's checking to make sure I'm still alive, but it's been so long since we've talked on the phone . . . "Did you need something?"

There's a long pause and then, "Do we have Advil anywhere? There's no more in the bathroom cabinet, but I don't want to go buy more if we have some someplace else."

I stand up so fast a spatula overbalances out of a mostly empty can of white beans and they splatter over the counter and floor. I turn away from them and plug the ear that isn't on the phone. "Are you hurt?"

Everything in my body has gone tight. I feel like I can see spaces in between atoms. Being an electrician can be so fucking dangerous. What if he's gotten an electrical burn? Or worse, what if he was electrocuted? He could have gone into cardiac arrest. He should be at the hospital, not home— The scar on Vin's back flashes in my mind.

"No, no." He hears it in my voice, the scattershot panic. "Not hurt. I have a fever. I'm just sick."

Better than graphically injured in an accident but—when I've got this many panic chemicals in my bloodstream—not by much. "What are your symptoms?"

He doesn't shake me off, thank God. He survived this last year along with me. He knows how it feels to need all the medical information and need it now.

"Sore throat, headache. Fever of 102.5. I just need Advil and sleep. I promise."

"There's Advil in the inside pocket of the blue backpack hanging on my closet door. I'll be there in forty-five minutes."

"Roz, I'll be—" But either he's heard the steel in my voice, or he's very tired, because instead of arguing, he just softens. "Okay. Don't rush. Be safe."

I do rush. Because I'm picturing him passed out on the floor, Advil spilled everywhere like the beans I'm cleaning up at warp speed. The oven dings, I burn myself on the dish and grit my teeth.

But the kitchen is cleaned and polished in record time. I grab my bag and rush out the door, texting Cherise to eat the lasagna and give me her honest opinion, and then I'm skidding onto the train and headed toward my husband.

When I slam through our front door, he's standing in front of the open fridge, filling a glass of orange juice. He looks wilted and pale, big blue smudges under his eyes.

"Did you take the medicine? How long ago? What dose?" I drop my bag and race to him, think better of it, and quickly wash my hands, wincing when the water touches my fresh burn.

"What happened to your hand?" he demands, reaching for it.

But I'm reaching for his face, feeling for his temperature.

"I'm fine," he says. "I'm feeling better. Show me your hand."

I'm not satisfied, reaching to feel his cheeks and neck. He's grabbing at my hand, trying to see it. I yank back and knock the glass of orange juice. It smashes against the floor like a firework.

I scream and jump backwards, because the shards of glass that have slingshotted across the kitchen floor are not from a juice glass, they're the plate glass front window of a café, and I'm on my back on a blue tiled floor, there's a truck wheel spinning idly a few feet above my head, and people are screaming. Vin's full weight is laid out over the top of me and he's not moving. My vision is in massive, lengthy blinks, and I don't think I'll ever breathe again. I look to my side and there's Raffi, facing away from me on the blue tile, his forearm cracked into a horrific angle. There's a man unconscious beyond him; I can see bone where his cheek is supposed to be.

I'm back in my kitchen now, ripping away from Vin's strong hands on my shoulders and standing over the kitchen sink. I'm sobbing, but there are no tears. I'm dizzy and nauseated. Gripping the cabinet, I sink down to the floor slowly, my fingers bearing all my weight because my legs simply can't.

I take long, deep breaths because everyone is always talking about taking deep breaths when you're panicking, but I don't even feel like they make it into my lungs. It's like trying to breathe through packed cotton.

Time passes and when I finally open my eyes, I see that Vin has taken up a mirrored position, seated on the floor, against the counter opposite me. He's watching me.

The orange juice is a sharp, treacherous ocean between us.

"Roz..." Vin pulls up his knees and rests his arms there, his head hanging down.

"Roz, this is so fucked-up."

It hurts, but he's not wrong. "I'm assuming other people can drop glasses without having a meltdown."

"No." He's shaking his head. "Not just you. That was me... I mean... This... I think... this is like... PTSD from the accident."

I'm taken aback.

Vin grew up pretty old-school. Work hard, get married, have kids, bury your parents, retire, die. No muss, no fuss. When he was a teenager and his mother found a nudie mag in the back of his closet, she rolled it up and walloped him with it. He's not exactly a psychology-terms sort of guy.

"I—" I shrug. "I guess I don't know."

"Because I don't think this"—he gestures to us on the floor—"is normal. For spilled juice and a low-grade fever and a burn that just needs some ointment."

"Yeah." I have to agree. There's an elastic band of pain around my head, tightening and loosening in rhythm.

We're silent for a long, long time. I'm about to stand up and insist that he go to bed, but then...

"Are you taking some sort of class?"

I freeze.

Art classes aren't exactly illegal or illicit, but I still feel like he's caught me doing something bad.

"I saw the art stuff in your backpack. When I got the Advil."

"Right. Yeah. Friday nights." I glance at him, and he's nodding.

"I get it. Anything to get out of the house." He stands up and I think I'm about to watch him leave. But he walks to the hall closet and gets the mop. "To get away from—"

He gestures to the broken glass, but then his hand just keeps on going, gesturing to our house as a whole. To—oh, God—our life together, I assume.

*Anything to get away*, he said. *I get it*, he said.

Anything.

The panic chemicals have started to freeze over. They're not racing and hot anymore, they're sluggish and pulsing with ache. I stand up on cold feet and try to take the mop from him.

"You should sleep."

He looks like he's about to protest, so I tug the mop away. "Seriously, Vin. It'll make me feel better if you sleep."

Well, he can't argue with that. And he doesn't. He nods, goes to the couch, and collapses. I can tell from his breaths that he's asleep in less than a minute.

I clean the mess quietly, cautiously.

*Don't rush*, he'd said to me on the phone. *Be safe.*

But ever since the accident I feel like my entire life is on the rush setting. I don't remember the last time I walked to the train. I jog the whole city. I'm late for work and bursting into Daniel's art class halfway through.

I'm always rushing. Except . . .

As soon as I finish cleaning the mess, I tiptoe to my room and grab my supplies out of my backpack. Thank goodness he's still sleeping when I get back.

I barely take my eyes off him while I draw him. I've haphazardly chosen a blue colored pencil because I didn't want to dig through my pencil bag and wake him. It takes twenty minutes for me to get every element down on paper, the tip of his head all the way down to his socked toes. The drawing is terrible. He's arched and looks like he's flying off the couch. His mouth is in the wrong place, his hands are laughable. His chest too big, his legs too short. It doesn't look like Vin at all. But . . .

I'm not rushing.

It really, really doesn't look like Vin. So I decide to give the drawing a caption, for clarity. *Vin sleeping*, I write, and then, after a moment of thought, add one word.

*Safe*.

# Seven

"*Will you come* over and make a dinner for me that will impress my date and make it seem like I'm an incredible cook, but also not *so* fancy that it's obvious I didn't make it? Also will you bring some bananas? I'm out of bananas." This is Raff over the phone.

"Is this date with the handsome lady bartender?" I ask as I pack up my bag. I'm in my gray little cubicle at work. Sadly, I didn't even have time to tinker in the kitchen today.

"No, she was a few nights ago."

"And how was it?"

"Transcendent. She's extremely into R.E.M. and once split a cab with Bill Murray."

"Did you have chemistry?"

"Oh, for sure. I met God for about three straight minutes."

"Gross. Are you going to see her again?"

"Hopefully! She rocks."

"But this date . . ."

"Is with my accountant."

"Raff! For the love of God, don't shit where you eat."

"Oh, come on. You only live once. And I love his tiny pants. I'd like to see what's inside them."

"So you need me to make you a dinner that will help you get into a man's tiny pants."

"Exactly."

"French omelet it is. I'll be there in an hour." It's a rare friend that you go to the grocery store for after work, come to his house to make him a dinner you will neither eat nor take credit for, and then vacate to give him the opportunity to get laid by an ill-chosen partner. But yes, Raff is that rare friend.

Raff and I met (of course) at a karaoke bar. I mean, can you think of any better best friend origin story than him needing a duet partner for "Islands in the Stream" and me, a perfect stranger, volunteering?

Well, sorry to disappoint, because that does sound amazing, but what actually happened was that we were both waiting on drinks at the bar and he held up the menu to me and said, *What do you think the odds are on these tater tots?* And I said, *The odds for what? Food poisoning?* And he said, *High? Bad? Like, need-an-IV sort of food poisoning or I-just-get-out-of-work-tomorrow food poisoning?* And I said, *Sounds like you need to quit your job.* And he was about to say something else but then got called up to the stage, where I watched him do (it won't surprise you) the most charismatic rendition of "Raspberry Beret" I've ever seen someone do, with the exception of Prince himself. He brought the house down. I paid for the beer he'd been waiting on and by the time he got back to his barstool there were tater tots, courtesy of me, waiting for him. *Tots!* he shouted. We shared them and chatted the rest of the night.

I never really believed in pheromones until I met Raff. Because he's tall and certainly slings a confident sexual charisma. He's a cocked-head, intense-eye-contact sort of guy. He's *Hey, do you wanna dance?* And then he *really* dances. But I never, not once, felt a romantic attraction to him. I met him and felt such a strong pull to him as a buddy . . . and him for me, too. Never once did he put the jets on. There are no lingering touches, there are no lingering glances, there are no *what if*s.

I used to wonder about this. Why I *didn't* want to date Raff.

He's hot, I'm hot, we spent all our time together, made each other scream with laughter, we (were) young, sexually active people. We fell asleep on couches. We even had a there's-only-one-bed situation when we got stranded overnight on Fire Island. But just . . . nada. I once told Raff that if we'd been in an arranged marriage, we would have been very happy together. In our little twin beds.

After I met Vin, I stopped wondering about this. Vin is spread legs that press into yours while you're sitting next to him. Vin puts himself between you and a crowd so they jostle him and not you. Vin steadies your elbow when your high heel slips. I'm not, like, a destiny sort of person, but . . . It was like my reactions to the two of them were inverse. With Raff, all we did was chat and laugh. With Vin . . . on our first date, I watched him slide his wallet into his back pocket after paying for the meal and something about it literally made me blush. His hand (big fingers, veins, you get it) holding the door open for me. He got me the last seat on the bus and then stood facing me, his belt buckle at eye level. I mean, *God*.

Vin is not an intense-eye-contact sort of guy, he's an intense *eyes* guy. He looked at every inch of my face on that first date. When our gazes crossed, he'd look away. Like he didn't want me to see his thoughts. When we got off the bus, it was this moment when either we were going to part ways or he was going to take me the rest of the way home. I was rattled, trying to work out how to tell him I didn't want this to be over but also wasn't ready to invite him into my bed yet. I'd been talking all night to fill in the silences but now I couldn't think of anything to say. The silence swelled. He was flustering me by (it felt like) counting my eyelashes from two feet away. I snapped, held two hands up, and blocked his gaze, like it was bright sun in my eyes. "I can't tell if this is going well!" I blurted out.

His hands gripped mine, his thumbs drawing quick circles against my palms. He lowered my hands and for just the barest of seconds, all of his fingers dipped between all of mine. And then he carefully slid his hands into his pockets. "It's going very well," he said.

This didn't help the flustered thing I had going on. "Well!"

And he smiled then, the first time I ever saw it. His full, happy smile. Me being all nervous because of his proximity gave him great joy. "Can I walk you home?" he asked. "And see you tomorrow?"

And that's Vin. He does not fill silences. But when he asks a question, it's *Can I walk you home and see you tomorrow?* When he finally has something to say, it's *I thought about you today.* (Second date.)

Or *Cold?* (Third date, after he'd just raised all my goosebumps by sliding some of my hair out from under my collar.)

Or *Let me.* (Fourth date, my earring got caught on my sweater.)

And then, when he couldn't fucking take it anymore: *Come here.* (Fifth date, first kiss, my apartment, him standing, hands in pockets, in my kitchen, and me with my back to the counter. As soon as I took the first step, he closed the distance between us. It was the sort of first kiss that ended up with me on the counter and my legs wrapped around his waist. He rested his forehead against mine. *Yeah,* he'd said, like he'd finally confirmed something he'd been suspecting all along.)

Anyways, *Raff.*

When Vin and I got married, I felt very strongly that I was becoming both a wife and a sister. Part of me worried that things with Raff might change, now that Vin was my number one, but not much makes a dent in Raff's self-confidence. Our relationship as in-laws only flourished.

Not exactly sure if that works in reverse. It makes me sick to think about the potential of finding out.

I push the thought from my head and concentrate on Raff handing me a glass of red, washing scallions, and watching me flip the contents of the frying pan with one hand.

"What about dessert?" he asks.

"You have some bread in the fridge. And you're already on a breakfast theme. Toast it with butter and add some cinnamon and sugar."

"You should charge for this," he decides. "Make an app. When people don't know what to cook for dinner, you FaceTime them, look in their pantries and fridges, and tell them what to make."

"Or a cooking show," I say. "I'd have a camera follow me around while I knock on neighbors' doors and make something from nothing."

"I would absolutely watch that." He's slicing scallions extremely slowly, his tongue poking out of his mouth. "Anyways, I think they're underutilizing you at work. Only having you come up with one recipe a week? It's like having Superman on your payroll and just asking him to change the lightbulbs."

He's been on this lately. My wasted potential. He's certain I'm a genius. I keep trying to tell him he's confusing genius with just being old-fashioned.

"It does," I admit. "It does bug me that our reach, my reach, is all so limited. There are so many people who need a meal. And so much food getting dumped. Right this very second, as you're chopping scallions. It just—yeah, I can't think about it too hard or I spin out."

"What about the cookbook idea?"

I wince. Oh, the cookbook idea. One drunk night last year I confessed a silly little idea I'd been playing with. That maybe a cookbook would be a way to help people figure out how to use their pantries to put dinner on the table any night of the week. I was trying to think of a way, any way, to do basically what Raff just described with the FaceTime idea. How do I take all the years of accumulated recipe-ing that's in my brain and transmit it to all the brains of all the people trying to feed other people? Raff latched onto it with gusto because who doesn't love someone else's ambitious little daydream?

But then I started really thinking about it, and then I started feeling really sheepish about it. Because, what's a cookbook without a set ingredients list? And besides, it's not like I make up recipes, I just poach them from other, more experienced people.

"That idea is a bust," I tell Raff. When I think of how to turn my skills into a book, let alone sell the idea to someone who would help me make it . . . "I'm all cook, no book."

"It's not! At least do one for your friends and family. Like a Christmas gift kind of thing. I'm sick of calling you every time I need to cook a decent meal. I want to feed myself for once."

"This is what YouTube is for."

"This is what a best friend is for."

"Are you wearing that for your date?" I ask him, to distract him, and it works.

"This? Yeah? Why? It's bad?" It's a Mister Rogers sweater, but he cut off the sleeves midbiceps. He's wearing it open-face with no shirt underneath. And cutoff jean shorts that go down past his knees. He's got a hairy chest and a shaggy cut down over his eyes. He can't really grow a beard but his mustache is currently flourishing.

"You know what?" I decide after careful perusal. "He's probably going to rip his tiny pants off the moment he sees you."

Raff pats his bare belly. "That's what I was going for."

When I finish cooking, I clean. When I finish cleaning, I clean a little more. I'm just checking the expiration dates on his condiments shelf when a big, heavy arm gets draped over my shoulder. "Darling, are we bored?"

"Bored? No, no." Scared of returning to my sad, cold house where no one loves me? Yes, yes.

His eyes narrow at whatever he reads in my expression. "Should I cancel with Stan? I'm canceling."

"No! Don't cancel! I'm leaving." I bop his phone out of his hands and jam it back into his pocket, maybe a little aggressively.

"Are you sure you're okay?" Something akin to fear crosses his expression. If there's one thing I've learned this last year, it's that Raff really needs me (and Vin) to be okay. If we're okay, then he's okay.

"I'm fine. I'm really fine. I'm gonna go home and crash."

"Okay . . ." He's still suspicious. Following me to the door.

"Probably I'll watch *Golden Girls*," I say, trying to throw him off the scent of my existential depression.

This does the trick. His face eases. If I'm watching *Golden Girls*, then nothing bad is going to happen to me. I kiss his cheek at the door, wish him well on his date, and jet toward home.

I'm grumpy, tired, a little torn open and I'm not totally sure why. A bus pulls up to the curb half a block in front of me and I know it doesn't make sense, but running to catch it actually sounds way more tiring than just walking the twenty blocks home.

I hope Raff's date is filling him up with joy. I hope they're laughing a lot. I hope they're happy and fed. I hope they have amazing sex and then get Raff's quarterly taxes filed.

God, I'm raw.

Next to me, a car performs an ill-advised and poorly timed

left turn and oncoming traffic slams on its brakes. The braking sound just shreds me. The long, angry horns just end me. Obscenities are flung out open car windows while my heart races. I'm covering my mouth with both hands. By the time I get home, I'm like a balloon that's had pins dragged across the surface all day long. One more thing and I'm just going to pop.

I stop at my front door and press my forehead there while I fumble out my keys. Dinner. Oh, yeah. I still have to make dinner.

When the door swings open, tears fill my eyes, instantly blurring what I've gotten a half-second glance at. Because there's a full dinner sitting on my kitchen table. A simple chicken and rice. I can see where Vin's already taken his portion. His bedroom door is open, so I know he's not home, but there's a note next to the chicken.

*Raff told me you're helping him make dinner for his date. Marcia sent chicken and rice home with me today.*

—V

Marcia is married to his boss, Esteban. About three times a year she sends Vin home with a meal for us. I, of course, reciprocate. And it really couldn't have come at a better time. Because Marcia is a boss in the kitchen. Seriously. Some people just have it. And she has it.

I quickly wash up and then make myself a plate, thanking the universe and digging in. I really, really needed someone to make a meal for me tonight.

But . . .

I chew, swallow, and then take another bite. This is . . . kind of bland. And kind of tough. A little zip goes down my spine as I rise slowly from my chair and survey my kitchen. I don't see any of Marcia's normal glass Tupperware out. And... there are dishes drying in the rack that I didn't use. I walk slowly toward my oven, like I'm in a horror movie and the bad guy is about to jump out and make me fight for my life.

There's a high, tingly, trembly feeling in my chest.

I reach out an open palm. A question. An open request of the universe. *Tell me.* And I press my palm to the oven door.

It's still warm.

# Eight

*Our model this* week is a young blond woman named Mel. She's a grinning, friendly good time until she strips naked on the model stand and then she's Death Valley serious. She's got soccer player legs that pin her aggressively to the earth, no matter what pose she strikes, and I get lost trying to draw them.

"That's two muscles, actually, not one," Daniel says over my shoulder, putting his terra-cotta pencil on my drawing and adding an extra bump where I hadn't noticed there was one. "It's hard to tell from this angle, but look at her right leg. See? You can see it there."

"Ah. Right."

"And, Roz?"

I look at him.

"We're drawing Mel today," he says in smiling, gentle admonishment. "Not just legs."

"Oh." I eye my drawing pad. Across which five pairs of legs dance, all in different poses. "Right."

I lift my pencil to try to give these legs a torso, a head, a—God, help me—*face*, and I just, sort of, get stuck. What am I supposed to be looking for again? Organic, repeatable rhythms? Mel doesn't have a penis. So now I'm not sure how to draw her nose. But that's my best trick! Wait, what other body parts happen to look like other body parts?

Daniel pushes my pencil forward until it connects with the paper. "Draw, Antonio. Draw."

I'm not exactly sure what this Antonio business is all about, but I've heard him say it to other students, who also are not named Antonio, so I assume it has some meaning that's lost on me.

The timer dings. Mel gets dressed and drinks a smoothie in the corner while Daniel gives us all an anatomy lecture on what he calls "the autonomous unit of the arm," which apparently goes all the way across your shoulder blade and down your ribs. When the lecture ends, Daniel doesn't immediately call us all back to our easels and I notice that other students are walking in a circle, eyeing everyone else's drawings.

"Care for a stroll?" Lauro says to me, one elbow cocked out for me to take. "I'll give you a tour of your classmates." We start strolling. "Here's Reggie. He's a structural engineer, if you can't tell."

Reggie, the middle-aged redheaded man who I saw carrying Esther's grandson to a cab after class last week, has drawn a very different Mel than I have. Reggie's Mel has every single muscle a human can have. She's an architectural marvel. His lines are single and dark.

"Stacia makes everybody look like they could fly," Lauro says, affectionately, as we get to the next easel. And he's right. Her lines are feathery and delicate. Under Stacia's hand, Mel has become big-shouldered but skinny-waisted, like a bird about to take flight.

"Esther loves everyone." Esther's drawings are cherubic and simple. She hasn't bothered with muscles or bone structure, really. Esther's Mel is well fed and happy.

"Cindy's got attitude." And, boy, does she. Mel looks like Jack Nicholson.

"Penny finds every model's best feature immediately," he says admiringly. Penny's drawing is anatomical and sure-footed until it gets to Mel's chin and neck, which are done with the flourish of a treble clef.

"Shan is . . . Shan." These are anime-style drawings, they look nothing like Mel, but that doesn't seem to bother Shan, who is propped in her chair, texting and eating Swedish Fish.

We circumnavigate the room. I'm charmed by every new drawing, and artist, we see. I think, in the back of my mind, I'd been thinking that every person, besides me, was an artistic genius. I'd been expecting them all to be drawing on Degas levels. But no, these are ordinary New Yorkers taking an art class, just like me. Some with more practice than others. Some with more talent than others.

"Everybody's drawings . . ." I say slowly.

Lauro stops circumnavigating and eyes me patiently. He looks genuinely curious. Which, I'm not gonna lie, is a good look for him. Much better than his usual tinge of sexy-and-I-know-it.

"Everybody's drawings seem . . . a little bit like *them*." I try to formulate the thought. "It's like . . . each person . . . some part of their personality does the drawing, not just their hand."

Twin matches are lit behind Lauro's eyes. He gives me a brisk nod. "Undoubtedly." He opens his mouth to say more but snaps it closed when Em pauses next to us.

"In short," she says, "I wanted to understand myself."

"Hm?" I ask.

"It's something Matisse said. When he was talking about why he drew. He studied the great masters and drew from them, to learn. To find himself. He thought that expressing himself through drawing . . . that would be the best way to understand himself. As a person."

"Oh," I say.

Em pauses for another beat, perhaps waiting for me to contribute to the conversation by quoting Picasso or something. But when I don't/can't, she just bobs her head and ducks away.

Lauro is looking after her, but then turns to me.

"I'm very smart!" I insist. "I'll show you my SAT scores if I have to."

He's smiling wolfishly at me. "Everybody is here to learn."

It doesn't soothe me and isn't meant to. I stick my tongue out at him and he takes me by the shoulders and steers me toward another easel.

Lauro's drawings. "Sexy, right?"

I stop and look. He's annoying for saying it about his own work, but he's right. Lauro's drawings have an effortless appeal. Long, elegant lines that start at the spine, sail perfectly around the hip, curvily twist to a heel. No scritcha-scratch for him.

"Art school?" I ask him.

He pumps his eyebrows. "Among other things."

I'm about to ask him if he fucked my best friend last weekend but we make it, finally, to Em's easel.

He doesn't say anything, and neither do I. Because there are no words. To my surprise, tears prick at my eyes. I'm not usually a cry-at-art type of gal but Em has *captured* Mel.

Five different Mels stand, sit, and slouch together on the page. Like they all existed at once, like Em wasn't trying to draw the mechanics of five different poses, she was trying to draw different sides of Mel, that only she could see, that only Mel could show her. It's not a perfect likeness, because it's not photorealistic, which would have been boring and impersonal. No, it's not just Mel on the page, there's something personal to *Em* in these drawings as well. In the groups of muscles that bunch just a little too far, showing Mel's athletic vibrancy and Em's celebration of it. The lines are slightly exaggerated, don't meet at the cross sections, Mel's energy bursts forth from the page and so does Em's. It's the two of them at once. Artist and model. Married in a moment that has already passed, can never be replicated again, couldn't have been photographed, can only be drawn.

I'm moved beyond words.

"Wow," I whisper.

"Exactly," Lauro agrees. Thrilled that I get it.

I scrunch my face down. "I need more practice."

Raffi comes over for dinner a few nights later. Vin and I are still committed to the ruse. We're not exactly loving, but we're not outright cold, either. If he's noticed that Vin and I have been falling to pieces, he hasn't said anything. It occurs to me that maybe it happened so gradually it seems normal. Normal that Vin didn't eat dinner with us. That he's sitting at the kitchen table on his phone instead of chatting with us on the couch.

"Hey," I say to Raff, my legs stretched out onto the coffee table and my hands curled around an after-dinner cup of tea. "Where can I find free nudes in this city?"

I feel Vin look up at me.

"Say more about that," Raff answers.

"I'm super into the figure drawing thing. And I want to practice more than once a week. But classes are expensive. I need free naked people."

"Everyone needs free naked people."

"See, that's the problem. This whole city is horny. Nobody will pose for me unless it comes with a happy ending."

"Where were you looking for these people?" Raff demands. "Tinder?"

There's a clatter from across the room and I think Vin may have just bobbled his phone.

"Of course I'm not using *dating apps*. I just googled *free figure drawing, NYC*, but everything seemed super sketchy. Like, in someone's living room. That kind of thing. All the well-meaning naked people are behind a paywall."

"Can you draw from photos? There have to be figure drawing websites, or YouTube channels or something."

"I tried that, but I feel like a lot of the magic gets lost when it's in 2D. There's no connection with the model. No spark of the here and now."

Raff cocks his head to one side. "Sounds romantic."

"Figure drawing *is* kind of romantic. Not in a . . . flirtatious way. It's just really personal. Vulnerable."

"Right. The model is naked for you. Totally vulnerable."

"And you're doing your stupid little drawing of them, which shows all your flaws and your newbie-ness. Also totally vulnerable."

"Yeah, I can see how drawing from some pics on the internet could flatten that experience a little bit. Well, you can draw me, if you want."

Vin straightens up, like he might stand.

"I don't want to see you naked!" I say to Raff. "But thanks. Hey, speaking of naked, what happened with Lauro?"

He rolls his head to look at me. "Nothing. I mean, nothing romantic. He's a cool guy. I like him."

"His art is really elegant and pretty."

"Just like him," Raff says with a smile.

"Lauro is in your art class?" Vin asks from across the room, inscrutable.

"Yeah, that's how I met him."

"Why are you sitting all the way over there?" Raff asks him. "Quit being a grump and come join us." When Vin still doesn't move, Raff lifts his arms. "I need someone to cuddle me and make me feel alive."

Raff rotates his arms over in my direction, he's leaning in for the cuddle, and then Vin is there, squeezing in between us and wrapping an arm around his brother. "Alive yet?" he asks Raff with a couple rough, affectionate pats to the cheek. I set my tea aside just in time.

"Ah! Gah!" Raff tries to wrestle free from Vin's grip but Vin gets him by the calf, charley-horsing him and making Raff scream.

Raff is the consummate little brother, shouting for Vin to stop but then poking him the second he does. They pinch and wrestle like kids and when they finally tire, I'm grinning. Raff squiggles down the couch, shoving Vin away from him with his feet. Which squishes Vin into me and me into the side of the couch. Vin quickly moves his arm up and out of the way. But that means he's surrounding me now, his chest at my cheek and his arm basically around my shoulders.

Here's the thing about Vin. Nudie mag shamings or not, he's a very sexually vibrant man. Not to objectify him beyond belief but . . . he is kind of built for good sex. His body, yes, wide and sturdy and strong. But that's not even what I mean.

He's Mr. Take-Care-of-It. If you need the recycling taken out? He's on it. The groceries purchased? He's already at the store. Have you seen this man change a tire? It's *porn*. And if you, like me, happen to be married to him, and if you, like me, happen to get horny on a Saturday morning, and if you, like me, happen to look at him in a certain way, then he drops the newspaper and picks you up and makes the neighbors regret moving to this building, you lucky bitch.

Not that that's on the menu anymore. But I can feel his chest hair under his T-shirt and his deodorant is bringing me back to some very sweaty times and my memories are no one's business but my own.

"Sorry," he mutters, and tries to switch his weight.

Against my will, I tangle my fingers in his shirt, keeping him from moving away from me.

He doesn't breathe. His eyes are painting lines on my face.

*Does she want me against her?* I can feel him thinking. *Yes, you idiot,* I feel like shouting back.

The lease bares its teeth at me from the fridge, hidden underneath the grocery list.

I use my grip on his shirt to rearrange my own weight, a little farther from him, and then unhand him.

Vin's eyes are still reading me, even though my face is turned away now.

"You two are freaks of nature," Raff observes from his end of the couch. "You've been married for eight years. How can the sexual tension still be this strong? Hey, let's watch that Arnold Schwarzenegger movie where he's a cop."

"That's the description of all Arnold Schwarzenegger movies," Vin says, gruffly, finally taking his eyes off me.

"You two knock yourselves out," I say. "I'm headed to bed."

I'm in a lazily colorful blur of a dream when I hear my bedroom door open.

"Roz?" Vin whispers. "You awake?"

"Sort of," I whisper back, rolling over with a groan.

"Can I come in?"

I push myself up to a sit and rub my eyes. "Yeah."

He quietly closes the door behind him and comes to stand

at the edge of the bed, hands in the pockets of his sweats. "Raff is sleeping over." He clears his throat. "He's in the guest room."

Ah. Meaning he's sleeping in the bed where Vin has slept ever since Raff moved out. Meaning Vin doesn't have a bed to sleep in tonight. Meaning if I want to keep this discord a secret for any longer, then Vin has to sleep in here.

"Okay," I say, answering the question he didn't ask out loud and scooching over to the far side of the bed. Which, actually, is Vin's side of the bed normally, so when he pulls back the covers and slides in on my side, it makes everything even more disorienting.

I realize, at the last second, that since he didn't get in on his side, the bed didn't make its signature Vin squeak. I resist the urge to ask for a do-over.

His breaths are long and even but they aren't his sleep breaths.

"Maybe we should just tell him," I say.

Vin is quiet for a few breaths. "I don't like saying it out loud."

Which plucks a string inside me. I feel it twang down to my fingertips. That is *different* than saying he doesn't want to talk about it.

Not wanting to say it out loud makes it sound like he wishes it weren't true.

I bury half my face in the pillow and hope he can't make out my next words. "I haven't told anyone yet, either."

He sits up, and so do I, and we're face-to-face, just two feet between us. I wish the lights were on, so I could see his face. But then I remember that it doesn't matter anyways because of the beard.

"If you were gonna tell someone . . ." He clears his throat. "What would you say?"

"Oh. Um . . ." I consider all the different facets of the truth.

Eventually, I go with "That you signed a lease. And you're moving out."

"I haven't, though."

"Well, yeah. The lease doesn't start until August fifteenth. I'm not going to make you find a place to crash until then."

"No. Not that I haven't moved out. I—I mean that I haven't—" He cuts off in frustration, his eyes flitting to me and then away. "I can't have this conversation with you sitting there like that."

"Like what?" I look down at myself. I'm in a baggy sleep T-shirt that has Christmas trees on it because we're not Rockefellers and I don't have enough money or closet space to keep my seasonal pajamas limited to their season.

"Like, *come to bed, Vin.*"

I'm gobsmacked. "This says *come to bed* to you? What, you have a Mrs. Claus kink?"

"Roz, you look like *you*. Like the *you* I've been married to and sleeping with for eight years. Yes, this says *come to bed* to me. Because when you've got those sleepy eyes and you're all . . . in blankets and you're talking to me in the middle of the night, usually it's a *come to bed* situation and it's—" He cuts off, searching for the right word.

"Distracting?"

He lets out a gust of air that's supposed to sound like a laugh. "Sure. Distracting." He's frustrated and pushing his tongue into the side of his cheek and glaring at the wall and facing half away from me and I would put a million dollars on red 27 right now that this conversation is completely over.

And then he flushes that bet down the toilet. "Confusing, really." He clears his throat. "Is what I meant to say. Because right now you look like the Roz I've always been allowed to . . . touch. But . . . I'm not . . . allowed anymore. And I know that. But even so, it's . . . hard for me."

I have never ever heard Vin be so articulate about how he's feeling in a given moment. Ever. And the fact that he's saying these words at all is almost as impactful as the words themselves.

I say my words the moment I think them. "Are you? . . . Not allowed?"

Like, *Says who?*

His eyes are on mine. There's no green in the dark, only shadows. "I thought . . ." he says. "I thought you . . ."

But he can't come up with any more words. His breaths are fast and spilling out between us. I'm suddenly understanding exactly what he meant by a *come to bed* moment. Because having Vin look at me like that, sitting in the dark, while I have no pants on—

He puts one set of knuckles on the bed between us and leans in toward me, balancing his weight. I think he's going to go in for a kiss but then his free hand comes up and just rests on my cheek. His eyes close for a moment as his thumb waves hello to the soft skin under my eye.

I fist my hands in his T-shirt the way I did on the couch earlier. *Yes, you idiot*, written in every tremble of my fists. His nose touches mine and he's tipping me back, my head into the pillow and his body over mine.

Our lungs are racing each other, pressing our chests together. His hand, at the back of my head, tightens in my hair.

Blue tile flashes in my head. A wall of sound. Vin still and heavy atop me. Blood when I touch his back.

"No!" I gasp, but even before I gasp it, he was already scrambling up and off me.

His eyes are pinned to the neck of my shirt, which has slipped off one shoulder, exposing the thin scar down my collarbone. The same scar that extends the rest of the way, fourteen inches, down his back.

He's got one hand covering his mouth and his eyes are a little wild, he's breathing hard, and not in the delicious way he was thirty seconds ago. "Jesus." He's tearing his eyes from mine and turning away, giving me his back. His feet on the ground and his elbows to his knees. The picture of defeat.

It's not a mystery, really, why we stopped sleeping together after the accident. First of all, because we were literally injured and needed a lot of time to heal. Me, a sprained shoulder from where I fell and the laceration on my collarbone, four inches long. And Vin's down his back, fourteen inches long. From the same section of windowpane that the truck crashed through. Vin's injuries were, obviously, worse. He also scraped a lot of the skin off the back of his right hand. And then, of course, there was taking care of Raff.

We were battered people. There was the medical stuff, and the legal stuff associated with the accident. We were lucky if we slept a few hours in a row. I challenge literally anyone in the world to feel sexy under those circumstances. That was just . . . not what our marriage was about during that time.

This is the first time, since the accident, that Vin has laid me down in a bed, with intention. And if this were pre-accident, I'd already be biting a pillow and trying not to wake up Raff.

Instead, Vin sits, facing away from me and looking like he's never felt more worthless in his life.

When I touch his back—the side without the scar—he's sweaty. His muscles tighten under my hand. I'm not sure I'm welcome. "Don't leave," I whisper, and he turns his head enough to give me his profile.

"Let's just try to sleep," I say, tugging a tiny bit at his shirt. "If you get up right now . . . I feel like it'll all, just, break."

His brow furrows. "Isn't it already broken?"

But still, he lies down next to me.

# Nine

"*Hey, Google,*" I call, sitting at the high-top table in Kitchen B.

"Whaddaya want?" Deb the nutrition educator responds with a scowl. It's lunchtime and she's just putting the finishing touches on some fried-egg sandwiches for me and Cherise. We decided to take an unsanctioned break from bean lasagna today and I'm feeling the reward of it down to my very marrow.

We've been referring to Deb as "Hey, Google" since we found out that not only did she graduate from Le Cordon Bleu in the seventies, she became a registered nurse in the eighties and traveled the world with Doctors Without Borders. Oh, and she has a pilot's license. She knows literally everything. Hence the nickname. She's basically Google if Google had a soul and a New Jersey accent.

Deb slides the sandwiches onto the table and Cherise puts away the grant application she's been working on for the last three weeks. I'm eating lunch with the two people who keep the roof on Harvest NYC.

"I was just wondering," I say, faltering for a second, only because I'm not sure I actually *want* the answer to this question. "I was just wondering what you know about PTSD."

Both Deb and Cherise look up at me over their sandwiches in unison.

Cherise's eyes are wide, Deb's are narrowed.

"I just mean . . . you know everything about everything. So. Is it real?"

"Is it *real*?" She's looking at me like she's finally realizing just how puny my intellect really is. Which, of course, is why I'm asking Deb of all people. If I wanted a clinical answer, I would have actually googled this. But what I really want is for someone to gruffly point out the obvious to me. "I take it you've never met a Vietnam vet?"

"No! No, I know *that* is real. But, like, what about ordinary people? Civilians." I'm starting to flounder. "It's . . . recently been suggested to me that . . . I might have it."

They both nod in immediate understanding.

"From the accident?" Cherise asks gently.

I put my sandwich down. My stomach has just tightened. The blood in my extremities has started to do that fluttery thing it always does when someone says the word *accident* to me. "Yeah. I guess."

"You didn't get screened for PTSD?" Deb asks with a frown. "The hospital should have at least offered some services."

"There was this, like, worksheet thing. I filled it out."

"And nothing came of it?" Cherise asks.

I'm embarrassed about this part. "Well . . . it's so obvious . . . which answers you're supposed to give . . ."

"Oh, my God." Deb is tossing her sandwich onto her plate and raising her eyes toward the heavens. "She lied on the worksheet. It's not there for you to pass, you dummy. It's there for them to know if you need help!"

"She's not a dummy, Deb! You can't say that to people! Jeez. And the hospital probably should have offered some help, worksheet or not." At first glance, everything about Cherise is round and sweet, even her voice. But don't be fooled. She's the boss for a reason. She's a tenth-degree black belt in ass-kicking. The interns have a not-so-secret photo of Yoda with Cherise's face taped on. "Nobody ever suggested a therapist?"

I try to answer and then shrug in frustration. "Maybe? I honestly can't remember. Those early days, when Vin and Raff were still in the hospital . . . when I try to remember specific details . . . it's like . . . sticking my head in a wind tunnel or something."

Cherise and Deb share a glance. "But someone recently suggested you look into it?" Cherise asks.

"Vin thinks we have it."

"Well, you'd have to get properly diagnosed with it to really know."

"I know . . ."

"But honestly, it would be *weird* if you didn't have it. Considering," Deb says. She's nudging my plate toward me. I pick up the sandwich to appease her.

"I mean . . . I don't know about PTSD. But it's just been the *worst* year." It's such a simple statement, but it makes the back of my eyes hot with tears just to say it out loud. "The accident, yes. But everything since then, too. You'd think—you'd think going through something like that would bring you *closer* to someone—"

This is the closest I've ever gotten to admitting that the accident itself was terrible, of course, but the actual hardest thing about the last year for me was getting so distant from Vin. The emotion momentarily cuts off my air supply and I'm gulping against tears.

Cherise does me the favor of removing the sandwich from my clutches and handing me my glass of water. "Things . . . aren't good with Vin?" she asks hesitantly.

"No," I whisper. "Things are not good with Vin."

It's that awful/wonderful feeling of removing a splinter. It has to come out, but it hurts so fucking bad.

A group of people are laughing and joking in the hall and

Deb gets up and closes the door to Kitchen B. She turns back with her hands on her hips. "Come on. Let's hear it."

"We—can't communicate anymore. Or maybe we never could. But it didn't used to matter. Now . . . he's like a stranger to me. But also . . . he's still Vin. He's still the man I married. And I *just don't get it*. How, in just one year, could we be *here*?"

I don't say that *here* is Vin moving out, but I can see from their eyes that I don't have to explain the details of how broken we are. I don't have to spell out that last night my husband and I tried to do what we historically do best and ended up freaking the fuck out and when he rolled out of bed for work this morning, I felt his warmth leave my back, felt his hand leave my hip, which is how I learned we'd been spooning and I just, for the love of God, want to know how he felt about that.

The PTSD is seeming more and more plausible. (See above.)

Cherise has one warm hand over my cold ones. Deb is pointing at me with her sandwich. "Honey, that is the *deal* with these Italian American men. PTSD or not. They'll die for you but they won't tell you one word about how they're feeling."

I laugh in a knee-jerk reaction, but then her words sink in and make me feel so instantly ill, feverish and foul-tempered and nauseated, that I have to just put my hands over my face and breathe through it. I'm feeling irrationally angry at Deb for using the concepts of *die* and *Vin* in the same sentence. Why would she think I'd want to hear that? Dying for someone is *not* romantic. It's sickening.

I take a deep breath and lower my hands. "Not all Italian American men. Raff tells me every thought that ever comes into his head."

Cherise quickly slides back from the table and goes to root around in the fridge. She comes back with a covered plate of sliced cheeses. "Courtesy of Tommy."

Her boyfriend is a cheesemonger and I like him because, personally, I don't think you can beat complimentary cheese.

But Cherise is now avoiding my eye contact and I think I know why. "Are you still mad at Raff?" I ask her as I choose between two stinky cheeses.

"I was never mad."

Deb and I raise our eyebrows in unison and it makes her laugh and crack and roll her eyes. "Okay, okay. When some rando fools around with your little sister, it's okay to be *skeptical* of them!"

"He had honorable intentions!" I insist. Because he's my best friend and I don't think it's diametrically opposed for sluts to have honorable intentions.

"It was a fling for him, but it was serious for her."

I concede this, because I'm sure it's true. "I will say this about Raff: His superpower is getting people to take care of him. But he does it without thought; he doesn't even want it half the time."

"Was that . . ." Cherise clears her throat. "Was that part of what was hard about this last year? Taking care of Raff after the accident?"

I consider this. "Hard? I mean . . . I think . . . when Raff was still living with us, everything was on autopilot, sort of? It was just . . . take care of Raff. Everything was almost, kind of, simple."

"Things can be simple and hard at the same time," Deb says. "And there's no way it was easy, taking care of someone in that position. For you or your marriage."

I lean my forehead on my hand, like I'm shading my eyes

from the sun. But in reality, I'm shading myself from everything they're telling me. I hate that it might be true.

Raff is my family. Of course I dropped everything to nurse him back to health. But . . . is it part of the reason that Vin is leaving?

Deb's watch starts beeping. "Damn. I've got a class."

"I actually have a meeting, too." Cherise is looking miserable to leave me here, crying into my sandwich.

"Go. Go." I shoo them away. "I'm fine. Really."

"No, you're not," Deb corrects me with two rough hands on my shoulders. "But you'll get there."

They leave the kitchen and I clean up after our lunch. I'm on autopilot again. Hollow and tired and feeling like a stranger, myself. The rest of the workday jostles me back and forth. I don't see Cherise again, which is a relief because if I did I'd probably embarrass us both by collapsing into her arms in a fit of tears.

I do happen to hear Deb teaching in Kitchen A on my way out of work.

"My greens ended up soggy," a student laments. "They should have been crispy!"

"Don't waste your energy over how you think things *should* be," Deb booms. "See things for how they actually *are*. Soggy greens are better than no greens."

I'm shaking my head and smiling as I leave the building. Don't waste energy on *should*.

It's good advice, especially considering I only have about two teacups of energy left in my entire body.

I make it the five blocks to the train and collapse onto the wooden bench on the subway platform. A young couple walks past me, not even glancing in my direction. He's walking backwards while he holds her, his fingers laced against her lower back. She's pouting with her arms crossed and her eyes on anything but his face. They're having one of those arguments that are actually foreplay.

"Babe, it doesn't mean *anything*," he's reassuring her.

"Of course it means *something*. She's your ex."

"Right, exactly. Thank you for making my point for me." He's charming and foppish, bending at the knee to catch her eye.

"What point?" She's catlike and fierce, her hair is slicked back in a perfect ponytail, and her top is shiny black leather.

"That she's my *ex*," he says triumphantly. "Not my girlfriend."

"And if I were your ex and slid into your DMs, would that be meaningless too?" Now, she's the one who's triumphant. Her logic's got him on the ropes.

He looks momentarily stymied. If he admits that some exes are meaningful, he's in trouble again. If he says that all exes are meaningless, including her, if she ever becomes one, he's in trouble again.

His confidence is restored and he goes for broke. "If you were my ex, I'd be the one sliding into *your* DMs. I'd be a lonely loser and I'd probably spend a week trying to figure out the perfect way to say *what's up?*"

She's trying to maintain annoyance but her face is looking mighty pleased. She can't think of a reply that doesn't undermine her previous stance on the matter, so instead, she just stomps off and he jogs happily after her, clearly forgiven.

There's a lot going on there, and frankly, I give them about three more months, tops, before the writing's on the wall, but oh, I remember those days. When you've gone absolutely loopy over someone and it's time to start figuring out if they have a secret shoebox filled with love letters from the one who got away.

A memory blossoms up before me. It's me and Vin, in a

hammock, at his mother's house, about eight months after we started dating:

*"Do you miss Yvette?" I ask, faux-casually. Yvette was his last girlfriend. They broke up about a year and a half before and we recently ran into her at the Union Square farmer's market. She's been stuck in my head since then.*

*"Miss? No." He's tucking my hair behind my ear. He's obsessed with tucking my hair behind my ear. He says I have ears like a fairy and the acoustics must be terrible.*

*"Well," I press. "You were together for six months . . . do you ever miss anything about your relationship with Yvette?"*

*"Um . . ." He thinks, his eyes on the stars and his thumb moving down to draw a circle under the sleeve of my T-shirt. "She was the only person who'd ever said they wanted to marry me. That was nice."*

*"Oh." I stiffen.*

*He stiffens too. "I mean—I wasn't—"*

*"Okay," I say. "We could do that. The getting married thing."*

*Silence. His thumb's gone still. The crickets are deafening. Even the breeze has fled.*

*And then, "Okay." And his thumb starts up that circle again.*

*"Wait. Really?" I prop up on one elbow, which is extremely difficult in a hammock. His eyes are too shadowed for me to see but he lifts his head and kisses me softly, meltingly, drawing me back against him and then settling me in the crook of his neck.*

*"I'll marry you," he says . . .*

I stand up off the bench and board the train that's just pulled into the station. I hold the bar and sway, staring into nothing. A realization is hitting me in slow-speed stages. I'm thinking of Vin. Of how he phrased that. He didn't say *Let's get married*. Or *Will you marry me?* (which would have been odd, considering I had pretty much just proposed to him). He'd said, *I'll marry you.*

The phrasing of that reminds me of something. It's catching at the edge of my brain. I can't fit the puzzle piece into the puzzle.

I'd wondered for years if I'd sort of cornered him into agreeing to marriage. Like I'd made it too awkward for him to say no . . .

But on our fifth anniversary I finally cracked and told him I'd been worrying about that. And I'll never forget what he said. That those eight months had been the longest of his life. That he was waiting to get to a year before he proposed because he worried I'd be freaked-out if he brought it up earlier.

What was it that Deb said about Italian American men? They'll die for you but won't talk about their feelings?

Vin never would have brought that up about our proposal if I hadn't come to him with tears in my eyes.

That's the way he is. *And he always has been. And I never used to mind it.* He doesn't say a lot . . . but maybe he says it all.

We pull into Grand Central, I get service, and my phone ding-a-lings. It's a text from Vin blinking up at me. A photo he's taken in the condiments aisle at the grocery store. A blurry close-up of jars of miso.

*Did you need red or white?* his text reads.

A warm confusion starts to spread over me, like waking up from a nap in a puddle of sunshine.

He doesn't say a lot but he says it all . . . And suddenly that puzzle piece clicks into place. I recognize the phrasing of *I'll marry you.*

*I'll marry you.* Said to me in a hammock a decade ago.

*I'll go.* Said to me outside Raff's door just weeks ago.

They *should* feel like bookends, but they don't. I can't explain it, but these two sentences, said by the same man, in completely opposite circumstances, *feel* like they mean the same thing.

I try a door inside my heart. I expect it to be locked, but the doorknob circles freely under my trembling grip. The nameplate on that door? It reads: You're Missing a Crucial Piece of Information, Roz.

I thought I'd understood it all and that there was only one possible reason for that lease. That my version of the story was certainly his version of the story because there could only possibly be one version of the story. But he's texting me from the condiments aisle because he . . . gives a shit about me getting what I need. Which, even though everything else is different, *is* Vin in a nutshell . . . And always has been.

I try the door again.

Still open.

Still free.

Still mine to step through.

So, what is Topic Roulette?

(Pick a topic out of the hat and then tell the first story that comes to mind!)

With no preparation? Jeez. You are hardcore people. Okay, then. My topic is— Oh, for the love of God.

(What is it?)

"Talk about losing your virginity."

(YES.) (Roz!) (Roooozzzzzz.) (ROZ!)

Oh, come on. I did not lose my virginity to Roz! We met when I was thirty-two! Although . . . I might have been more nervous sleeping with her for the first time than when I actually did lose my virginity. Which was when I was sixteen. At a movie theater. By the way.

(Vin!)

(Big Vin!)

(Vinny gets it done!)

Yeah. Yeah. So, did I do it? My turn is over?

(Pick a different one!)

(Yeah, that one was stupid, who put it in there? Bill? Did you put it in there?)

(It's a topic with potential for tension, intrigue, embarrassment, triumph. What more could you want, Irene?)

(New topic!)

Okay, new topic. This one is . . . wow. Okay. It says, "The end is the beginning." Right . . . I'll try.

A story where the end is the beginning . . . Let me think . . .

So . . . No one ever actually gets what they want. Let's just start with the fact that I understand that.

Now, here's the story of how I thought I was actually about to get everything I'd ever wanted.

(Yes!)

(He's finding his rhythm, people!)

(Tell 'em, Vin!)

And how, for seven years, I had it.

I asked someone to marry me. And she said yes.

And I don't know about anyone else. But for me, asking someone to marry me made me think a lot about death.

And I don't mean that in a, like, oh-I-secretly-hated-my-wife sort of way, like I couldn't wait for the sweet relief of death. I mean that in a, you know, till-death-do-us-part sort of way.

I . . . I am not someone who . . .

I . . . have always known that I needed to live for a very long time.

In fact, I needed to live long enough to . . .

Does anyone else have a complete dumbass for a little brother? Yes, okay, based on the laugh that got, I guess I can see that almost everyone who has a little brother thinks he's a complete and utter dumbass.

Well, mine is a dumbass but he's also . . . like Bambi? Like a butterfly? He's . . . he's a colorful and precious soul and needs to be protected. He'd hate that if he heard it. I'd hate that if someone said it about me. It probably says more about me than it does about him that I'd classify him that way.

But here we are.

He once got severe pancreatitis from eating too much fruit. As a twenty-eight-year-old man, he almost fruited himself to death.

This is what I'm saying.

I have always known that I needed to live a very long time so that I could outlive him. Because what would he do without me? It was my job, as his older brother . . . I was there the day he was born. There are Polaroids to prove it, and I would be there to help him to the other side someday, I just always sort of knew this . . . without thinking too hard about it . . . I knew it.

But then I met a woman.

(Roz!)

(Roz!)

Oh, fine. Yes. I obviously talk too much about my wife. You've heard the stories. I get it. Get a life, Vin. Well, yeah. You should be so lucky to love someone as much as I love her.

ANYWAYS. I met a woman. And she has this way about her. For the first time in my life, I wasn't the only one changing the pillowcases. She was choosing the soap she thought smelled best. Someone else was thinking about tax season. Someone else . . .

So, for me, marrying someone, it felt a little bit like infinity? Like, yes, obviously forever just means until you die. But I took her hand and it occurred to me that I might get hit by a bus. I might . . . get cancer. I might have a heart attack. I might die tomorrow. And it would be all right, because she would be there for my brother. Loving her meant loving him. Meant putting my heart into someone else's body because she loves him too. She's not going to let my brother be alone even if I'm dead . . . Even if we get divorced. Loving her has felt . . . like immortality? I was giving myself, extending beyond my, whatever, my body, my, my, my mortal confines! That's what it's called. My mortal confines.

And here's the thing. Because I stopped thinking, for the first time, that I'd have to outlive my brother just as a matter of course, because I was suddenly able to just die whenever I'm gonna die, suddenly . . . I realized that I might not die alone.

Look, I haven't spent a ton of time picturing this. And I know this makes me sound so sad and like Beetlejuice or whatever, I'm just saying that in the back of my mind, I always thought I'd die alone.

But I asked Roz to marry me and it suddenly seemed like I probably wouldn't.

That there would be somebody to make sure there were flowers on the grave. And I just . . . I just got used to that really fast.

I put my heart in her chest and she carries it around. And she'll put flowers on my grave.

And from the moment I realized that I wanted to marry her, I was already thinking about the end. Not the end of our relationship, but the end . . . of it all.

Loving her made me think about death. In a good way. It was a gift. It was because I wasn't scared to go. Not when I had her.

So, that's . . . Yeah. It's not a story, really. It's my thought. She's my "the end is the beginning."

# Ten

*Last week, after* seeing Em's work, I left this classroom feeling excited and inspired. Nevertheless, this week I'm glaring at some truly awful drawings on my drawing pad. There is nothing to be found of the model in these drawings and I certainly hope there's nothing to be found of me because these are ugly, stunted scribbles.

Can I blame it on Vin and the fact that I'm starting to see some things I hadn't been able to see before, yet I've not actually seen *him* since we fell asleep in bed together? Sure, yeah. That sounds plausible.

Our model is Pavel again, and you'd think it would be easier to draw someone familiar, that you've already drawn.

But—big bummer—I'm not finding myself spiritually connected to his vulnerability. I'm finding myself irritated at him because drawing is hard.

Which is obviously not fair. But here we are.

My pencil gets pressed to the paper by Daniel's hand. "Draw, Antonio, *draw*," he says.

I put my hands on my hips and face him. "But I don't know how to draw!"

Apparently Daniel has got a little sweet-and-sour sauce of his own because he puts his hands on his own hips. "And you think you'll learn from me telling you how?"

"Well!" I shake my head at myself and let my arms go limp.

"Obviously not. Obviously I can only learn from *draw, Antonio, draw*-ing."

He laughs. There's affection in his eyes. He's sensing yet another teaching moment, courtesy of the noob. "Do you know what I'm quoting when I say that?"

I shake my head. The timer beeps and Pavel puts his basketball shorts back on.

Daniel walks to the big chalkboard at the corner of the room and roots around for some chalk. There are still his notes from earlier in class (about the position of ribs and sternum and what it means for the pelvis), so he flips the board to the clean side. And is confronted with a comically excellent drawing of an enormous, hairy dick and balls.

"Ha ha," Daniel says, erasing it.

"It was a nose and ears!" Lauro calls from the back of the classroom.

When he's erased our collective defilement, he writes in big letters on the board, *Draw, Antonio, draw*.

"Does anyone know who this quote is attributed to?" he asks.

"The one," Esther says, snapping her fingers. "The one guy. The famous guy."

"Yes, he was very famous," Daniel prompts.

"This guy," Esther says, and does a saucy little pose.

"The *David* pose! So, yes! You are correct, this was said by Michelangelo."

"Nice, Esther!" I go up for the high five and she wins my heart for life by kissing her own palm before high-fiving me back.

"Okay. So this is the first half of a quote that Michelangelo said to his apprentice, Antonio. Does anyone know the second half of this quote?"

A chair scoots out and Em stands up. She's almost six feet tall, by the way. Today she's wearing wide-legged jeans with a hand-embroidered orca whale on them and a tight black tee. "Draw, Antonio, draw, Antonio," she quotes, her voice so sure I feel like I'm listening to someone sing. "Draw, and don't waste time."

She sits back down and all of us, to a T, applaud.

"Yes." Daniel points at her. "He tells him to draw three times in the span of two sentences. Seven, eight, *nine* words total and three of them are the command to draw." He turns to the board and studies it, lost in thought, his head cocked to one side. "'And don't waste time' . . . as if . . . as if all the time in Antonio's life spent *not* drawing is a waste."

"Harsh," says Shan.

"Okay, right. So, maybe it's not every second of Antonio's life that's a waste." Daniel is gathering us around, pulling out a chair for Esther, moving an easel so that Reggie can see him.

"Let's picture it. Realistically. Michelangelo is probably not shouting this out a window to Antonio while Antonio is playing basketball. No. *Really* picture it. Michelangelo is almost certainly saying this to Antonio while Antonio is about to draw . . . but hesitating. While Antonio is deliberating over whether to start at the torso or the feet. While he's remembering his last drawing that didn't go so well. While he's telling himself he's no good. Or that he has to be better."

I gulp a little, my eyes stinging, yet again, in this classroom.

"Michelangelo," Daniel continues, "master that he is, already knows the secret. The only time you ever get better at drawing is *while you're drawing*. He knows that hesitating is nothing more than, I don't know, preemptive lamenting! And Michelangelo knows that attempts are *it*. The whole point. Sacred. There *is* no lamentable attempt!"

He's pacing in a large oval now, his hands behind his back. We're a group of prairie dogs, all pivoting our heads in unison to watch him.

"I love when he's like this," Penny says, and I look back to see their elbow resting on Lauro's shoulder. Both of them smiling affectionately at Daniel as he corrals his thoughts.

"Which!" Daniel says triumphantly, when he's gotten a hold of his thought. "Leads me to the concept of attempts. The only reason we hesitate to draw is the fear of failure. So . . . let's start there. Drawing shows you, graphically, all that you don't understand. This is why artists study anatomy. If, when you're drawing Pavel's leg, you don't understand where the shin bone connects to the ankle bone, and you draw it lining the outside of his leg instead of the inward slant, you're going to end up with ogre legs in your drawing. Which is fine. It's *fine* to draw ogre legs. Awkward drawings are wonderful!"

He's gesticulating purposefully and staring into nothing.

"They're a formulation of thought. An *attempt*. And that is what is so wonderful about drawing. It *is* thought. It's not Tetris. It's not autopilot. It's an active playtime, between what you already understand and what you're learning in the moment. And most importantly what you're *seeing*. Draw, Antonio, draw! Draw what you see and show yourself what you don't understand yet! What a gift! Every drawing a road map to what you need to learn? Is there anything else in life that gives so generously? Don't waste time! If we can't even put pencil to paper, then what are we doing here? Go, go knit a sweater. Eat pizza! Live and don't waste time! But if you are here, if you have the pencil in your fingers and Pavel on the stand . . ."

*Draw and don't waste time.*

"Whoa, you're home early," Vin says with a start as I bang through the front door and throw my bag on the ground. "I thought you had art class?"

"I did! I ran home after!"

"Wow. Are you all right? You're looking a little . . ."

"I'm not all right! I'm wasting time!" Daniel has exposed a glaring passiveness in me. I've been sitting on a folding chair and watching my life slip past me. It's time I jump on a motorcycle and chase it down.

"You're late for something?"

"No! Yes! I have to do something." I open up my and Vin's laptop and navigate to NYC Craigslist. After Daniel's lecture, Pavel got back on the model stand and I locked in like I never had before. My drawings were not drastically different than the ones I'd made earlier in class, with one main exception: I did not hesitate. I was calm and happy just trying.

So now? Now, I'm going to find someone else to draw naked if it's the last thing I do. I've never been so motivated to get better at something in my life. Drawing is leading me toward something. It's so close I can taste it.

Vin is drifting toward my back. I feel his eyes flick to the computer screen and away. And then back. He steps into my eyeline and lifts one eyebrow. "You're taking out a Craigslist ad?"

"Yeah."

"For what . . ." He already knows. I can feel it.

"Naked people with pure hearts."

The laptop gets closed, nearly chopping my fingers off. "Roz, no."

"Quit it!" I attempt to yank his hand away from the laptop.

"This idea is not good."

I'm laughing because the way he phrased that makes it

sound like such a simple yet epic burn. "Well, I'm out of other ideas! I can't afford another class. I want to draw more than once a week. I've been thinking about this for a while. At first it was just a thing I wanted, and I wasn't sure the added complication of finding a model was worth it. But look, these classes are important to me. Drawing is . . . I'm into it! I want to do as much as I can! And the figure is a pretty important part of *figure* drawing."

"Well, it's not going to be a *figure*," he says with one gigantic hand still flat on the cover of the closed laptop. I'm attempting to open it and failing completely. "It's going to be a *man* with a *boner* and a *Polaroid collection*."

I burst out laughing again. Vin is funny when he's funny. "Well, what am I supposed to do?"

"Go to an art museum and draw the marble sculpture people." He's gesticulating, trying to come up with the right words. His cheeks are slightly pink above the beard. He puts a hand on the back of his neck. "That's probably better than 2D, right?"

I get a tickle of intuition. "Did you . . . did you research this for me?"

Drawing from the marble sculptures at the Met is a long tradition for art students. One that would have never occurred to me before if Daniel hadn't talked about it last class.

"I . . ." He's palms up. "I get why this not having people to draw is a problem for you! But I . . . don't want you mixed up with strangers."

These are long sentences for Vin. These are feelings and desires. *Doesn't say a lot but says it all.*

My phone ding-a-lings. It's a text. Cherise. "Oh. The ingredients list came in," I mutter, clicking into the photo she sent of what they've been able to rescue this week.

I normally get it early on Saturday mornings, but it can get so down to the wire with whether I can actually come up with something by Sunday, I really don't mind at all that she's texted me about work at ten o'clock on a Friday night.

"Zucchinis, beets, and bell peppers. Hmm. Dang. I don't think we have any of these right now. I'll have to buy them." I slide the laptop aside and stand up and Vin's shoulders loosen, he falls back a little.

I really hate when I have to go out and buy the ingredients that we have such a surplus of in the refrigerated Harvest NYC truck parked somewhere in Harlem. But it doesn't often make sense for me to schlep across the city and back for something I could usually buy for less than ten dollars at the grocery on the corner (which is open until eleven).

"I'll go," Vin says. "Just text me the list."

He's walking backwards. Eyes on me. He grabs his house keys off the hook.

I decide to test a theory. "Hey."

Vin pauses.

"Will you pick up some cookies, too? From that place I like?" (An all-natural bodega two neighborhoods away, the only place in the city that carries this particular brand.)

"Sure."

"Oh, and also Raff said he had some Tupperware of ours. Do you mind grabbing it?" (Another half an hour on his trip.)

"Okay."

"Oh, and I said I'd feed the fish at Surya's house while she's in Tampa." (A high school friend who Vin doesn't even like and who lives on the Upper West Side. This will add at least an hour, maybe more.)

"Oh. Uh. Sure, do you have her keys?"

"Oh, my *God*!" I throw my hands in the air. "Vin!"

He's scratching at the back of his neck. "What?"

"What the hell?"

"What?"

I'm inflating like a puffer fish, filled to the gills with that warm confusion I first discovered when he texted me about the miso. "Why are you doing all this crap for me?"

He blinks.

"Seriously." I'm literally pulling at my hair. "I don't get it. You're texting me about miso. You'll go feed Surya's fish? *Do you want me or not?*"

He puts the house keys back on the hook and says the only thing that it's possible for him to say in this scenario:

"*What?*"

I do understand this reaction, even if it utterly infuriates me.

"No, because let's do some math here, okay?" I'm standing now, ticking things off on my fingers. "You decide to move out without any conversation. Right after you move to the guest room *without any conversation*. So I'm thinking, okay he wants out. He's over me."

Vin inflates. He's suddenly grown three inches. He takes a step toward me but I hold up a stop sign and plunge on.

"But then, a couple weeks later, you're all of two seconds away from pulling a wedding night Edward Cullen on me in bed. So, maybe *not* so over me."

"Who is Edward Cullen? Wait, the vampire?"

"You wanted to fuck the headboard off the bed, Vin! I was there! You can't fool me! So . . . you want me but you're leaving. You want space but . . . you'll run errands for me at ten o'clock at night? You'll feed the fish at Surya's house, Vin? At 131st and Amsterdam Avenue? Are you kidding me? What is this? Do you want me or not? *What am I to you?*"

His mouth opens and then closes. He throws his hands up and then lands them at his sides. He very obviously cannot find the words. Eventually, instead of answering my question verbally, he lifts his left hand and shows me his wedding ring.

It's gold and substantial, used to be his grandfather's. Vittoria brought it to him after we eloped. I don't wear one and never have. It never seemed important to me. And besides, I like to switch up my jewelry. There was never something I could imagine wearing forever.

I'm shaking my head. "*No.* No, that's not an actual answer."

"It's . . . it's a symbol."

"Vin. I don't want to be a symbol. Symbols can be interpreted in a million different . . . And I just want to know what *you* . . . You know what? Let me explain something I learned in my art class." I reach across the counter and grab the lined pad of paper we use for the grocery list. It's a clean sheet. On it I draw a stick figure with a skirt on. "See that?"

"A stick figure?"

"You know what my teacher said about them? That even a bad drawing, even a laughable attempt at drawing what you're seeing, what's really there, is superior to a stick figure. Even if your drawing is so deformed you can't even tell what it is." I'm pointing at myself. I'm the thing that's gotten so deformed. "You know why? Because even if a stick figure, or any symbol, is instantly recognizable, it's not *honest.* It doesn't show you what's actually there."

"You're saying—"

"You can't even say the word *wife* out loud. You show me your ring and think I should just get it? How you feel? Maybe if you weren't *moving out.* But . . . Vin. I mean. Sure, sure, you wear the ring and it's recognizable to the whole world what exactly it means. But to us? To you and to me. Is it *honest*, Vin? Does showing me that ring say *anything* about how much we've changed this past year?"

His mouth opens and then closes. He twists his wedding ring one full revolution around his finger. "I . . . never imagined . . . the symbol of it . . . would make you feel dishonest."

"Well . . ." I hesitate. I almost don't ask. But . . . *There are no lamentable attempts.* "How does it make *you* feel?"

He scrubs his hands over his head and then twists his ring again, his eyes glued to it. "Calm . . . Settled . . . It . . . for me, it doesn't *need* words."

*Draw and don't waste time.* "For me it does."

He flinches, his face staying all crunched down on itself, then he lets out a long breath. "I get that you need me to say . . . to tell you . . . and I'm practicing. I swear to God I'm practicing. But when *you* feel something you just tell me. But my thoughts . . . don't . . . go in a straight line . . . You want answers . . . But that's not what comes. What comes . . . is a cloud. Feelings I don't have words for."

This is not news to me. We've been married for eight years. I know that my husband is not a verbal processor. Insights into his thoughts and feelings historically only come when he's relaxed and open, not when I'm demanding answers. Right, it's not news, it's not a pivotally new piece of information. But . . . hearing him say it out loud. Hearing him reach for a description that feels accurate to him . . . My breath is catching. Holy shit, Michelangelo was really onto something. Drawing is the only time you're actually getting better at drawing. Well . . . turns out talking with Vin is the only time I'm actually getting better at talking with Vin. There is genuine traction in this conversation.

"Roz," he says in a low voice. His eyes are suddenly red and slitted. "I know . . . it's bad with . . ." He points at his heart and then at mine. "And usually I . . ." He points at his heart again, and then, again at mine. "But since . . . since the accident . . . the cloud . . ." He taps his temple. "It's like a tornado."

I'm immediately winded. Aching for him. I think of his inscrutable exterior, thoughts like a tornado on the inside. How painful it must be to keep that permanently contained.

"But you want to know how I *feel*," he continues. "Why I'll do errands . . . and the headboard thing . . . and also the lease . . ." he tries, his voice low. "Well. You are my wife . . . To me . . . We are having a tough time . . . but that doesn't mean . . . I won't do for you."

Emotion rises in my throat. It's not the answer I was (yes) hoping for. It's not *I want you, I love you, I'll never leave, let's forget any of this happened.* But in some ways it's better.

Picture Vin with a gigantic treasure chest filled with heavy steel letters. He just painstakingly rooted through that chest and laid each letter for me on the table. I'm his wife and he's going to do for me.

I scramble to come up with a reply and only find the ever-genius "Well. Now I know!"

Somehow my hands are thrown out to the sides.

I wish he'd stop looking at me.

He catches his left hand in his right. Under his fingers his wedding ring slides in a smooth circle around his finger, like it's been trained to spin and spin and spin and never stop.

"I know because you *told* me," I say on little more than a whisper. "So thank you. Because you don't *normally* tell me. So I don't *normally* know."

I'm feeling relieved. Like I've just set down a twenty-pound grocery bag. I needed something and I asked for it and he gave it to me. Look at us! It's working— But when I look up and take in his expression, I read . . . dismay.

"But . . . but you *do* normally know," he says in a low voice. "You can tell what's . . . going on with me. You . . . you were like the first person who just got me. Without . . ."

*Without him having to say anything.*

Tears spring up from deep within, pinching behind my eyes. "Oh, good. Another thing I'm failing at."

"No. No, I— See! See, this is why it's a bad idea for me to say this stuff. Because when I do, I just end up making you sad."

"News flash. I was sad before."

"I know."

"And so were you."

"No. I was determined. I . . . thought I could fix it . . ."

By leaving? Or . . . I suddenly remember the sign on that door I discovered the other night. *Roz, there's something extremely important that you're missing.*

"Vin . . . how did you think you could fix it?"

"I thought . . . space . . ."

"Right. Space." I'm not sure if I'm offering it to him, or asking him why he's already taking it. "You want space. I mean, obviously you do," I mutter. "You're the one who signed a lease."

He's turned half away from me. I can tell from the stubborn set of his jaw that this conversation is coming to a screeching halt. It occurs to me that it's not stubbornness. It might just be fatigue. He's been very clear that he's not good at this.

I'm not good at running up a hill with a forty-pound sack of flour on my back. If you asked me to do that for twenty minutes after sundown, I'd probably cry uncle myself.

His chin comes up. "That lease doesn't start until August fifteenth."

It's the second time he's mentioned that explicitly. And this time . . . I have to ask. "What are you saying?"

"I'm just saying . . ."

I wait. *Please say that you're not going.*

"That I'm still here."

# Eleven

**Only Raff would** host a housewarming party at a bar fourteen blocks from his actual house and almost three months after he moved in.

"My apartment is too small!" he'd insisted to me when he'd floated the idea.

"Then call a spade a spade, Raffi. This is just a party."

"No, no," he'd said. "I want people to bring me houseplants and colanders. It *has* to be a housewarming."

Thus this jade plant balanced inside a vegetable steamer that I carry into Bar Samantha. Which is a romance-novel-themed bar, complete with pink velvet barstools, stacks of books for anyone who comes here to have a drink and read, and, of course, women in reading glasses seemingly confused by the hive of men buzzing in the back corner.

Raff's friends are cleanly cleaved into two groups. There are his work friends—fellow engineers in button-downs, drinking neurotoxic IPAs and following Phish around the country during their PTO. And then there are his nonwork friends—every age and gender, tongue-pierced poets and musicians, the couples who live in Brooklyn Heights and ask Raff to spice up their marriages, the broke college kids he meets when he thrifts on the NYU campus, family friends he kisses on the lips, his former neighbor whose dog he walks because her arthritis has been acting up, and yes many of them also follow Phish around the country with their PTO.

I march straight up to Raff—where he's being petted by a woman in a five-thousand-dollar necklace while her husband watches—and shove my gift into his free hand. "Hi, I love you."

"Hi!" He takes his other hand out of the woman's back pocket and gives me a big hug. "Laurel, meet my best friend Roz. Roz, meet Laurel."

"Hi," I say, and shake her hand. And then I quickly point toward the bar and head in that direction because if you start letting Raff introduce you to people, pretty soon that's the only thing you do for the next hour.

I detour on the way to the bar, distracted by the presents table. It's overflowing with gifts. I spot one in particular that makes me smile.

The bar is getting crowded with Raff's associates. An ex-girlfriend of his is clearing some armchairs back, I think she works here. She's turning up the music, doing some nonsubtle ass-shaking in Raff's direction.

Once again, I'm doing a hell of an impression of myself.

Yes, technically, I'm standing here in this bar, nodding and smiling at a few of Raff's friends. But mentally . . . *I'm still here,* my husband says.

I don't know what you've been thinking about since yesterday, but that phrase has been on constant repeat for me. And tonight, apparently he means it literally. Because after one more scan of the room, my gaze catches on Vin's gaze where he leans his back against the bar, hands in his pockets. He is one hundred percent green eyes and dark hair and calmly watching me pretend to breathe.

He wore a collared shirt and his nice jeans to his brother's party because he's a respectful and thoughtful son of a bitch.

*I'm still here.*

Something in me snaps.

I narrow my eyes at him from ten paces. He narrows his right back at me.

I put one hand on my hip. He raises his eyebrows.

*I'm still here,* I mouth at him from across the room.

*What?* he mouths back.

And so I know it's safe to go ahead and ask him the question. *The* question. The only question.

*I'm still here, for now?* I mouth at him. *Or I'm still here, no matter what?*

He cocks his head to one side, his brow furrowed. He's staring at my mouth. *What?* he mouths at me again.

Look, a new life has started whether I've realized it or not. I draw on Friday nights. I ask my coworkers about PTSD. The terrible truth is that I don't actually need him to answer that question. I need to know what I would even *do* with either answer.

*If you leave,* I mouth at him, warning him. *It'll tear my heart out. But I'm going to keep on living.*

He's still staring at my mouth, trying to parse out the words I'm mouthing at him. Now his hands are out of his pockets, and he's straightening up.

One of Raff's coworkers leans over and says something to him, but Vin outright ignores him. He can't take his eyes off me.

I'm calling this a new life but . . . I feel a swell of something familiar. It feels . . . like me. Me pre-accident. Like the old me. Like the person who didn't used to sit around wondering if her husband still loves her.

He's right. I used to just know. But these days, I have to ask.

And look at me go. I've just said exactly what I meant to Vin. Across the room, granted. Where he definitely couldn't hear me, sure. But staring into his eyes, nonetheless.

For the first time in a very long time, I'm feeling strong. I think I'd like to test my wingspan.

I swagger over to the bar and straight to the open area at Vin's elbow. He keeps his back to the bar and looks down at me. I wave at the bartender and she winks to let me know I'm next.

I lean back and peer around Vin's chest, ignoring the fact that his eyes are following me. "Hi, Sidney," I call to the previously ignored coworker.

"Roz!" He's delighted. He leans across Vin as well and busses my cheek. Vin's eyes keep following me as I order my drink, make small talk with Sidney, shoo Sidney off when his wife arrives at the other end of the bar.

And then it's just the two of us in a crowd full of people we vaguely know. I've got my eyes on the mirror behind the bar, which gives me the perfect view of the impromptu dance floor that's heating up over my shoulder. And the even more perfect view of the back of Vin's head as he leans next to me, looking out at the room. That's one thing about Vin, you can put your back to a room full of people and he'll keep an eye on the whole world for you.

"So, uh," he finally says, and I can't help but smile to myself. I feel like I won some small competition, getting him to speak first. "What were you mouthing at me?"

I lean back and raise an eyebrow. Our eyelines meet like magnets. "Oh," I say airily. "You'll never know."

He recoils slightly, trying to get a read on me.

"So," I say, facing back to the bar. "Your brother is living on his own. In a nice apartment. With a vegetable steamer."

For a moment he's still trying to read me, his eyes all over me. But he seems to give in to the conversation. "And way too many houseplants," he says with a frown over at the gifts table. "Where the hell does he meet all these people?"

"Not just houseplants," I say. "Did you see that someone brought him a goldfish?"

"Oh. Yeah. What'd you think?"

"What'd I think? I mean, what an incredible housewarming gift for Raff! He needs constant company. I wonder who—"

Vin is scrubbing at the back of his neck and glancing at me. He looks simultaneously pleased and embarrassed.

Here's another thing about Vin. He doesn't directly tell you he's leaving you, but also he buys his little brother a goldfish so he won't be lonely.

Help.

Apparently the universe hears me because seconds later there are two heavily essential-oiled arms around both Vin and me. My temple is against Raff's temple is against Vin's temple. Raff pulls back with a grin. "Hi, family."

My stomach tightens.

"You're the belle of the ball," I tell him. "Everybody loves you. Everybody wants you."

"I know!" he says with delight, and then his brow comes down. "Actually, I think I kind of botched the invite list."

"How?" Vin asks. He's started scanning the room, taking stock of the attendees.

"I invited way too many hopefuls. I can't possibly please them all."

Vin stops scanning and rolls his eyes. This, apparently, is not a problem he's concerned with solving for Raff.

"Oh, who cares!" I tell Raff. "Give it your best shot." I plant two hands on his shoulders and start slow-shimmying them. "The dance floor awaits."

And it does. I've never met a dance floor that wasn't waiting for Raff. He slides backwards, licks two fingers, and makes them sizzle against his eyebrows. I bark a laugh and enjoy the view of Evan, Raff's boss, dancing like he's plunging a toilet.

The bartender asks Vin if he likes the beer she recommended to him and he responds with a firm negative. She laughs, thinking he's flirting. I laugh, knowing he's not. His eyes are on the side of my face but my eyes are still on the dance floor.

From my vantage point I can see at least three different people currently in love with Raff. He's either blissfully ignorant or blissfully in the know. His arms roll up toward the heavens and he shakes his tail feather. Did I mention he's in carpenter jeans and a tight black tee and a big silver chain? He draws one hand down to touch the sweat on his neck and the surface tension breaks, the three lovesick lovebirds converge in unison, clearly wanting to claim him for their own. I watch as he clocks all three in his peripherals and then beelines straight for me.

And then I'm twirled onto the dance floor by my brother-in-law, laughing involuntarily and happy to provide the assist. Raff and I . . . helping each other dance alone by dancing together . . . this is what we do.

It's sharply wonderful to dance. It's been too long. I feel the wax crack off my spirit. Oh, that's right, life is supposed to feel good.

My eyes ski around the dance floor. It's a warm summer night and it's hot in here anyhow, so I'm spotting quite a lot of glistening shoulders, the waterfall of collarbones, inner thighs giving way to audacious butt cheeks where shorts just can't contain our collective will to live. I get lost, for a moment, in the elbow next to me. I can never draw elbows! And now I can see why, because what shape even is that? I scan for more elbows, each one so different and so similar to the last. I wonder if it's possible to draw a dance party.

How to build an experience like this onto a blank white page? How to take one whole moment and run it through the kaleidoscope of my brain and out through my hand? How to take a pencil and scratch against the blankness of the page, and find all these elbows waiting for me just on the other side? All those knees, all those noses and right-angle feet, all those hands on other hands and lips with just a kiss of negative space between them. How to draw music, if not by drawing those hips right there, popping like that, to this beat? How to draw desire, if not by drawing the one successful lovebird with their fingertips one knuckle deep in the front of Raff's waistband? How to draw solitude, if not for drawing my own two feet on their own little island of dance floor?

One of Raff's old roommates appears at my shoulder; I turn my head to see what he's up to back there. Thank goodness it's fleeting. He's rolling away, cologne in the wind, looking for a different butt to spider-monkey. I gratefully rotate ninety degrees and trip over someone's big foot.

It's Vin's big foot and Vin's big arm looping my front half, keeping me from falling. I straighten and my eyes meet Raff's over Vin's big shoulder. Raff is now the butter in a coworker sandwich and looking thrilled to be alive. His eyes land on my hand, braced against Vin's shoulder, and he starts grinning at me. He's always loved when Vin and I flirt in public. I mean, he's completely misinterpreting this right now, but still, he thinks I'm intentionally in Vin's arms.

If I push away from my husband right now, pricked and smarting, because it's painful to be held by him . . . Raff will know it all, all at once. I just know it. So maybe that's the reason, when the song changes, and the dance floor tightens and heats, that I let my other hand find Vin's other shoulder. Maybe it's because tonight, I'm still testing my own wingspan. Maybe it's because my favorite Beyoncé song of all time comes on. My hands find each other at the back of Vin's neck and my eyes ricochet off his and his eyebrows have lifted in surprise.

He resituates his arms around me and it's so familiar, such well-trodden territory, that a lump forms in my throat.

Vin's dance moves have always been both economic and confident. No wasted movements. Total focus on you and a strong hand at your back. He dances with the same effortless swag he uses to pop open a jar no one else could untwist. Like *Yes, hello, you're welcome.*

Anyways, somehow I'm in my husband's arms on a dance floor for the first time in over a year. His spread hand on my lower back guides my hips where he'd like them to be. It's a patient song, hopeful and somehow heartbreaking. *Your love is bright as ever, even in the shadows,* the lyrics insist to us. The song wraps around us. Her voice is plaintive and raw. *You better kiss me, before our time has run out.* My fingers involuntarily tighten against Vin's shoulders. August fifteenth and our time will have run out.

This song is about imminent doom around the corner, about not missing your chance, but somehow her voice has every bit of hope laced through it. She's been through something terrible and still wants to see how it'll all end. How can she make something so beautiful out of pain?

Vin slides me closer, his forearm replacing his hand at my back. Oh, why am I dancing this close with the man who is preparing to leave me? His chin grazes the top of my head and I want to cry with relief that he's not trying for eye contact.

My eyes prickle and my view changes from high-def to sparkly. Everyone on the dance floor is swimming, bejeweled, adorned in crowns of tears.

"Don't cry," he murmurs, his mouth lowered to my ear. And how did he even know?

I sniff and scowl, my face twisted away from his. "I can cry if I want to."

"You're right," he amends. "Go ahead and cry."

"I don't want to!"

He laughs, because he's always liked me ornery.

"I said," I tell him, because this night might be in danger of meaning absolutely nothing if I don't tell him. And the heat of him underneath my fingertips is so precious that it has to—*has to*—mean something. "I said that I'm going to keep on living my life. A full life." I pause, because I realize that I'm not talking about choosing a new life without Vin. What I'm really talking about here is hope in the face of doom. What I'm really talking about here, ultimately, is survival. And so I finish my own sentence with the one thing I most want him to say to me: "No matter what."

He's gone still despite the music. He knows exactly what I'm talking about. He knows I'm telling him what I'd been mouthing across the bar earlier.

"That—" His voice is at my ear, vibrating through us where we're pressed together. "That's what I want the most."

# Twelve

"*Roz! Hi! What're* you doing right now?"

"Who is this?"

"Lauro."

"Oh. Hi! How'd you get my number?"

"Raff."

"Right. What's up?"

"A few of us from class are going to Daniel's art opening tonight but I forgot to invite you yesterday."

It's the day after the housewarming party, Vin's voice in my ear, his desire for me to live my own, big, special, one-and-only life. (Is he there with me during all this life-living? He didn't elaborate, the tight-lipped jerk, so now I'm determined to keep up my half of the threat. I shall have a sun-drenched existence. With fabulous people doing fabulous things. I'll draw and smoke cigs and quote famous artists with Em. Mental note: Wikipedia famous artists and memorize some crap that they said.)

How are Vin and I, you might ask? Well, when I came out of the bedroom this morning, Vin was washing his cereal bowl. "Raff wants a ride to Morristown to pick up some Nintendo gear from some guy. I think we'll have lunch at Mom's on the way back. Do you want to come?"

His mother would sniff out our issues like a drug dog at the airport. She'd have me in handcuffs and a headlock, demanding answers about the state of our union. Vin would have been dispatched to change the oil in her car. He'd have no idea.

"I'm going to pass," I'd said. Which landed like way more of a rejection than I'd planned. And he'd left and I'd thrown myself into work.

"Seriously?" I say to Lauro. I stop chopping sun-dried tomatoes. (Orange pesto. This week's recipe is going to be fire.) "I didn't know he was having an art show!"

"It's his first in a few years. I don't think he expects many people to be there. I think it'll be me, Em, Reggie, Shan, and maybe Esther if she can get a babysitter. Wanna surprise him with us?"

"Yes! I'm in! *Absolutely.*"

When I hang up with Lauro, I send off the recipe to Cherise, complete with photos and extra-careful step-by-step instructions, and clean up the kitchen. I zoom through a shower, blow-dry, makeup, and then for the outfit. It's a tall boots kind of night. And ooh! Faux-leather shorts. And that one tank top that crosses against my neck. When I survey myself in the mirror, I see I've put together an all-black ensemble. Like a caricature of an art student. But I don't care! With the boots up to my knee and the short shorts I look tall and hot for once.

I speed out the door and pass Vin in the hall. "Hi," he says, eyes glued to my thighs.

"Hi! How was your mother's? I'm going out with art class friends. Pesto pasta in the fridge. Be back later. Bye!"

And I'm gone.

The venue is a converted church in Brooklyn. Daniel and two other artists. Their paintings are displayed grandly on the altar and after perusing them, Shan, Reggie, Lauro, and I drink wine in the pews.

Daniel's paintings are enormous. He'd need a ladder to paint them. They're of people, of course, crowded and luminous and painted with gradations of just one color each. Somehow, I'm equally reminded of landscapes and figures.

Daniel stands beside his paintings with his hands clasped behind his back. He's in a bow tie.

"He hasn't moved at all," I observe, eyeing him over my wineglass.

"Yeah," Shan agrees. "He must be super nervous?"

"He said he doesn't want to be a distraction to the art," Lauro says. He's looking for something, glancing over one shoulder.

"Well, it's very distracting!" I say. "Having the artist stare at you while you look at their art."

"Go tell him, then," Lauro says with a smirk, apparently giving up on what he was looking for and settling back into the pew.

Just then, Esther waddles through the crowd, green church dress on, Fabi tugged along in her wake. She makes straight for Daniel. When she gets there, she says something to him and his pose relaxes for the first time. He reaches down and high-fives Fabi. Esther straightens his bow tie. He laughs at something she's whispered.

"Good job, Esther," Lauro says with affection. "Come on. Now's our chance. She defrosted him."

We all get up and file over.

When we first got here, Daniel saw us, his eyes widened, and he bowed his head to us. But that was it.

Now that Esther is here and teasing him about his pocket square, when we approach, Daniel actually goes in for a light hug of each of us. "Thank you for coming."

Daniel, Shan, and Lauro start talking about the exhibition, but I take a chance and sidle up next to Fabi and Esther. "Another gallstone?" I ask her.

She laughs. "No. This time I just wanted to take my grandson to see some art."

"Where is the art, Abuela?" he asks, looking around at his own eye level.

I point up, to where Daniel's paintings are suspended, ten feet in the air.

"Oh. Wow."

While he's looking up at the sky, I can't help but do the old tap-the-shoulder trick. He looks to his opposite side and then to me. I shrug, innocent.

Fabi looks up at the art again and I go to tap his opposite shoulder but this time, his little hand snakes up and catches me, pinching my fingers.

"You're fast!" I crow.

He eyes me critically and unhands me. "I know kung fu."

I love this answer. "Oh, me too."

He steps back and eyes me. "Really?"

"Yeah. I can break a cinder block with my face."

He senses the game immediately. "Well, *I* can break one with my pinky."

"I can catch a hummingbird with one hand."

"*I* can juggle twenty-five grapes at once."

"Oh, well, I definitely can't do that. You must be better at kung fu than me."

He's very pleased with this exchange. "I actually *can* do five roundhouse kicks in a row."

"That sounds really hard."

"It is. Abuela gets mad when I do it in the house."

"But where else are you supposed to do it? The grocery store?"

His eyes grow round, he's seen me anew. "That is a *very* good point."

"Quit making trouble," Esther says to me with a scowl. "Fabi baby, go get Abuela a cup of water over there. And be good."

He follows her directions immediately. Roundhouse kicks or not, they've got a good thing going. She's eyeing me quizzically.

"You have kids, Roz?"

"Oh. Nope." I honestly don't know why I volunteer this next bit, other than the fact that Esther is a little bit magic, of course. "My husband and I thought we'd try, but then . . ." *Then we got into a life-altering accident.* I shrug instead of saying anything.

"There's time. I didn't have Fabi's father until I was forty. And then, if you think about it, there's even more time. You never know what the world is gonna give you. Because I didn't think I'd be raising *another* baby at sixty."

"He's been with you since he was a baby?"

"Yup. His father is overseas. Back a few times a year. Gracias, chico." She takes the dangerously full cup from Fabi as he returns, his knuckles wet.

"Shan knows a place around the corner," Lauro says as he returns to us, putting his arm around Esther's shoulders and kissing her temple. "She says kids can come."

"Nah, nah." Esther waves a hand. "Fabi and I have a date with a couple milkshakes at home."

He straightens up like she's electrocuted him. "Really?"

"Let's go look at the art first," she says, mock sternly, leading him away and waving to us. "See you on Friday."

"Bye, Fabi!"

Lauro is looking at his phone. "Daniel said he'd meet us at the restaurant in a bit, if you're interested."

Shan and Reggie are already sidling toward the door. "Sure."

We go to a taco joint for a late bite and I get the shock of my life when I hear Reggie speak for the first time and hear his New Zealand accent. He peels off after tacos but Daniel still hasn't joined us and Shan knows another joint around the corner.

"I know all the joints around all the corners," Shan tells us.

"You must have a very rewarding nightlife," I say.

"No." She shakes her head sadly. "I work for a food and drink distributor."

The three of us get to the next bar and it's a real sexy beast. The drinks take eight minutes to make and the clientele all look like they're extras in *Eyes Wide Shut*.

Before the drinks even come, Shan is checking her phone. "Oh, Em just texted."

Lauro is scrambling out his phone, sees no notifications, and frowns. "What did she say?" he asks Shan.

"She's taking a cab home from the venue. We live in the same building." She says that last bit to me, by way of explanation. "I'm not gonna miss a ride home!"

Shan leaves some cash for her drink and sweeps out of the bar.

Leaving me and Lauro.

Alone.

I turn, expecting him to be grinning like a tiger. But instead, he's frowning down at his phone, sliding it away, catching my eye, and *then* grinning like a tiger. "Guess we'll have to finish Shan's drink too," he says on a sigh, as the bartender delivers three gorgeous tumblers, all in various shades of glowing amber.

What am I supposed to do? Run out the door? I lift my drink. "To life." (The one that Vin wants me to live.)

Lauro lifts his drink and clinks mine. "To tonight," he says. "With you."

*Shit.*

Two hours later, I literally fall into my own home. My purse is caught on the doorknob and the floor has risen to greet my hands and knees.

"Whoa. Jesus." That's Vin.

Oh, good. He's here to see this.

I'm up and trying to hop out of my ridiculous boots but I accidentally upend the umbrella stand.

"I hate the umbrella stand! Why are we constantly preparing for rain! It should be a sunscreen stand! Of course we were always gonna fall apart!"

Suddenly he's next to me, one hand on my elbow. I jolt at the strength of it. He stands there like a pillar of cement, his eyes on my face, his hand steadying me.

I'm seized with the need to knock him off-kilter. I take two hands and plant them on his chest. Give my best attempt to push him over. The only thing that happens is all my breath comes out at once. Unfortunately in a gasp.

"Hey." He's very concerned.

He removes my hands from his chest and it topples me forward, my forehead planting itself against his sternum. I roll my head to one side and the world tips. I feel his palm press between my shoulder blades but I'm still spinning, still floating away.

"Roz. What happened?"

I'm dizzy and wretched. It hurts not to hold on to him.

So I do.

I tip up and grab him around the ribs like he's a dock in a roiling ocean.

"I—" I gasp. "I—accidentally—went—on—*a date*."

And then everything just releases. My nerves and dismay. Even the excitement I felt about going to the opening and spending time with my new art friends. It's all in a slushy pile of disappointment and embarrassment, dripping off the boots I still haven't managed to get off. I cry unseemly tears. There are bad noises and fingers twisted in his shirt and I can physically feel my makeup hotly displacing, melting across my face.

My lungs squeeze for breath and I try to calm myself a little, letting it out in a choppy stream. That's when I register the rumble underneath my cheek. He's shaking. Both hands around me and shaking. With laughter.

"Hey!" I tip my head up and sniffle. "Why are you laughing!"

There's hair in my face and then it gets slid behind my ears. "I don't know. I'm happy to see you."

"I just told you I went on a date and you're *laughing*? What the fuck is that! And I can't get these fucking boots off! Don't the people who make boots understand that eventually they must come off?"

He unclamps my hands from around his ribs and reclamps them against his shoulders, kneeling in front of me. The night we decided to get married, I stepped on a nail in the yard at his mother's house, and he knelt in front of me just like this, studied the puncture wound, rose with me in his arms, carried me to the car.

A loud *zip!* jolts me from the memory. He easily slides one boot down my calf and off my foot. "Oh. Right. The zipper," I grumble.

He clears his throat and I think he might be hiding another laugh.

"It's not funny," I insist. "I can't believe you're laughing."

"Right." He clears his throat again. "Must have been terrible for you."

"It was!"

"How do you accidentally end up on a date?"

"I thought my drawing teacher was going to be there too. He was supposed to come. But he bailed. Everybody bailed. And then it was just me and Lauro and there was, like, velvet and eye contact and the bartender made me a drink based on my laugh and Lauro took a sip and said it was delicious and did I mention the eye contact?"

*Zip!* The other boot slides off and my sock comes halfway off along with it. I start to bend to fix it, but he's already there, fingers firmly straightening it back up my calf, fixing the front seam so that it neatly aligns along my toes.

He stands, slowly, steadying me at the elbows even though he's the one moving. "So was the eye contact with Lauro or the bartender?"

I go to answer but then pull up short. Because now that he mentions it . . . "Both? Oh, God. Why did it all have to be so sexy?"

Now that I'm boot-free, I'm fancy-free, so I tumble past him and to the couch. It's warm. He must have been lying here when I fell through the front door. I grab a blanket off the back of the couch and promptly suffocate myself in it.

"It was sexy to you?" he asks low, from a distance, and I realize he's still standing at the door.

I'm continuing to fight for my life under the blanket, so it takes me a moment to register both the question and his placement in the room. When I blink it into focus, it's a gut punch.

"I can't look at you on that doormat without thinking of the time you left me the lease. And then you walked out the door without a word," I say.

His face doesn't even move a centimeter. "Which part was sexy to you?" he presses. "The situation? Or him?"

My heart is still racing, thinking I'm going to watch him walk out the door again.

"I like a dimly lit room as much as the next gal in heeled boots and lipstick!" I say with a scowl. "I *like* getting called 'baby.' I like being told I'm delicious. I—" I realize my feet are exposed at the bottom of the blanket and immediately pull them closer, inside, where it's safe. "I just didn't want to be on a date with him."

Vin's hand reaches up toward the doorknob, and metallic chemicals start pumping through my bloodstream. I feel instantly sober. Everything is bright and outlined in black pen. I've just told him I'm (accidentally) dating, so now, of course, I'm about to watch him turn that doorknob and leave again.

His hand lands on the brass knob. I watch for the twist, preemptively feel it in my gut. But then his fingers move two inches north. *Clunk.* The lock turns and he steps off the doormat, into the house, locking us in.

(Hey, Vinny! Somebody's happy tonight!)
(What's the smile all about, Vin?)
Nothing, nothing. It was just a good night. Is all.
(Come on, Vin! You better spill!)
All right. All right. Well. You know how that story I told before was called the Cat Doesn't Come Back? Well. Uh. I'm smiling because . . . for the first time in my life . . . I think I waited long enough. I think the cat might have come back on her own.

# Thirteen

*I wake up* feeling shockingly fine. Probably because Vin force-fed me Gatorade and ibuprofen last night. But I've never been more nervous to talk to him in my entire life.

I'm doing a killer impression of making pancakes while he's in the shower. Every time I hear the water splash off his head onto the shower floor I nearly scream.

At some point this shower is going to be over. Vin will smell pancakes and emerge.

We'll have to discuss—sober—that I accidentally went on a date last night. (Lauro leaned in and ate the cherry out of my drink! And I almost took his eye out with my elbow.) And then I came home and snotted all over Vin and he literally had to button my pajamas and tuck me into bed.

If I were him, I'd be checking into the Holiday Inn.

Vin emerges from the bathroom in a puff of steam. He's in athletic shorts and a T-shirt and his toothbrush is hanging out of his mouth. I think he says "Smells good."

"Yup. Thanks. There's plenty, if you want."

He nods and turns back toward the bathroom and I can't help but shout at his back. "I spent seventy-five dollars last night! On tacos and fancy drinks."

He keeps walking, spits and rinses in the bathroom sink, and comes back with a little smile on his face. "Lauro didn't foot the bill? What a cheapskate."

"Ack!" I'm so mortified over all of this, practically melting down the counter. "What a waste of money."

"It wasn't a waste of money."

"Why?"

"Because I got to see you like that." He comes up behind me and grabs a pancake off the stack. "I forgot how cute you are when you're shithoused."

*"Ack!"*

This is the sort of mortification people don't survive. They just, simply, cease.

He's chuckling, I can hear it, but when I glance at him, his face is serious.

"Hey," he says.

I flip the last of the pancakes onto the stack and turn off the griddle, turning to give him my attention. "Yeah?"

"I'll do it."

"You'll do what?"

"I'll be your model."

I'm leaning back on the counter, and when he drops that bomb, I slip and bang the crap out of my elbow. "Ow! Shit! What?"

He's there in a second, gently rotating my arm, leaning in and inspecting.

"Are you okay?" His brows are so low they're practically melting into his beard.

"Yes. Just my funny bone. What did you say?"

He's still bent over my arm, inspecting, and I get impatient. I poke his shoulder with my free hand. "*Vin*. What did you say?"

Finally satisfied that my arm isn't going to fall off, he lets go of me, steps back, and crosses his arms over his chest. His eyes land on mine. "I'm offering, is all."

"You'd let me draw you?"

"All I have to do is sit still, right?"

"Naked."

His eyebrows rise a half centimeter.

"Nude, I mean," I continue.

He clears his throat. "Right. Yeah. I knew that when I offered."

He's still got his arms crossed and his eyes boring into me and it makes it very hard to have this conversation.

"Even . . . even with all this going on, you'd let me draw you naked? Like *naked*? In front of me?"

His brows kick up and his arms finally uncross. "Roz, I'd trust you to figure out whether to pull the plug if I were in a coma." He takes one step toward me and for a diamond-sharp moment I think, no I *know*, he's going to put his hand against my cheek again, like he did in bed just the other night. But then his hands slide into his pockets and he holds, a few feet from me. "Of course I can get naked in front of you."

*I trust you.*

"Look, Vin. I won't do the Craigslist thing. You were right about that. You don't have to get naked just to stop me from doing something dumb."

Now he's looking at the floor. "I'm not allowed to help you?"

And what am I supposed to say to that? No?

Of course not! Nor can I say yes.

I go with a good old-fashioned foot stomp. And then I say the only thing I really can that doesn't proclaim either *I don't want your help*, which feels incriminating, *or I do want your help*, which also feels incriminating.

"Well!"

"Look, you said classes are too expensive. Strangers on the internet are a bad idea. And based on your reaction to your accidental date last night—"

"*Ack!*"

"—it seems like finding someone *else* to see naked isn't..." His eyes glitter with something I can't name. "Isn't... what you want. So..." He throws two arms out. "I figure, you've got a husband. It's a person and, uh, territory you're... familiar with, at least." He pauses, looking like this conversation has just shaved a year off his life. "Right?"

"Right. Well... fine. Thank you. We can try. *Try.* If it's weird, we're bailing."

"All right." He nods and his face has gone full marble again. "Where do you want me?" He looks around. "The kitchen probably has the best light, yeah? But that seems kind of weird, somehow." He scratches at the back of his neck. "Living room is probably best, huh?"

I'm gaping at him. "Now?"

"I mean... yeah? There's time before work."

How can he be so cool about this? I'm slowly disintegrating on the inside and he's all, yeah, sure, what's the big deal about showing you my dick?

I want to demand that we do it next week, next month, *never!* in fact. But if I delay, then he'll know that I need to mentally prepare myself to see his naked body and if he knows that then he'll be able to figure out how much the idea of him naked affects me and if he knows *that* then he'll know that when I can't sleep I imagine him naked in my bed next to me, his leg between my legs, his chest under my cheek, his big hand moving up and down my back, his nose in my hair...

Okay, he probably won't be able to figure out that last part but he's going to get *vibes* if I delay this, so—

"Sure! Living room!" I (accidentally) shout. "Let me get my drawing stuff."

I scurry to my bedroom and pull out my drawing bag. See!

This is normal. Look at all these drawings. I do this. I'm a draw-er. I . . . can totally do this. My drawing pad under one arm, I look down at my selection of pencils and immediately hit a brick wall.

Which drawing utensil to choose?

"Roz!" I pinch the bridge of my nose. "You're not choosing lingerie for a big date. Grab a number two pencil! Draw, Antonio, draw! Draw and don't waste time!"

I must look like a professional athlete with a gold medal on the line because as soon as I march into the living room, Vin's eyebrows rise, his spine straightens, and his shoulders draw back.

He's already stripped down to boxers and is sitting on our coffee table, knees spread, fingers loosely laced between his legs.

He looks *comfortable*.

"I, uh . . ." He coughs. "I don't actually know how to pose. Now that I'm thinking about it, I assume it's more complicated than just *hold still*."

He coughs again.

Okay, so maybe he's not comfortable. This helps.

"Well . . . I guess I'm not sure? I'm definitely not an expert. In class, in a round, we usually do four or five short poses. Like around two minutes, and then a long pose, ten minutes, max fifteen."

"Sure."

"Just try not to choose a pose you'll have to break. Like don't do anything acrobatic. Or that you'll have to like, flex for."

"No flexing. Got it." There's a ghost of a smile on his face as he puts his thumbs in the waistband of his boxers. He pauses and his eyes flash to mine; the smile is gone. "Yeah?"

"Um. Sure?"

His brows come down and his hands slide back up to his hips. "Roz." He waits until I make eye contact.

"Yeah?" he says again. He's asking me what I want.

"Oh, what the heck?" I toss my arms up. "Whip it out."

He laughs and shakes his head, but his boxers slide to the floor and he bends down after them, picking them up, neatly folding them, and setting them aside. I don't look directly at him, but I can tell he's frowning, hands back on his hips, and looking down at the coffee table.

"I was picturing doing a sitting pose, but . . ."

"Having second thoughts?"

"Standing here bare-assed . . ."

I laugh a little hysterically.

"I varnished this coffee table by hand," he says. "It just seems wrong."

I'm swallowing my laugh and trying to get in the zone because, yes, he's my husband, and yes, I've seen him naked hundreds, if not thousands, of times, but, if there's one thing I've learned from drawing class, it's that this kind of nudity is a rare and valuable gift.

I quickly walk to the linen closet and bring him a towel, handing it over as a peace offering.

"I'll set the timer. Do whatever pose makes you feel comfortable. Seriously."

"Two minutes?" He spreads the towel out on the floor.

"Yup. Four two-minute poses."

"Okay." And then he lies on his back on the towel and stares at the ceiling.

I click the timer, set up my paper, and then, finally, let my eyes actually fall to him. All of him.

He's bigger than he used to be. There are more shadows,

more muscle, a soft layer over the top. He looks like he could lift a Buick if your bouncy ball rolled under there.

There he is. Lying there naked. My husband. No! Right now, he's the model. It almost helps a little that he looks different.

I shake my head and reach into the satchel for a pencil. Any pencil. I won't get in my head about this. Except . . . a lying-down pose is actually really hard. Everything is foreshortened and there aren't really any angles to draw. The human body becomes mostly a straight line with just a few squiggly bumps that if you don't draw them in the exact right place, your drawing ends up looking like calligraphy gone bad.

The timer goes off.

Oh! New pose already. Okay. I'd barely done one shoulder and half a rib cage of the last one.

I'm surprised when he sits right up. I'd kind of thought all his poses would be lying-down poses. They're the easiest for the model and probably the least vulnerable. I've got his profile now, his elbows resting on his drawn-up knees. His back is a curve, his feet bent at an angle I can't make believable before the timer dings again.

And now he's on his feet. I've still got his side. I think he might be feeling shy about giving me the full show. At the last second, one of his hands comes up and his forehead inches down to meet the palm. This . . . is a sad pose. I lose twenty seconds to blinking and therefore only get one leg from the hip down before the timer is off again.

And now, finally, the butt. His scar is a stark purple line down his back and I make myself focus on absolutely everything else. He faces away from me, hands on hips and his head dropped back to look at the ceiling. Another sad pose. No, not sad. Exasperated? Or maybe . . . distraught? Hard to say. This time I'm determined to get something from each hemisphere of his body on the page at the very least, so his head is too egg-shaped and too low against his shoulders and his spine goes a little too much to one side and his legs are too long, even for leggy Vin, but the feet come out looking weirdly, serendipitously perfect. And I do, in fact, get a whole human on this page.

When the timer dings, he immediately starts swinging his arms at the shoulders. "Fifteen minutes, you said?"

"Fifteen minutes is really long . . ." I warn him. "You'll be dying by the end."

"Let's give it a shot. Anything in particular you want me to do? Or not do?"

I hesitate.

"What is it?" he asks. "You can say it."

"The lying-down poses are the hardest to draw. For me. But I know they're the easiest to do, so—"

"No problem. I'll just sit, then."

He grabs the towel and lays it out over the coffee table, assembling himself into pretty much the same pose he was in when I entered the room. Legs spread, fingers laced, oh, boy, right in front of the crotch, which means I'm going to have to stare, *there*, very hard in order to decipher fingers and thumbs from carrot and plums.

Shockingly, I can feel myself starting to blush. Which is ridiculous. Ridiculous because, not to be crude, but me and Vin . . . me and Vin are *acquainted*, okay?

I've had literal conversations with that particular part of his body. Much to his delight and laughter.

But right now . . . it's all feeling very new and very different and context is everything, okay?

He's got his head cocked to one side, studying me, and then he glances down at his hands. "Oh. Is the fingers-crossed thing too complicated?" He smooths his hands over his thighs. "Better?"

"Yes. Great." I clear my throat. "Comfortable?"

"Yup."

I set the timer and get to work.

The thing about having a one-on-one session with a model, whether or not you're married to them, is that when you're in a class, there are a ton of people and the model doesn't really look at any of you. But Vin is facing me square on and he's watching me draw. I can feel his eyes as tangibly as I'm sure he's feeling mine.

These are not sexy times. Not exactly. But they are extremely intimate.

"You're so focused," he says.

And I jump. A big graphite mark mars the paper, but luckily not over the top of what I was drawing. His ear, by the way.

"Sorry," he says, and coughs a little before resuming his position exactly as it was.

"No, no. It's okay. You can talk if you want."

"Telling someone they're focused is kind of an asshole thing to do because it breaks their focus. Or so I've just learned. I'll shut up now."

I'm smiling against my will, and so is he and it's all so shadowed and awkward and comfortable all at once. We're here, in my living room. And he's here, my husband. But he's naked and I'm drawing and we've never done this exact thing before and that angle, there, right where his nose casts a shadow against his cheekbone and my pencil goes and I just *nail* it and his eyebrows, I know those eyebrows, or at least I thought I did because I have to draw them twice to get them right.

I'm constructing Vin from nothing. Well, not nothing. But I'm taking the Vin I see and running him through the underground tunnel network that leads from my eyes to my brain to my hand. And yes, okay, my heart. Of course, this figure on my page isn't actually Vin. This is an idea of Vin. And perhaps extremely importantly, *my* idea of Vin. I think of Em's drawings. If I'm using that same theory, *in short, I wanted to understand myself*, then there is as much of me on this page as there is Vin.

I wondered on the dance floor how I would draw music, and the first idea was "dancing hips." Well, now that I've got Vin pinned between my pencil and paper, what is he *actually* showing me how to draw?

Oh, jeez, I glance at the clock and eight minutes have passed and he's just a floating face and hair, not even a jawline yet. Which I kind of botch, and then connect awkwardly to his neck. I bail on the top half and make an attempt at the knees up to the hip, give him ribs and a strong shoulder. I try for like four seconds on each hand and leave them mostly blank before dropping my eyes to his crotch. To ignore or elaborate? Oh, fine. I quickly draw what I see. A body at rest, familiar and foreign all at once. Sometimes I look at a penis and I think, *Really?* Really, *that* was the best possible design? I digress.

I get something passable down and move along to his feet. Again, for some reason, I'm getting feet today. Even two feet that are flat on the ground and facing me, which turns them from their normal long, triangular lines into a bunch of squishy U shapes on top of one another, but they're real life, they're giving feet, baby, and when I go back and add in the toenails, I blink because they're not just giving feet, they're giving *Vin's* feet. I'm just flourishing over that pairing of not-quite-even ankle bones when the timer dings.

Vin immediately rises to his feet and stretches.

"I could do a few more two-minute poses," he offers, one hand holding the opposite ear and stretching his neck. He's full frontal now, and everything that looked restful and nestled moments ago, suddenly looks much more present and I glance down at my drawing. I just drew Vin's feet and they look fantastic. I can see the other poses. Sad, distraught, exasperated, patient. Vin's eyes on me while mine are on him.

These are feelings. This is connection. This is him doing, yes. But this is him vulnerable, too.

"No!" I flip the paper over on itself before he can see what I drew. "No, that's okay. I think that's enough for today."

"Really?"

His hands are on his hips. I wish he'd put his underwear back on because with the drawing pad closed I don't know where the heck to look.

"Yeah, that's good. Thank you."

"Once a week, then? Or is twice a week better?"

"Once is fine!" I squeak. "See you next week!"

He recoils with a laugh as he steps into his boxers. "Or in like ten minutes. In the kitchen."

"Right. Yes." I recover a skosh of my composure and fall back on humor. "I wasn't talking to you. I was talking to *him*."

He glances down at his now-covered man area. "Oh. Right. Well, if *I'm* in the kitchen, *he's* in the kitchen."

"Yes, but he'll be minding his manners."

"He minded his manners just fine this morning!"

I'm at the doorway to my room, halfway through. I look back over my shoulder. "He certainly did." I knock on the doorframe, not sure whether I want to go inside or turn back around. "Thanks, Vin."

"You're welcome."

I close the door behind me, with the funny feeling that I've left something behind in the living room.

# Fourteen

*After work on* Tuesday, I finally nail the bean lasagna recipe. (Hint, there's an inhuman amount of garlic. Garlic covers almost every cooking sin.) I've been cooking with unusually fierce verve and when I come to, I've got twice the food Vin and I could possibly eat in a week.

"Damn."

I get an idea, text Lauro, and then text the number he sends me. My phone almost immediately rings in my hand with a callback.

"Esther!" I answer.

"Bean lasagna? Sounds awful. Bring it over. How'd you get my number?"

I'm laughing. "I swear it's not awful. Lauro has everyone's number. He's Mr. Social Skills, apparently."

"Did he try to kiss you after the art show?"

"What? No." (I don't mention the cherry in my drink or the subsequent accidental elbow to his face.) "Why?"

"I've known him a long time. He had that I'm-gonna-kiss-somebody-tonight glint in his eye."

"Well, if he used the glint on somebody, it wasn't me."

"Good. You're married. Or so you say."

I laugh again. She's funny over the phone. "Right. And even if I didn't say, I still would be."

She hums. "I'm at 103 and Lex. Don't get excited, it's not fancy."

"What time should I come?"

"Before dinner, obviously."

And so I'm just strapping the extra lasagna into a wide-bottomed tote when Vin gets home from work.

His Mauricio Electrics T-shirt is dusty with drywall, his Yankees cap pushed up loosely—which he does when he's driving the work van—so it doesn't block his view. He stands in the open door and it must have been a hell of a workday because I can smell sweat from here. Which, ladies, let me tell you, is not actually a bad thing.

"Hi." He closes the door behind him.

"Food's warming in the oven, if you're hungry."

He glances at the bag over my shoulder. "Headed back to work?"

"No. I made too much by accident, so I'm gonna drop some at my friend's house. She's at 103 and Lex."

He frowns. "Trains are terrible today because of all that rain this morning. I guess there's flooding in the system."

I quickly take out my phone and check the recommended route. "Yeesh. You're right. It says I should take the B and then walk across the park. Maybe I'll drive— Never mind, traffic is *horrific*. Dang."

So I'm looking at a twenty-minute train ride and then a twenty-five-minute walk. With a five-pound lasagna.

"You got a sec for me to shower? I'll go with you. Carry the food."

"Oh." Maybe it's because he's standing there, big and bearded and dusty, but the offer makes my stomach flip. "Not much of a relaxing night for you . . ."

He shrugs.

"Okay. Sure, then. If you're sure."

He nods and then crouches down to take off his boots. The laces make little snappy noises as he slides them out of the worn-shiny divots across the tongues. I make note of his shoulder placement, his knee bent like that, I'd never get the hands right, even if I were to get him to freeze exactly like that for an hour.

Once I hear him kick the shower on, I grab my drawing pad and try to draw that pose from memory. It's a bird's nest of lines, as I search and search for the right ratios and proportions. It's discouraging. So instead, I turn my eye to the boots he's left on the front mat.

They're high-quality and a million years old. He's had them re-soled twice. The leather loyally retains the shape of his foot no matter how long he's been gone. They're set on the ground in the exact footprint of his, well, footprints, and even if they sit there overnight, or two weeks, they always give the impression of Vin having *just* been there. I choose my smoothest lead and the pencil curves on the page the way the heel curves away from me, into nothingness. I pool the laces, tip up the toes toward the ceiling. The shower shuts off and I jump. This is a decent drawing.

*Vin Home from Work* I title it.

"Ready?" He's damp and tugging a T-shirt over his head. I catch a glimpse of his stomach. It occurs to me that people probably see him on the street and have daydreams about his sexual competence.

It's slightly cool out—one of those sweet summer days, like a drink of cold water in the warm sun—and as we get off the train at Central Park, he points across the street to a little café with gigantic bunches of eucalyptus in baskets out front.

"You want a cup of tea for the walk?" he asks.

I'm still slightly ill over the wasted seventy-five dollars this weekend, so I shake my head no.

He reads my mind with a laugh. "Roz, it's a buck fifty."

He hands me the lasagna and comes back across the street

three minutes later with a steaming paper cup and a scowl on his face. "Apparently it's three-fifty now. For hot water and a bag of grass clippings."

"Thank you for my grass clippings." I'm absurdly happy to get a cup of herbal tea from the hands of my husband.

Vin's phone rings as he takes back the lasagna. "It's Raff."

"Go ahead."

He answers and I listen as they catch up. His brow is furrowed when they hang up.

"Everything all right?" I ask.

He nods as we enter the park, green and blooming, just starting to dim with sunset. There are little kids in giant backpacks, teenagers on motorized scooters screaming with laughter, a pack of elderly women tiptoe-jogging at a clip. "Yeah." He glances at me. "I think he's lonely."

"He was having fun at his party." I supply this, but it feels a little thin.

"Okay, so maybe not lonely . . . But searching? I get the feeling he's been looking for something he can't find."

Perfectly said.

*Maybe he should move back in,* something in me tries to say. I practically have to clap my hand over my mouth to keep from saying it.

"He keeps talking about Marine . . ." Vin says, like he's finishing a thought.

"Yeah, he's mentioned her to me too. Why . . ." I glance up at him. "Why *now*, do you think he's suddenly missing her?"

"She used to take care of him. Then we took care of him. Now he's on his own. He's missing having somebody."

Oh! That . . . is . . . shockingly insightful.

"It's interesting that you bring that up . . . I . . . actually was just talking about this the other day. With Deb and Cherise."

He nods to show he's all ears.

"Cherise mentioned that . . ." There's no direct route through the park, so we meander along some smaller tributary paths on our way to a bigger one. His T-shirt sleeve is brushing my shoulder. My heart is definitely still galloping. "She . . . wondered if maybe taking care of Raff the way we did . . . made things harder for us, as a couple."

His eyebrows dip up toward the brim of his hat. He's as protective of Raffi as I am, so at first I think he's going to reject that statement out of hand. But then, "Actually, I've had a similar thought."

"Wait. Really?"

He clears his throat and reaches around my shoulder, guiding me across his path and to his other side while a biker blaring Panic! At the Disco blasts past us. "Well, we didn't have sex once the entire time he lived with us, so . . ."

I stop walking and stare at his back. He takes a few steps, his back to me. I watch his body expand with a deep breath and then, only then, does he finally turn and look me in my face. There's a mixture of vulnerability and resignation there.

I feel oddly . . . zippy. A chemical rush, no doubt. "You've never said anything like that before."

He gestures with his chin for me to walk alongside him again. I do, but he doesn't say anything else.

"You never mention our sex life," I prod. "Or lack thereof."

"Well." He scratches the back of his neck. "Seemed . . . like . . . it was okay to mention it?"

"Yes! Of course. I . . . would actually love to hear your take on it."

We walk in silence for thirty feet and I can tell by the way he's watching his feet that he's gathering his thoughts. "At first . . . at first it was the accident, you know? Of course we weren't gonna have a lot of sex right after something like that. But then, you know, six, seven, eight months later . . . I think . . ." He clears his throat. "I think because those rooms . . . well, you can hear everything in that apartment. I think we just stopped while he was there because it felt . . ."

"Rude? Or embarrassing or something?"

"Right. Yeah. Even though Raffi would not have given a shit. Still . . ."

"Yeah. Still."

"But because we weren't having sex . . . I think all the things that weren't working with us . . . got really obvious."

*All the things that weren't working.*

"But Raff was just always there," he continues. "So there wasn't a lot of space or time to figure any of that out and we just had to keep on going and going."

"And we found this different rhythm. One that had more to do with taking care of Raff than with us."

"Right. Yeah. And . . ." He glances at me and snaps his mouth shut. He's physically stopping himself from saying something. But I've just mainlined his thoughts and feelings and I'm greedy for more. I need more.

"No, come on," I say. "Finish your thought. I don't care if it hurts."

"Look. Roz. The first thing I ever loved about you was how you were with Raffi. I . . . rested easy knowing that if I ever screwed something up with him, you'd be there to pick up the slack. And I . . . I still feel that way. Even if . . . you and me . . . whatever. I know that no matter what, you'll be there for him."

My heart fell out of my chest twenty steps ago when the words *first thing I ever loved about you* came out of my husband's mouth. But I can't be deterred. He hasn't finished this thought, I can feel it. "But . . ."

"But." His face is constricted. He looks like he really doesn't want to say this next part. Or maybe, that he wishes it weren't true. "But after the accident, we were both so focused on him being okay . . . we didn't really check in with each other. And there were times—"

He cuts off, or rather, emotion cuts him off and he looks, fiercely, away from me. I don't need him to finish that sentence out loud. I can finish it myself and it makes me sick to my stomach: there were times that Vin needed me but I was helping Raff.

I don't know what to say. I'm searching around for anything.

But Vin's not quite done.

"And then, those last few months that Raff was with us, when you started getting really depressed, I wanted to be the one—but Raff was so excited about getting you back on your feet. All the Groupon stuff. I just . . . didn't know how to fit myself back in. And then he left and . . . nothing worked *without* him anymore either."

"Wow."

"I know." He's grimacing. "All pretty ugly."

"That's not ugly! That's . . . human! And I'm so glad I know. And I'm—"

"Don't say sorry. Really. I'm serious. How much you love Raff is a part of . . . it's part of what makes you *you*. So don't apologize."

My brain is circling this. Having Raff stay with us seemed like such a no-brainer at the time. He's family. He was drowning and needed us. Of course we'd do that for him. But maybe once his arm was healed and he was back on his feet, maybe it would have been kinder to all of us to just launch him.

"If you could go back . . ." I prod.

"Oh, I definitely would decide not to care if he heard us having sex."

I burst out laughing. "WOW. Okay! Not where I thought that was headed."

He's smiling, glancing sideways at me, one hand in his jeans pocket, and I just get catapulted back to our first or second date.

"Do you remember—" I start.

"Yes."

I laugh. "You don't even know what I was going to say!"

"Doesn't matter," he says gruffly. "I remember it."

"It *does* matter! I was gonna say it was our first or second date. And we were walking in the park."

"Second date, then."

"Okay. Second date. And I laughed and went to put my hand on your shoulder but then you ducked into it so that my hand ended up on your cheek instead?"

He laughs, grimacing, the tips of his ears pink. "Yeah."

"I thought that was so smooth."

"Gah." He's pinching his face closed at himself.

"Why does that embarrass you?"

"Because . . . I didn't mean to be smooth. I actually didn't mean to do it at all. I just . . . I was so into you and when you reached out to me . . . I just . . . the idea of you putting your hands on my face . . . like you were gonna kiss me . . ." He clears his throat and some of his pinchy embarrassment seems to be ebbing away to make room for a different, weightier emotion.

My blood is pounding hollowly through my veins. I knew we were into each other when we first started dating. This isn't news, but to hear him say it, with pink ears, *I was so into you.* It makes it feel oddly fresh. Like maybe those two hearts brushing shoulders while they strolled through the park actually haven't been beaten to death by the specter of a breakup.

"We didn't kiss then, though."

"No." He clears his throat. "We didn't kiss for five dates."

"Wow! You really got those stats memorized."

"No one made me wait five dates for a kiss before you."

"*Made you wait*. Oh, please. Because *that's* how *that* works."

He's smiling again. "All right, all right. I kept choking."

"Choking?"

"Yeah."

"How were you choking?"

He lowers his brow while he looks down at me. "I wanted to kiss you so many times on those first few dates but I kept chickening out at the last second."

This actually *is* news. Because he's many things, but sexually intimidated is not one of them. Difficult communicator though he is, he has a very easy sexual charisma. Every kiss, every progression or push, it always felt so natural with him. There was never: *And now! the moment he touches my boobs for the first time.* Or: *There he goes trying to get my jeans undone.* Not that things were never clumsy or funny, because sex is often both, but more that he always seemed like whatever was happening was exactly what he wanted to be happening, exactly the way he wanted it.

"You thought I'd reject you or something?"

"No. Not really. I guess . . . It was more like, I knew I was only gonna taste it once, that first kiss."

I catch my toe on a cobblestone and Vin lunges forward to steady me.

"Mind the lasagna!" I shout, and it makes a lounging group of skateboarders laugh.

"Sounds like a sex move!" one of them calls to us.

Vin is still clutching me by the elbow, eyes narrowed at them. "The fuck that kid knows about sex moves, he's like thirteen."

"I'm actually kind of intrigued by this," I say. "Which body part is supposed to be the lasagna, you think?"

"Oh, for the love of—" Vin shuffles me along.

"Thanks for coming, Vin," I say happily, almost looping my arm through his but just patting the lasagna instead (an alternate, more tame sex move).

"So, who are we bringing food to, again?" he asks.

And so I tell him about Esther and Fabi, which leads me to Reggie, which leads to Shan, to Stacia and Cindy, to Penny, to Em, a brief word on Lauro (to which Vin raises his eyebrows and says nothing), and lastly to Daniel.

Which gets us all the way to the stuck buzzer of Esther's building, onto her elevator that smells like soup, and through her front door, where she's beckoning us and demanding we put our shoes *there! No, there!*

"Well, come in," she says. "Good lord, you're tall."

"Sorry," Vin says.

"Why would you be sorry about that?" Esther asks.

"Oh." He's stymied. "I guess I'm not?"

"Good. Fabi! Company!"

Fabi emerges down a long pink hallway decorated with gilded family photos. His eyes light up when he sees me, but he stops in his tracks when he sees Vin.

"Who's that?"

"This is my husband, Vin," I tell him. "He's *terrible* at kung fu."

Vin is handing off the food to Esther, *yes, ma'am*-ing her, but he does a double take at me. "What did you just tell him?"

"Nothing. Oh, Fabi, do you play the trumpet?" There's an open case in their living room. It's sitting atop a floral print couch under a windowsill where they're growing basil.

"No, that's Abuela."

Esther's back from the kitchen with two cups of something for Vin and me. "Horchata," she says to me, handing one cup over. "Horchata," she says to Vin, handing the other cup over.

"Thank you," Vin and I say in unison.

"Esther, you play the trumpet?"

She points to a photo on the wall and I lean in to see a young dark-haired Esther, raising a trumpet to the sky, grinning, with her arm around a man with a saxophone. They're on a stage, sweaty and exhilarated and obviously in love.

"Mr. Esther," she tells us with a smile.

"He's dead," Fabi informs us solemnly. "Abuela says he rolls over in his grave when I eat spaghetti with my fingers."

"Wanna hear me play?" Esther asks. "I'm a better musician than I am an artist."

"I love your drawings, Esther!"

She waves one hand in the air and trots toward the trumpet. "I do the drawing class for something we elderly call 'enrichment.' And because Daniel would forget to charge anyone for the class if I wasn't the registrar."

She picks up the trumpet and turns to Fabi. "54321," she tells him.

I think she's telling him to count her down, but she jumps directly into playing, tearing into those first euphoric, jaunty notes of "My Favorite Things."

"Five," Fabi says. "Four."

Esther's fingers are curved and strong, her eyes closed. There's a knot in my throat when she goes up an octave and trills.

"Three, two, one."

*Bang bang bang!* A little dust falls from their light fixture when the upstairs neighbor stomps from above.

Esther tears off midnote and glares at her ceiling. Then she resumes the trumpet and finishes the phrase she'd been in the middle of. On principle, it seems.

She carefully lays the trumpet back in its case. "It's not as bad as it seems," she says. "I get two hours to play on Sunday afternoons while he's playing pickleball at the Y."

"Is two hours a week enough?" I ask her.

She shrugs.

"You want me to go up there and talk to him?" Vin asks.

When I glance at him, I double-take with a start. Esther glared at the ceiling, but Vin is trying to incinerate it with his gaze. His hands are on his hips and his eyes are narrowed darkly.

Esther's mouth is dropped with glee. "Roz, your husband is flirting with me."

That drops his eyes back to her, a little light returning to his gaze. "You should be allowed to play at least a little bit every day. He can't expect you to be quiet at all hours."

I glance up and see Fabi still lingering at the edge of the living room, his eyes returning and returning to Vin.

I elbow Vin and mutter out of the corner of my mouth, "Quit being intimidating."

Vin's hands drop from his hips so fast his arms nearly fall off. He folds them in front of him in an absurd attempt to look smaller. If I handed him a tutu right now, I'm positive he'd put it on.

"Hey, while you're here, change a lightbulb for me," Esther says, puttering past Vin and assuming (correctly) that he'll immediately follow along in her wake.

"Fabi, wanna get dinner on the table with me?" I ask, and he scampers after me.

Esther's kitchen is clean and dated. I'm positive that in thirty years, Fabi will see plates exactly like these ones in an antique shop and clutch them to his chest and shed tears for his wonderful, perfect Abuela who raised him so well.

He and I slap a salad together. "Cut up a peach for Abuela," he tells me. "She likes an after-dinner peach."

And then we get everything plated for the two of them, complete with ice in the water glasses.

"Well, looky here," Esther says, coming back into the kitchen. Vin is wiping grease off his hands with a rag, so I'm assuming her list of while-you're-here's extended a bit past a lightbulb. "Somebody made me dinner."

"Who's your super?" Vin is grouching. "That light fixture is dangerous. Call him and— You know what? Never mind. I'll come back tomorrow with my tools and fix it. Just don't touch it in the meantime. Hey, Fabi, you like Messi or Reynaldo?"

Fabi jumps at being directly addressed by the frowning giant washing his hands at his Abuela's sink. "Oh! Um. Messi."

"Of course. He's the greatest soccer player in the world. I would say in history but then there's Pelé and Marado—"

"Maradona!" Fabi finishes his sentence, brightening up quite a bit. "Do you play soccer?"

"I did in middle school and my little brother did all through high school. But I didn't keep up with it, so now I'm old and bad."

This makes Fabi laugh.

"You have a soccer ball or should I bring one tomorrow?" Vin asks. "After I fix the light fixture, we can go down to the park and kick the ball around, if that's okay with Abuela."

It's moments like these that put Vin's young adulthood in context for me. He's only six years older than Raff, but that means they were eleven and five when their dad died. Which means that Vin has spent a lot of time kicking a soccer ball around with a kid Fabi's age.

"I have two soccer balls," Fabi says quietly, his eyes going to his Abuela to make sure this plan is good with her. He's already bouncing on his toes.

"Good luck," says Esther to Vin. "He's fast. Like a mosquito." She does a buzzy-buzzy-mosquito finger as she walks over to Fabi and gets it stuck in his armpit, tickling him to within an inch of his life.

"Abuela!" he gasps, hysterical and weakly falling halfway to the floor.

"Wash your hands," she says to him. "And you two, either make yourselves a plate or scram. I'm hungry."

We give hugs and waves and excuse ourselves out the door, and Vin gives Fabi a fist bump.

I'm happy and overfull with things to tease Vin about. I poke him in the elevator. "You want me to go up there and talk to him?" I drop my voice low to mimic his.

His ears are pink again. But he puts his palms up and shrugs. "What?"

"Big Vinny DeLuca was gonna go up to the neighbor's house and list his options for him?"

He's laughing. "I wasn't going to *threaten* him, I was going to negotiate quiet hours for her!"

"With that beard, everything is a threat."

His hand goes up to his facial hair. "A little old lady can't practice her trumpet because the asshole upstairs is making a big deal about it? Come on. You can't tell me you weren't mad about that."

"Well, sure, but this is life in New York City. I was mad but I wasn't about to go knock on the guy's door."

"Good." He's alarmed. "You should not be knocking on a stranger's door."

"You're the only one who offered that!" I'm throwing up my arms, mock exasperated. I soften. "Thank you for helping her. You don't have to go back tomorrow."

He shrugs. "She's your friend. And I want more horchata. It was good."

We step off the elevator and back onto the street. I check my phone for train status. "Oh, it looks like the 4/ 5/ 6 is back up and running. We can catch it at 96th."

He nods and we start strolling down Lex. There's the tiniest little bubble of disappointment in my chest. I sort of wish I hadn't checked my phone and we were retracing our steps across the park instead of walking to the train.

Walking with Vin through the park felt like a little vacation from our normal lives. I want more.

# Fifteen

"So," Vin says, clearing his throat as we walk toward the train. "You don't like the beard?"

I turn toward him sharply. His hands are in his pockets and he's not looking at me.

"Oh. I—"

"Roz," a man's voice calls.

Both Vin and I turn to see St. Michel sitting at an outdoor restaurant on 100th, just off the bustle of Lex. He's got a glass of frosty orange wine in front of him because of course he does.

"Hi! You remember Vin? You've met a time or two. So, back from Montreaux?" We walk over and he stands to kiss my cheek and, to my deep delight, Vin's.

"Always, always, back from Montreaux," he says on a sigh. "Join me for a drink?"

I'm about to explain that there is a bean lasagna getting cold on my counter back home, but Vin is already pulling out a chair for me, and then for himself.

The server sprints over to us, eyes bouncing back and forth between Vin in his T-shirt and ball cap and St. Michel in his jean button-down with a silk scarf tucked in at the collar. Daddy and French Daddy. This is clearly the server's lucky night.

"What can I get you to drink?" they ask Vin, plainly wishing they could sop him up with bread.

Vin just points at me. In all the times we've ever dined out together, he's never once ordered before I have. So it's probably silly that it makes my stomach flip just a little. But also, this is a fancy wine bar and I'm not in any way, shape, or form prepared for this order. I'm a "house red" girly. I flip the menu from one side to the other.

"Taste this," St. Michel says, sliding his goblet of juicy wine toward me.

I follow instructions. It's light and cool and tastes like just a whiff of summer on the wind. "Well, it barely tastes *orange*," I say to him, and he laughs.

"A glass for her," St. Michel says. "From my bottle. Vincent?"

The glass gets slid his way as well and to my surprise Vin takes a sip too.

"Sure," Vin says to the server. "Thank you," Vin says to St. Michel.

The sky's started on its journey from orange to purple and I'm glad I wore a sweatshirt.

The server promptly delivers our matching drinks and Vin glances at me, nostrils flaring. I turn away from him so I don't laugh in St. Michel's face.

Vin squints his eyes into the yonder while he takes a sip of the wine, sets down the glass, and—God, help me—swirls it.

That's all it takes. I burst into laughter.

"What's the joke?" St. Michel asks.

"Sorry. Nothing." I'm pinching the bridge of my nose, trying to stop giggling, reaching hard for dignity. "We're just . . . we're really trying to fake our way through the fact that we are not fancy wine people."

Vin is chuckling too. He lifts his glass to St. Michel. "This would go great with pork rinds."

St. Michel has just completed the cheers but immediately

looks as if he'd like to take it back after that statement. He can't tell if Vin's joking.

And then all three of us are laughing, together, but most likely at different things.

St. Michel's eyes flick between us. "You two really *should* stay together."

This sentiment, said from a lightly accented tongue, on a warmish Tuesday night in June, with this wine and this lighting, weirdly *doesn't* stab me through the heart. When St. Michel says it, he makes it sound like a concept, like a choice, like *Don't go to Florence, go to Venice instead.*

Vin hasn't stiffened either, though he's looking back and forth between St. Michel and me, probably trying to figure out when the hell I dumped my marital issues on the custom framing guy.

If anything, I'm just a little surprised. This is a different take than he had before. And besides, his nose is rarely even in his own business, let alone ours. "I thought you said breaking up was fine."

He purses his lips and signals to the server. "It is. But so is marriage. The artichoke tartines, please." The server salutes and disappears.

"Ringing endorsement of holy matrimony," I say on a laugh. Vin is now watching him with a lowered brow.

St. Michel shrugs. "It's all fine. Everything changes anyhow. Everyone thinks that their relationship should reach stasis. And most of them want it to reach stasis right after they start dating. So they can have that new-love feeling for the rest of their life. How boring."

"You don't enjoy falling in love?" I ask him, slightly teasing him now, because he can't be this over *everything*.

"Of course I do, but it takes so much energy. If you felt new love the entire time you were married to someone, what a waste of a life. Obsession takes up all the time. When would you ever write your novel? Or paint your masterpiece or . . ." He looks over at Vin with pursed lips. "What do you do again?"

"He's an electrician," I answer for him, because he's got his quiet face on.

St. Michel rolls his eyes without actually moving them. "Yeah, I can't make anything from that."

Vin and I both laugh and St. Michel tumbles on. "I just mean that life is work, work is life. We are nothing when we're not working. Bored and depressed and asking existential questions that don't need to be asked, because who cares? Stay busy. Eat when you're hungry, fuck each other, work hard, and rest when you die. This is the key. You'll get happy again someday. Just stay busy."

Vin's eyebrows are up. Either he's completely skeptical or he's kinda buying it. I seriously do hate his beard.

"Besides," St. Michel says. "There is no hell for you to burn in. If your marriage isn't working, restructure it. What you do in your marriage is between the two of you and whoever else you invite in. It's fine if it's not conventional. This is how we make these things work."

"St. Michel," Vin says, leaning forward on his elbows, eyebrows down, finally breaking his long silence. "Are you trying to find a way to fuck my wife?"

"Vin!" I screech, mortified beyond—

"If she comes knocking at my door, I won't turn her away," St. Michel says coolly.

Well, shit!

"There will be no knocking! What the hell?"

St. Michel holds his Euro-bored expression for about two more seconds and then it unfolds into a smile. "Life is long. I enjoy an interesting woman."

The aforementioned mortification is still incinerating me.

Vin, however, is smiling, eyes on me. I get the distinct feeling I'm being teased. By both of them.

St. Michel reaches over and pings a fingernail against Vin's wineglass. "You never came back to pick up your frame."

"Well, you called her instead." Vin is glowering at him and it's suddenly clear to me that they know each other, maybe even well.

"What did you have framed?" Another thing I apparently know nothing about.

Vin waves a hand. "Nothing. Not important."

"Not important?" St. Michel's all eyebrows. "At this rate she really might come knocking at my door."

"Not important *right now*." Vin cuts his eyes to me. "Important later."

"Are you two having an affair?" I demand right as the server is returning with two plates of tartines. One tartine ends up in my lap. I've just spoken into existence the porn of a lifetime.

St. Michel is smiling at me like a cat. "Fate has not been so kind to me. But—" He's ticking his finger back and forth at me. "If he comes knocking at my door . . ."

Vin and I laugh. "Yeah, yeah," I grumble. "I get it. Use it or lose it."

We finish the bottle of wine and the tartines, which I dissect with a fork and a (metaphorical) magnifying glass in an attempt to reverse-engineer the recipe. Tartines are hard because you need—

Vin's hand touches the back of my neck. "She's going into her work world," he explains to St. Michel.

"It's not attractive," St. Michel says affectionately, motioning toward the pile of tartine I've deconstructed. I scoop it up with a spoon and clean my plate.

St. Michel is leaning back in his chair, turning his face toward the breeze that curls across our table and makes the napkins dance. "Children," he says to us, eyes closed. "Return home."

I try to get him to return to his home as well (he lives in an impossibly stylish and tiny studio apartment above his framing shop) but he insists he's got more wine to drink and jazz to go see.

I look at the time. "You're going to a show *later*?" I ask, mildly scandalized. On a normal night I would have been in bed an hour ago.

This gets him to finally crack his eyes at me. "You are aware you live in New York City, yes?"

Vin slides his well-worn wallet out of its well-worn home in his back pocket and places well-worn cash between the salt and pepper shakers.

Two men start yelling at one another down the street and St. Michel takes the distraction to slide Vin's cash into my front pocket. I start to protest but he kisses the back of my hand and firmly shakes his head.

The two men are yelling at one another still, but walking backwards and the yells are fading and Vin turns back to the table, standing and tugging me to my feet. "Bedtime," he says, and makes my stomach flip. St. Michel would probably roll his eyeballs right out of his head if he knew that Vin meant *separate* bedtime.

We cheek-kiss and then he's waving us down the street. I'm loose with wine and happy. Unless it's with Raff, Vin and I almost never socialize together. Like ever. And tonight he charmed the pants off Esther and tried to buy St. Michel a bottle of wine.

"Hey." I nudge him lightly with my elbow. "St. Michel was flirting with you."

"Sure."

"Well, what the hell?"

Vin laughs. "He helped me out with a project. We spent a few hours talking. Became friends. Sorry I didn't tell you."

"Seriously, what is this project you got framed?"

He's obviously irritated that St. Michel even brought it up in the first place. "Baby, it's really not important right now. I'll show you later."

That *baby* runs me through. It's been so, so long. And it immediately transports me back to clean-shaven Vin, eight years younger and rolling over in my bed the morning after we slept together the first time.

Was he going to be weird now that we'd slept together? I'd wondered.

I'd had sex take me all sorts of directions in the past. You never quite know how it's going to land. He'd pursued me in such a straight line, no wavering or game-playing, that part of me wondered if it actually *had* been a game. And now that he'd gotten what he'd wanted . . .

But Vin is Vin, not some other guy. And he rolled over and tucked me into him, sort of under him, kissing my neck, pushing my hair behind my ears. "Can I make you some coffee, baby?" he'd asked.

And that's how I'd known he was sticking around. The way he said *baby*.

Like it had been my name all along. Like we'd always been together, and always would be.

You hear about a moment that changes someone's life. Sometimes it's a bad thing. A missed connection at an airport or the wrong fight at the wrong time and then you can't put everything back together again.

I've had a few bad versions of that moment. I've only had one of those change-your-life moments and it was a good thing. I know it's corny. But I started thinking about it, calling it in my head The Smile Moment.

My wife, well, she wasn't my wife then. Then she was just my little brother's best friend, of about two years. I'd heard about her a lot from him. And I guess I wasn't actually expecting much. My little brother, he's the sort of person who walks into a train station bathroom and leaves with a new best friend. He was always stumbling into these friendships. And they'd be, like, so intense and either he'd be so obsessed with them or they'd be so obsessed with him. And I'd hear about this person nonstop for a year, like Vin you have to meet them, they're the funniest, smartest, yadda yadda. And then I'd finally meet them and they'd be like, you know, funny, yeah, but kind of mean? Or, smart, sure, but kind of mean. And now that I'm saying it, out loud . . . that really was the common denominator. He apparently is really into people who are like brilliant and attractive and mean.

So, yeah, that's the primer. That's the background. That's what I was expecting. I'd been hearing about this Roz person for about two years. Vin, she's so smart and funny and you're gonna love her, no seriously, this time you're really, actually gonna love her. And I thought, Sure. Right.

So, anyways, back to the story. We're at this restaurant. And it's this big celebration. Raff, my brother, he'd worked his ass off and gotten his master's in engineering. First in the family to even graduate from a four-year college and then he just decided to put a cherry on top and continue on through grad school— Sorry. Sorry. Obviously I'm proud of him. He's sort of a—never mind. This story isn't actually about him. Okay! So, we're in this restaurant in Brooklyn. Old Italian joint out in Sheepshead. Like, waiters in the penguin suits and a live piano player playing, like, "Fly Me to the Moon." You can picture it.

And, first of all, I was already surprised because when he told me he was having this party, well... a Raff party is usually a blowout. Like, he'll get a clown and then the clown ends up in a threesome in the back bathroom. That's a true story, by the way. For another time.

So I was expecting a huge thing. Every person from his graduating class or something. Or all his professors. But it was small. It was me and my date, Raff and the girl he was dating, this new guy friend he was excited about, and then an empty seat for Roz, his best friend.

She was late. I was not impressed. And I was hungry. We were waiting for her to get there to order, so I was grumpy. And I'd been wanting to get this introduction out of the way. Here's the thing. We have this pattern, Raff and I, where when things start to get too intense for him with one of his new friends, the friend gets too mean or too controlling or they want to date and he doesn't... a bell dings inside his brain and he's like, I know, it's time for them to meet Vin. So. He brings me out to the bar and I meet the friend, the friend is an asshole, I tell Raff that I don't like the way the friend is treating him, and he breaks up with them, or whatever, and he breathes a big sigh of relief. We've never actually acknowledged this as the pattern, but this was the pattern. For like twenty-five straight years. Since he was like five years old.

So, anyhow. I'm hungry, I'm annoyed, and I'm anxious to get this little meetup out of the way because I figure the same thing is going to happen.

I should mention, because it sounds weird that I'm telling it this way, I should mention that he does actually have good friends too. He's got friends from when we were kids, the neighborhood, he's got friends from college, he's got friends from work. It's not like I'm telling him every single one of his friends is an asshole and then he doesn't have friends. He's got tons of friends. It's just this one thing, this lightning-strike thing, this I'm-obsessed-with-you thing that's never worked out.

Okay, okay. So, I guess this isn't that much of a story because there's only like one moment of plot. And basically the plot is that she walks into the restaurant.

I looked up, I'm not sure why, because it was a busy restaurant and waiters were running around and people were coming in and leaving. But she stepped in and instantly I looked up and just knew it was her. This Roz person.

She didn't know anyone else who was going to be at the dinner. So she was looking around the restaurant, trying to spot Raff. And then she did. Her eyes landed on him, she recognized her friend, and then she just broke into this smile.

You hear *smile* and you think you know what I'm talking about. But you don't. Some people have a smile that just . . . it's like a knife but in a good way? You see it and it's like suffocating, but in a good way? It's something that you can only see in real life, in a real moment, when someone is experiencing actual happiness and calmness and . . . goodness. And it's rare. Some of the best actors have come close; you see it on a screen and you think they nailed it. Because they have beautiful smiles. But that's not what I'm talking about. They can't actually do it. Because then you see it in real life, this kind of smile, and you realize that an actual smile, a true one . . . it can only happen when there is truly zero artifice.

She was just happy to see Raff.

I knew a lot of things in that moment. I knew Raff had found somebody who actually loved him. A proper best friend. And . . . and I knew that I wanted to know what it would feel like to be on the receiving end of that smile. That exact smile from that exact person.

That was the moment that changed my entire life.

# Sixteen

*I draw Vin's* boots on Wednesday night and Thursday night too.

Each drawing is titled *Vin Home from Work*. The Thursday night drawing I spend almost an hour on. I try my hand at cross-hatching and turn the paper into a smudgy indecipherable hair ball.

*Vin Home from Work*. I'm building him from nothing. Conjuring him from thin air onto white paper. When I look at these drawings, I can hear the groan he does when he steps inside and the workday is done. I can feel how hungry he is for dinner. I can hear the front door locking behind him.

*Vin Home from Work*. Vin, my husband who retreated away from me because I'd retreated toward his brother.

"Oh, cool," Vin says from behind where I stand at the kitchen counter, filling in the last few lines on my drawing. His voice makes me jump a foot in the air.

"Why are you sneaking around?" I'm irrationally, hotly angry at him for making me jump and I'm clutching my drawing pad to my chest like a shield.

"Sorry?" He's got one hand on the back of his head. "I thought you'd have heard me come into the kitchen."

"Well . . . okay!" And that's all I got.

"I didn't mean to . . ." He clears his throat. "I liked your drawing."

"Oh." The drawing pad comes down half a foot and I peek

at my drawing to see what he saw. One is bad and one is good. "Which one?"

He points to the good one. "But . . . I thought that you only drew people?"

I'm frowning and grumpy. "Your boots basically *are* people."

His brow furrows in (very reasonable) confusion.

"I mean . . . they have a lot of personality. They . . . are like an extension of you, or something."

"Ah." He's nodding like he understands, which would be a miracle considering *I* don't understand. "Like your glasses."

"My glasses?"

"Yeah. Whenever they're lying around, I feel like you can see me still. When you leave them on the bathroom counter, I face them toward the wall."

I burst out laughing at this very delightful piece of trivia. "Are you serious?"

He shrugs, half-embarrassed and half-pleased at making me laugh. His hands are in his pockets and he's rocking back on his heels, looking at his toes. "Are you . . . in the drawing mood?"

"Are you . . . offering to model?"

He shrugs again. "Yes. I mean, I know we said once a week, but I'm . . . not busy."

"Okay, yeah. Same setup as before? Did that work for you?"

He's nodding, already headed toward the hall closet for a towel, already pulling his T-shirt roughly off over his head. This time we both plunge right in. This is old hat, you know, for us. Me, the seasoned artist. Him, the seasoned . . . nude.

Vin jumps right into a seated pose with his legs extended and crossed at the ankle, leaning back on his palms, and I jump right into absolutely botching this drawing. Draw, Roz, draw! Michelangelo would be so proud of this yeti whose feet get chopped off by the nothingness at the edge of the paper.

On to the next. He's standing, one arm up, palm at the back of his head. I like this pose because it comes naturally to him and I see him do this all the time, clothed. But I never realized before that it tipped his rib cage to one side like that, compressing half his midsection and elongating the other half. I never realized that his armpit stretched so open like that or that he'd have to shift his weight to the opposite leg of the hand in his hair. This time it's his arm that runs into the edge of the paper.

He does another seated pose, a lying-down one, and then one last standing. In this one he's twisting around, like he's looking for something over his shoulder.

"Vin . . ." The only thing that moves are his eyeballs in their sockets as he brings me into his eyeline. "Did you . . . research poses?"

Now the only thing that moves is the rush of color to his cheeks. The timer dings and he shrugs, shaking out his hands and feet in preparation for the fifteen-minute pose.

I switch to a clean sheet of paper, leaving all the chopped-up Vins in the past. I don't know why I can't keep any of them within the framework of the paper today.

This is the long pose, so I expect him to go for something lo-fi. But instead he hits one knee. And then I expect him to lean his elbow on the other knee, at least. But he doesn't. His torso remains upright and straight. He puts one hand on his thigh, and the other hand he extends, palm up.

"Vin." I've got my hands on my hips.

"Hm."

"Your muscles are going to be screaming by the end of these fifteen minutes."

"Hm."

He's got his stubborn face on, so I walk to the couch and grab a throw pillow. "At least put this under your knee."

He catches it, places it, and then resituates into the same position.

It's a complicated one. The legs are making the same right angles but extended from the pelvis in different ways. His shoulders look level at first, but the extended arm turns out to be lifting one side up. His back toes are turned under, lengthening the bottom of his foot and jutting his heel backwards. One hand disappears against his thigh but the other hand is unforgivingly stark against the negative space. There are hollows under his collarbones, the hips talk to the shoulders, the shoulders frame the neck, the neck cradles the head, the head houses his face, which has a dark and plaintive expression. He's . . . remembering something. I'm sure of it.

*What are you thinking about?* I need to know.

But I can't know.

So instead I draw.

I imagine.

I create an idea that exists somewhere halfway between Vin and me.

My brain is calm and productive, I'm churning through this pose, this leads to that, leads to oh, nope, draw that again, lower, sharper, there, good. There's the network of the knee that has his scars from his past ACL surgery that I can't actually see from here but I know they're there. There's the stepladder of hip, spine, shoulder, where he's piggybacked me so many times. There's the dip between his shoulders where my chin sits when he's carrying me.

His hand lowers an inch in the air and then lifts back up. His muscles are starting to strain with the work of it, but his facial expression doesn't change.

This pose, I realize, isn't an idea. This pose has a story. It's the classic will-you-marry-me pose, sure, but that has no history with me and Vin. So what is this story? In his mind, is there something in his extended hand? Is he offering something? Or is he holding his hand out expectantly? Waiting for something he's owed?

The time is ticking down. I get lost in the whorls of his ear, the hairline, the connection of nose to brow, the shadows where his eyelid lovingly curves around his eye.

No, it's not will-you-marry-me. So what is it?

Maybe it's the strain of holding the pose, but I think his hand might be actually extended farther than when he started. He's definitely not handing something over in this story, no . . . he's reaching for someone. I'm sure of it. In his mind, his fingertips are centimeters from someone else's.

I'm on to toes, toes, and more toes, who ever needs this many toes, and then back to the rise and fall of that hidden hand against his thigh. I know it's a hand, you know it's a hand, so how do I make a few simple lines look like a hand?

Twenty seconds left now, and I feel his eyes on me. At the top of my gaze, I feel his chin rise. A question, for me. I finish the skateboard of a shin, correct the railroad of his sternum, and then let my eyes take in the entirety of the pose, one last time.

Just five seconds left now.

And I see it. The whole structure of the pose, all its illustrative details, the way he melted into it, like he was partially resisting at first, but can't fight it anymore. His eyes on mine. His hand out for me. He's waiting. He's patient. No. It's not *will you marry me*. No. It's simply:

*Will you.*

"Wow, you're kind of a nightmare today," Raff says cheerfully as he tears into the enchiladas I brought over. It's an early dinner for the two of us because I've got to head out to art class in a minute.

"Rude!" I start to say, and then reconsider. "Fair!" I amend.

I worked at Harvest this morning and it was a special treat because the computer system was down, so I did all of the volunteer juggling by hand. There will be approximately nineteen mistakes, I'm sure, and I don't even want to consider what that means for the rescue food. When I got home, I slapped the shit out of two pans of enchiladas and then decided that I simply could not sit around and wait for Vin to get home. I took one of the pans and absconded to Raff's.

"So." Raff finally comes up for air, chewing and then actually swallowing before he stuffs more food in his mouth. "What's your deal?"

"What's your brother's deal is more like it."

I say it playfully but this is the closest Raff and I have ever gotten to actually addressing my marital problems, and it makes my heart kick into gear. Vin hasn't told him, and I haven't told him, but hinting around is kind of telling him, so *urgh*!

"Trouble in paradise?" There's a lightness in his tone that belies the anxiety behind it.

I decide to swerve this and get straight to the heart of the matter. "When you were kids . . . I mean, as someone who has known Vin for the longest . . . did he ever used to say one thing and do another?"

Raff pushes his lips out and considers. "Growing up, Vin used to say *nothing* and do *everything*."

"Right." He was putting Raff to bed and getting him up for school and then taking him to school, going to school himself, going to work a part-time job, doing his homework, and then doing the whole thing over again. All, apparently, without much discussion. "Wasn't that . . . lonely for you?"

Raff's eyes flick to mine. In the span of one sentence our entire year flashes between us. The accident, the pain, the recovery, the paperwork paperwork paperwork. Vin and I babybirding Raff back to life. Not even discussing it. Just doing it. Just going, going, going. Saying nothing, doing everything.

My question hangs between us. It elongates and echoes, his eyebrows lift and without even saying anything back, it's like he's reflecting that question right back to me.

*Isn't that lonely for you?* his eyes ask me.

*Yes,* my sad little shrug replies.

"Just tickle him," Raff advises, and the tension disperses. "That's what I do, when I'm sick of his strong-and-silent routine."

I laugh, trying to picture that. "You really think it's a routine?"

"No. I think he really is both. But nobody is just one way, you know? I used to worry about that, before he fell in love with you. When does Vin get to crumble? When does Vin get to turn into soup and have someone who loves him come around with a mop? These are things I've never been allowed to see, really. Vin in pieces. I assume he's made of pieces like the rest of us. I have to assume that or else I'm really a failure."

"Failure! What? You're the first person in your family to go to college. Let alone get a master's degree."

"Oh, don't remind me." He waves me off. "I was talking about real stuff."

I blink at him. "What real stuff? Marriage? Kids?"

"I can want that!" He's indignant and wagging his spoon at me. He eats enchiladas with a spoon, by the way.

"Well, yeah!" I agree instantly. "I just didn't *know* you wanted that. What about your threesomes in Brooklyn Heights?"

He grumbles and pushes his food around. "Those wouldn't have to end just because I got married, you know. People live all sorts of ways."

"They would if you got married to Marine." This is a test of sorts. I've just poked a sore spot with a long stick. Hopefully a very long stick.

He props his forehead up on his palm. "I gave up on Marine. She updated her substack with this long essay about her new boyfriend and he seems like good people. I wasn't right for her."

I splat more enchilada on his plate. "She's not right for *you*! I mean, she's wonderful. But she can't handle your heat, Raff."

He gets a little smile on his face. "My heat?" The smile falls away. "You mean my unintentionally wandering eye."

"She was the only person you've ever dated who didn't treat you like a trash bag. But there are nice people in the world. You just need to find one who . . . gets a kick out of your inclinations."

"This is what I mean. It would be really nice to be a carbon copy of Vin. All I'd have to do is go to work and come home and fuck the one person on earth I want to fuck and also I'm married to her. See, *that's* life."

"That's a fairy tale," I admit.

"Exactly!" he agrees, totally missing my point.

I'm about to say more when his closet door creeeeeeeaks open behind me. I jump and turn just in time to see an Everest of laundry come tumbling out. "Ahh!"

"Oh, it does that."

"You mean it does that when your laundry pile gets so big the door just gives up on life?"

"I'm busy." He shrugs.

"Raff, you just got done telling me that you watched a nine-hour *Ancient Aliens* marathon last weekend!"

"Oh, fine. You and Vin are perfect for each other, by the way. You're both the cops."

"Finish eating and we'll drag that crap to the laundromat before my art class."

Which we do. Raff insists he wants to come with me to the art class to say hello to Lauro, but I force him to stay and do his laundry. I almost, almost remind him to fold it and not just jam it all back into the bag, but then I consider that maybe he's right and I am the cops. So I don't say anything and just hug him goodbye.

Lauro is leaning against the outside of Nine Five Four when I stroll up for class. He's looking at his phone and frowning. He double-takes when he sees me and slides his phone away. "Hey, beautiful."

He's leaning forward, tiger smile, hands in his pockets.

I cross my arms. "Quit flirting."

His eyebrows come up. "Really?"

"Yeah, we're just friends. Art friends." I hold out my hand for a shake but he gives me a little high-five slide-and-squeeze instead.

"Bo-ring."

I laugh against my will. "And if we ever go out for drinks together again, don't eat the cherry out of my glass. The cherry is the best part."

"Oh, yes," he agrees, with big solemn eyes. "The cherry is absolutely the best part."

I roll my eyes, plant my pointer finger on his forehead, and forcibly remove him from my line of sight.

"Well, there's no point in being a gentleman anymore, then," he says, and jostles me as we both try to squeeze through the doorway of the building.

"Get a life!" I'm laughing and shoving him. This is the most physical contact Lauro and I have ever had, but he's keeping his word, it's not flirtatious. I wonder, for a brief second, if it ever really was genuinely flirtatious. I think come-ons might be his first language. Everything else is a translation.

"Excuse me," a quiet voice says from the sidewalk behind us.

Lauro and I turn in unison to see Em waiting for entry to the building. Her eyes flick to us and then past us, down the hallway. We are not classmates, we are merely obstacles between her and class.

There's an absence at my side and Lauro has turned into vapor. He's stepping back out onto the sidewalk, holding the door wide open. "Sorry," he mumbles.

I'm through first, Em follows me, and Lauro trails behind.

"Hi, kids. Hi, kids," Daniel calls from his desk, feet up, nose in *The New Yorker*.

I decide to take the easel next to Em's. She's quietly setting up her supplies and, oh, cool! Today she brought watercolors.

"I like your shirt," I offer.

She's wearing a long silk duster over bike shorts and a Haim concert tee.

"This is the sort of outfit tall, young people get to wear and look like runway models," I say. "If I wore that, everyone would assume it was laundry day."

To my great delight, she gives a surprised chuckle.

Across the circle of easels, Lauro glares at me. *Quit flirting*, he mouths.

I roll my eyes.

"What're we working on today?" Daniel asks, hands in his pockets, strolling around toward Em and me. He's talking to Em, of course.

She wordlessly opens her drawing pad to show him some of what, I assume, she's been working on this week. They are watercolor paintings of a pug. Done in every shade. There are a few hurried ones. Rushed lines as he bends down to a water bowl. One where he's got two paws up on a windowsill, the neighborhood watch. Another where he's sitting patiently at the door, clearly waiting for someone he loves to come home. And then there's one where she had more time. The colors are vibrant, the details luxurious. He's backstroking through a nap in a warm pool of sunshine.

"Holy smokes," I can't help but murmur. They are gorgeous.

"These are great!" Daniel says happily.

"Jesus Christ," Lauro whispers from behind me. He's got his arms crossed, one palm covering his mouth. His eyes are somber and, maybe, a little wrecked.

Lauro drifts back to his easel and Daniel and Em jump into a technical conversation about color theory and perspective and my God there is so much to learn.

How come I can't effortlessly turn *my* number two pencils into absolute stardust?

I set up my easel and prop my drawing pad up. The front cover swings open and the papers accordion out from the spiral binding.

"Oh," Daniel says.

I reflexively look up to see which of her drawings he's talking about, and then give a start of surprise when I realize he's looking at *my* drawing pad. He's talking about *my* drawings.

My drawing pad has swung open to my drawings of Vin from last night. All the chopped-up ones.

Daniel's head is cocked to one side and he doesn't say anything. I start to get a little self-conscious and fiddle with one corner of the paper.

"Shan brought raspberry pie!" Shan calls as she bursts through the classroom door.

The pie takes precedence over all, because duh, it's pie.

The other students file and scramble and shuffle into class. The model is new, a twenty-year-old self-proclaimed football player ("Call me Teddy") with muscles only previously discovered in medical textbooks.

Maybe it's Teddy's ability to hold a naked fifteen-minute headstand or maybe it's just a warm summer Friday, but there is an electric breeze, the classroom smells of raspberry pie, and everyone's pages are lavishly filled.

Reggie calls to the class toward the end of the fifteen-minute break. "Class potluck at the park tomorrow night? My wife has been wanting to meet you all."

"Shan, bring more pie," Esther agrees, by way of demand.

"I'm in," Lauro calls.

"I've got my kids . . ." Daniel says. "Will Fabi come?"

"We'll bring some stuff for them to play with. Roz, bring Vin, he'll entertain the kids for us." That's Esther again, making more demands. I nod, because what else am I supposed to do? Explain that I'm not sure how to ask him to join me for something like this because he's endlessly confusing to me?

Then the break is over and Teddy closes us out with muscleman poses à la Arnold Schwarzenegger. It is glorious.

"Hey, Roz," Daniel says. "Would you mind staying behind to talk to me for a second?"

"Oh!" I'm surprised. "Sure."

Everyone is packing up, Em taking the longest because of her paints, and I think Lauro is lingering at the door for me, but when I look up again, they're both gone.

Daniel is propping the classroom door fully open.

He plops onto Em's stool and folds his hands. "The drawings of yours that I caught sight of earlier . . . I didn't recognize the model."

"Oh. Right. It's, um, actually . . ." For some reason the words *my husband* have become the two most embarrassing words in the English language. Do other people get their questionably estranged spouses nude in the living room in order to (minutely) level up their figure drawing skills?

"Someone very close to you," he supplies. "Not a stranger."

"Right. But . . . how did you know that?"

He gives me a smile. "You're not in trouble. I'm excited for you. These drawings . . . Can we look at them together?"

I scramble my drawing pad out and flip past all the Teddys to get to all the Vins. Daniel takes them from me and leans in close.

"So," he says, straightening back up. "You want to know how I guessed you were close to this model? Well, look, here. The lines. Nothing sketchy or unsure. They're the longest, truest lines I've seen you use. You were comfortable. There's a confidence here. And see, here, the key point. See how he extends off the edge of the page?"

I wince. Daniel is probably a very laid-back teacher, all things considered, but he's a stickler for two things: 1. Don't draw pieces of the model (*we're drawing Mel today, Roz, not just legs*), and 2. Use just enough forethought to get the entire model onto the page.

"Right. I didn't start in the right place on the page. I didn't plan it well enough to be able to fit him all in one place." I try to admit my mistakes before he can point them out to me in detail.

"Sure, sure." He waves off my words. "Next time try to think in planes, how to position each drawing so that they're all in conversation with one another, not just slapped on the page, et cetera. These are the considerations of an artist who wants to continue to improve. But . . . I have to say that I quite like the effect you've gotten here." He playfully wags his finger at me. "You're hitting on your finest quality as an artist again."

I screw up my face. "Penis nose?"

He laughs. "I think that needs a rebrand, but yes. What I really mean is that it's not always accurate but it is always *honest*."

I'm blushing with pleasure at the compliments but for some reason I'm also determined to point out the flaws in the drawings that irritated me so much yesterday. "Well, one hundred percent to the *not accurate* part. Not only does he fly off the page. He gets too big, here, the scale is all off."

Daniel seems equally determined to argue the merits. "Too big? That's one perspective. For me, I think you've made this model *expansive*. He's . . . opening. You couldn't fit him all on one page because, maybe, he *doesn't* fit on one page. For you."

"Oh." I feel a little socked.

"Yes, you didn't consider the framework of the sixteen-by-twenty piece of paper, and as a general rule, you should, it's part of composition. But the beauty of the fact that you didn't consider it, the beauty of these drawings, is that you never once minded the edge, the lines just kept going. I love this. Once you realized he wouldn't fit on the page—which you must have, mid-line—you continued to extend on, preferring to keep drawing instead of bailing out. Look here. The lines are strong and constant straight through the edge. This gives the viewer the feeling that the story is not over."

*The story is not over.* "Oh," I whisper.

"The chemistry here . . . you drawing *this* model . . . it makes me think of infinity."

"Oh," I say one more time, because it's not socially appropriate to pull your head into your T-shirt like a turtle.

Daniel is handing the drawings back to me carefully. I think he's sensing that he's just tap-danced on my insecurities. "This . . . seems like it might be . . . bad news?"

He's got a look on his face like *Please don't let this lady weep in the classroom right now.* I laugh at his expression and don't answer his question. Instead, I ask one that I know is childish. But I ask it anyhow.

"Do you think I'll ever be capable of making art like Em's?"

His eyebrows jump up. I've surprised him. His head cocks to one side as he considers. "Well . . . no. And I mean that as a compliment! There are plenty of artists out there with heaps of technical talent. They're the copycats of the world. They can look at Em's work, find the points of interest, and probably do a fairly good job of imitating them. But I really don't think that's you, Roz. Look, when I said before that I was excited for you . . . Some people take my class to fill time in their week. To socialize. Or to practice, maybe. They have an idea of what they want their drawings to look like and so they spend time getting closer and closer to that vision. All of these are wonderful students and I wouldn't trade a single one of them or ask them to be different. But I'm excited for you because, sure, you have a long way to go with the technical skills, but you come to this class and let the drawings be what they're gonna be. You let the drawings show *you* what's there, instead of the other way around. One of my favorite artists, an NYC legend, Jim McMullan, he once said something like 'Drawing leads the artist out to the edge of what she sees and understands.' And I look at your drawings and . . . I just think you're open to that. You are willing to learn from your own drawings. I love that! This is exciting for me as a teacher! This is how I know you'll continue to improve. Because there are clearly moments, ideas, concepts, memories in your head that are dying to be drawn. And you'll understand them differently once you do. You won't make art like Em because you'll make art like Roz."

There's a knock-knock and I jump. A man wearing a blazer and a smile is leaning up against the doorway of the classroom. "Interrupting?"

"Oh! Elias! I forgot."

Daniel has plans. "Oh, go, go," I say to them, shooing them off. "Have fun. Thank you for chatting with me, Daniel."

Daniel shows me how to lock up after myself and seems to sense I'd like a moment alone with my drawings. I wave them off and do just that. First I look over all the Teddys. Everything I drew tonight, trying to see it through Daniel's eyes. And . . . I take the compliment. Things are wobbly and off, no one could say that these are anything but the drawings of a beginner. But there is learning here, there is allowance, I am not forcing these drawings to be something they, simply, can't yet be.

With a lump in my throat and a flutter in my chest, I flip back to all the Vins from last night.

I take one look, through this new and terrifying lens, and a sob bites me in the throat. I cover my eyes with one hand.

*Expansive.*

*Not over.*

*Infinity. Infinity. Infinity.*

There, drawn by my own hand, the terrible, undisputable truth:

Even if he's leaving, I still love Vin desperately.

# Seventeen

*The next night* I'm just pulling Vin's favorite chicken and rice out of the oven when he comes through the front door, home from helping Raff haul and assemble a new bed frame. I wasn't sure I'd see him before I left for the potluck. I haven't invited him yet, and I thought I'd feed him first, in case he doesn't end up wanting to go. And here he is, groaning, hungry, locking the door.

"*Damn*, that smells good," he says. And then, casually, like he's not performing open heart surgery: "Hi, baby," he adds as he looks through the mail on the counter.

This *baby* thing that he reignited on Tuesday has not let up. *Baby?* he calls from across the apartment. *What's the password for our ConEd account?* Or, *Baby, my mom's on the phone and she wants your lentil soup recipe.* Or worst yet, *Let me, baby*, he said as he popped out of nowhere on the sidewalk outside our laundromat, taking the laundry bag from my hands.

He's been slowly tenderizing me with these endearments. You'd think that would mean I'd be gently softening up. But no. Have you ever even seen what a tenderizer looks like? It's a serrated *mallet* that you use to beat the shit out of a piece of meat. And that's exactly how I feel. Like something that's pliable only because I've had the shit kicked out of me.

(*Expansive, not over, infinity*, and now this: *baby*) . . . Help me.

"Baby?" he calls, now, from the running shower.

I place my forehead on the closed bathroom door, squeezing my eyes closed. "Yeah?"

"I forgot my towel."

"Sure, sure," I'm muttering to myself as I storm into his room and rip the towel off the back of the door. I'm smoldering and sore. "People get towels for other people. It's the human thing to do. The decent thing. It's what people do for each other."

I'm turning to leave when my blood freezes over. I can barely make myself believe what I'm seeing as I stand there, rigid and icy.

How do I emphasize what I'm looking at strongly enough? Just imagine I write the next words with daggers, and on each drag of the blade, a line of blood blooms in cursive:

Leaning up against his wall are a line of just-bought *moving boxes*.

The air goes out of me on a jagged gasp. I would not have been more shocked if there had been a Playboy bunny in Vin's bed.

I guess this move is still on!

So, why fix Esther's light fixture? Why get a drink with St. Michel? Why feed Surya's fish? Why, why, why, baby, baby, baby if he was always going to leave, leave, leave?

I know he wants to "do for me" but this is just cruel.

On autopilot I hand the towel in to him without looking. I walk stiffly to the kitchen and put the finishing touches on dinner. When did he buy them? How long have they been in there?

And most importantly, when is he going to put *things* in those boxes and then take those boxes away?

He's out of the shower now; it won't be long until he's sitting down at the table.

I'm muttering to myself, trying to talk myself down from

opening the fridge door and screaming into it. "The *when* isn't important, Roz. He's been very clear that it's going to happen. *I'll go*, he said. And he will."

I wait until he's seated. I've placed warm bread in front of him, next to the chicken and rice, beside the salad. He's leaning in, eyes closed, inhaling the scent.

He's soft, open, definitely not expecting it.

"What are you planning to eat once you move out?"

His eyes pop open and he scans me. *What's going on here?* I can hear him thinking.

"I mean," I continue, arms crossed, plate empty. "I'm just curious. When you signed the lease, were you thinking about that at all?"

He clears his throat. And, to his credit, takes a scoop of chicken and rice. Brave man. "I haven't," he says.

"Well, maybe we should think about it now. I can write down some easy meals for you. Things you can make a bunch of at the beginning of the week and then eat for a few days."

"No," he says with a shake of his head, "I meant that I haven't si—"

But I cut him off, too scared he'll call me *bab*y again.

"Because you can't do microwave meals or instant noodles every night. It's not good money management and it's high sodium." To my horror, my voice cracks. I've revealed way too much. The fact that I give a shit about Vin's sodium intake makes me feel so transparently injured. But who could blame me? I just found moving boxes after being pounded with a serrated mallet all week and I'm weak with it, tender and sore and *mad.* A very dangerous combination.

I expect him to read the flashing neon *shark sighted!* signs and stay the fuck out of the water, but to my surprise, he wades in. He swallows a mouthful of chicken and loads up his fork. "I cook," he says. "Which you know. Because I used to feed myself before I met you. Just like you can change a lightbulb. Like you used to do before you met me."

"Cooking is way harder than changing a lightbulb!" I say, but all the iron in my tone is oxidizing in my chest. "But fine! I guess you'll just be fine. I'll die falling off a stepladder trying to change a lightbulb. But you'll still be eating home-cooked meals. So, fine. You'll be fine."

He chews and swallows, eyes on his plate. "Do you really think," he says finally, "that if I moved out I wouldn't come back to change the lightbulbs?"

And how, *how* could he say that to me right now?

It all piles up on me. The goldfish he bought his brother, him wiping beer off my shirt, the chicken he made and pretended it was Marcia's so that I'd accept it, *Let me, baby*, and him posing for my drawings.

But that lease is still up on our fridge. Space, he says.

I'm out here dying for infinity and he's buying moving boxes.

"Do I really think you wouldn't come back to change the lightbulbs?" I say slowly.

He stops eating. Like he's finally sensed the danger.

"If you're *divorcing* me, then yes! Vin! I think you probably won't come back to change the lightbulbs!"

He's breathing hard, he's staring right through the table. "Who said divorce?" he says in a low voice.

"Well, not you! So I'm out here guessing! And it didn't take Sherlock, Vin, to see a lease on the kitchen counter, left out for me to find, with a move-in date. It wasn't exactly a stumper to find *moving boxes in your bedroom and figure out what they're for*. I get that you are moving out. Okay, I get it. This is fucking *devastating* for me but it isn't *confusing*."

"Baby." He's standing, so I stand too.

"No! Let me finish. Because this part?" I point at my drawing pad on the counter. "*This* is the part that's confusing me. What the fuck is this model thing you're doing, Vin? You're posing for me? You're letting me draw you and calling me baby and carrying the laundry and food for me? You're sharing a glass of orange wine on a Tuesday with me? What *is* this? You're trying to make sure I'm all right before you go? Because if that's the case then I'd really, really rather you just left. Because this is not making sure I'm all right, this is screwing me up before you leave. So just go and let me take care of myself."

"Roz—" He is moving toward me slowly, sucking oxygen, his eyes intense like—like—like I don't even know what because I can't see his fucking face through the beard. "They're for the last of Raffi's things. The boxes. He asked me to bring over the books and picture frames and shit he has in the corner of the room still."

"What?" I need him to repeat that.

"The boxes are not for me." He's standing directly in front of me and now I'm the one who's sucking oxygen. He seems to have used the trip to my side of the table to get perfectly calm and . . . tender? I can't tell. "And . . . I didn't know you've been devastated."

This sentiment, said from his lips on a warm Saturday night in July, with our set dinner table and this familiar living room lighting, *does* stab me through the heart.

The boxes are not for him. They are not for him.

I feel sick with relief. Emphasis on *sick*. "Didn't know I've been devastated?"

"You're doing art classes. Going out with friends. Laughing with Raff. You—" His eyes flick to the fridge but he cuts himself off. "I know this has been confusing. I've been trying to communicate. And to show you . . . But things have just gotten . . . so far . . . off track."

Okay. Well. When he puts it that way, I guess I have been

trying to hide my pain from him at every turn. It just didn't occur to me that it was *working*.

"What if . . ." I'm hanging off a skyscraper, my nail polish chipping as I hold on for dear life. "What if I asked you all the questions I need to ask and I . . . could assume you'd answer me."

He looks very concerned. "You don't already assume that?"

"I mean the whole answer, Vin."

His brow comes down. "Ah. Well. I'm working on it. But I don't always *know* the whole answer."

"Then just say that! Tell me as much as you can and then report back when you figure out the rest!"

"Okay."

He's agreed to this so readily I can't help but be humbled. I've been thinking this whole time that my questions are obvious and that Vin just hasn't willingly answered them. But laying it out like that, having him say "okay" immediately . . . if I'm really thinking about it, when Vin understands what I need . . . he gives it to me. No hesitation.

"Okay." I signal him over so that we're both sitting on the couch and facing each other. Much better than facing off with the dinner table between us. We're here. We're making headway. I'm determined to plunge us on through the tundra. "When I saw the lease, I understood that you wanted out . . . And you clarified that that means *space*. So, okay. But now . . . Vin . . . everything you've been doing for me lately . . . are you . . . trying?"

He picks at a hangnail. "Trying at what?"

"*Us*."

He stills, nothing moves except for his green eyes slicing to mine. "And if I was?"

"If you were . . . I'd be . . . confused."

His eyes drop back to his hand. "Why?"

"Because you asked for space! Our marriage is in shambles! You sleep in the guest room, we are never on the same page, we haven't slept together in a year and—"

His eyes are still on his hand and I just can't take it anymore. I can't believe that I've been in a cold war with the person I, apparently, *infinity*.

"Vin!" I shout, about to snap right in two. "Lease or not! Are. You. Leaving. Me?"

Green eyes. "Literally never."

And I just absolutely break.

"What. The. Fuck?"

These are the same ugly tears I cried into his shirt last weekend. This is the bad stuff fighting its way out of me with dinner forks. I'm shaking and disconsolate, hiding my face in my arms and praying for air. My muscles are seizing, my fingertips digging into my biceps as I hug my legs. When I open my eyes, Vin is staring at me desperately, his hands folded on the top of his head, his eyes wide and stressed.

"Well." I point at my general devastation. "Help!"

He lunges across the couch and gathers me up in a ball. He's pushing my hair behind my ears, squeezing me, rubbing my back in big circles. He's telling me I'm all right. He's saying I'm doing a good job. He guides my face into his neck and it's so scratchy-warm-familiar in there that I nearly start these terrible tears anew.

"How could you say *literally never* when you signed a lease to move out, Vin?"

I pull back and even the beard can't hide the worried tenderness on his face when he swipes his thumbs below my swollen eyes, brushing away the tears.

"I keep trying to tell you. I didn't."

"What? Yes, you did, you *just* said it!" If he's taking it back, I swear—

"No. No. That's not what I mean. I mean I didn't sign it. I never signed the lease."

I flash back to the other times we've talked about the lease.

*When you signed that lease,* I said. *I didn't,* he'd replied.

*Well, you're the one who signed this lease,* I said. *I haven't,* he answered.

I scramble up off his lap and he resists for just a moment, like he doesn't want me to get off him. But I can't be stopped. I'm through to the kitchen, lifting trembling fingers to the Coney Island magnet that keeps the grocery list pinned over the top of the lease. Gravity sweeps the papers to the ground and there, poetically, on top of my bare feet is the last page, signature line completely blank.

"I . . . I never checked," I say dully. "I never checked if you signed it."

And then he's there, in the kitchen with me, lifting me out of the wreckage of the hated lease, and setting me on the countertop.

"I tried to tell you over and over that I hadn't signed it."

I'm stumbling over concepts here. "Tried? What do you mean you tried?"

"Whenever you brought up the lease, I tried to explain— I wanted you to see it the way I see it. I didn't want you to think that I'd already signed it."

"I'm sorry." I've got two hands up. "What do you mean *the way you see it*? And if you didn't intend to sign it, then why didn't you *tell* me that? Vin, it's only three words! *It's not signed.* That's it! You couldn't have said even that?"

"Roz, you're so quick in arguments. Making sure you understand what I'm saying is *hard* for me."

"I get it, Vin. I mean, I'm starting to get what you mean by that. But this is just a few simple words! Extremely important words that could have changed everything for me if you'd just said them!" I'm equal parts irate and elated. I want to scream.

He's nodding, his hands on the counter on either side of my hips. Resolve is forming in his expression. "You want to talk about words? Let's talk about words. *Fine* was your word," he says in a low voice. I'm eye level with those baby greens and, baby, they are killing me right now.

"What?"

"Just now. When I said the thing about how I know how to cook and you know how to change a lightbulb. I wasn't saying *So therefore I'll be fine if I move out.* Those were your words. I was saying the opposite."

"What? Explain! I don't get it." I'm shivering. He's rubbing big hands slowly up and down my arms, trying to warm me.

"I was trying to say that the reason you cook for me isn't because I literally can't. Just like the reason I carry groceries and retile the kitchen floor isn't because you can't. I do it because that's what I do for you . . . And . . . And if I really did leave, because you wanted me to . . . I wouldn't be fine. But I would feed myself, if you didn't want to anymore. And I would still do things for you. Everything that you'd let me."

Tears and more tears, but these ones are the kind that everyone wishes they could cry. Big, fat, and demure, rolling down my cheeks and over my trembling lips.

"How can you say the most romantic thing ever about *moving out*? Jesus, Vin! What's wrong with us?"

"I told myself when I married you, Roz, I'd give you anything you needed. I'm like . . . hardwired to do that."

*The boxes are for Raff. He didn't sign the lease. He'd do everything I'd let him do.*

I can't help it. My body takes the wheel and thanks, girl, because what a great idea. My legs go around his waist, my arms around his neck.

I'm mad. I'm confused. I'm holding him so tight I'm not even on the counter anymore. It's got to be painful for him, this hold, but he just nuzzles into my hair, one arm under my butt and the other cinched against my back.

I feel a quake against my chest. One big compression and a throat clear. I release him, to see for myself, and sure enough, Vin's eyes are squeezed closed. When he opens them, they overflow. I treat my thumbs to being *his* windshield wipers for once.

"I missed you so much," he whispers, pressing his forehead into mine.

He sets me back on the counter and we're hugging in all the positions a person could possibly hug. If it were sex, it would be unrealistically pornographic, but as it's just hugging, it's incredibly soul-healing. His hands slide up my arms, to my shoulders, to my neck, to my chin. He's holding me, his green eyes as clear as tide pools. His gaze drops to my lips, he's leaning in—

"Hold the phone."

He freezes, his gaze lifting from my lips to my eyes. Holding.

"We have not gotten to the bottom of this motherfucking lease."

He laughs, probably because I look ornery and grouchy and dizzily in love all at once. "Let's clear it up," he says.

I tug at his shirt for emphasis. "Well, I get that you didn't sign it. And that's nice. Wonderful. A really, you know, *crucial* piece of information. That I would have liked to have had when I first found it. But why did you have it *at all*? If you weren't going to sign it, then why was it in our house in the first place?"

"Right." Vin's eyes are downcast. He's daunted by all he's about to have to explain to me. I wish I could set him up like a movie projector and let his brain just shine the story on a blank wall. Alas, we're humans. Alas, words.

"Okay. So . . ." He picks me up and walks me across the apartment, dumping me with a bounce on the guest bed. He steps back and looks at me, hands on his hips. Then he turns on his heel and walks to his closet, pulls out a big blue sweatshirt, and stuffs me into it. "I can't watch you shiver anymore."

"Vin!" I clap my hands. "Focus!"

"Okay." He nods again. I'm starting to think *okay* is his power word. "So . . ."

He drops to his knees in front of me. At first I think, *Bold! I didn't let him go in for a kiss and he's going straight for gold.* But no, he's just digging under the bed for . . . the wrapped frame I picked up from St. Michel right before Vin's mother's birthday.

"Vin!"

"You never opened this." He hands it to me.

"Why would I open it? It was for your mother."

He shakes his head. "No, it wasn't."

I'm slightly irritated. Because I was the one in charge of the whole project. "Vin, this was your Mom's birthday gift."

He shakes his head again. "No . . . My mom's birthday gift was mailed to her house."

Now he's got my full attention. "What are you talking about?"

"The family portrait you had framed? The one of all of us on the beach?"

"Right . . ."

"St. Michel mailed that to her house. Gift-wrapped and all. It's over her mantel right now."

"What?" My incredulousness is so exaggerated he laughs. And then pulls out his phone. He scrolls for a second and comes up with a photo. It's of his mother grinning from ear to ear with one hand on her mantel. Above it is the framed photo that, for weeks, I've been thinking was in this brown paper package. I zoom in on the framed portrait. The one I've been avoiding even thinking about. There we are, Vin's mom, Vin, Raffi, and me, all smiling with our arms around one another. The lighting, ambient and diffused, is lovely. The ocean is a dignified gray in the background, we're all wearing shades of blue, as mandated by me.

The feeling I had that rainy night returns. It's a family photo. Of a family I was about to exit.

My fingers tingle just looking at it. It's all so surreal. I zoom out and see Vin's mom's smile. It hurts. She loves us so much. Her entire, intact family.

Vin's peering over my shoulder at the phone. "I never thanked you for that."

"For planning her gift?"

"Yes. For considering her birthday. Choosing the photo. Choosing the framing that would look best. But . . . you organized that photographer too. Told us all what to wear. Picked the perfect location on the beach."

My fingers are tingling even harder now, my gut flips. "It's the beach. Any location is the perfect location."

He ignores my casual belittlement of myself. "You did all the work for this."

I hand his phone back to him. "I didn't have St. Michel mail it, though. He wouldn't have even had your mother's address."

"Right." He slides his phone away and clears his throat. Stepping back from me. "I did that part."

"Why?"

"I . . . I wasn't sure . . . I wasn't sure I was going to make it up there that weekend and I wanted to make sure she had her gift."

This is news to me. All of it. "Going up for her birthday was always the plan . . . wasn't it?"

"Yeah. Until . . . I actually had this different idea. Like . . . a surprise, I guess?"

He's getting flustered. The words aren't flowing, his brow is going down. He doesn't know how to explain this to me.

"Just tell it linearly."

His eyes shoot to mine.

"Don't worry about getting any background in, or whatever. You can fill it in later. I'm listening. I'm not going anywhere until you're done. Just tell it in the order it happened."

He considers this, his eyes on the ground. Not being obstinate, I can see now, but slowly gathering thoughts, putting them in the right order.

"Okay. So," he starts. "St. Michel called you a while ago to tell you that my mom's gift was finished. But you didn't answer, I guess, so he called *me* to come pick it up. When I got there, he was like, *She always checks my work,* so I opened it up to check." He laughs a little. "And then I saw the photo. The one you chose. And Roz . . . I hate that fucking photo."

"What?"

"I'm sorry. I do. It's obviously perfect and everyone else loves it, especially my mother. And I knew she was going to love it. So I had him gift-wrap it and mail it up to her house, but yeah. I hate that photo."

"Why?" It's lovely. Flattering. We're all smiling. The angles hit. What could be wrong with it?

He pulls his phone out and brings up the photo of the portrait one more time, zooms in. Just looking at it makes his eyes sad. He lets out a long resigned breath. "Look at the way we're standing."

I narrow my eyes at the photo.

"The way we're *arranged*," he prompts.

The second I see it, I can't unsee it, and all the blood rushes away from my heart. "Raffi's standing between us," I whisper.

He nods. "When I saw this, when I realized that of all the hundred photos the photographer took during that shoot, *this* was the one you chose, I knew we were in trouble."

"I . . . I can see why you'd feel that way."

He lets out a big breath that I realize now he's been holding. He comes and drops down on the bed beside me, a respectful distance away, but his weight makes me bounce and I tumble into him.

"Oh!"

"Sorry," he says on a little laughing grumble. But then both of his arms come up, around me, in a firm squeeze, his cheek resting in my hair. "But not that sorry."

I mentally file away the information that all it took was me saying *I can see why you'd feel that way* for Vin to walk over and put his arms around me and his cheek in my hair, but for now, I can't be stopped. I need the rest of this story and I need it now. I scramble up to a full sit, his arms fall away, and I arrange myself crisscross applesauce, facing him.

"So, you hated the photo . . ." I prompt. "And you're there in St. Michel's workshop . . ."

"Right. And . . . this idea came to me. I wanted him to frame a new photo. I showed it to him and he told me it was a terrible photo and it would take a genius to frame that and make it look like anything."

I laugh. Because that is a very St. Michel thing to say.

"I wanted it done ASAP," he continues. "But he told me basically that the fastest he could get it done was by my mom's birthday weekend and that he'd be going out of town right after that. Marseilles?"

"Montreaux."

"Right. So. Yeah. I thought maybe it was a sign. That I would physically have to be present in NYC to pick up the project that weekend. It was like the universe was telling me, *Don't go to your mother's. Stay with Roz. Fix this* . . . And from there, the rest of the plan sort of fell into place."

"This surprise . . ."

"Right. Yeah. I . . . was going to pick up the new framed photo and give it to you. And then take you out to the beach for the weekend. Montauk. Just the two of us. That was the plan. To sort of get us back on track, after Raff moved out. But while I was waiting for the project to be done, things got even more awkward between us. Everything I was trying just seemed to make it worse. I just kept thinking, *If I can just give her this photo* . . . Honestly, this sounds fucking stupid. And it made me feel fucking stupid ever since then, but I just kept thinking that since I didn't have the words to explain how I felt, if you saw the photo, then you'd just *know,* and I wouldn't ever have to explain it."

"So . . . you waited."

"I thought, I can't just have this photo, because that whole thing, starting over, that's what *I* want, but I didn't want to, I don't know, corner you? I wanted to give you the ability to . . . decide. If you wanted me, I wanted you to come to me on your own. Not because I forced you. Which means I had to bring options. One option of what I wanted." He holds up one hand. "The photo. Us getting closer. And one option of what *you* might want." He holds up the other hand. "Me moving out and giving you all the space you might need. And I wanted to show you that I was serious. That I was taking whatever you wanted seriously. So, in my mind, I thought that if I showed up with the photo and vacation in one hand." His eyes hit mine. "And the lease in the other . . ."

"Then I could choose which one I wanted." I hug my knees and try to bear this joyous pain. On one hand, oh, God, how did we ever end up in a place this mangled? On the other hand . . . He wasn't secretly preparing to leave me. He was trying like hell to guess what I wanted and provide it for me.

This information unfolds inside me like a paper flower much too big for my chest. I feel every petal, every stretch, as it opens itself to the sky.

*Vin hasn't stopped loving me.*

"Right. Like I said. Fucking stupid. I should have just . . ." He shakes his head. "So, I got the lease, like, as a symbol to you, and left it in the guest room. But then I was out with Raff, and remember he was still on a month-to-month then? Well, he told me that he'd found the lease in the guest room and he went on this whole thing thanking me but he was going to find his own apartment when his short-term was up and I realized that *he* thought that I was renting this new apartment for *him*. And then I asked him what he'd done with the lease, because I don't know how, but I just *knew* that you were about to find it and misunderstand—"

"Which is exactly what happened." I think of Vin's face when he came through the front door that day. I'd mistaken that intensity for determination. I'd mistaken his commitment to *me* for commitment to *leaving*.

He'd been out of breath. Like he'd been running. Nothing ever in half measures.

"I got home and you'd put it up on the fridge."

"Oh, *Jesus.*" Tears pinch my eyes so hard it physically hurts. "I acted like it was fine. Like I didn't care."

"Like it was natural, for me to leave."

*And I didn't know you've been devastated*, he said to me, earlier tonight. I guess this impression of myself is better than I thought.

I bite my lip. "You didn't correct things. Or cry. You acted like it was fine, too. You just walked right back out the door. And every time I've brought it up since then, you didn't explain!"

"I was scrambling, Roz. I thought . . . I thought you were mostly just mad that we hadn't talked about it. That I made the decision unilaterally. I didn't think you . . ."

"Were dying inside? Because yeah."

"Oh, baby." My hands are cupped in his hands. "Seeing that lease on the fridge . . . I had, well, an epiphany, I guess. Sure, sure, actions speak louder than words, and that's how I've lived my life. But in this case, I was only *ever* using actions and never words and it meant that you thought I wanted to move out. And . . . I knew I had to get a new skill set like fucking fast. So I walked out that night, yes. And I walked directly to a therapist's office."

"What? Are you serious?"

"Dead serious. I waited three hours until he could see me for an emergency appointment."

"Did you go back?"

"Once a week since then."

"You . . ." I am not breathing. "Are." Still not breathing. "Seeing." I might not make it to the end of the sentence. "A *therapist*."

He laughs at my delivery, or maybe at the fact that I almost pass out at the end of it. "His name is Dr. Elias Colewood and he's helped me a lot."

"Wow." I'm staring into nothing. "In that case, then you're definitely earning a higher grade than I am at marriage."

"Let's start with *not* grading each other." He can't help himself anymore. He's gathering me up like a rag doll, holding me so tight I have to tap-tap his shoulder when I need an inhale.

"This whole time . . ." My head is spinning a little. "I thought you were the one who needed space. But . . ."

He's shaking his head. "After the accident . . . You were just so . . . hurt. In like every sense of the word. You were suddenly sleeping like all the way on the edge of the bed, and you were barely talking to me and we weren't even eating together anymore. So I thought I'd try to give you some time, sure. I'd sleep in the guest room, fine. It was never what I wanted, I just . . . was trying to read you . . . and I thought that's what you needed. Space. But you were miserable still, just like me. So, turns out I didn't know what you needed and I didn't know how to give it to you . . . And then, a few weeks ago, something changed. Suddenly you were lit up again. You were the old Roz. I wasn't sure what it was. I heard about the art class, and I thought *Okay, that must be it. The thing that's making her happy again* . . . I thought maybe I'll try again with the framed portrait. Maybe I'll figure out a way to explain this whole mess with the lease . . . But then I meet this Lauro guy . . ."

"Vin, no."

"I know. But still, I thought to myself . . . if she wants him . . . what's the move? Well . . . I talked Raff into staying the night. So you and I could share a bed. I hoped maybe you'd remember how it used to be with us . . . but then *that* didn't happen the way I wanted . . . And I thought that was really the end. Right? Can't sleep with your husband and you have feelings for someone new . . ."

"Vin, *no*."

"I know. Just let me . . . And then you're mouthing words

at me across the bar, telling me that you were going to live your best life, whether I'm there or not—"

"I didn't say whether you were there or not. I said *no matter what*."

He's confused. "Is there a difference?"

"It's . . ." How to explain this? "It's basically the one phrase I wanted you to say to me. You were already on about *I'm still here, Roz*. And . . . I didn't get it. I was hurt and confused—"

"Confused? How could that be confusing?"

"I was trying like hell to figure out if you meant *for now* or . . ."

"No matter what." Either he's quoting me or he's asserting it, with his very molecules. And based on the fact that I'm pretty sure I can see his soul burning through his eyes, I think it might be the latter. "I meant *no matter what*."

"Well, how was I supposed to know what you meant?"

"How was I supposed to know what *you* meant?" he tosses right back at me, with fierce eyes and a smile. "From my perspective, you already were moving on. Your life was so . . . separate from me. You were going to art classes and looking beautiful and dancing at Raff's party like you didn't have a care in the world."

"Pretending I wasn't mortally wounded," I inform him, tugging on his shirt so he'll hear me, really hear me.

His hands cover mine. "Well, I got that. Eventually. But not at the time. At the time, I was pretty sure you were falling for someone else."

"Vin."

"Which . . . if it made you happy . . . made you okay again . . . I mean, it might have killed me, but if you were happy . . ." He's scraping a hand over his hair. "I didn't know what to do other than dance with you and tell you I wanted you to be happy. But on the inside, I was *sick*. I didn't sleep that night . . . But the next night? Well, that was the best night of my year, Roz. I have not stopped thinking about *that* night."

"Which night?"

"Your date with Lauro. You coming home drunk and squeezing the hell out of me. Crying on my shirt."

"Oh, God."

"No, don't be embarrassed. It's my favorite. The best thing that's happened to me in so long."

"*Why?*"

"Because you were so grossed out about having gone on an accidental date . . . with someone else. Because . . . he probably thought he was making progress but you ended up in *my* arms, asking for comfort from *me* . . . You told me what you wanted . . . And it wasn't him. And it was something I could give you."

"I told you what I wanted?" I'm racking my brain, trying to remember when in my drunken state I told him to tear up the lease.

"*I like getting called 'baby.' I like being told I'm delicious,*" he quotes. "Look, we've been so beat-up this year . . . and after Raff moved out, you were fried. I thought that if I could just keep myself as . . . compressed as possible . . . If I could let you live your life however you were wanting to be living it . . . Then you would have some room to . . . get back to your old self . . . But it turns out you took that to mean I don't want you. You'll never know what I felt that night, watching you say that to me. That another man calls you 'baby' and tells you you're delicious and it quenched something for you. Something I've been withholding. Roz . . . never again. *I* give that to you."

I sway toward him, handfuls of his shirt and his exhales on my face.

The boxes . . . are for Raffi. The lease . . . was a gesture of goodwill. The space . . . was a gift to me, not because he wanted it. The wrapped portrait . . .

"I wanna see this damn portrait!" I say, scrambling off his lap and across the bed to retrieve it.

"I'm not sure I'd call it a portrait. It's a pretty crappy photo." He looks very nervous.

So I pull the paper off all at once. Because we've all waited long enough, and because, frankly, I'm dying to see it.

The photo he's chosen is revealed and I burst immediately into tender, stinging laughter.

It is, objectively, terrible.

The original photo—which I recall immediately—was too dark, a little blurry, a thoughtless composition taken by a careless hand. But this one has been further cropped in, so it's extra blurry.

It's immediately my favorite photo ever taken.

"St. Michel must have been *appalled*," I say in a watery voice.

Vin laughs. "He really was." He clears his throat. I can feel his eyes on the side of my face. "Are *you* appalled?"

"I love it, Vin."

How could I not. It was the night we first met, Raff's graduation party thrown at a fancy restaurant. I barely said anything to Vin that night, but then, right before we left, Raff made all of us squish in at one end of the table to document the occasion. I'm doing a passive protest at this mistreatment, crossing my eyes and pulling the sides of my face down in a deeply unflattering grimace. Vin, serendipitously seated next to me, is leaning back in his chair. In the original photo, it looks like he's deadpanning the camera. But zoomed in, you can see that his eyes are actually on me. Zoomed in, you can see a softness in his expression. Zoomed in, you can see . . .

"Dang, you already had it *bad* for me," I tease him.

He chuckles and tucks my hair behind my ear. "I did. Still do."

And then he leans in and takes one long sip from the newly exposed skin of my neck.

"Raff took this picture, you know."

"I know," he says quietly. "That's part of what makes it perfect."

And he's right. Raff is an enormous part of our life. And always will be. Fixing us will never, ever be about extracting Raff from our lives, only about keeping him on his side of the table, where he probably wants to be anyways.

Either way, it's just me and Vin here now. He carefully removes the picture frame from my hands and sets it on the floor. And then he does the most Vin thing ever. Namely he cups my cheek, tips my head to one side, and starts kissing me from my collarbone up to my ear and back.

You wouldn't know that this is the most Vin thing ever because you've never had sex with Vin. But he's got this way about him that just ends me. He's gentle and bossy at the same time. He gets you all worked up and dying for him and bent into a pretzel and somehow it all ends up seeming like it was your idea in the first place.

For instance, right now, all he's done is lace his fingers into my hair and lean me to one side so that he can walk his teeth over my throat and somehow I'm the one who ends up in his lap with my hands under his shirt. See? He's the master of escalation.

His shirt is old and soft as a kitten. It used to be midnight blue but he went and used it so hard that now it's dusky gray. I've had a crush on this shirt for as long as I've known Vin.

Right now I do myself a favor and lift it up over my head

and lock myself inside with his chest hair. He's laughing and holding me tight.

"I love . . ." he starts, and I still so I don't miss a word. "I love . . ." He clears his throat. "I love how when you get horny, you just do whatever the hell you want."

I resurface with an outraged laugh. "Me? Come on. You're the one who *invented* T-shirts. I mean, Jesus. What am I supposed to do with all this?" I'm feeling up his shoulders, grinding on his blue jeans. There is so much Vin and I'm going to need an IV before the night is over, I can feel it.

His response to all this? He falls backwards on the bed and kicks his hips up into me. Punishment and reward for being such an incorrigible flirt. Next he plants his pointer finger underneath my chin and draws me toward him with nothing but the power of his green eyes, which telegraph his very inappropriate catalog of thoughts about me. He's going in for a landing, our lips are centimeters apart, and then, at the last second, he turns my head and sucks on the pulse point under my jaw.

The sound I make is obscene. It earns me another kick of his hips and two firm hands on my ass, grinding me down on him.

Well. Two married people get all horned up in a bed. I bet you can guess what happens next.

Wrong!

What happens next is my traitorous phone ringing loudly from the kitchen. "Forget it, fuck it, I don't care." I'm gasping and rolling my neck to the other side, dying for him to kiss me more, everywhere.

But then it starts ringing again.

"Raff?" Vin asks, lifting his head.

"Not his ringtone and don't say your brother's name when you're making out with my neck."

And then it rings again. "Lemme just check," he says.

I grab him with every bit of my strength and try to hold him in place, but he dumps me to the side, stands up, and walks away as if he didn't even notice. I should probably hit the gym every once in a blue moon.

"It's Esther!" he calls from the kitchen. "I'm gonna answer it."

"Esther!" I sit up all at once and find the digital clock on the nightstand. "Oh, shit!"

"She wants to know where the hell you are. You're late for the potluck."

"I'm late for the potluck!" I appear in the doorway so tousled and off-kilter that Vin laughs. All he did was kiss my neck but I must look like he crawled underneath my petticoats and shredded my pantaloons with his incisors.

My first instinct is to drop my panties and crawl back in bed with Vin. "Tell her I'm not going."

"She'll call you back," he says into the phone, and puts it on the counter. And then he's got his arms around me, one hand on the back of my neck, tilting my head up to the sky. "You should go."

"I'm not going," I say mulishly. "You love me again. I'm staying right here where I can squeeze you." And I do just that.

I've got my ear to his chest so I can hear the stuttered inhale. My head rises and falls like it's riding on a wave. When I look up, his eyes are red and slitted again. "Go to the potluck. It's temporary. But this—" He taps his breastbone where my ear was just resting. "Is not. It'll be here when you get home."

"Now I'm definitely not going."

He's frustrated and so pleased. "Roz!"

"Come with me, then."

"Wait. Yes. Really?"

"Really. Come on. I want to show you off to all my new friends. Shan is going to shit a brick when she sees what a hunk you are."

"Jesus." He's standing behind me, untuggable, with one hand over his eyes. At first I think it's because I've embarrassed him by calling him a hunk, but when he lowers his hand there's a glowing emotion there, like nighttime sunshine, the kind that bounces off the moon from the other side of the world. "If . . . if six months ago . . . or two months ago . . . or two days ago . . . you'd told me that you'd be running out that door to go meet with new friends . . . and that you'd . . . you'd want me there with you . . . there's nothing I wouldn't have . . ." He steps up to me and cups my face in two gentle hands. "I could have endured anything, baby, if I knew it was going to get me here."

# Eighteen

*Vin must have* gotten the hint when Esther handed him a mesh bag filled with footballs and Frisbees, et cetera, because he's been playing with Fabi and Liam and Sari (Daniel's eight-year-old twins) for the last hour.

He stops by every so often for some bites of the hamburger and corn and watermelon and casserole that I piled onto a plate for him when we got here. As soon as Shan cuts that pie, I plan to snag Vin a slice.

By the way, I decidedly have my back to Vin because he's throwing a football and I already told you about his T-shirt.

Reggie and his wife, Carina, have been talking to me for the last nine minutes about a vacation they took to Connecticut and I have, sadly, not been listening at all. Sadly, I say, because now there is a break in the conversation where a normal person would have something up her sleeve, say, a reply, but I can't even come up with nouns right now. *Vin is not leaving me. Vin still loves me. Vin pushed me down on his boner and almost made me black out.* I feel like a high schooler who is pretty sure she's going to lose her virginity after school today. Sorry, Reggie and Carina, Connecticut can't compete.

"So," Lauro (in a silk floral-print button-down) says, flopping down in the grass beside me and eating grapes like the lecherous lout that he is. "That guy. Vin."

Oh, never mind, I love Lauro. He's just brought up the only subject I have any interest in at all right now.

"Yeah?"

"He's Raffi's brother, right? That's how you know him? Why'd you bring him?"

Reggie and Carina get up to greet Stacia, who has just arrived.

"He seems pretty into you," Lauro prods me when I don't answer him.

"Oh?"

"Yeah, he's looking at you like he'd like to test how flexible you are."

"He knows exactly how flexible I am."

"Oh, reallllllly." He chomps grapes with a grin. He's gotten the information he wanted and now he's very pleased with himself. "So you two are hooking up? He's wearing a wedding ring, you ho."

To lie or not to lie? Which would be more fun? "He's my husband."

And now I have the incredible satisfaction of truly gobsmacking Lauro. It almost looks out of place on him. Like seeing a tiger slip on a banana peel. "What?"

"Yup."

"You are *married*?"

"Yup."

"To *him*?"

"Lauro, yes." Surely, it can't be that shocking.

"And here I thought I might actually have a shot." He says it in a friendly way, one that says more about his confidence in himself than anything about our supposed (nonexistent) romantic connection.

"Nah, never had a shot."

He takes this with aplomb, seemingly more interested in my marital life than in the rejection he's just been administered. "That night I first met him I did *not* get married vibes from you two."

I sigh. "Well, it's been hard times. We thought we might be splitting up."

"He does not want to split up with you. Trust me."

"He was the one who was leaving! Sort of."

"Well, he's not leaving now. Actually, he's coming over here. Bye." Lauro does a backwards somersault and skedaddles. If Vin were frowning at me like that, I'd probably do gymnastics to get away from him too.

But he's not frowning at me. He's smiling at me. It's his we-have-a-secret smile. I know this smile well. And the best part? The only secret it ever is is how much he wants me. I expect him to sit where Lauro was just sitting, on the grass beside me. But instead, he pulls an old-school Vin and parks himself behind me, legs spread in a V on either side of me. His hands trail up my thighs, over my belly, he gives me a squeeze and then just holds me.

This is going to get indecent and we're in a public park, so I choose the most effective sexual defuser known to man. Hamburger.

"Mmrgh," Vin says when I shove it over my shoulder and into his mouth. "Vis is goob."

"Esther's on the grill. Thank her later." I lace my fingers with his free hand to fully demonstrate that I don't want him going anywhere right now.

"Hi!" Daniel says, standing above us.

"Hi," I say, though I've already greeted him earlier.

He's holding out his hand to Vin. "It's Mr. Infinity," Daniel says with a grin.

Vin shakes his hand. "Sorry?"

"Nothing!" I fill in quickly.

"I'm Daniel. The teacher. Glad you could make it. Let me know if you ever want to make a few bucks modeling for the class. Oh, Em's here." Daniel is waving and wandering off.

"What's Mr. Infinity?" Vin asks me.

"Oh, it's really nothing. Just something he said after he saw some of the drawings I've done of you."

"Oh. That person has seen a drawing of my dick," Vin says, and takes a big bite of his burger. "Not quite sure how to feel about that."

"If it makes you feel better, that person has probably seen more drawings of dicks than almost anyone else on earth."

I wait a long time for Vin to respond. And then finally . . .

"Good stuff," he says.

Which for whatever reason just really cracks me up. I'm wiping tears from my eyes when Shan comes to sit next to us with her pie. She's brought the slicer and a stack of paper plates, too, bless her.

"Soooo." She's grinning and slicing at the same time. "How'd you two meet?"

"Bachelorette party," I say. "He was the stripper. Fireman costume."

She's laughing but then sobers, leaning forward confidentially. "Wait, really?"

"She's my brother's friend. I met her and asked her on a date."

"Oh." She's fatally disappointed. "Pie?"

And then we're swarmed with classmates seeking pie.

Vin has to unhand me to eat his, a concept he clearly disapproves of. Which makes me very happy.

Fabi and Liam and Sari chase the first few fireflies. A softball game is dramatically lost within hearing distance. Reggie's accidentally gotten way too drunk and Carina thinks it's hilarious. Penny and Lauro are sitting on either side of Em, watching her draw everyone's slow disintegration toward blankets on the grass.

When the pie is gone, the universe does a backflip and treats us to a rising crescent moon so thin you could pick your teeth with it.

Vin leans back on his palms and I lean back on Vin's chest. Let's cast it in bronze, all of it, even Stacia's very dry brownies.

I'm so filled with fluffy gold clouds I could cry. I tip my face up toward Vin. He tips his face down toward me.

"I have to pee," I say.

"Wow, I really thought you were going to say something, I don't know . . . *lovely*," he says on a laugh and then helps me to my feet.

I go to the bathroom and on my way back toward the group (now just a silhouetted blob in the dim distance) I hear a familiar voice speaking in a very unfamiliar way.

"You can't *really* have thought I'd like this, Lauro. Not in your heart."

That's Em. And she's . . . seeming quite fierce.

"So I drew a portrait of you, Em. What's the problem?"

That's Lauro. And he's . . . seeming quite timid.

They're just ahead of me, around a bend of trees. I'm not a total asshole, so I make myself known. "Sorry, guys, I'll just pass—"

Neither of them even acknowledges me.

"What's the problem? The *problem*? Roz!"

I jump a foot in the air. "Yes?" I squeak.

"Come over here for a second." I really can't stress how odd it is to be hearing Em berating a wilting Lauro.

I immediately follow directions because, if it's not obvious by now, I'm totally scared of her.

"Here." She thrusts a piece of paper in my hands and I tip it toward the circle of coppery streetlight a few yards away.

It's a beautiful portrait, done in Lauro's typical style. Flowing cursive that wraps around form. It's clearly Em, but a softened version. She's bent over a drawing pad like a nymph might touch her fingers to a crystal-clear lake.

"It's . . ." I fish for a word and find Vin's. "Lovely."

"Right," Em says with a vicious nod. "But *I* am not."

Lauro straightens. "Em, you're—"

"Don't give me that, Lauro. There is absolutely nothing of *me* in this portrait and you know it. I'm erased."

She's trying to shove the drawing back into his hands. He's refusing to take it. "Nothing of you—"

"You've been doing this since NYU. You come to class with a smile for everyone, flirting and, and, and *whatever*. You buy drinks and pretend you're the party. But I see you, Lauro." She pokes two fingers against his chest so hard it makes the drawing crinkle where she's pinning it against his heart. "I *see* what you're drawing. How you see people. This silhouette bullshit. Continuous line around the outside. You don't come to class to give or . . . or to *learn*. It's disrespectful to the model. Who comes to class and strips naked for you. You offer nothing in return." I wonder, for a moment, if it's really the model she's talking about. But she's plowing on. "If you were really looking, Lauro, really trying, if this drawing were actually an offering to me, I would *not* look lovely. I would *not* look graceful. I know myself. I am neither of those things. I hunch over the drawing pad. I frown and look ugly and I *draw*. I draw what I *see*, Lauro. But you? You are not trying to draw people. All you're trying to do is contain them."

Lauro isn't blinking, his chest is moving up and down under his shirt. He's clutching at his heart and the drawing has crumpled terribly under his fingers.

"Em—" His voice is just a husk.

"It's all just stylized flatness," she says, and now he shrinks back. This more than anything has sliced him to the bone. She's clearly touched something fearfully tender for him. "It's *pretty*, Lauro. But meaningless."

His breath comes out in the sort of exhale people do when they lift their bloody fingertips and realize they've been stabbed.

"I think . . ." I whisper gently, and touch her shoulder with my fingertips. "I think that's enough."

It's obviously not my business, but turns out I do like Lauro after all and he seriously looks devastated.

She jumps under my touch and turns her wild gaze on me.

"Hi?" I squeak because I'm scared she's about to rip my heart out.

"I'm—I'm leaving now," she says artlessly. "I'm going. So. Bye." And she turns on her heel and speedwalks away from us and onto the bike path that rings the park.

When I turn back toward Lauro, he's turned away from me. His shoulders are heaving and his hands are over his face.

"Go away, Roz. I'm sorry I'm an asshole. I really am. But please."

"Yes. Right. Okay."

He grunts and I take that as my cue to do as he wishes and leave.

"You okay?" Vin asks as I settle myself back down on the blanket beside him. "I was about to come find you."

"Yes. I'll explain later," I whisper back, because I don't want Shan overhearing; she apparently took my absence as an opportunity to sit right next to Vin. He looks weary. And happy. We've got a whopping three whole New York City stars in the apex of the sky and it's time to go home. But Vin and I are Vin and I, so instead of leaving with our empty casserole dish, we scour the area for trash, use Vin's key ring flashlight to help find Reggie's wallet that he dropped in the grass. We're in the middle of the park, so Vin takes ten minutes and carries Esther's bag of lawn toys to the east side for her, putting her and Fabi into a cab. By the time he gets back, Sari has fallen asleep on one of the blankets so Daniel hoists her and Vin hoists the portable grill. Only Penny and Stacia are left to walk with us and Penny eventually takes pity on Liam, who is sleep-walking, and lifts him up too. We make it to an old crappy pickup truck parked on Central Park West. There's a terrible approximation of *Starry Night* painted across the side.

"Nice," I tell Daniel in surprise. Somehow it doesn't quite seem like his style.

"My ex-wife painted it a long time ago," he explains in a low voice so he doesn't wake up Sari. His eyes are friendly and sad. His cheek nestles gently into his daughter's fall of dark hair. "Hold on to that infinity as long as you can."

We get all of Daniel's picnic stuff (and his kids) packed into the truck and then it putts off down the street. Penny and Stacia wave and head off in opposite directions.

And then it's just me and Vin.

"So, what happened?" Vin prods the second we're on the B train, both holding the pole and swaying.

I try to tell him about the fight, but he can't stop touching me. He's sliding my hair behind my ear. He's pushing my glasses up the bridge of my nose. He's untangling my earring. Is it just me or did he get taller since the last time he physically adored me?

"Are you even listening?" I demand, which makes the kid in AirPods and a backpack (who is also holding this same pole) laugh. I turn to the kid. "He's not even listening."

"Lauro got yelled at! I listened," Vin insists.

"Yeah, but it was the context that was important!" I say.

"What context?"

"Em isn't someone who normally yells," the AirPod kid supplies. "Plus, it sounds like they were probably dating at some point."

I point at the kid. "He gets it."

"Okay, okay," Vin says, with a smile for me and for New York. "I get it. It's big. Lauro and Em. Who'd have thought." Now he's straightening the straps of the tote bag against my shoulder. With a frown, he realizes I'm the one carrying the casserole dish and takes the bag over to his own shoulder. And then I guess that messed up my shirt because now he's smoothing it down.

I roll my eyes at the kid. "I guess I'll just try again later."

The kid is laughing and looking back and forth between us. "Have a good night." He waves and gets off at Bryant Park.

A crush of people board the train and Vin takes the opportunity to crowd me. A suitcase rolls over my toe and Vin lifts it like it's a shoebox, handing it from a teenager to their father. Elbows and high heels and packs of people who just got out of *Frozen*. The world is an obstacle course but I've got a bodyguard. Vin plants his forearm across my shoulder blades and curls us away from the pole, which has gotten too crowded. He holds the overhead bar for both of us and I hold his ribs.

It has been a very long day and my feet are tired but I wouldn't mind if this train ride were six hours long.

But it ends, as all things do, and now we're headed down our block, back to our apartment, where the worst year of either of our lives mostly took place, and to the two separate bedrooms that nearly tore us in two.

"Vin—" The entrance to our apartment building opens its yawning mouth. This building has been here for a hundred and fifty years, it's seen it all. It doesn't care about quarreling couples. It's six stories tall and six units wide on a Saturday night. Someone is almost certainly getting banged into their headboard in there as we speak. Dropping a cake on the floor, fresh from the oven. Singing in the shower. Deciding whether or not to fuck your husband? It's not fazed. Nothing would surprise this rent-controlled building. These are nerves, I realize, at going upstairs, just the two of us, and seeing exactly what's worth fighting for. "Vin—"

But he's not listening again. He's suddenly got one arm braced across me, stepping in front, yanking me back behind him. There's a large man lunging up from the stairs of the building, jolting toward us on feet like roller skates.

"Roz!" he chirps, and reaches for us. "And Hot Vin."

"Lauro?" I duck under Vin's arm and steady the unsteady mop of a man who falls into my arms. My heart, meanwhile, is a race car. Perceived danger. Vin putting himself in front of me. Blue tile and an accident that can never be undone. But it's fine, it's fine, of course it's all fine. It's just my friend Lauro, drunk. "Are you okay?"

I say this to Lauro, but I glance back at Vin. Who is definitely not okay. He doesn't love a danger surprise any more than the next man who's had a brush with death in the last year. I make sure Lauro is steady on his feet and then immediately return to Vin's side. His fingers slide over my shoulders, to my elbows, to my hands. Verifying, for his touch memory, that I'm safe, I'm fine, we're all fine. I lace my fingers with his and give him a squeeze.

"Okay?" Lauro muses, blissfully unaware of anything that he's just triggered in us. "Well, sure. But the mushrooms were a bad idea."

"What mushrooms?" I'm thinking about everyone's potluck dishes and coming up mushroomless.

"These ones?" he says, and pulls a little baggie out of his pocket. In it are about an ounce of wrinkly gray-brown magic mushrooms.

"Oh. *God*."

"No, no," Raff says (materializing from nowhere) as he resurrects from a pile of what looked like clothes on the stoop. "It was *these* mushrooms."

A second baggie of mushrooms is produced.

"Did you know he was there?" I muse to Vin.

"If there are mushrooms, he's always there," Vin says with a sigh.

"So you left the park," I say to Lauro. "Found Raff. Raff gave you shrooms. But how did you end up *here*?"

Lauro opens his mouth to answer but then winds up staring at the streetlight. Raff moves him aside. "The mushrooms were here. In your house. In my stuff. Hey, has one of you been sleeping in the guest bed? Because both Lauro and I have broken hearts. That's part of why we like each other so much. But I think it's a two-person thing. I mean, I don't want you two to join. That's too many broken hearts. And my heart . . ." He puts a hand on his chest. "My heart . . . I think is like . . . an apple? A really ripe apple? But not too ripe." He hooks one finger into the collar of his shirt and checks things out. "Too ripe is bad. Don't get too ripe."

"Jesus Christ," Vin grumbles.

"Tuck them into the guest room?" I ask Vin. "Or punt them off toward Raff's?"

Vin drags a hand down his face. "I'll take them to Raff's."

I loop an arm through his. "Me too."

Because—I verify with a palm on his chest—his heart is still regulating and I'll be damned if we're going our separate ways right now.

He seems to pick up what I'm laying down because he doesn't argue. And so we all trek off toward Raff's.

Getting these two bozos to 28th and Ninth is like trying to get toddlers to sit down and do their taxes.

But eventually they're through Raff's front door. I make two bowls of ramen while Vin sets up the pull-out couch.

When we're departing through the front door, Lauro intercepts us with two aggressive and mildly insulting thumbs-ups. "Thank you, Mom. Thank you, Dad."

Raff is headlocking him back into the apartment. "Just ignore them," he advises Lauro. "If you fight them on anything, they make you buy dental insurance."

"Are we really *that* bad?" I ask Vin on the walk home.

He considers this. "Bad? No. Overbearing? . . . Well."

"I know how *you* ended up this way. You've been a parent since you were eleven years old. But how did *I* end up this way?"

"Aunt Therese" is his immediate, and astute, answer.

"You think?"

"Sure. Your mother farms you off and who steps in but a woman who teaches you how to love with cooking, cooking, cooking."

"Ugh. How boring. I wish she could have shown me something more chic. Like how to love with world travel, travel, travel."

"She left you an apartment in the West Village. How much more chic could you want?"

"It's hard to feel chic when the toilet literally screams for its life every time you flush it."

"So it's got some personality." He's all shrugs.

And now we're back. To our fifth-floor walk-up, held together with duct tape and Vin's elbow grease.

As soon as we step through the street entrance, those nerves kick in again. By the second floor, my stomach is doing a dance step. By the fourth floor, my muscles are screaming for oxygen. By the fifth floor, it all hits. Today I made squash soup for work, the potluck casserole, and Vin's chicken and rice. Then Vin and I had the most important and hardest conversation we've ever had. We finally, *finally* made up. He showed me the framed portrait. We rolled around on the bed. We went to a night picnic in Central Park and helped close the thing down. Then we corralled two inebriated ding-dongs twenty blocks north. And now we're here.

He puts the keys in our door and lets us through. It's orange and blue in our apartment, everything sidelit by streetlights. There is a low thrum between us and, unfortunately, I think it might be how much our feet ache.

"You know?" I say as I shuck off one shoe and then the other. "I'm starting to suspect that in all the ways that *actually* count, forty is definitely *not* the new thirty."

He's toeing out of his sneakers and laughing. "Oh, yeah?"

"Hey, Vin." I lock our front door and then catapult myself into his arms. "Whaddya say we *don't* have sex tonight?"

And you can tell we've been married for eight years because he grips me close, buries his face in my neck, and groans: "That's the nicest thing you've ever said to me."

I'm laughing while he carries me through the apartment. "If I'd been all horned up, you would have totally done it, wouldn't you have?" I'm delighted with this aching, exhausted, nearly middle-aged husband at two in the morning.

"Happily," he says, and then he sits my ass onto the bathroom counter. "But instead, just imagine *brushing your teeth.*"

"Oooh, yes. More."

He's running the faucet and handing over my toothbrush.

"Picture hot water in your hands. You're washing your face."

"More, big boy."

"Now you're applying eye cream and lip balm."

I'm laughing with the pure joy of being known by him, and thus, getting this joke.

"Don't stop," I say, and then hock toothpaste into the sink beside me.

"You're stripping in the bedroom. You're digging through the bottom drawer, your favorite drawer. You're . . . sliding into those wrinkly yellow shorts with Snoopy on them."

"Mmmm."

"Add a sweatshirt, but, baby . . ." His voice has gone all low and rumbly.

"Yes?"

"Don't forget the socks."

I'm laughing as I slide off the counter and proceed to go about my bedtime routine in pretty much the exact way that was just described to me.

We're slipping past one another in the bathroom, he's handing me my headband I use for washing my face, I'm peeing with the door open while he chucks clothes into the hamper. We are so fucking good at this.

Finally, we're washed up and grinning, standing on our respective sides of the bed. He turns his back, I hold my breath.

And down he goes.

*Squeak!*

I feel that exclamation point in my soul.

We meet under the covers. "Welcome home," I whisper.

"I never left," he whispers back.

# Nineteen

*Well, sunshine, bluebirds,* I'm sure you can imagine.

Actually, it's kind of cloudy from what I can tell and we don't wake up to the sound of bluebirds chirping, we wake up to Vin's phone ringing.

"Hi, Ma," he says, gravel in his voice as he rolls over and half sandwiches me between him and the mattress. I'm on my belly and his cheek is on my back. I can feel his voice reverberate through my own rib cage. "Oh, yeah? Right . . . right . . . Well, let me ask her . . . He's not picking up? I'm sure he's fine. I was with him last night . . . Okay. I'll call you back."

He tosses the phone to elsewhere on the bed and I roll to my back. He tucks one arm over my hips. "What was that about?"

"Everil canceled their Fourth of July plans. I guess he's going on some retreat out west."

Everil is Vin's mom's "man friend." He knits his own sweaters and wears secondhand Crocs. I'd call him a real find except for that about six times a year he goes on spiritual retreats where self-proclaimed gurus feed him lentils and tap water and take big wet bites out of his retirement fund in exchange for enlightenment. If you want my opinion, if you have to purchase it with all the money you saved from your lifetime position as a bank teller, it probably isn't all that enlightened, whatever it is.

"So she wants us to come keep her company?" I guess.

"So she wants us to come keep her company."

I squint at my phone and Vin reaches one gigantic arm across me and hands me my glasses. "The Fourth is tomorrow," I say. She'll want us to drive out today—Sunday—and spend the night there.

"I have off work." He clears his throat.

"Traffic's gonna be a nightmare," I groan. And then I toss the blankets off. "We better get going."

And so we race off to his mother's, at a glacial pace. Just outside the Holland Tunnel eight different cars honk at Vin for the high sin of . . . changing lanes. He pushes his Yankees cap even higher on his head and leans over the console for another bite of the breakfast sandwich I'm holding for him.

A little question mark forms between my brows as I watch him select the longer route on Google Maps.

"Why are we going the long way?" I ask him.

He glances at me. "Less traffic. Less stress."

This is very unlike the Vin of yore. I mean, he's a born New Yorker. Traffic does not bug this guy. Get there and be done with it, that's his motto. But . . . he's choosing the path of least resistance. I ponder this. This and broken glasses of orange juice. This and Vin's reaction to Lauro jumping out at us last night. But really, I'm just pondering Vin. Vin post-accident.

"So," I ask him after we're out of the hairiest traffic and onto the two-lane highway that leads to his mother's pretty little house on the side of a hill. "Less stress . . . Is that because . . . Are you . . . This PTSD thing, you really think we have it?"

"My therapist thinks that I do."

"And based off that . . . do you think that I do, too?"

"I don't know. I know that . . . you are different than you were before the accident. And not in a bad way. But . . . you . . . used to come to me with all your problems. And not to have me solve them . . . but just to lay them down somewhere . . . Which I loved. That I could be that person for you . . . But . . . you don't do that anymore. And . . . I've wondered if the . . . rift between us wasn't . . . so much because of the accident itself . . . but because of the things we've had to do *since* the accident . . . personally . . . individually . . . to heal from something like that." He's glancing at me as often as he can peel his eyes from the road. "Does that make sense?"

I consider this. "Are getting super stressed out at the drop of a hat and never knowing why you're so fucking off-kilter signs of PTSD?"

He quirks his eyebrows and I laugh. "Oh, fine," I say. "I probably have it, too."

I survey him. So familiar it hurts. "You want my problems, you say? You miss hearing them?" I ask.

He nods.

"Well. You asked for it. Here I go. You could feed all of New York City every night with the food that restaurants and cafeterias toss into their dumpsters. That's a problem I have. I want to feed the whole world. I want to be beautiful. And not just for me but because you're aging like a fine fucking wine and it's a perpetual fear that people will look at the two of us and think, *Why the hell is he with that hag?* I want to look at someone and know *exactly* how to draw their collarbones. I want the sort of fine motor control that Degas had. I want to understand how I'm feeling at any given moment and not take it out on you because you're there and you love me and you, apparently, won't leave me. I want to go back to the day before we got these scars and hug you and tell you that in a year everything will be okay."

He nods after each point, laughs after some of them, and holds my hand after the last one.

I don't pester him while he gathers his thoughts.

"If one of us is aging like a fine wine," he says, "it's you."

"Oh, please!" I crow. "Check out what these diabolically strategic bangs are covering." I lift them and show him my forehead. "It's like an accordion up there."

"Everyone has an accordion up there if they do *that* with their eyebrows."

"Well, someday soon it'll be an accordion whether I'm doing that with my eyebrows or not." I'm brushing my bangs back down with my fingers.

"Roz, you know that getting old with you was like the whole reason I signed the paperwork, right?"

"Did you just refer to our wedding as 'signing the paperwork'?" I'm glowing, burning, twisting on the inside, but playing it cool on the outside.

"Name one other thing we did at our wedding besides sign paperwork."

Well, he's got me there. Eloping is desperately romantic when you're leaving behind a jilted fiancé and racing to the other end of the country to start your new life, or something. Eloping in real life is just showing up to the county clerk with your marriage license and waiting in line like you're at the DMV. Vin and I repeated after the nice lady and then signed the papers. After that she leaned forward and told us we could kiss.

"Kiss!" I tell him. "That's one other thing we did at our wedding."

He assents. "It was a really good kiss."

"You know, at the time," I say, "a small part of me wondered if *that* was why you were signing the paperwork."

"What's the *that*?"

"The physical stuff. Our chemistry. It was so good and so easy . . . I think I worried that whenever the sex faded . . ."

It occurs to me that the sex *did* fade. More than fade. It

evaporated this year. And all that was left was our problems. But . . . that's not right. If all that was left was our problems, then we wouldn't be sitting in this car together. Having this extremely productive conversation with each other.

"You know what? Never mind. Don't even reply to that," I tell him. "I'm not worried about that anymore. Maybe I never was. Speaking of sex, I'm really looking forward to getting back in the sack with you."

He's staring out the windshield, likely a little whiplashed from this conversation and who could blame him.

But a few minutes later, he's still said nothing in reply and I begin to suspect he's hit an internal roadblock over there.

"Vin? You all right?"

"I. Am. Thinking," Vin says.

And if you could not laugh at that delivery, then you're a better human than I am. "Thoughts. Are. Happening."

He finally glances at me, treating me to a light flick. "You said you need more words from me! So this is the type of poetry you can expect."

"Well, what are you thinking?"

"I'm thinking . . . I . . . want you . . . a lot . . ."

"Yes, great. Love where this is going."

"I . . . am also . . . scared."

I stop needling him immediately. "Wait, really? Of what? Sex?"

The car is on cruise control. He's leaning back in the seat, one hand on the wheel, his legs spread as wide as they can and one knee jumping. "Look, Roz . . . when I . . . As much as it makes me want to fucking puke to say this . . . but . . . I'm different. Since the accident."

Ah. I flash back to the last time we attempted anything like sex. Vin on top of me. Both of us pushing the other away, breathing hard, stinging tears, the defeat in the set of his shoulders.

"Okay," I say, to show I'm listening.

"Dr. Colewood says . . . that the reaction I had . . . that night . . . in bed with you . . . Look, I've struggled with this PTSD stuff a lot. Which makes sense, you know? The accident was . . . terrible. But for a long time I struggled with PTSD . . . without . . . without realizing that's what it was . . ."

"Okay."

"Turns out I've been getting . . . what's called a freeze reaction. There's fight-or-flight but there's also freeze. So . . . when something puts me . . . triggers me . . . like loud noises . . . or yelling . . . or sirens . . . or, you know, tension with you . . . or . . ." He looks so sad on this last one that it brings tears to my own eyes. "Or seeing your scar . . . it makes me freeze up and freak out . . . Like what happened the last time we tried to have sex. I freaked out and panicked and couldn't . . . get control. And it . . . scares me . . . the idea of that . . . getting in the way of . . ." His eyes flick to mine. "Being with you. And . . . it makes me feel . . . really . . . small . . . the idea that I couldn't take care of you in that way. All because I'm having this stupid fucking reaction."

When someone is closed off from you, all you can think about is closing yourself off from them. You see their brick wall and imagine how much it would hurt to run into it. But the second you see that door crack open, even an inch . . . well, you have to open your own door to even check and see, right? And Vin's done more than open it a crack. Vin's just used a garage door opener. I could park a pickup truck in that wide-open vulnerability. I've just witnessed a true act of bravery. And now all I want is to protect him and reward him at all costs.

"Vin, when we dropped the orange juice and I was crying on the floor, was that fucking stupid?"

"No. Of course not."

"And when I pushed you off me in bed and cried and panicked, was that fucking stupid?"

"I didn't . . . I didn't realize that happened. I was . . ."

"Freaking out yourself. Yes. But now that you know, was my reaction stupid?"

"No."

"So don't say that shit about yourself. None of this is stupid. It's awful. It's . . ." I search. "Wretched. Unfair. Bad luck. Onerous. Poisonous. Excruciating. Almost too heavy to bear. But it's not *stupid* and neither are you. And I understand what you mean about being scared."

"Are you scared?"

"Of having bad sex with you? No. So what if we have bad sex for a few years while we get this all straightened out again."

"A few *years?*" He tips his head back and groans.

"Well, you promised me eternity, so what's a thousand days or so?"

He reaches his hand across the console and tucks my hair behind my ear. I pull his hand into my lap. If it were his other hand, I'd spin his wedding band.

"Can I ask . . ." I glance at him.

"Anything."

"Okay, so . . . That night in bed. You laid me down, you were on top of me. We were about to kiss . . . And then you saw my scar?"

He purses his lips, thinks, and then nods. "I . . . hadn't seen it for . . . well, since you didn't need the bandages changed anymore. So that was my first time seeing it . . . you know, as a scar."

"Oh. Jesus." Funny thing about brick walls. Sometimes you don't even realize you've been bricking yours into place. "It's really not bad, you know. As far as scars go."

I think of Raff's scar down his arm. Vin's enormous purple line down his back.

He's looking like he has an awful lot to say, but he just purses his lips, lets out a deep sigh through his nose. "Okay."

I decide to veer away from the topic of conversation that clearly pains him the most. "Okay, another question, then. About sex."

The smile is back in his eyes. "Shoot."

"So, you don't want to see my scar when you're feeling frisky, got it. But . . . is it . . . are you also talking about, like, a boner issue?"

He grins at my discomfort. "No. Well, maybe, but I don't think so. I just mean . . . Okay . . . sex for me has always been this clear, calm lake that I can go swim in. I can float around, I can swim, I can . . . you get it. I just get in the water and play around and . . . even when I'm all . . . turned on, my mind is . . . peaceful. I'm just in a different place. There are no . . . obstacles." He points to his head. "But . . . PTSD has made everything more . . . prickly? So . . . now if I want to go to the lake . . . I have to get through, like, some thornbushes on the way. Worries, stress, annoyances . . . all these things that just didn't used to be there."

I'm gaping at him. "You . . . you just described how *everything* feels to me. Like life is just a million miles of thornbushes. Even things I normally love . . . *everything* makes me so fucking scratched up. I can't . . ."

I break off because he's pulling into his mother's long, winding driveway. Instead of driving all the way up to her house, though, he idles the car around a curve and I find myself pulled into the two biggest, strongest arms I've ever had the honor of knowing. "I know," he says low, his nose in my hair.

"But sometimes I can't tell if life is prickly or *I'm* prickly. I'm like . . . I'm like a porcupine who keeps bumping into cactuses. I'm a PTSD porcupine!"

He laughs now. "Yes. Me too."

"Well, how are two porcupines supposed to make marriage work?"

"I'm pretty sure they manage it in the wild."

"I love that you think porcupines get married in the wild. New life goal, witness a porcupine wedding."

And then Vin's mother comes walking around the curve of the driveway, shading her eyes against the sun. She likely heard us crunch the gravel and then came to investigate why we didn't pull up to the house. Vin rolls down the windows.

"Hi, Ma."

She kisses his cheek. "Well, pull on up."

We do just that and as soon as I step out of the car I'm swarmed by miniature dachshunds by the names of Allen and Rhoda. Vin's mom adopted them as a pair after visiting them at the shelter for weeks. They were bonded, so the shelter wouldn't let just one of them go, but Rhoda has diabetes and requires insulin injections, so no one else wanted the burden.

Vin grabs our bags and tiptoes into the house, trying not to step on any tails. "Allen! Dammit!" He stands there, helplessly frozen, while Allen vigorously humps his sneaker. Allen's had an unrequited crush on Vin for years.

I remove the lovesick pup and pick up Rhoda as well, so she doesn't feel left out. All of us tromp into the house.

Ramona moved into this tiny little farmhouse nine years ago when she finally got sick of her building in Brooklyn never having hot water in the morning. She wanted to stay in the city, but anything within her price range was so far out in Brooklyn or Queens that it was literally going to be the same hour-and-forty-five-minute commute to her boys that this beautiful little house is. Besides, she'd always wanted a vegetable garden. How'd she afford it? We have no idea and she's never told us.

She feeds us minestrone for lunch and then sics Vin on her broken washing machine.

Ramona's got me in the vegetable garden wearing a gigantic visor. She sits on a little folding chair and points out all the weeds I've missed.

"So," she says, face tipped toward the sun. "You look less like shit these days."

I can't help but laugh. "Okay? Didn't realize that was a battle I was fighting, but okay."

"What?" She's eyeing me. "You looked like shit for a while after the accident. Was it supposed to be a secret?"

"Glad I can trust you to be candid."

"I'm allowed to say things like this, sweetheart. I'm your mother." *I'm ya motha.*

Well, mother-in-law, but she's never made a distinction there, so why should I? "I've . . . been feeling better recently." As in since yesterday.

"Vin says you're in art classes."

"Oh. Yup."

"Says you're a genius."

"Wait, really? That's sweet, but I'm definitely not."

"He says he sees your heart in everything you draw."

"I . . ." The heart that Vin can apparently see starts beating double time. "When did he say that?"

She shrugs. "Couple of weeks ago."

A couple of weeks ago? When would he have looked at my drawings? Back when he found my stuff in my backpack?

When everything was cold between us? He could look at some crappy little sketches and see my heart?

"He must have been looking really hard, then," I say, my voice slightly scratchy.

"With you, he always does." There's a distinct pause. And then, "How are my boys?"

I glance up at her. She never asks me about Vin and Raff. She wouldn't need to. They talk all the time. Vin is up and down from her house a few times a month for this or that. She and Raff watch episodes of *Dancing with the Stars* over the phone together.

I know she's talking about this year. About the accident. It strikes me that my answer today, Sunday, is very different than what my answer might have been on Friday. "Better every day."

"Yeah?"

I nod. "Yeah."

"You taking care of my Vin?" Some might view this as an annoying question from a mother-in-law. After all, doesn't she care that Vin is taking care of me? But of course . . . she knows Vin. Of course Vin is taking care of me.

"I'm trying," I say, and if it's not completely true, I immediately resolve to rectify that.

"You know . . ." She spots some weeds she can't resist and gets off her folding chair to kneel in the dirt next to me. "You're the only one he ever lets."

"Take care of him?"

She gives one brisk nod. "It was like, his father died one morning and then by that night Vin had decided that he was just going to take care of everything. I was too . . . I was so . . . I couldn't see it . . . at the time. And by the time I started recognizing the pattern, it was too late."

"He was already Mr. Take Care of It."

"But not with you."

This is so surprising it rings as dead wrong. "Oh, he's absolutely Mr. Take Care of It with me."

She's pursing her lips at me and tossing weeds into my pile. "He calls you when he has a fever. He wears the clothes you buy for him. He eats your food and asks for more. You make him comfortable. You make him feel at home. And—" She clears her throat. "I relied on him too much. To work. To take care of his brother. Growing up, he didn't have a place to just . . . be. To feel at home."

"Well." I'm clearing my throat too. "Well, you don't have to worry, Ma." Mostly I call her Ramona. But every once in a while, because she's old-school Italian and it delights her and it's the way she thinks things oughta go, I call her Ma. "If he didn't feel it when he was young, he's gonna feel it when he's old. I'll make sure he gets taken care of. That he has a place to come home to and someone there who lets him rest. Even when we're old and gray. Especially when we're old and gray."

"Ma. Iced tea?"

Both Ramona and I jump at Vin's voice behind us. We were facing away from the house and didn't hear him pad up to us through the grass.

"It's in the fridge, dum-dum," she says, fighting to her feet. "Where do you think I keep it? The toilet?"

He helps her to her feet and she heads off to rustle it up. And then he's there, next to me, two hands on mine, pulling me to my feet. His eyes are bouncing between mine but I can't tell if he heard our conversation or not.

Later, the three of us are sitting on the back porch, drinking iced tea and watching dachshunds frolic, when her phone rings. "Hi . . . Okay . . . Yes." She hangs up. (This is where Vin learned his conversation skills, by the way.)

"Your brother is taking the bus in," she tells Vin. "I'll go get him from the depot."

"Oh, he's coming? What time?" Vin asks. "I'll get him."

She waves him off. "He gets in at four. But Loretta lives over there. I'll stop in for a bit first."

She heads to the sliding door. "Roz, do something with those tomatoes, will you?" She points to the patch in the corner of the yard. "See you at five."

By "do something" she means pick them and then turn them into dinner, which, it won't surprise you, sounds fun to me.

I finish my tea and head down there. I'm just washing a bowl of green and yellow and purple heirloom tomatoes in the sink when I hear Vin walk up behind me in the kitchen.

"I'm thinking linguine alla cecca. Your mom loves it and it's pretty easy—"

I turn and drop a tomato.

Splat.

Because Vin is standing in the kitchen, hands in his pockets, with a freshly shaven face.

I try to say anything. Anything. But—

Instead, I just fling myself across the kitchen and jump into his arms. He catches me by the butt and laughs.

"It's Vinny Green Eyes!"

Because here he is. *Here* he is. My husband. The one I married. Vin of the jawline, Vin of the firm mouth, Vin of the smile, of the—yes! Smile lines. Smile lines, I see them now, outside the corners of his mouth and there, mirrored next to his eyes. He looks older without the beard and his face is fuller than the last time I saw it fully revealed. And I love it, I love it, I love it. Because he's gotten older just like me and because he is so right. The reason we signed on the dotted line with each other was so that we could have the *privilege* of these faces, only getting line-ier as time speeds on.

His eyes are squeezed closed. "It has been so long since you called me that," he whispers.

"It has been so long since I've seen this face. Why'd you shave it?"

He sits me on the counter and uses his now-free hands to cup my face. "Because we're growing old together. Changing together. It didn't seem right to cover it. Besides. You didn't kiss me on the mouth once since I grew that beard. And I'm really fucking sick of not kissing you on the mouth."

Well, sometimes joy is so big it hurts.

To ease the passage of this enormous emotion, I do the only thing I can think of. I tug on his T-shirt and he bends to me. When our mouths connect, I make a groan so guttural that Vin stops kissing me to chuckle. But not for long. He presses my jaw, opens my mouth, firmly seeks out my feelings for him. He's so warm and tastes like iced tea and *him*. Like my big, safe man.

He turns the kiss gentle in a bossy way. We're going his speed, whether I like it or not. And I do. I like everything. Any way he wants to give it to me.

He's got one hand on the back of my neck, tilting me up to him. He's kissing me softly but he's pushing farther in with each slide. When I fully yield, he grunts and his forearm slides me forward on the counter. I wrap my legs around his hips and he grunts again. We're twisting, I'm leaning, he's holding us both up, thank God, because if it were up to me, I'd be free-falling.

He breaks from my lips to kiss at my neck but is almost immediately drawn back to my mouth. He's warming me, petting me pliant. I'm soft as a fresh bloomed flower, and he's trying to taste what's at the center.

Well, maybe not completely soft, considering I've just started climbing him. His shirt is slipping, stretching under my fingers. I've got my arms around him so tight I'm trembling. Or maybe I'm trembling because he's just sucked my bottom lip, lifted me off the counter, taken three steps, and pushed me up against the hallway wall.

It's a high-speed slide show, a delicious rapid-fire, all the times Vin has slid my panties down my legs and pinned me against a wall.

"Do you remember?" I pant as he starts making out with my pulse point. "Do you remember your birthday?"

He lifts his head and I read in his green eyes that he remembers exactly which birthday I'm talking about. A long time ago, a weekday. He'd come home from work grumpy and tired and I'd dragged him out to dinner and a movie, teasing him the entire time, priming him. Little touches, pretending to brush something off the back of his neck, pressing my chest into him when someone was trying to move past me. Eye contact at dinner, drawing my toe up and down his leg during the movie. I wound him up so tight that he started undoing his belt in the hallway outside our apartment. The door was still swinging closed when he lifted me up and made me pay for working him up so badly.

"Rob's wedding," he grunts in reply. And I moan remembering going down on him in a hotel room, and afterward him putting my palms against the cold glass of a window.

"New Year's three years ago," I counter. One of Raff's friends had mistaken me for single and hit on me so aggressively that Vin took me home and kept me on the edge for an hour and a half. I literally begged him to fuck me and when he finally did, I came about forty times in about forty different ways.

Well, that precious memory has him pulling me off the wall

and striding down the hallway toward the bedroom. We're making out like this might be our last kiss. We're using our greatest hits as foreplay.

He kicks the door shut behind us and the slam feels final. Like nothing is allowed in this room but him and me. We're hashing this out one way or another.

This isn't his actual childhood bedroom, but it might as well be. There are old family photos lining the walls, a row of yearbooks on one shelf, a faded poster of Yankee Stadium. Now that me and my scar are in this room, everything that has made him into Vin is present and accounted for. I'm surrounded by him in every way possible. Brick by brick, this room and its contents are a scale model of his heart.

Bright sunshine and a little dust. It's all so, humblingly, *seeable*.

Here he is, lit from the side, clean-shaven and drawn in clear, expansive lines. Loving the absolute hell out of me.

Also, he's extremely turned on. He's just given me a hickey, I can feel it burning on my neck, and now he's tugging on my shirt, biting at the little heart that holds my two bra cups together. My shirt is slipping against my skin and I'm gasping his name. The button on my jeans slides like velvet and then his hand is under my panties, finding me.

"Fuck." His voice is harsh and unforgiving, like he's mad that I've been this wet for him and didn't tell him. His big middle finger slides into me and I arch up into him. He bites my lip and moves his thumb in circles while his middle finger gives me the old come-hither.

This motherfucker knows all the magic tricks that work on me. He's everywhere, kissing my mouth, nuzzling my ear.

"More," I cry, and he gets what I mean. He puts his mouth at my ear.

"The first time we came out to this house I fucked you in the back seat of our car so we wouldn't wake anyone up."

A spike of pleasure rockets through me. I'm very, very close. "More."

"Fucking you on the floor when I get home from work." His words are getting choppy and his hips are pushing into my thigh. I'm almost there.

"More."

"The first time I put you on your hands and knees you said nobody'd ever hit it like that before."

And that's the one that gets me. Because I wasn't lying back then and I'm not lying now. I'm screaming through clenched teeth, arching and gasping. Even though the only words I can say are *fuck* and *Vin* over and over again, it's pretty much the truest thing I've ever said in my life.

He teases every last little jump out of me before he pulls back and stands, ripping off his belt and undoing his pants. "You got hopes and dreams for this, baby?"

He's always pretty dominant, but every once in a while he really hulks out and I am here. For. The. Ride. "Anything you want," I gasp.

"Good."

He pulls me by the ankles, yanks my jeans and panties down to my knees, and flips me onto my stomach. My ass gets a friendly slap and then he finds me with his fingers again.

But not for long because holy shit that's a lot bigger than his fingers and he's pushing, pushing, pushing into me. His hands plant on either side of my shoulders and his hips start working me inch by inch up the bed.

I'm sensitive and soft and still electrified by fireworks and every slap of his hips against mine is multiplied by a thousand. For a moment I can feel it. Everything he's held inside this year. Every second that he's wanted me, needed me, and couldn't have me. I fist the sheets and take it all.

"Give it, Vin."

I can't fix his pain, not really. But anything he needs to let free into me right now, *that* I can take. Yearning, I can fix for him. It's absurd to think that this could be an answer for us, but also, of course it is. We're one thing, Vin and I, a unit. We're best when we're on top of each other, in rhythm, taking charge of the other's needs.

And right now his needs are feral. He collapses down, gives me his weight, slides his arms around me, he couldn't be closer if he tried. His breath is hot on my neck, my name is on his lips. He's holding me in place. I'm so his I know he's about to come before he does.

"Fuck. Fuckfuckfuck." He kicks his hips forward and holds. Pushes deeper and then deeper. "Baby."

As usual, he immediately becomes the most affectionate man on earth right after he comes. He's kissing my ear, brushing my hair out of my face. Gripping me close and sliding us off the bed.

He falls backwards and I fall with him, his back lands on the floor and my back lands on his chest. He slips out of me and everything he's left behind starts dripping down my leg.

We're panting, fighting for breath.

I'm about to make some joke, some silly *And we're back, baby!* comment. But his chest is stuttering underneath me. I try to turn and see what's happening back there but he pins me in place with his arms.

"Words, Vin!" I demand, because if he's not going to let me see his face, I have to know what the hell is going on.

"Just . . . happy."

And now, not even his arms can stop me. I spin and hold

him. Our sweaty, twisted, wrinkly clothing is an impossibly annoying impediment, but I don't want to unhand him to remove anything.

"I . . ." he continues once I've got my face pressed to his neck. "I was so lonely without you."

I kiss him with no tongue. It feels like a hug, a look-at-what-we've-been-through kiss. I give him another. A look-at-us-now kiss.

I try to move, to cuddle him more, but my jeans constrict me. Sweat trickles down my back and Vin trickles down my leg.

"Ugh. God."

He's laughing.

"Good thing you fixed the washing machine," I grumble.

"*Almost* fixed the washing machine," he corrects.

"Oh *no*."

Now he's laughing even more. Probably at the genuine horror and concern on my face. "You take a shower. I'll finish it up real quick and get our clothes in the washer."

Fifteen minutes later, I'm just rinsing the last of the shampoo out of my hair when the bathroom door opens. I freeze.

"I'm naked, Vin!"

There's a pause. "I . . . assumed?"

"No, I mean that . . . my scar . . ."

The shower curtain comes back. "That's okay. Thanks for reminding me."

Vin steps in. He's one of those men that somehow look bigger when naked. He's quickly wetting himself down and then crowding me back under the water, where it's warm. He's got my back against the wall again and he doesn't waste time, dropping to his knees and putting one of my legs over his shoulder.

Vin has always been really into this. Going down on me

well after the sex is said and done. He says it's when I'm silkiest. He says it's when I'm sweetest. He says he doesn't like to be rushed. He says—

"Fuck."

Yeah, he says *fuck* a lot (when we fuck).

I say it a few times, too. For good measure. He's tongue-kissing me down there, petting, soothing. His way of saying thank you, I think, for making my softest place take all that passion. He takes a long, gentle time and then I'm whispering his name into the curls of steam, gripping his hair, balancing against his shoulders, shaking with tension and then with release.

I'm pudding by the time he comes back to his feet. I'm pudding and he's smiling.

"You need a nap," he decides, and dunks his head under the spray.

"I need a honeymoon. With my hot husband."

He's still smiling. "Go. Sleep for a minute while the laundry finishes."

I do, and he doesn't. He keeps puttering around his mom's house, fixing things, straightening up, delivering my clothes in a neatly folded pile. The shadows are different each time I open my eyes. My body is soft and still buzzing when he comes in and gently touches my cheek, his hands smelling like basil.

"Dinner's on, baby."

I push myself up to a sit and the covers fall away. I'm groggy and shocked. "You cooked."

He's quiet while I rub my eyes. When I finally focus on him, he's on one knee beside the bed. He leans forward, forward, forward, and plants his forehead against my heart. "I'm so in love with you," he whispers.

"That's just the sex chemicals talking," I say happily, hugging his head with both arms.

"Sure," he agrees easily, lifting his face to mine. "But that doesn't make it less true."

They're waiting for me on the back porch, dinner in a spread. Ramona is "just commenting" on Raff's new mullet-ish haircut. ("It's a fashion mullet, Ma.") ("Just saying the word *fashion* doesn't make it fashion, sweetie.")

We eat pasta with just-picked tomatoes, basil, and mozzarella so milky fresh we have to close our eyes to chew it.

Raff is unusually quiet, but that might be because he ate an entire bag of mushrooms last night and probably hasn't fully recovered.

The mosquitoes come out, so Ramona lights a hundred candles. She brings out a pound cake with fresh peaches and more basil.

"What is this, a wedding?" Raff asks.

"Apparently we don't have weddings in this family," Ramona replies, so ice cold that both of her boys just gripe, "Ma!" (For different reasons, of course.)

The three of them watch the sky deepen while I scour the kitchen clean. Seriously. I even use her preferred white vinegar solution on the stovetop. I'm guilt-cleaning, partially because I was supposed to make dinner but slept through it and partially because me and her son just did some very dirty things under this roof.

Ramona goes to bed first with a lot of very detailed instructions re: the candles. Vin, who is used to Raff and me burning the midnight oil, throws in the towel next. But before he goes, he slides one hand to the back of my neck, tips my head up, leans down, and kisses me softly, deeply, lingeringly. And then two more for good measure.

I expect a friendly jab from Raff, some comment on me as a wife or person with a private life or as a lady who kisses, but . . . he waits for Vin to close the sliding door behind him . . . and then he bursts into wrenching, ugly tears.

"Raff!" I jump into Ramona's chair, where I can reach him, and throw my arms around his shoulders. "Raff, what is it?"

He twists and puts his arms around me. The shoulder of his short-sleeve flannel (don't ask) is soft as butter under my cheek and he smells like incense. "You—" He gasps. "Have—" Another gasp. "A hickey!"

"Oh! Shit!" I forgot about that. I unhinge from the hug and put my hand over it. "Oh, Jesus. Do you think your mom saw?"

He's laughing through tears at my horror and discomfort. "Of course she did! It's, like, bright as a stop sign."

"Oh, Jesus."

"This is a good thing, Roz. *This is such a good thing.*" And then he's weeping again, his face in his hands and his elbows on his knees.

"*Raff*," I say again, unhanding my hickey to lay a palm on his back, make big, sweeping circles.

"I thought," he says, trying to take a deep breath and failing. "I thought you might be splitting up or something . . . I thought . . . I thought I'd fucked everything up for you two. And I was all ready to . . . never forgive myself."

"Raff!" He's back in the circle of my arms again because he can't stop crying. It occurs to me that he sounds just like Vin right now. Only, the pauses between Raff's words are filled with bursts of tears. Isn't it the same thing, though? A pause for a swell of emotion that forces the words to one side or the other? "You've been feeling this way all along?"

"Well, neither of you were *saying anything*. Which made me think it was a secret or something. That I wasn't supposed to know. So I just . . . pretended not to know . . . but that pretty much meant I watched in silence while you guys split up."

"Raff, first things first, *we are not splitting up.* We've had a lot of trouble this year. But we love each other. We're getting back on track."

"I wanted to move out so bad, Roz," he's saying into his hands. "I could tell that it was a strain for you two. But . . . the thought of being alone. Of ever being alone . . . It took me too long to move out. I know. You weren't sleeping together anymore, barely even talking. And still, I stayed. It took too fucking long. I know it. I am such a fucking coward."

"*Raff!*" And now I've said his name in pretty much every inflection one can use. This time I'm angry. "You were terribly injured. Just like we were. Fine, you stayed a little too long, but what do you think it would have done to me and Vin if you'd left too early? You think that would have been the magical answer? No way, me and Vin have to find our way through this together, no matter if you're there or not. And you are not a coward for not wanting to be alone." A thought occurs to me. "Even though you're alone now and seem to be doing pretty fucking well."

He's glaring at me because he wants to be glaring at himself. "I'm having random sex with random people and wishing—" He cuts himself off. "This is not the point. The point is that you and Vin are sleeping together again. And I'm so happy."

"I don't think most people are this involved in their siblings' sex lives."

"It's not about the sex! Well, I mean, of course it is, because when is it ever *not*, really? But I just mean that he kissed you good night. And clearly wanted you to come to bed with him. And actually come to think of it, why didn't you go to bed with him just now?"

I pat his shoulder. "Because I'm talking to *you*."

"Forget about me! Go! Cuddle your husband! Tell him how much you love his jawline."

"How'd you know I love his jawline?"

"Girl."

We both burst out laughing. And then I sober a little. "I . . . didn't know you'd been worrying about this. Or, honestly, noticing this."

"Raff has eyes and ears, you know! Raff has a high IQ and a high EQ, you know. Raff doesn't only think about himself, you know!"

"Well! Okay! I know this!"

He props his chin on his hand. "Do you? Because sometimes you and Vin really do treat me like your nine-year-old son. *Don't tell the baby that Mommy and Daddy don't love each other anymore.*"

"Hey!" I point an aggressive finger at his chest. "Vin and I love each other very much."

He bangs the table. "And you have the hickey to prove it!"

"Ugh." I bring my knees up and hide my face. "So embarrassing. We're almost forty years old."

"You could have told me, you know. That you were having problems."

I unhide my face and study him. I see a lot more hurt there than I would have predicted.

"But I get it," he continues on. "I probably wouldn't have told me either. Nobody wants relationship advice from someone like me."

I bristle. "Someone like you?"

"Oh, don't make me spell it out. You already know."

I've seen Raff sad plenty of times. Occasionally mad at himself, but this totally defeated, low-grade-despisement thing he has going on feels very foreign and unnatural.

"I do *not* know."

He twiddles his thumbs and tips his head back to watch the stars.

"Hey." I wait until he looks at me. "Just now, when you said 'having random sex with random people and wishing' . . . Did you mean . . . Wishing you were different than you are?"

His knee jumps. "No. I don't know. I mean . . . I know we were joking about it the other night. That it would be so much easier to be like Vin. To just want the person you have. But . . . it's not a joke. Because I see what it means to *you* to be who Vin wants. To be the *only* thing that Vin wants. It's . . . magic, right? Like, the rarest, most special gift you can ever give to someone? And . . . I don't know if I can ever give that. I just . . . I don't think I'm built that way. To only want one person at a time."

"No, no, no. You've got it backwards. You started at the wrong side of the equation. The rarest and most special gift is loving someone the way *they* want, or need, to be loved. And . . . Vin and I . . . we're *still* working on that. I meant it when I said that what you described was a fairy tale. There is no magic spell that makes all this easy for us, just because we've made a monogamous commitment to each other. Raff, there's nothing wrong with random sex with random people! Random people love you! You make random people's month. But if what you're saying is that you want partnership or companionship or a commitment of some kind with someone *and* you want to keep plowing through New York . . . well . . . it's New York, go find someone who would be okay with that! Or who wants to do that *with* you. You know what? I'm just going to say it. You are *forbidden* from getting married, being monogamous, and having kids. You don't want it! If you tried to do it, you'd just ruin your life. And the life of whoever you married. Just have random sex with random people if it makes you happy! Fall in love five times a week. Date everybody. At the same time!"

"That's exactly what Lauro said," he grumbles.

"Then take his advice if you can't take mine," I grumble back.

"Lauro is in love with one person and wants to be monogamous and get married and do oil paintings of each other's butts. This disqualifies him from giving advice on this matter. Same as you."

"Fine, fine. It's above my pay grade. All I'm saying is that you wishing you were different can, in no way, shape, or form be the catalyst for Vin and me having had trouble this year. It doesn't even make sense. Quit blaming yourself."

He collapses back into his chair and looks at the stars. His head rolls to me. "Are you two really fucking again?"

"Mind your own business!"

He's grinning at me.

"Go," he says. "I'll do the candles."

And so I do.

Vin rolls over and pulls me into him the second I slide under the covers. His eyes are closed, his face is clean-shaven. It all sends a warm jolt through me.

"Good conversation?" he asks on a low grumble, his eyes still closed.

"Always," I reply, snuggling closer because he is so warm and so big and so mine.

"Thanks," he says. "For taking care of my brother." And then he cracks one eye. "He doing okay?"

"Oh, my God! This family! Why don't any of you ever ask *each other* how you're doing? Always with the *Hey, Roz.*"

He's smiling. "It's a game of telephone. You're the telephone."

He's petting my hair now, pulling the blanket over my shoulder, testing my pillow, deciding his is better and trading them.

"What would you ever do without me?" I ask.

"Please, please don't make me consider that," he answers. And then there's no more movement. We're just staring into each other's eyes, a foot apart, tangled under the blanket. And it's all so familiar. The feel of him against me, the shadows that nestle into his face. The curve of his eyelid, the dark fringe of his eyelashes. He's thinking his own thoughts and also trying to guess mine.

I know because I *know*. Because I've spent the last eight years working for the privilege of looking at him and knowing what he's thinking.

"How," I whisper through the tremble in my voice. "How could I have forgotten, Vin?"

"Forgotten what?" He's whispering too.

"That I *do* always know what you're thinking." Not the details, of course. Rarely the specifics. And PTSD has made it, maybe irrevocably, more murky. But at the core of it, of course I know what he's thinking: *I love her. I want her. How can I help her? What can I do for her today?* That's my man. This is what is written in his heart.

He moves and I move. We meet in the middle, where the pillows overlap. Our lips greet and then slide gently, his hand searches under my shirt for the smooth skin of my back. He's rubbing a big, slow circle there.

If, earlier today, he turned me on from the inside out—full heat and speed—well, tonight he works from the outside in. Long, slow touches, every place but between my legs. He never stops kissing me. He kisses the scar on my collarbone but leaves my shirt on, sliding me out of my bottoms and one of my legs over his hip. It's a long time later, when I've been slow-burned until I'm gasping, that he pushes gently into me. He starts to roll me to my back but pauses, reads my eyes, remembers my triggers. Instead, then, he rolls to his own back and takes me with him. I pin myself against him and he holds me so tight our heartbeats talk to each other. He's got both hands on my hips and his tongue in my mouth.

And I just don't care that we're in his mother's house. That there are other people here. That someone might hear us. I mean, yes, not ideal. But there are some things more important than propriety. And sometimes you just say, you know what? My marriage comes first tonight.

We kiss and gasp and make quiet love on a squeaky bed. Afterward, when I'm listening to his heartbeat hammer in his rib cage, and the world is mixing with the other world, and I'm floating away, sinking in, warm and Technicolor, he says something.

"What?" I murmur, startling awake for a moment.

"Nothing," he whispers. "Sleep. I'll tell you later."

# Twenty

Look, Vin and I are not movie stars. We're not civilian detectives or real detectives. We're not surgeons or even all *that* attractive. We're normal people. So after we drive home early on Tuesday the fifth, Vin goes to work and I go to work.

I grocery shop and when he gets home, he's dirty and stinky and takes a shower. I feed him burgers and fries and salad. We watch two-thirds of *What About Bob?* curled up on the couch together and Vin falls asleep. And then he falls asleep again, this time in our bed.

Did I mention he brought home a carton of gorgeously ripe cherries because he knows me? Because he's in love with me. Because he knew I wouldn't want flowers.

It's not flashy. But this is life, baby. And it's the happiest consecutive four days I've had in over a year. Absence makes the heart grow fonder, and all that. And Vin, my Vin, has been very absent. Up until now, of course.

Wednesday night we transition very smoothly from sitting on the couch to having sex on the couch and I almost cry it feels so good.

Thursday, though. Thursday, Thursday, isn't it always a fucking Thursday? The volunteer roster is a nightmare this week. So many people called in to change their shifts that all the work I did on Tuesday had to be redone.

It's not my fault. It's just one of those weeks. But when I

drag my ass into Kitchen B, I'm really feeling like it's my fault. Especially when I open the fridge there and find some kale that smells like old socks and two plastic bags filled with mushrooms too slimy to save. I toss the food in the compost bin and this one really is my fault. I'm pretty much the only reason they stock this fridge.

I screw around, trying to put a new spin on bean soup and end up with . . . bean soup.

When you're in my line of work, there's a ninety percent chance that whatever you set out to cook, you're going to end up with bean soup.

Deb has to toss one of her students who came to class drunk. Cherise is fighting with a vendor over the phone.

I leave work in a foul mood. The train is crowded and loud. I'm finally headed up the street to our building when the toe of my sneaker catches the curb and I totally bite it.

I'm fine, definitely fine. But the shock from the fall punches up from the ground and through my arms. My palms throb and so do my shoulders. I'm on all fours on the street like a total klutz and two high school kids stand about five feet away and stare at me. My heart bangs, my stomach has started churning with the kind of adrenaline that happens when something—anything—unexpected happens, and my head just . . . aches.

"Oh, honey." This is an elderly man. He carefully puts one knee on the ground and grips me by the elbow to help me stand. Look, I just don't have very many elderly men in my life. Certainly not one who would get on the ground and help me stand up. And the whole situation just sort of shreds me. The high school kids have either grown consciences or they've realized the situation is not as funny as it first seemed, because here they come, grabbing my other arm.

"Is she okay?" someone asks from behind.

"Get her bag for her," someone else calls.

All of New York has turned out to see my embarrassing trip and fall. Oh, joy.

"Thank you," I'm saying to one person and the next. "Thank you. Thank you for your help."

"I'm afraid we can't save the tomatoes, honey," the elderly man says, handing me the brown paper bag of tomatoes that I brought home from work. I was gonna make dinner with them tonight.

They're dripping out of the bag, lopsided from being ground into the dirty street.

"That's okay," I say. "Thank you."

I wave everyone away and gingerly pick my way through the entrance of our building. And then I stand at the bottom of all the stairs and just weep. There's no other word for it.

"It's not a big deal," I say to myself, over and over, through tears, as I trek all the way up. "It's not a big deal."

I'm through the front door and dying to throw myself into Vin's arms. God, wouldn't it be so great to just walk straight into the safest place on earth and fall asleep?

But, of course, it's still too early for him to be home. My apartment is still and quiet. And lonely.

I shower off, testing the bruises on my palms (no scrapes, thank goodness), and continue with my refrain. "It's not a big deal. It's not a big deal."

I get straight into pajamas and when I'm just hanging up my towel, Vin finally comes through the door. I run into the main room, about to vomit my feelings all over and ask him to clean it up.

But then . . . his face. Lined and tired and . . . something else.

"What happened?" I ask, and I need the answer now. "Vin, what happened?"

"Nothing," he says, toeing out of his boots. "Not a big deal."

And that's when the weeping starts up again. "Whatever. It. Was. It. Was. A. Big. Fucking. Deal. *So tell me! Right now!*"

I don't mean to be shouting at him. Or even crying. And I certainly don't mean to be swearing. But here we are. In the bright/hollow light of early dusk because neither of us has turned on the lights yet.

"Why are you yelling at me?" he says back in a low voice. This is the closest that Vin ever gets to yelling. And it rocks me a little.

"Why are you yelling at *me*?" I demand.

His hands go out to either side. "What the hell?"

"Vin, what happened. Just tell me what happened."

He approaches me slowly. "It wasn't a big deal, like I said. Everyone's fine. I'm fine. But somebody rear-ended the work van today and—"

His voice suddenly fails and he rips his head to one side. Probably so I don't see his face twist with severe emotion. But I see it. I *feel* it.

"Oh, Vin." I close the distance between us and pause.

A fender bender is never fun. Definitely something that you replay in your head for a couple days. But for us? After what we've been through? The sound of tires screeching. The crash of *any* two things together. Being shoved forcefully by a lethal metal box . . . It's definitely enough to make you cry in the kitchen the night it happens.

For a moment, there's a pause.

The muscle memory of this year is very strong. This is the moment that he goes into his bedroom and I go into mine, right?

He reads my eyes. I read his. I'm assuming he's seeing my heart right there, just like he did in my drawings. His expression softens.

I open my arms and he goes immediately into them.

His forehead rests on my shoulder and he takes long breaths, in his nose and out his mouth, like someone must have taught him to do.

"Baby," I whisper into his hair, and the endearment makes a shudder of emotion wring free of him.

"It's not a big—"

"Yes, it is," I assert. And the funny thing is, when I'm defending Vin to Vin, I also end up defending myself to myself. "It might not seem like a big thing on the outside. But on the inside, it absolutely is. I tripped on the sidewalk today and it ruined my day. My week. I cried the whole walk up to our apartment."

He straightens and tugs me close. "Are you okay?"

"I'm fine. I landed on my hands. But I got this shot of adrenaline or whatever and now my head aches. And I'm in a bad mood. And I didn't make dinner. And I just feel like the world peeled me like a banana today. But I don't want to be a peeled banana. I want to be an *un*peeled banana. And it seems like everybody *else* gets to be an unpeeled banana, so, what the fuck!"

He's laughing. "I'm definitely a peeled banana, too. Let's order Chinese food."

I'm tapping my temple. "I knew there was a reason I married you."

"Yeah. I always know when to order Chinese food. It's my superpower."

I order the food while he takes a shower and then, in his boxer shorts, he comes to find me lying on my side of the bed, trying to read a book, but really just watching my thoughts play out on the page.

"Hi."

"Hi," I whisper. He was in a (minor) car accident today. My

eyes fill involuntarily. I know that emotions don't make you weak, but it sure is hard to feel strong when you're leaking out of your paper bag like a smashed tomato.

He crawls across the bed and lies on top of me, his head resting on my chest. It's such a nice position. It's so friendly and warm and husband-ish. It's countless, the number of times he's cuddled me just like this. Given me his perfect weight and let me hold him.

But . . .

The awful truth is that his chest pressed atop me like this might always make blue tile flash through my mind. My hand on his back, warm with sticky, fresh blood. *Vin,* I said, over and over. But he didn't answer.

"Vin."

"Hm?"

*Vin.*

"Vin."

"Yeah?"

*Vin.*

"Vin!" I plant my two aching palms on his shoulders and shove him off me. "Off!"

Our nice, safe moment is ruined, scratched to ribbons. He's scrambling back, breathing hard, eyes on my face. I can't stop myself. I grab his pillow, strap it across my face, and attempt to scream my soul clear out of my body. I drop the pillow and inhale fiercely, sucking my soul back inside.

"Wow." Vin's eyes are wide. He's reaching out for me, brave man.

I lunge forward and collapse on top of him.

"Baby, what's going on?" He's clasping me, scrubbing a hand up and down my back.

"Sorry! I'm just! You can't lie on me like that anymore!" And, yes, all the weeping from earlier takes a right turn into straight-up sobbing. The weeping didn't help. The sobbing does. Every ugly quake pushes handfuls of this unfairness out of me. My new refrain? "It's not fair. It's not fair. It's not fair."

"I know." This is Vin's new refrain. "I know. I know. I know."

"I can't believe I can't handle it when you lie on top of me anymore. I love when you lie on top of me."

"Deep breaths, baby. You're triggered right now. I didn't think— I even *knew* that that was a trigger for you, but I forgot. I'm so sorry."

"It's *okay*." And it really is. Even though the situation just so isn't. My sobs have descended into hiccups and Vin goes to the bathroom and comes back with tissues. "Is this how you feel when you see my scar?" I ask him through gasps.

"Yeah." He's rubbing feeling back into my hands, brushing my hair back. "But I can prepare myself for it, now that I know it's a trigger. I literally say to myself, *Vin, you're about to see Roz's scar. Which makes you feel all sorts of panic and anger and fear and sadness because you and she were in an accident where you thought she might die.*"

"Well," I consider. "When you say it like *that*."

He smiles a sad smile. "I literally say that to myself. I know it's clunky. But it helps. It makes me feel less like I should be over it already."

I scramble up onto his lap. "What if . . . what if we're never over it?"

"I . . . I don't know. Then I guess we'll just have nights like this."

"It's not fair," I say one last time, but the gasoline's already been all burned up.

"It's really not," he agrees.

The doorbell rings, which makes both of us jump and then laugh at ourselves. "Food," he says, lifting me off his lap and then going to give cash to the very sweet kid who climbed four flights of stairs just to feed us tonight.

We're both tanked. Emotionally and physically. We're already in our PJs and eating Chinese food in front of the last third of *What About Bob?* I literally can't remember the last time Vin and I finished a movie together.

After we're brushed and in bed together, meeting in the middle, noses almost touching, I whisper to him through the dark, folded shadows of our familiar bedroom. "I guess nights like this are how the porcupines do it, then. Marriage."

He's smiling. "They have big fights and cry a lot and hug."

I run my hand over his stubbly cheek, which he shaved this morning before work. For me. "They have to be careful when they hug, so they don't prick each other."

"They do," he agrees solemnly. "But that's not so bad."

"It's not so bad," I agree.

# Twenty-One

*There's a 106-piece* set of oil pastels in an art supply shop on Eldridge Street that would cure my PTSD, I just know it would.

Why? Oh, I don't know. Maybe because I'm pretty sure a drawing class saved my marriage. Perhaps if I learn to use pastels, everything else in my life will get fixed right up, too.

There are samples out on a pad of paper to test. The reds and greens and blues and purples are the confident, saturated, celebratory hues of a late August window box flower garden.

If only I had a spare two hundred and seventeen dollars lying around, I'm sure I would create passionate and cathartic art. Still lifes that really live, portraits with emerald shadows and spots of white in the irises.

But, of course I don't have a spare two hundred and seventeen dollars lying around.

"Those ones are not worth your money," says Lauro, unexpectedly coming to stand at my shoulder. This is the shop just down the street from our drawing class, and it is Friday, half an hour before class starts. "The pigments don't give. If you want the real deal, go with those. Hi, by the way." He kisses my cheek and then points at a different set. There are only eighty-five pieces in it and it's two hundred and ninety-five dollars.

"Who are you, Jeff Bezos? Hi to you too."

"Yeah, they're expensive. You can borrow mine if you ever want to use them."

For some reason, using someone else's oil pastels doesn't seem like it would cure my PTSD. I'm beginning to suspect it's not the oil pastels.

I wander away toward the pencils section. They sell them in singles over there and the whole thing is a little more my speed. Lauro wanders along with me.

"Here for supplies?" I ask him.

"I saw you come in."

I pick up a chalk pencil and draw a swirly on the test pad next to it.

He picks up a lead pencil and quickly draws a nude woman lying on a couch. He plucks the blue chalk pencil out of my hand and gives her a recognizable heart-shaped diamond necklace.

I raise an eyebrow. "Draw me like one of your French girls?"

"You know," he says, handing the pencil back to me. "I've been figure drawing since I was fifteen years old and I *still* think of that scene every time I sit down to draw somebody."

"Where do they let you draw naked people at fifteen?"

"France," he says matter-of-factly. "My parents sent me to a French drawing atelier. Boarding school, sort of. I mostly just learned how to go down on girls. In my spare time I occasionally attended class and learned how to draw."

"I do not believe that for one second."

"Which part?" He's grinning at me, pulling one pencil out of my hand and replacing it with another brand. It's a much smoother, richer ride and I resolve to give him my art supplies shopping list before I buy every time.

"The part where you only occasionally attended class. I'm willing to bet you actually worked your ass off."

Now his brows are furrowed. "What gives you that impression?"

"Obviously you're talented, but nobody gets *that* good without decades of practice." I nod toward his drawing of Kate.

He's frowning now. He adds a mustache to his drawing. "Maybe I tried hard," he concedes. "To get so good that I wouldn't have to try hard ever again."

"Yeah. Trying is terrible. Smart to get it out of the way. How's that working out for you?"

He gives me a pout and moves us down the aisle. "You need to throw your pencil sharpener in the trash. Every time I see you use it I want to tear my hair out."

"What's wrong with my pencil sharpener?" I demand.

"The same thing that's wrong with every pencil sharpener. Uniformity! A pencil should give you a unique line, every time. Sharpen with a blade instead." He selects and then hands me an X-Acto knife. I hand it back.

"I'm not going to chop my finger off."

"Just try." He takes one of the pencils I've (he's) chosen and gives a few quick shaves to show me how.

I follow directions and, dammit, I see what he means. It's given me an angled Ichabod Crane sort of pencil tip and when I drag it along the paper, I'm gifted a line with both clarity and personality. "Oh, fine," I grouch.

We've moved along to the paper aisle. "So," I say, rubbing a fingertip along all the different textures and weights of paper. "Raff says you're in monogamous love and you want her to shove wedding cake in your face and make babies and tie her shoes for her and—"

"Raff's an enormous blabbermouth," Lauro grouses. He's got hands on his hips and the scowl to end all scowls.

"You admit it!" I crow. I feel like a third-grader. But this is fun.

"What? There's something wrong with wanting that?" He's defiant and prickly.

"Of course not. I just didn't see it coming. I really couldn't tell you had feelings for Em."

"Well." He kicks his shoe at the parquet floor. "For a while that was kind of the point. I thought if *she thought* I was over her, then she might . . ."

"Over her, you say. So you dated?"

He has the good grace to wince a little. "We . . . dated?"

"Lauro." I'm admonishing him, but he's clearly already admonishing himself. "She doesn't strike me as the kind of person who could easily . . . deal with you sleeping around."

"Well, she's not."

"Did you cheat?"

"No. We weren't exclusive. But after about a month, she asked me why we had to do it my way. Why we couldn't do it her way. And I . . . there wasn't really an answer besides that I didn't *want* to. And . . . that was enough of an answer for her. She stopped picking up my calls."

"And you got your heart broken."

"I don't know about *broken*." But then he folds a little. "But she's special. And I miss her. And it bugs me that I fucked it up for both of us."

"Well, if you want her back so bad, then why the hell have you been flirting with me so much? And flirting with everybody?" I can immediately recall at least five different instances of Lauro tying smocks around Shan's neck, giving Stacia a back hug, opening his mouth for a bite of Penny's ice cream off Penny's spoon.

"I don't *know*. Was I just supposed to stand next to her with tears in my eyes? I didn't want to look like a *loser*."

"It doesn't make you a loser to come to an art class and take it seriously! You didn't need to try to sleep with anyone who breathes!"

"I didn't sleep with anyone! I . . ." He clears his throat, glances around, and lowers his voice. "I haven't been sleeping with anyone. Well, besides falling asleep with Raff while we were on shrooms."

"So." I do the math. "You've been signing up for the art classes you know she'll be in. You come to class wearing mesh. You flirt in order to show off your desirability. You make these effortless sexy little drawings . . . This entire time . . . have you been *peacocking* for Em?"

"I mean." He raises his hands and lets them flop to his sides, like *So what?*

"It's just . . . it's so obviously the wrong strategy for her."

I'm reevaluating everything I thought I knew about Lauro. I love this. I thought he was a smooth operator. I thought he knew what the hell he wanted and how the hell to get it. Turns out he's a bozo like the rest of us. Delightful.

"Well, I'm not, you know, Will Smith in *Hitch*, okay? I don't actually have a ton of tools in the toolbox!" He's looking flustered and embarrassed. The matching linen shorts and button-down (mauve, by the way) that he's chosen to wear now seem terribly contrived. I imagine a pile of tried-on and discarded outfits on his bed. It's Friday for him. Em day. He'd better make it count.

I suddenly realize that I think Lauro is going to be my friend for a really long time. We have a solid chemistry. He cares about me and I care about him.

"If this is the only tool in your toolbox . . . Okay, so, you mean that peacocking is the only way you've ever made a move on someone before? And it's just always . . . worked?" My skepticism is radioactive and it obviously inflames him.

"When you're beautiful, you're allowed to be inept!" he practically shouts.

And it makes me roar with laughter because he's actually *not* joking. "Oh, Lauro, old age is gonna hit you like a ton of bricks, God willing."

"No." He's defiant. "No, I'm a Clooney."

"Not even Clooney is a Clooney. I'm sure there's a saggy butt and penile shrinkage under those tailored pants."

He's been stabbed through the heart. "Don't talk about Clooney that way!"

"Lauro. Em doesn't give a shit about people who look cool. She literally only cares about one thing."

He's caving in on himself. "I know."

"*Sincerity.*"

"I know."

"So quit being such a politician, you slut."

This finally cracks him back into Lauro-ness. His tiger smile comes back and he slings an arm around my shoulder, bringing our temples together. "Fine, fine."

He's walking us to the checkout.

"How'd you two get together in the first place?" I ask, out of sheer nosiness.

"I heard that she does this storytelling thing. At this one bar, not far from here, actually. So I wandered in one night. I was just curious, I guess, to see her do anything that wasn't drawing." He puts all my supplies on the counter. "Turns out . . . she was drawing."

I study his expression. And I see it all. His tenderness for her, sure, but also . . . his tenderness for someone who freely shows how much she cares for the thing he also cares so much about, but pretends he could take or leave.

Every drawing for him is perfection, but he acts like he could toss it in the trash and not care. Every drawing for Em is a gorgeous work in progress and she treats it like it's sacred. For both of them, it *is* sacred. It's language. It's point of view. It's their inner selves, in physical form.

No wonder he's in love with her.

"And . . ." I prompt him, hip-checking him away from the scanner, this little scamp is trying to pay for my art supplies.

"And . . . I went and sat next to her. And didn't disturb her. Just watched her draw. And at the end of the night . . . she turned to me and . . . just, like, started kissing me."

The look on his face right now . . . He's like a thirteen-year-old boy who witnessed a magic trick and wants to re-create it but has no idea how the magician pulled it off.

I decide to throw him a bone. "*Sincerity*, Lauro. You sat and watched her draw and didn't throw any bullshit her way. That's why she kissed you."

"Okay, okay." We're back outside in the July evening air. It's like stepping into a fire-warmed blanket. He aggressively points between his own eyes. "Grow new personality. Immediately."

"It's not a new personality!" I'm certain. "She was drawn to you in the first place because you showed her that side of you. Just show it to her again."

We're walking into Nine Five Four now and he's glancing behind us. If Em were to walk in, I get the feeling he'd stiff-arm me into a trash can.

So I spare him and head in first. Reggie and Daniel are already here, and they give me a wave. I choose an easel in a part of the circle I've never been before. Lauro goes to sit over next to Reggie. None of us chat.

The rest of the class files in one by one. Esther flies solo today. Em is still not here. Lauro is glancing at the door, willing her to appear. I can feel his thoughts. If she doesn't show up . . . if she stops coming to this class because of their fight last weekend, then it *really is* over . . .

She's the last one through the door.

There are a few empty easels. She surveys them all and chooses the one next to me. She sets up quickly and some of her pencils fall. I get the feeling she wasn't going to come and then changed her mind at the last second.

I gather up the fallen pencils and hand them to her. She takes them, her eyes on mine like flame. They're hazel eyes, almost yellow around the iris. Damn, she's intense. "I'm sorry," she says bluntly. "For last weekend. I . . . was really fired up. It was probably uncomfortable for you."

I look away because her eye contact is too high-octane for me. "It's okay. But . . ."

I'm not sure how to say this. *But . . . you should give Lauro another chance? But . . . you should talk to him at least one more time? But . . .*

The fact is, none of this is any of my business, no matter if Lauro and I are friends or not.

My *but* hangs there until Daniel saves the day by ruining the day. He's been talking on the phone, but now he hangs it up and stands up, screeching his chair against the floor.

"Hi, everyone. Unfortunately, I just got word from the agency that there was an error and they didn't book anyone for us today."

I glance around. Sure enough, no model. There are collective groans of disappointment. Daniel is leafing through a notebook.

"I have a lecture prepared. But without a model . . . It'll be an early day, folks. Sorry about that."

"I'll do it," Lauro says, stepping out from behind his easel. Every head has turned in his direction.

"No. Lauro, I couldn't ask you to—"

"You didn't," he says with a shrug. "I volunteered. I'll sign the consent form."

He's already stepping into the middle of the circle, toward the model stand.

Daniel pulls him aside, they talk for a minute, and then Lauro signs a form. The class is abuzz with the idea of drawing someone they know. (And maybe with the idea of seeing Lauro full monty.)

I glance at Em. Her eyes are slightly narrowed as she watches Lauro step up onto the model stand and start to unbutton his shirt.

He's obviously staunchly ignoring our side of the classroom. But when he sticks his thumbs inside his shorts, I transmit thoughts so strongly in his direction that he glances at me with a start.

*No peacocking.*

He has an amazing opportunity here. Either he's going to build a bridge or build a wall. If he swaggers through this, he's going to end things with Em here and now. I can feel it.

He gives me an almost imperceptible nod and drops his shorts. They are—oh, good lord—black silk boxers.

And then, the moment of truth.

One of his hands goes up to the back of his neck. "I'm gonna leave my boxers on. If that's cool."

He's not swaggering. He's not whipping it out for classwide fawning.

He's . . . a little embarrassed.

A little vulnerable.

He's *trying.*

His statement is greeted with every single one of us loudly reassuring him that that is *totally fine, wonderful, thank you, you're the best.*

I chance one more glance at Em and her eyes are not narrowed anymore.

Lauro is, of course, a fantastic model.

If he's been doing this since he was fifteen, then he's certainly picked up on what makes an interesting pose, a rewarding pose, a challenging pose. And, yes, duh, he's beautiful. A pleasure to draw. He's got shadows and hollows and grace and charisma. Each pose tells us a story. In one, he's chest out and ambitious. In the next, he's guarded and contracted. In the next, he's buoyant and conversational.

Daniel walks a big circle around us all, with his hands clasped behind his back, eyes on all of our easels. He's talking today, where he usually gives us silence. I think he's doing his best to pillow Lauro's (potential) discomfort as much as he can. "Yes, very good, Esther. More space there, up through the sternum. It's not a single line, it's a plane. Yes, wonderful. It's fun to draw someone we know, isn't it? It's a special experience because you have to unknow what you already know and learn fresh everything else. Some artists believe that the very act of drawing is taking something apart in your mind and putting it back together again on the page. Or in the case of our beloved Lauro, taking some*one* apart in your mind and putting him back together again."

Em makes a sound, and it might as well have come from me. I know exactly what she's going through over there, taking apart the man you love and reconstructing him using nothing but your two eyes, one hand, and bleeding heart.

Em's been working with her pencils but she stops drawing on the words *beloved Lauro*, chucks her pencils back in their bag, and switches to—be still my beating heart—a black fountain pen. And now Lauro is currently being immortalized in luscious, stark lines. He's bleeding down the page. He's wrapping himself in her heart right before my very eyes.

Excellent.

"It's not really the final product that matters, is it?" Daniel goes on as he passes behind Em, and then me. "It's the thought process that's *exposed* by the drawing that compels us." He pauses behind me, then taps my drawing with one finger, right over where I drew Lauro's hand, decided it was in the wrong place, and then drew another halfway over the top of it. Daniel gives me a thumbs-up. "We want to draw, because we want to understand."

A memory pops up for me, unexpectedly, yes, but also, it was right there at the surface. It's blue tile, the screech of brakes, smashing glass, screams. It's Vin on top of me. But . . . I'm not triggered and wretched and out of control. No. I'm drawing Lauro's shoulder, arcing and overlarge, and trying to figure out how to connect a collarbone to a throat, but also, really, I'm drawing Vin's shoulder, the way it looked over the top of me, my hand pressing his wet back and coming away bloody. *We want to draw because we want to understand.*

Tears pool and gloss over my vision because I *do* understand. Finally. Even if I didn't understand yet, in my living room, while I was drawing Vin himself. I understand now, drawing Lauro and standing next to Em drawing Lauro, watching her draw him. I must have looked just like her. Whatever is drawn on her heart, she's transcribing it onto paper before my very eyes. And isn't that *just it?*

We draw what we want to understand. We draw what we want to *know.*

Vin flashes before me, his pose in the living room on one knee, his unwavering love. I was drawing it before I even knew for sure it was there. But then, again, flashing, blue tile and him on top of me. Because there are the easy things to set down on paper: Vin's boots and *home safe.* They shimmer at the surface waiting for me to sketch them into plain black and white. And then there are the things that are buried deep inside me: the worst fifteen seconds of my life, culminating in Raff unconscious on a stretcher, Vin bleeding in my arms. Those things . . . they're caustic and leaking battery acid somewhere deep inside. I have to dig them out. And I think the shovel . . . I think the shovel is this pencil in my hand.

The things I want to understand—need to understand—in order to live, are waiting for me in the blank pages of my drawing pad. I think . . . I have to dig them out. One scratch of the pencil at a time.

When the fifteen-minute break starts, I jump when Em grabs my wrist. I turn to her and see red, shiny eyes. "Talk to me," she whispers. "So that Lauro doesn't come over here."

In a very un-Em-like move, she's already covered up her drawings. I'm assuming so he won't see them and know that her heart is his for the taking.

"Oh. Um." What should I talk about? The bone-deep epiphany I've just had about trauma and art? No, of course not. I default to my factory settings. "What are you going to have for dinner?"

She chuffs out a breath, receives my awkwardness with gratitude. "Ramen. I always just go home after class and make a quick bowl."

"Do you ever crack an egg into it? That's Korean style. With kimchi. Or you can add green onion. And a swirl of sesame oil if you have it."

She shakes her head. "No. I go plain. That sounds good, though."

"Eggs and noodles. Nothing is better," Shan says beside me.

"Oh, I know. Carbonara. Pad thai. There's Chinese-style with spicy tomatoes and eggs."

"Wait. Are you a chef?" Penny asks, peeking around their easel.

"No." Esther saunters over, eating a tuna fish sandwich. She gives them a brief and mostly accurate rundown of my job.

"Wait. Really?" That's Reggie.

I'm blinking around at everyone. Since when is my job interesting?

"Because my wife's been on me to cook more often. You have any easy recommendations?" he asks me.

"Oh. Sure. What kind of stuff do you keep at home? Like in the pantry?"

He gives me a three-point list and I give him four quick dishes he could make. He scribbles them down.

Apparently this is a party trick because Shan gives me her pantry. I hand her two recipes straight from the brain.

Em goes next and her pantry is hard. Because it's almost exclusively snack foods. But I pull out my trusted tomato and pinto bean soup in a blender and everyone oohs and ahhs.

"The enchilada dish you described," Daniel calls from across the room. "Is the sauce in layers?"

"No," I call back. "It's sort of . . . hold on."

I wave him over and do a little scribbling on my drawing pad, digging around for my colored pencils to show him the way the two sauces should alternate in stripes.

Em hands me some of her pencils. "Hey. Draw the ramen you described to me."

I can't imagine she's never seen a bowl of ramen with various toppings in it, but I do what she asks, figuring it couldn't hurt. The bowl ends up with wonky perspective and the green onions look like they're attempting to jump ship.

But as soon as I'm done, I turn and see Daniel and Em grinning at me. The rest of the recipe-conversation-havers have mostly floated away, continuing different conversations elsewhere.

But not Daniel and Em.

"These are good," Daniel says with a tap to my pad.

"Really good," Em agrees.

I'm agog. To me, they're messy and amateurish.

"Personality, charm, familiarity . . ." Daniel lists.

"They look," Em decides, "the way food should feel when you're eating it."

"*Exactly*," Daniel corroborates.

It is, hands down, the best compliment I've ever received.

Something old and familiar, new and exciting, flutters to life within me.

"Really? Wow. I . . ." I got nothing. Instead of replying, I just absorb the happiness.

Shan calls Daniel over and he drifts away.

I'm incapable of speech right now. I think I'm happy? I think I need to draw. I think I need to run home and crawl into my husband's sweatshirt. I think I'm hungry. Regardless, Em and I must be looking pretty lonely over here and Lauro (clothed once more) is glancing in our direction.

"Quick! Talk!" Em requests of me. Those eyes of hers are burning me up. Let me tell you, Lauro has a *type*.

"Oh. Um. Uh. So, I heard you do a storytelling thing at a bar?"

"Oh. Right. Yeah, you didn't tell me your husband is Vin. We recognized each other at the picnic but when he didn't say hi, I figured he was shy."

"Huh?" I'm blinking at her non sequitur, trying to catch some footing in this complete left turn.

"He's becoming kind of a legend over there. The newbie to end all newbies. The girls would all be taking a shot at him if he didn't just talk about you every time."

"Em. *What?*"

She's reading my face, likely clocking some desperation. So she rewinds. "The bar, Sooth? Over in the East Village? Its whole thing is that it has a story open mic every night. Anyone who wants to tell a story can. But it's a scene. A crowd. There are regulars. I go because it's a good way to draw people without them caring. Vin started up maybe six weeks or so ago? He goes a few times a week. Though I've been missing him a bit because I come here on Fridays and I've heard that's the night he usually goes."

"You . . . are telling me . . . that my husband . . . goes onstage. And talks about me. In public."

"At Sooth. In the East Village," she repeats, like I'm slow. And then she glances at her watch. "The open mic started like twenty minutes ago."

*I've been practicing. I swear.*

His words thrum in on every side. It's the final thing hidden behind the door labeled *Roz, You Are Missing Something*. Therapy, yes. PTSD, yes. Clouds and tornadoes and the maze of his wonderful Vin brain. But . . .

He's been giving me speeches recently. Complete thoughts. *Practicing.*

He's been telling me the story of Vin.

"I—have to go. Now."

"Oh. Shit. Did I . . ." Em is trailing off, glancing between me and my hands packing my things so furiously that pencils are flying all over the place. "Did I fuck this up?"

"No! No. I just have to go."

"Are you okay?" That's Lauro. He's bending down next to

me, gathering fallen art supplies and helping shove them into my bag.

"Yes. Fine! See you next week!"

I realize all at once that as soon as I run out of this classroom, I'm going to leave the two of them standing awkwardly together. Exactly what Em has asked for help trying to avoid. But . . . (It's my *but* from earlier, resurrected, hanging once again in the air.)

"Hey," I say to her, quiet enough not to draw the other classmates' attention. "Just in case you need someone to say it out loud . . . Em, what if . . . what if that drawing he did of you, where you're lovely and graceful and you took offense because you felt like it erased you? Well . . . what if that's *actually* how he sees you?"

And then I turn and run.

# Twenty-Two

*Sooth is just* a really bad bar. Divey and sticky. It still reeks of decades-old cigarette smoke. Someone's spilled a beer on the floor and no one seems to care. There are blinking neon lights behind the bar and a dirty mirror. Almost everyone I can see is drinking beer out of the can, I assume, because to drink something on tap would be to send a party invitation to botulism.

What is *not* really bad is the clientele. It's a real smorgasbord of people in here, from (probably) every borough and every walk of life. Some of them have their arms around one another, others are sitting on laps. A few people are sitting directly on the bar because seats are very scarce. There's a small stage in the back and ten or so high-top tables with people on barstools crowded around each one.

A woman with a wolf cut and a purple satin bomber jacket is on the mic, telling a story about going hunting with her uncle Ira. People are laughing and shouting commentary.

I go on tiptoes and scan the bar but don't see Vin.

"You want to sign up for the open mic?" a man with a mustache whispers to me. He's handing me a sign-up sheet. "There's a few spots left."

"Oh. Thanks." I take the sheet. Big block letters at the top read *Tonight's Topic: The big bad wolf.* And then there are twelve lines for people to sign their names. Ten are filled out. The second-to-last name? Vin DeLuca.

The crowd erupts into applause and makes me jump. "Aaaaaaaand, let's hear it one more time for Tammy Talia. Thank you, Tammy." The man with the mustache is holding the mic with two hands and romancing the crowd. "Next up we've got the one, the incomparable, the inimitable LaVoya Loach!"

The crowd erupts for this person and I study the list. Tammy Talia was number six and LaVoya Loach is number seven. Which means there is only number eight before number nine. Number nine being Vin DeLuca. Vinny Green Eyes, to those of us who share a bed with him.

I scan the bar again and this time, I see him halfway up the room, leaning against the wall (not taking up a stool, of course), eyes on the stage. His arms are crossed.

A woman ducks around him and pokes his arm for his attention. He leans down to hear her and then shakes his head. She walks back to her seat and he recrosses his arms.

LaVoya is telling a story about an aged punk rocker who used to live in her building that everyone referred to as Cousin Wolf. It's funny and sad. At least I gather that it's funny and sad based on watching Vin's facial expressions. Because I cannot tear my eyes away.

This is exactly how he must have felt when he found out about my drawing classes.

Hello, heretofore invisible other side of my partner, nice to meet you.

Next up, after LaVoya, is a guy named Bill. When he takes the stage, everybody says *Biiiiiiillllllll* and it sounds like a round of booing, but he's clearly loving every minute of it. He has a high, miniature-sounding voice and he talks a mile a minute. His story is about visiting this little island in the middle of Lake Michigan where scientists are apparently doing some sort of population study on wolves.

I'm starting to understand tonight's topic. Basically, it's just "whatever you think of when you hear the phrase *the big bad wolf.*"

Bill's story is sad. The people in the audience are shouting things like "Get 'em, Bill!" and "Tell it like it is!" At one point he mentions a cat and someone rings something called the cat bell. His story is about his parents' messy divorce and spending a night with no sleeping bag and hearing wolves in the distance. But a full moon makes a special feature, and later, a girl he'll come to love. So when he's on the ferry ride back to the mainland (and we're there with him), there's a whiff of hope.

The mustached MC takes the stage and my stomach drops to my toes. Next up. Next up. Next up.

Oh, my God. Vin's never interacted with a wolf in his entire life. What the hell is his story going to be about? What if it's bad? Or, perhaps even scarier, what if it's good?

Also, it occurs to me all at once that Vin is for sure going to see me from the stage. I'm standing here, in the back, but everyone in front of me is seated. Crap! Where to hide?

"Psst." I whip around to my left and there . . . is Raff. He's beckoning me over to the bend in the L-shaped bar. If I stand right next to him, we'll be hidden by the line of people sitting in front of us.

"What the hell are you doing here?"

"I used to date Tammy," he whispers. "She told me a few weeks ago that she spotted my brother here. I've been sneaking in since then. He doesn't know I come. *Shh.* You'll miss his intro."

He tucks me in front of him and I peek around the shoulder of the enormous man in front of me. I can see the stage, but hopefully the stage can't see me.

"Now, this next reader, despite being a bona fide newbie, needs no introduction. Why no introduction necessary? you might ask. Because every single woman in this bar has already clocked him. But laaaaaadiesssss, he's maaaaaarrrrried. He's *so* married he makes the rest of us look a lot! more! single!" This intro is garnering a lot of hoots and hollers, and Vin has one hand over his eyes like he wishes he could blink out of existence.

Also, a lot of the hooting and hollering is from me. This is like going to Barnes & Noble and stumbling on a shirtless calendar starring your husband.

Also, *also,* I'm so nervous I could puke. Thank God that Raff is here because if I didn't have his hands on my shoulders, I might shoot off into space like a bottle rocket.

The MC is looking like he's planning on going on for a long time, but Vin has decided to clear him out. He's walking up onto the stage and headed for the mic.

"Give it up for Big Vin DeLuuuuuca!"

And they do. Everybody screams. Everybody hollers. Everybody wants to hear what Vin has to say. And join the club, bitches! Because me too!

"Hi," Vin says into the mic, and his deep, familiar voice heard in such a new and resounding way makes tears spring into my eyes. He's adjusting the mic stand and asking people how they're doing tonight.

I turn one-eighty and face Raff. "He knows how to adjust a mic stand," I say behind my hands. Raff turns me back.

"Just watch," he whispers.

And then Vin pulls a folded piece of paper out from his back pocket. He unfolds it, and the creases in the paper interact with the stage lights. For just a flash, there's the shadow of a heart on that paper. And then he starts to talk.

There were three of us. Me, my wife, and my brother. We did good together. Because that's family.

We don't have a lot of money.

Actually. Never mind. I'm pretty sure my brother is secretly rich and he probably bought my mom her house in Jersey.

(Intrigue!)

(We got a rich brother, people!)

But that's not the story I'm telling. What I'm trying to say is that we did not live, and never have lived, fancy. We're the sort of people that if you break your phone screen, well then you have a broken phone screen until two years from now when you're eligible for an upgrade.

(These are facts!)

(Eat the rich!)

Anyways. In retrospect our lives were just very simple. The three of us ate dinner together three or four nights a week. Me and Roz—

(Roz!)

(ROOOOOZZZ!)

(Who has Roz on the bingo card?)

Me and Roz went to work, came home, spent time together, thought about Raff. Thought about having a kid. Thought about what to do for my mom on Mother's Day. This was life. And I, honestly, wouldn't have changed it. If you'd given me the option to go live on an island. Or inherit a yacht. Or whatever. I would have said, Nah. I'm good.

But there was a big bad wolf. And maybe everybody has a big bad wolf? Like, maybe if you live long enough, you just get a big bad wolf.

Ours . . . was maybe a little different than most people's.

We were three of four people who were sitting in a café this time last year when a truck drove through the front window and almost killed us.

(Oh, Vin.)

(Shit.)

(You got it, Vin!)

I know, I know, I'm not trying to lay out all my bad and terrible moments onstage. I know that this isn't therapy. I think a lot about what CJ said to me right before I went up onstage for the first time. "We don't want anybody bleeding out onstage. Take care of yourself up there, man." And so I've just kept not telling this story.

But here's the thing. I think . . . I think I'm kind of stuck. Like, every day, at some point, not all day, but at some point, I realize that I'm pretending it didn't happen. That I'll drive home and not jump out of my skin whenever someone honks at me. That I'll get home and walk into the house and Roz won't have a scar under her shirt. And she and I won't cry at loud noises. Or yell at each other because we're all panicked about absolutely nothing. Or that I won't have to see my brother do his PT where he picks up a pencil, draws a circle, puts the pencil down, and then does the whole thing over and over again. And he's an engineer, for Chrissake. He needs to be able to—

Sorry. Sorry. Wow. You can hear a pin drop in here. I can't tell if this is a good thing or a bad thing.

(It's a good thing!)

(You got it, Vinny!)

Anyways. I thought that telling the story might be a way to remember that it happened. And that's life. And we're all okay. So here I go. We were sitting in this little café on the corner of Hudson and Worth. We were too early to meet some high school friends in Rockefeller Park, so we decided to duck in there and get coffee. It was raining. So we sat in the café. Roz was trying to figure out how they got their corn muffins so moist.

And this is life. One minute you're laughing because your brother burned his tongue and the next minute everything is in slow motion.

I learned something very important about myself that day. It's the only good thing that came out of it. I learned that I'm someone who would die for my wife. Did learning that come at way too high a price? Yes. But there it is. We heard screeching tires, I looked over my shoulder, a truck came through the window, hit the side of the building, and went on its side. And in those two seconds I'd jumped across the table and covered her. Which meant that even though she was really hurt, she was okay. Mostly okay.

Oh, shit.

(What?)

(He's freezing up.)

(Why is he freezing up?)

(I don't know, Irene. Why don't you ask him?)

(You okay, Vin?)

I . . . didn't . . . Shit. Hold on. I just . . . saw someone I didn't expect . . . Oh. Two people I didn't expect . . .

You okay, baby? Can I go on?

(Wait, what??)

(Is Roz in the building?)

(Where is she?)

Don't everyone look at the same time or she's going to leave and never come back. Baby, really. Is this story fucking you up?

(Finish it, Vinny Green Eyes!)

(Vinny Green Eyes!!)

(She calls him Vinny Green Eyes!!!!)

(Finish it, Vin!)

(You got this, Vin!)

Okay. Okay, then I'll just read from the paper. Exactly what I wrote. Okay.

When a terrible thing happens to you, it happens and then it's done, right? Wrong. That's why I'm calling this the big bad wolf. Because when the truck smashed through the building, that was the first time the big bad wolf came around. But the big bad wolf in the story comes back over and over, right? And it has. It's on me. I think I'll carry it with me forever. And there were some really dark days. But there was one thing that helped. One little light that I hold. Right here. I would have died for her. And that makes me feel good. At least . . . at least, now that I've got the rest of my life to live . . . At least I know that I've got something to die for.

# Twenty~Three

*Vin steps off* the stage to raucous applause and makes a straight line for me and Raff. By straight line I mean he skirts in and out of the crowd. People are stretching this way and that, trying to figure out which people are the infamous wife and brother.

I think for a moment about Em and Lauro. Loving one another in secret code. Putting pieces of themselves down on paper and saying *Look, here I am.*

Em immortalized Lauro with a fountain pen. Well, Vin just immortalized us with a folded-up sheet of printer paper and a microphone.

He's getting closer and my heart is in my throat. And then he blurs out of focus because my eyes are filled. And then I don't *have* to see because his arms are around me. His scent fills my nose. His chest jumps under my cheek. One of his arms unwraps from me and I look up in time to see him wrap it around Raff's head, tugging his brother close. Vin kisses his forehead, like a good Italian brother. Raff clutches at as much of Vin as he can get his hands on, which isn't much because I'm not giving an inch.

There's more of the show to see, but Vin tugs us out of Sooth and onto the street. He unhands us on the sidewalk and then his big arm goes up and he covers his eyes with the inside of his elbow. He's sobbing. Like me in bed the other night.

I take the ribs and belly area for a hug and Raff takes the shoulders area. We both hold Vin while he quakes.

He takes a few enormous breaths and then starts patting our backs, reassuring us that he's okay. "Sorry," he says gruffly. "Just . . . it's a lot to be onstage. To try to tell that story. And then to see you two . . ." He scrubs at his tears with the shoulder of his shirt.

And then the three of us transform into that one Spider-Man meme where we're all pointing at one another. Trying to answer all forms of the question *How did you get here?*

I explain about Em.

Raff explains about Tammy.

Vin says that his therapist thought it would be good for him. Sent him as homework. And it worked so well he kept coming back. His therapist (by the way) is the one whose office is in the hallway of Nine Five Four. Vin saw his name on the door when he went to pick up the lease. The night I put the lease on the fridge he just walked straight back to that door.

"Was it really okay?" Vin asks again. "To hear me talk about it like that? When you weren't expecting it?"

"Shit, I've been hoping you would," Raff says. "I want every detail, man. You know I don't remember it."

"Wait." I hold up a hand. "You told me that you don't 'really' remember it. I just thought . . . I thought you meant that it was kind of foggy and you'd rather not comb through it. But . . . do you mean that you actually don't remember any of it?"

"I had a concussion," Raff says with a shrug. "I remember glimpses of the ambulance. And then waking up after the surgery."

"Raff . . ." I'm struck. Silent. Shocked. "I didn't realize . . .

And we *never* talk about it. Jesus. You must have been going nuts."

"Like I said, I've been waiting for Vin to talk about it onstage."

"I still can't believe you've been coming for weeks." Vin scrubs his hands over his face. And then he looks at me. "You swear this is your first time?"

"You think I could keep something like that a secret?" I point back at the bar. "I would never *not* be able to talk to you about it all. You were onstage, Vin. You made people laugh and shout for you! You . . ."

I run out of words and just clutch him to me again.

Vin is bashful and pleased. He feels bad about leaving the show early, but it's clear we three need to be alone together. So Vin ducks back in and pays his and Raff's tabs and then, just the three of us, we walk home.

It's an odd walk. Nostalgic, the three of us together like this, but also . . . very new. Because we're never going to be like we were.

We're changed forever. As individuals and as a group.

But also, we're still us.

When we get home, I make pancakes and Vin makes bacon. Raff sits on the counter and makes us cry.

"Look, not to state the obvious here," he says. "But this year really sucked."

We give a soggy laugh.

"And I'm . . ." he continues. "I'm, like, a very happy person? I don't wear angry well. It doesn't look good on me. So I've just, sort of, pretended like my arm doesn't hurt all the fucking time. That it's, like, *fine* that my life got destroyed. But . . ."

"It's not," I supply.

"Yes." He points at me like I've just said something completely genius. "It is *not* fine. And it's not like I needed anything else to make me . . . more complicated. Look, I know this has been a tough year for you two, but you still had each other. You still had the home you'd built together. You still had the option of rebuilding. Me? Seriously, I think I might be in too many pieces for someone to want the whole package."

"Raff." That's Vin. And he's not happy his brother feels this way.

"I'm not asking for you to make me feel better," Raff insists, showing us his palms. "If you never did another thing for me for the rest of my life, I'd still be eternally grateful to both of you. I just need to say it. Thank you." His eyes are liquid and squeezing shut. "Thank you for being there when the truck— I know it probably makes me selfish. But if you two hadn't been there with me . . . I just feel like the thing would have killed me. I just . . . I know it in here—" He thumps his chest. "That I wouldn't have survived this without you two."

Vin takes him by the shoulders in a rough, big-brother sort of way. "Everything you're saying is wrong," he tells Raff. And it breaks through Raff's spiritual dysmorphia like two hands ripping a sheet in two. Raff is laughing through tears.

"Well, what do I do now, then?" Raff asks. "If I'm wrong about all this, then what the hell *is* wrong with me?"

Vin gives him a weightless, certain smile, made possible by a clean-shaven face. "Nothing, dude. You're perfect." And he kisses him again, on the forehead.

"That is *not* helpful," Raff says, but he's got a wry smile on and one hand against his chest. He's locking it inside, I can tell, this assessment from the person he trusts the most in the world.

I loudly crunch bacon and they both turn to look at me. "What? It's getting cold!"

And so we eat. And then Raff goes to bed in the guest

room. And it feels good. It feels like, every now and then, he belongs here. Because he *is* perfect. And so are we.

When Vin (and the Vin squeak) join me in bed, I, unfortunately, have a little river of tears drip-dropping off my nose.

"Oh no," Vin says, sliding over to hold me.

"I'm okay," I reassure him. "But your story . . . this night . . . I finally realized something."

"Tell me." His arms tighten around me, our legs tangle together.

"I realized . . . and I hate it, Vin. And I don't want it to be true. But I realized . . . I'm *so* mad at you."

"Wait. Really?" He's pulling back to see my face. Because this wasn't what either of us was expecting. And also, because I'm calm and sweet. Not how one usually tells another they're so mad at them.

"Your story tonight . . . It reminded me of something and I think . . . I think a lot of the prickliness I've been having . . , I think it's because I'm mad at you."

"Okay . . . well . . . what did it remind you of?"

"It was something I heard in the hospital. What you said tonight in your story. Your *beautiful* story . . . it brought back this memory . . . I heard one of the paramedics who brought us in talking with the ER doctor. They were talking about me. The ER doctor said, *It's a miracle she doesn't have a head injury.* And the paramedic said—" My voice breaks and I lift Vin's hand to my lips. "And the paramedic said, *Yeah, her husband was able to get his hand under her head to break her fall.*"

"Right," Vin says slowly, trying to read me.

"And then I looked at your knuckles, they were bandaged, and I wouldn't even know until the bandages came off a few weeks later how bad the scrapes really were, almost down to the *bone,* Vin. But it was enough, then, just to see the bandages."

His eyes are everywhere on my face. "And it made you mad?"

"Vin, it made me *irate*. And for a long time, I thought it was anger at, you know, fate. Or the driver, even though it was an accident. But . . . no. No, Vin, it's anger at *you*."

He's stroking a hand from the top of my head down to my back. We are so not fighting right now. We are so tender and open. It's so hard to hold it all at once, the low-lying torrential rain of an emotion that's been on my heels for a year, and this sweetness for the person I love the most in the world. How do I feel it all? How does anyone live for decades? Life only gets more and more complicated. The good never unmixes with the bad. It only tangles more and more.

"Vin, I'm so mad you got hurt. There's a fourteen-inch scar down your back, for God's sake. And your knuckles. Your poor knuckles." I lift his hand to my forehead and I just hold it there, feeling his warmth.

He does what he does best and doesn't say a word. He waits. He lets me fill the silence because he knows that when I do, it won't be trapped inside anymore. It'll be between the two of us, where he'll help me carry it.

"You are *not* allowed to die for me, Vin. And I'm so mad that you almost did. It falls under the same category as dying from drunk driving or dying because you were base jumping or doing something stupid and dangerous that you should *not* be doing."

"Baby, all due respect: dying for you is not stupid."

We laugh because I don't know why. "If you'd died for me, do you know how awful my life would have been after that? *I would never get over that, Vin. Never.*"

"Sure, yes, but you'd be alive."

"Look, I'm not saying that my anger is rational. Anger is almost never rational, right? I'm just saying this is how I feel.

When I think about that day, remember that moment, I just want to scream *Vin, get out of there!* Because it feels . . . it feels like I almost lost you. And you were so *still* on top of me, and I know it was just a moment. But it felt like forever that you didn't move. Like maybe I *did* lose you. And my brain goes back to that moment, over and over, trying to make you wake up and be happy. But it took paramedics to lift you off me, Vin. Even after you were responsive again, the laceration was so bad you weren't moving . . . And I know now that you're proud of it. And I know it's the best thing that anyone has ever done for me. It's the most loved I've ever been. But it was also *the worst moment of my life.* To be saved and then think that I had to live an *entire* life without you."

"Baby." Even if it's a moment he's proud of. Even if it's the light he carries, he can see that anything that ends with him being torn from me is something I can't help but hate.

"And the worst part . . ." I'm hiccuping now. "Is that . . . in your arms, you on top of me, one hand under my head, that's always been the best place in the world, Vin. *In the entire world.* And nothing bad happens to me when I'm there. I know this. I know this in my soul. But this time your arms were around me and something bad happened to *you.* Which, Vin, don't you get it? Something bad happening to you is the worst thing that could ever happen to *me.*"

He's tranquil, tender, his eyes searching my face and his fingers tucking my hair behind my ear. "You would die for me, too," he says quietly.

"Of course I would! Gladly! A fourteen-inch scar! And I thought you were dead! And now I can't even *think* about you holding me like that again. Being on top of me like that. That *fucking* accident took that and made it terrifying for me. Can you even—"

I cut off at the flash of expression on his face.

"Can I even? Roz, you have a mark on your chest because something almost—" He cuts off. "I know a lot about what you're talking about. Okay? You're my favorite place too. Being able to be against you like that. It's . . . the best I'll ever feel in my life. And yes, that's gone for now. God. Sometimes . . . I still . . ."

"Can't believe it even happened?"

"Yeah."

"Maybe we'd have a crib in that room over there, if it hadn't," I say quietly, finally saying out loud something we've never directly talked about. "A little crying raisin. Instead of a gigantic sleeping Raff."

We had just started trying to get pregnant like a month before the accident. After the accident, well, you already know we weren't trying anymore.

Vin is nodding. "That's the thing about stuff like this, it changes your future in a million little ways. Not only are you different, but your *life*, your *circumstances*, are different. All because a truck driver had a seizure at the wrong moment. That year, for us, it's just . . ." He snaps his fingers.

"And for Raff," I say quietly.

"And for Raff," he agrees. "And for Ethan."

"That's his name? The other guy who was in the coffee shop?"

"Yeah." Vin rubs my back and holds me on his lap. "I reached out to him. He invited me to his bar. I'm gonna go tomorrow. I think that's part of why . . . I think that's why I wanted to tell the story tonight. I'm trying to get it all out, Roz. All these little painful jabs from trying to keep it in. I'm trying to set it all down now. And I think meeting him is part of that. For me."

He doesn't ask if I'm coming with him.

A few minutes later, when he's still rubbing my back and I'm flopped against him, docile as a kitten, he speaks again.

"Still mad at me?"

I stiffen and scramble up to look him dead in the eye. "Look, Vin. Everybody wants to be the person who runs back into the burning building to save the box of kittens, but nobody wants to be *married* to that asshole."

He laughs. "Okay, okay. I get it. No dying for you."

"I'll never forgive you if you die for me."

He kisses my temple. "Understood."

"Not even a scratch from here on out."

He kisses my cheek. "Got it."

"If you die for me, I'm gonna die for you, just to spite you."

"Okay." He's laughing when he kisses my mouth.

He lifts my hands to his lips and kisses my knuckles. But he pauses midkiss. He's arrowing in on something extremely important and extremely new. I'm already humiliated. Grand gestures are excruciating.

"What the hell is this?" he asks low, scrubbing one thumb over the pearl ring I'm wearing on my left ring finger.

"Oh, who cares?" I scowl.

"*Roz.*" He's nearly tugging my arm out of its socket, trying to get a better look at this thing.

"It's one of the pearls Aunt Therese left me," I tell him, because, after all, even if I'm the one wearing it, this whole thing was for him. "Something beautiful made from the irritation of a grain of sand, et cetera, et cetera. You get it. I took it to the jeweler down the block. He set it."

"You're wearing a *wedding* ring." His voice has been rubbed over sandpaper.

"What a stupid name," I gripe. "It should be called a marriage ring."

"You're right," he agrees, his eyes shiny. "Should I have thought of this? Gotten it for you?"

"No! That would have defeated the whole purpose! You wear yours for me. I should wear mine for you."

"A marriage ring, huh?" He looks so young right now. His eyes are open and uninjured. He's hopeful. He's got an entire life ahead of him.

"Hey. No halfway proposals this time," I tell him with a bossy finger. "No misunderstandings. I'm saying this once. And I'm saying it in black and white."

"Okay." He nods obediently.

"Will you stay married to me for the rest of our lives?" I very nearly demand.

He's laughing at my ferocity.

He pulls me in so close that he says the next part against my lips.

"I will."

Vin goes to meet Ethan on his own. I send him with enough enchiladas and fruit salad to feed twelve.

While he's gone I do a totally casual, almost meaningless, no-big-deal Google search. The keywords? *Therapists in my area.* Oh, boy.

The second he comes home I pounce on him. "Did you tell him he can freeze them? I forgot to tell you to tell him that you can freeze the enchiladas!"

He's smiling down at me, arms around me. "You think I've never delivered someone your enchiladas before? Three-fifty for thirty minutes or until the cheese is bubbly. Freeze what you don't bake and defrost it before you bake it."

"I love you so much."

He's tucking my hair behind my ears. He takes a long breath, looking into my eyes, but his thoughts are clearly far away.

I watch him while he walks to the sink and washes his hands. Pulls down a glass and takes a long drink of water.

"How . . . was he?" I'm not sure I want to know the answer. It's why I didn't go with Vin today.

Vin turns and leans against the sink, setting the water aside. "He's . . . good. His scarring is . . . bad. The whole left side of his face is just . . . fucked. But . . . he says the pain is a lot better than it was. Plus, his daughter was with him. And to her, he's Superman. She was squishing her face against his and playing with his cheeks and stuff."

I'm smiling through tears. "How old is she?"

"Three?"

"God, I'm so glad he has her to love him like that."

"That's exactly what he said. And about halfway through, his daughter's stepdad showed up."

"Oh, he's not with the mom?"

"I guess not. Because the stepdad showed up with all these watermelons. Like five watermelons. And he said hello and then took Mimi, the daughter, to the playground. And I was like, *That's a lot of watermelons*. And Ethan was like, *Oh, don't get me started*. Because I guess Shep, the stepdad, has been doing all this research on foods that are healing for tissue injuries. And so he makes Ethan eat all these special recipes since the accident, and this week he's on about watermelons."

I'm smiling because Vin is smiling.

"I guess you had to be there," Vin says with a shrug. "But . . . I just got the feeling that he's all right. Or he will be. He's got his people. And he says he's almost got full function of his face back . . . He actually seemed even better than we are. To be honest."

"Well," I say, leaning my elbows on the counter. "You can't expect him to fall apart in your arms. I'm the only one who does that."

"And Raff on occasion. Where'd he go, by the way?"

"He went home. He said he wanted space."

I raise my eyebrows at Vin and he raises his back at me. "They grow up so fast," Vin says, and makes me burst out laughing.

"I'll wait until dinnertime to check on him."

"Progress," Vin says, and goes up for the high five.

And honestly? I think it really is.

I draw so much over the next few weeks that I start YouTubing hand and wrist stretches. Vin has been very patiently performing both modeling duties and taste-tester duties.

His only request was that I conclude my section on anchovies.

I'm working my way through the pantry ABCs. Anchovies, beans, crackers, couscous, chicken broth, you get it. Basically, I make a dish, I write down the recipe, and then I draw a little picture of it.

Then Raff scans it into the computer.

When we're done, I'll have a gigantic PDF titled *Roz's Brain*. From there, maybe I'll apply for a grant so that Harvest NYC can produce the book and start selling it and make a little extra dough. Or maybe, gulp, I look for a publisher on my own.

"Maybe you'll get TikTok famous!" was Shan's guess.

"Why does she need to be famous?" Esther grouched. "And send that PDF over to me. I need it."

But Vin and food have not been the only things I've been drawing.

"Rafael!" I shout one Wednesday night. "Get your shoes on."

Raff scrambles up from his pretzeled doomscrolling. "What?"

"Go do an errand for me."

"Okay!"

I've been pawning off errands and tasks to Raffi left and right these days. I'm humbled by how fast he obliges. I guess nobody wants to be the baby brother for the rest of their life.

I give him directions, explicit instructions, and cash. He puts the cash back in my hand. "Please. What is this, milk money? Either let me pay for it or Venmo me later. Cash is just embarrassing."

"See? Old-fashioned." I point at myself.

"Old-fashioned is cute," Vin says, coming in through the door and taking his boots off. "I wouldn't know what to do with you if you were cutting-edge."

"Back in a jiff." Raff scoots out the door.

"Where's he going?"

"You'll see."

Tonight, I join Vin in the shower because why not? He's my husband, after all. He's in love with me, after all. Because somebody has to wash this day off him. Somebody has to open their arms wide for all that care, all that persistent love.

Of course, he's the one washing me. Of course, we end up on the bed, turning the bedsheets translucent with my soaking wet hair. Of course we get back in the shower and are so hopped up on endorphins we just can't stop smiling.

I'm smiling for another reason too.

We're in pajamas and chopping vegetables at the counter, side by side, when there's a noise that makes us both jump.

It's just Raff. Rattling back through our door. He comes in with a dazed expression on his face.

"What's wrong?" Vin is bristling, stepping toward him, but I'm pretty sure I already know what's happening.

"Nothing . . ." Raff says, kicking off his shoes, crossing the room, and handing the package off to me. "I just . . . met someone."

"On your errand? Jesus Christ, you can't swing a dick without finding somebody to flirt with," Vin says, hands on his hips.

"I think the dick-swinging might be why he meets people to flirt with," I say, with a grin, because I know exactly what happened and I'm determined to relish every second of this.

"No, no," Raff says, sitting down at the table. "I think I, like, *really* met someone. Someone . . ."

He's run out of words to describe this someone, so I helpfully fill in some blanks. "Was he about this tall? Salt and pepper? Probably wearing some silk garment worth more than a monthly mortgage payment? French accent? Somehow made you feel like dirt and ten feet tall at the same moment?"

Vin looks from me back to Raff. "You met St. Michel?"

Raff spins in his seat. "You know him too?"

Vin shrugs. "Sure." And then he turns to me. "What'd you have framed?"

"I'll show you once Raff is done turning into Jell-O. This is fun."

"I'm done, I'm done," Raff says with a wave at me. But he's not. He's thinking about St. Michel with a blush in his cheeks.

I can't help but get Raff in a headlock. "St. Michel is good at loving people in pieces," I tell him. "He says relationships should work for the people who are in them."

"Stop!" Raff is covering his ears and melting down toward the table. Then he's jolting upright. "Should I ask him on a date? No, he's way too cosmopolitan for that. I should follow his business on IG and—and—"

"Raff, I sent you over there in short shorts and a sun hat. With this mustache? And your thighs? I'm *sure* he's clocked you. Play it cool for a few days. Then go back and get something framed. He'll be feeding you oysters and tying you to his bed frame in no time."

"Do I like this?" Vin asks no one in particular. "Hard to say."

"Okay." I unhand Raff and pick the package back up, walk it over to Vin. "You got one for me framed. And now I got one for you framed."

He takes the package and holds it, his eyes flicking to mine. He doesn't even have to see it yet, to confirm. My heart is in this package, he just knows it.

He pulls the paper off all at once and his eyes instantly fill. Raff comes to look over his shoulder.

It's a drawing of a thought. Of a hope. Something I'd like to understand.

It's the three of us, sitting around a table, maybe at a café, drinking coffee. And in this drawing, we are older. In this drawing, we are perfectly fine. In this drawing, we are living very, very normal lives. Which is to say, layered lives. Lives shot through with crimson. Lives with pillowy, inviting shadows in the corners of darkened rooms. Lives that sometimes wake us up in the night. And lives we talk about, and draw about, when we have to set them down.

Daniel's voice fills my head. *Roz, there are clearly moments, ideas, concepts, memories in your head that are dying to be drawn. And you'll understand them differently once you do.*

"This, I think, is the reason I've been so pulled toward drawing," I tell them. "I needed to get this idea down. Us. Together. Old. I think I needed to see it to believe it, you know?"

Vin wipes his eyes on his sleeve. "I know exactly what you mean. It's the same reason I've told the story of *that* night"—he points to his framed photo, of the night we met, on the wall—"a few different times at Sooth," Vin says in a gruff voice. "To explain how I feel about you, Roz. But also because I go back to that night. Over and over. I need to tell it to believe it. That we were ever that young. That we were—"

"Safe," I supply, and point at the title of my drawing, written in the corner. "It's the same thing I write whenever I draw you. Like I can protect you, by enshrining the moment or something."

"The end is the beginning," Raff whispers, and puts his head on Vin's shoulder. "That was the name of one of Vin's stories about the night you two met. The end is the beginning. That night was the last time you two were ever not together. That part of your life ended. And the rest began."

And the accident, that was an ending. A very clear ending.

But right now, in this moment, when Vin gets his tools out from the closet and puts up the framed drawing next to the framed photo on the living room wall, it also feels like it was a beginning.

*What if we never get over it?* I'd asked Vin.

And I think . . . I think the answer is in that drawing and in that photo. Maybe we never really get over *anything*. It just becomes . . . a part of your drawing, a part of your story. You adapt, you grow, you think about it less. You form new habits. You meet new people. But getting over it? Making it like it didn't even happen? I don't know. If you want it like it never happened . . . that's just denial, right? We have to learn how to accept it. It happened. It's real. We're here on the other side. We're smiling from the other side. Crying and wailing from the other side. Yes, cooking from the other side. Holding each other and feeling perfectly fine on an awful lot of days.

Later, when Raff goes home, Vin and I lie on the couch and look at the art on the wall.

"It's so cool, baby," he says. "That you're learning how to draw."

"I feel like what I'm doing is learning how to *see*."

"Me too," he agrees. "Storytelling, it's like I'm learning how to think."

And I pull him down, over the top of me. He knows better now than to give me his weight. So he just cages me in with his elbows. We become our perfect unit. Our two becomes one. Me and Vin against the world.

But no, that's not right.

It's me and Vin, a *part* of the world.

Me and Vin, thank God, here, alive, together, injured and healing.

You can't delete a chapter and get the same ending. And I no longer want to try. I want all of it. Every tangle. I'll draw right off the edge of the page.

Him and me, we're shooting for infinity.

# Acknowledgments

*When I look* at the cover of this book, I feel the warm glow emanating from inside their home. And that, more than anything, is how I wanted this book to feel. Like a safe and warm room for a reader to spend some time while we talk about marriage longevity and how we navigate life's inevitable bouquet of wounds and bandages. Which, when I think about it, falls squarely in the domain of something good friends might do with one another.

So, reader, I thank you for spending time with me as a friend. Not only do you make it possible for me to have a job *at all*, you are, most importantly, the person on the other end of the tin can telephone line. Writing a book can feel like screaming into the void. But I am NOT screaming into the void. I'm writing a very long letter to you! I thought of you quite a bit while writing this book. This book is about mental health and trauma and how to stay light in a heavy world. And more than anything, I wanted all the words I wrote to add to your lightness, not your heaviness. You have given me the gift of your time, your thoughts, your eyeballs (or ear-balls, if you're listening to this), and I hope I have given you the gift of lightening your load, whatever load that may be.

I also want to specifically thank Stephanie Jedlicka, who has been a constant source of support and excitement for me over the years. And thank you to @rknuckles, who named Puma Thurman. As Vin would say, good stuff.

I can't really explain how hard my agent, Tara Gelsomino, works, because frankly, she does her job so well I don't even know the half of it. She protects me, advocates for me, guides me, and cheers me on. Long story short, if I didn't have her, I'd be selling my books out of a suitcase in a back alley and none of you would ever have gotten to hear about Roz and Vin banging (twice!) at his mother's house.

Noah Arhm Choi, goodness gracious, what would I do without you? This is not the place to explain what it's meant to become family over all these years, but if it were, I'd tell you that you are irreplaceable and inimitable and I'm so grateful to be able to have you on speed dial. Most relevantly though, Noah is incredibly good at their job, and I have been so lucky to work with them as an authenticity reader. Their skill set is the product of decades of study, thought work, grinding, hustling, and most importantly, a wide-open heart and mind (and an extremely sharp intellect). Thank you, Noah.

Emma Caruso is somewhere, right this second, wearing about ninety different hats and having the audacity to simply call herself an editor. Quick explainer: Editing a book (as well as she does) turns you into a therapist, an interpreter, a dreamer, a problem solver, a cheerleader, a coach, a project manager, a diplomat, a politician, and it helps if you have flawless common sense and a good eye for color. Also you need to be able to spin a hundred plates on very long sticks. Needless to say (but I'm going to say it anyhow), without Emma, what you've just read would not have qualified as a book, it would have been a pulsing mass of exposed psyche and thoughts only five-sixths of the way finished. Let's *all* thank Emma for making this book a book.

Talia Cieslinski . . . How do I say this lightly? I can't, so I'll just say it: Talia edited this manuscript three different times.

Every time we thought we were almost done, I decided to rip the manuscript into five sad little pieces and then stitch it all back together and then hand the mess back to Talia. Talia could have told me to go jump in a lake. She could have sent me a thumbs-down emoji the size of the Empire State Building. Instead, Talia edited this manuscript, top to bottom, three different times and then bought me a cup of coffee and told me how excited she was about the changes. Can you *imagine*? When I was a runaway horse, Talia guided me back to the barn and made it seem like my idea. From the bottom of my heart, thank you, Talia.

To Whitney Frick, who has expansive vision and elaborate dreams for the future of every book she publishes (and still manages to care deeply about all the minute details as well), thank you. Thank you so much to Brianna Kusilek, Madison Dettlinger, Debbie Aroff, Avideh Bashirrad, Cindy Berman, and the entire team at Dial, who do their jobs with ruthless efficiency and wildly good cheer and somehow find the time to drop notes of encouragement to their impressionable and sensitive authors.

Thank you to Sarah Kaye, who made me so excited to do the hardest part of all, actually putting my book into the world where people can read it.

To Fernanda Brigneti, you do literally everything I'm too distracted, scared, overwhelmed, or confused to manage on my own. Seriously, Fernanda takes care of everything, what would I do without Fernanda? Thank you, Fernanda!

Thank you to Camille Kellogg and Hannah Sloane for the support and friendship and for being there from the very beginning. How wonderful to be on the journey with you.

Tarah DeWitt and Ali Rosen and BK Borison, thank you for mirroring my experiences back to me with unique and illustrative flair. Thank you for the support from every angle, the frank perspectives, and most of all, for reading my dang books. Wow. How could I have gotten this lucky?

To Stephen Gaffney, Elise Engler, Janette Beckman, I hope you see your fingerprints all over this book, because the way you've taught me to see the world (and draw it) quite literally changed the course of my life.

To Karin Arizala, Jeanne Kabenji, and Vivien Schapera, I cannot ever quantify how much you've all helped me on my journey, because your positive impacts continue to snowball. Each of you has helped me to grab hold of, digest, and ultimately alchemize the experiences that have been the most unwieldy and difficult in my life. You have given me the framework to be able to treat myself with grace.

To Kathy and Josh, we wouldn't have made it through the last few years without your constant care and guidance and your guest bedroom. I love you. Thank you.

For my Sands fam and my Ambrosino fam, thank you so much for caring and cheering and checking in and audio recording NPR segments that talk about my books. You are my most important people.

Kate, you flew halfway around the world just to drag me outside. You fed me pastries and took half-day-long walks and never once felt like I'd lost something integral to who I really am. You saw the me hiding inside of me. How do I repay something like that? I guess I'll just have to keep trying until we're old and gray.

To Mom and Dad, you've helped me make sense of the senseless, and don't care if I'm talking nonsense. Reader, if you see glimpses of unconditional love, if you see the characters love themselves in spite of their flaws, if you see people deciding to do the hard work of living their everyday lives after unimaginable tragedies and accidents and unfairness, that's because my mom and dad taught (and are still teaching) me how to do that.

To Frank and Sonny, you two are the whole point. My constant companions, my living, breathing, sticky, quietly whispering, gently tugging at my sweater while I type this companions. I am the person I am because I get the honor of raising you. Let's do it all again in the next life, every single second. I love you infinity.

To Jon. Oh, Jon. My life raft *and* my shore. This book has a pulse because of you. When I was drawing to understand myself, because it was the only thing I could bear to do, you gently brought me back to writing. Writing (my first language, our common language) has repeatedly saved my life, and without you, I might have forgotten that. I love you. Let's go to the future together.

# Behind the Book
## ON DRAWING

*The book is wonderful, but my biggest question is why would the main character be led toward drawing?*

This was the big note from my editor after reading the first draft of *No Matter What*. A novel about a woman who turns to drawing to help herself parse out troubles in her marriage and, ultimately, deal with a recent trauma.

Honestly, I was a little flabbergasted. *Why drawing?* The whole book was the answer to *why*. But then, as I read through that first draft again, I realized, as I always do, that Emma was right, and though I'd answered over and over how drawing is *valuable*, I had not thought to answer the question of why *drawing*. Drawing over knitting. Or dancing. Or running marathons.

I, I, I who had been called, called, called to drawing, drawing, drawing.

Let's start here: I've never had good hand-eye coordination, or good handwriting, or good color sense. (Once when expressing disappointment that the Empire State Building wasn't lit up with a "real" color tonight, my sister—an interior designer—asked me what color I thought the lights *were*. I don't know... building color? I answered. She pertly informed me they were, in fact, champagne. Which is, apparently, a real color.) All this to say, I have always been deeply moved by fine art but never thought it a real possibility that I could create it.

And then... life.

I moved my family to Buenos Aires for a few months.

Orange vermouth, chilled, in a juice glass while I cooked. Dinners were rice dishes with onions and beans and tomatoes purchased an hour earlier from the open-air market down the block. Fresh pink shrimp from the Italian-owned pescadería. The owner loved my children's names: Frank and Sonny. Cooking with the radio playing and our twelve-foot windows open on cast-iron hinges. The sky that distinct and unnameable (for me) color between blue and pink.

Does it sound lovely? It was. Often.

But I should mention that I was tender as overripe fruit, racked with sharp tears at the turn of any phrase. My phone would ring with a message from a well-meaning loved one and I'd get nauseated and tingly.

Grief, it was. Fresh grief, of course.

Fresh grief in a new country. Less than a month after losing one of my best, dearest, greatest friends of my lifetime. There are no words. There are no words.

I fed my children. I bathed their warm bodies in warm water in a clawfoot tub. I stared hollowly at my husband's sleeping profile in the blue hours of the night. I jumped at unexpected shadows in the unfamiliar apartment, certain I'd see my friend's silhouette.

Our bed, rented temporarily from the actual residents of the apartment, had a thin velvet coverlet over crisp white sheets. In a different dimension, one with a more poetic scientific framework, the solid form of water would not be ice, it would be that bluebell velvet blanket. It rippled over any form. Never smooth, but who would choose "smooth" over a Monet pond? I'd sit upright in the nascent gray of yet another morning, and I'd draw the ripples of the blanket on a five-by-seven drawing pad with a poorly sharpened pencil.

And then I'd move my feet, see new patterns, and I'd draw

those. I became very compelled to understand the drape and fold of textiles. The tensile hang, for example, of the thick curtains, somehow both stubborn and graceful. The pouchy, sullen couch pillows (feather, ancient) after my children had dive-bombed them.

I drew the clothes drying on the racks, the dish towel crumpled and dejected where it found itself on the tile floor.

Over and over I turned to drawing and found blank calm for the space of a few breaths. I found that ideas (*no words, no words, no words*) could still travel the etheric tube from my brain to my hand, even when badly thought and badly drawn. Poorly formed on both ends, but an idea realized, nonetheless.

But I'm painting a misleading timeline here. I didn't actually pick up drawing in Buenos Aires while grieving. I first picked up drawing as a hobby, years before, in early motherhood.

I, trapped underneath my nursing child, verklempt with love and boredom, tried very hard to capture the surface tension of his perfection with my phone camera. It won't surprise you that the photos were uninteresting and didn't, in fact, capture his essence. Also . . . all of the mystical and (frankly) mind-blowing poetry of what it means to feed your child *of yourself* was always reduced down—in these blurry and overclose images—to just boob-in-mouth.

I had an inkling there was more. One day, on a whim, I made sure I had my journal at hand and I gave it a shot. The closed lines of his eyes were two lumpy crescent moons, meaningful only in their relationship to each other, not because I'd gotten the shape right. His nose was a mushroom. His mouth, and the part of me his mouth touched, was expressed with just one squiggled line. In this drawing, his form is a part of me, and my form is a part of him.

Well, I was hooked. I didn't want the *Reader's Digest* version (the bad photo), I wanted the full Jane Eyre. I started drawing a lot. My drawings lacked technical skill and knowledge. I was frustrated. So, I took online classes. I took in-person classes. I drew flowers at the Botanic Garden and did poor watercolors of wine bottles. I felt certain that by excellenting my technical skills, I'd find enlightenment.

But the truth is (as with the drawing of my kid nursing), most of my best drawings are my worst drawings. Scribbles with one hand and whatever pen I could reach at the time. The fastest approximation I could manage of whatever beloved moment I happened to be witnessing.

I'd often title the drawings. *Frank body-slams Sonny.* Or *Sonny shouts to Daddy out the window.*

I can't stress enough my lack of technical skill and knowledge. But I once had a teacher tell me that no drawing is "bad," instead they are only ever "awkward" or "cute."

Well, sure!

I have reams of awkward and cute drawings in notebooks on my shelf. In a bout of determination to build art school from nothing, I enlisted my husband to pose for a series of nudes for me. The drawings are energetic, occasionally hilarious, and probably say more about the Knicks (which he was watching while posing) than they do about my husband. (In case this sounds familiar to anyone, this series of drawings and the conversations with my husband leading up to these drawings inspired the novel that precedes this essay.)

My oldest got the stomach flu and I have the drawing to prove it. Here he is, flat as a pancake, eyes glazed, practically swimming off the couch.

And then there's my youngest, jaunty chin and tense fingers askance as he takes trembling and tentative steps.

There's my dad, asleep in a lawn chair, more beard than grandfather.

There's my nephew being eaten by the couch, his knees at ear level and his face replaced by a cellphone.

There's my curly white poodle, somehow wonderfully described by scratchy black graphite.

Here's one of me. In the mirror after losing my temper at my housemates (aka, the family of my blood, bone, and heart). In this drawing I'm too wide and too sullen. My remorse is not palpable except for in the very fact of the drawing itself. I've chosen to immortalize one of my worst moments. Eternal punishment for Mom.

I attempted many times to draw and paint the sky before realizing I could just draw the arced V of a bird in flight and then the entire blank page becomes the sky.

Okay, now the timeline has righted itself and I can take us back to Buenos Aires. I already had an established drawing practice, but it had taken on a layered (and obscured) meaning while I grieved in a foreign country. I wondered if this repetitive drawing of textiles was good for me. I mean, what was it? Just someplace for my mind to rest? An opportunity to understand the world through the careful grouping of observable patterns?

Over the course of five days, from a chair on our apartment's roof, I drew our small rooftop garden, attempting to faithfully capture—literally—every single leaf or petal I could see. It was obsessive, but I convinced myself I was "doing art." However, the obsession grew. When I started counting leaves, something sort of snapped within me. This wasn't right.

I was imitating drawing, producing drawings, yes. Perhaps I was improving my technical skill, increasing my knowledge of form and shape, sure. But what I was doing lacked something integral. Whatever I had discovered when I drew the single line of my baby's mouth and my breast (when I blurred the reality, thus *capturing* the reality) was completely void in the persnickety drawings I was doing now.

Fortuitously, my husband—desperate to give me oxygen—had just given me a book on Ruth Asawa and her drawing process. I turned gratefully toward reading. Which is the third corner of that triangle labeled *How I Make Sense of the World*. The other two corners are (hopefully obviously) drawing and the thing I'm doing right this very second . . . writing. Anyways, reading and Ruth Asawa.

Though observational drawing was a big part of her practice, she also drew a great deal from her imagination. Her hand/eye was remarkable. Her handle on color was modern and wieldy. She was able to produce exacting patterns freehand. She could draw perfect circles. Part of the secret, she revealed, was not to look at the point where your pen touched the paper but rather just ahead, at where your pen was about to be. To look at what you were about to draw. She was looking ahead on the page, bringing the end of her pencil to meet the eye.

Very new for me!

Drawing has always followed this pattern for me: Eyes (see Frank's socks on his sleeping feet), Brain (turns sock shapes into drawable sock shapes), Hand (puts some shapes on the page, oh no, they don't look like socks, try again, okay, that's better).

But! This new (to me) sort of drawing doesn't go Eyes→Brain→Hand.

It goes Brain→Eyes→Hand.

An entirely new order of operations.

This might not seem like a big deal, but picture relearning how to do *anything* under a new order of operations. I invite you, for instance, to imagine putting on your socks before you put on your underwear.

Drawing from my imagination felt new and, honestly, terrifying. What if it turned out there was nothing in my imagination to draw? Or what if there was great stuff in there, but without a literal representation in front of me, I would get confused and attach elbows to asses (et cetera). It all pretty much felt like, *Oh good, a new avenue for discovering my own inadequacy when it comes to drawing.*

But still, the next morning I went to an Argentinian café filled with antique clocks. It was cavernous and completely empty except for me and the barista who'd been incredibly patient with my bad (awkward, cute) Spanish. I pulled out my notepad. Drawing from imagination . . . does that mean, like, I should draw a unicorn?

Terror.

But then an image swam up. A jacaranda tree fallen ninety degrees onto a rusty old VW. Not from my "imagination" exactly. Because it was something I'd just walked past not ten minutes before on my way to the café.

Ohhhhh. Of course. Rather than "imagination," I should think of this as drawing from my mind's eye. Well, I could do that! That's where I write from! I have lots of keys on a ring in my back pocket and I know exactly which ones (brass and substantial) open the door to my mind's eye.

And so, I drew a miniature. The tree in sure lines, my eyes painting a path a millimeter in front of the tip of my pen. The car was squashed and angular beneath the biologically sweeping lines of the tree. I was surprised when my hand swiveled, tried for the texture of the bark without my permission. What came up was practiced and familiar. These lines were the same shorthand I'd been using to obsessively describe the rippled, velvet bedspread.

*Oh, so all of this has been going somewhere,* I thought. And so it was.

Later that night, I put my kids to bed and *then* drew a picture of them in the bath (now drained and dry and silent).

Drawn from above, their shoulders became two pairs of parentheses around their hearts. Their legs were spread and stable, like roots from a trunk.

I loved these new drawings, this new style. I tried my hand at every (any) thing I could think to draw. Just the light off the river but no river itself. The infinity tiles of a garden path. Lovers sharing a chicken dinner.

And then I flew home (across the world) for his funeral.

I've done a disservice if, for even a moment, while reading this essay, you've forgotten about my friend who died. Because I sure hadn't. The drawing of the tree and the car, the drawing of my children in the bath, the chicken dinner, the light on the river, well, there I am, pen on paper and breathing through broken glass. Clouds of pain and shock, lost in circuitous thoughts that (still) don't make sense. An unendurable reality.

By moving briefly to Buenos Aires, I had ensured that I'd skip springtime in New York and instead have three autumns in one year.

It fit, as endings go.

He had died in Japan just two weeks before my (previously scheduled) sabbatical. It took time to plan his funeral in the States. There was no choice but to fly to Argentina with my family, leave them in another hemisphere, and return home on my own for the funeral.

Anyone who's grieved knows that things happen while you're grieving that don't make sense and you just accept them. In the Houston airport, on a layover between Argentina and Michigan, I ordered a veggie burger at TGI Fridays and was instead served a crispy BLT. I, decades into vegetarianism, just ate the damn thing. Me folding my morals and eating bacon for him would have put a maniacally joyful glint in my friend's eye. He would have been heady with certain power and laughed, sinister and charming and annoying. (And then, the joke safely made, he would have leaned forward precipitously, *You don't have to eat that, just order something else.*) In the year since, I've had three BLTs, because . . . because I miss him. Because part of me will always be lost without him. Because a BLT on a plate, in front of me at a restaurant, even the ones that I actually order, will always feel like an inside joke between me and him that I still get to experience in real time, and not just in my memory.

I'll skip any description of the funeral. I'm back on the plane now, this time out of Houston and back toward Argentina. Window seat. My nice drawing utensils are at the bottom of my purse and I don't care to dig for them. So instead, I use the readily available pack of markers I keep on hand for my kids, so they have something to do while we wait for food at restaurants.

The sun is rising over the Amazon. I do an eyes-on-the-paper oval, careful to emulate the shape of the plane window. And then I carefully select my colors. And I do an eyes-on-the-sunrise capture of that mountainous cloud, the blue fire of impending morning. I am very small, flying over the earth. I'm probably not supposed to be here, I assume. Seeing the clouds from above. This is surely a privilege reserved for those who have ascended on from their earthly confines.

Beliefs about the afterlife aside, I feel extremely close to my friend in that moment. Physically close, I mean. He's seeing that cloud too (burning peach on the bottom, crowned in glassy black and a few remaining stars), I'm sure of it.

But look, all I have are markers. Unmixable and I don't know enough about building color to have mixed them anyhow. So the colors are what they are. They'll never be the sunrise that he and I (maybe) watched together, me through the plane window, him in blazing person, freed from body, all him, pure concentrate, no water, nothing mixed or diluted.

Riding on a cloud? Sure. Maybe he was riding on a cloud. He died on a mountain, so okay, he probably was riding on that cloud, free of fear.

I called it our goodbye, but these days he almost certainly knows a lot of things I don't, so he should probably have been the one to name that moment, not me.

The drawing I did on that plane *burns*.

It hurts to look at it.

Even right now, this second, I can feel it pressed between other drawings on the shelf behind me.

The great artists, they understood the power of drawing.

Dangerously distilled, the idea is this: We draw because we want to understand.

"Drawing is the clarification of thought," said Matisse. And then later on, "In short, I wanted to understand myself."

Ouch.

("I'm drawing textiles in order to understand textiles." *Sure*, okay.)

Bridget Riley says, "In earlier times, I used to draw the thing seen; now I see the thing drawn."

She's not saying that the product is more important than the process. I think she's saying that the product (the drawing) is never how we planned it to be. It is always altered from what we had envisioned in our mind's eye. It always ends up being uniquely itself. And in that journey from brain to eye to hand, a cosmic and unplanned alteration is added, something that we can only accept as a gift, and, upon seeing it on the page, learn from it.

There is always something to be learned from a drawing.

And home from Argentina (several months after the airplane sunrise), I sat on Coney Island Beach, drawing my son asleep under a towel, and I finally realized what my drawings had been trying so hard to teach me.

First, I'll explain the drawing. Only his face and gently tousling curls are visible against the towel. Everything else is safely tucked in under green and white stripes.

The thing about drawing a form underneath a textile is that you have to have a handle on the form *itself*, minus the textile. Anyone who is seeing lumps under a towel and then just trying to approximate the lumps in relationship to other lumps is going to get a (shocker!) lumpy and illegible drawing. So, perhaps it's obvious, but if you can't draw my son's shoulder, you can't draw my son's shoulder under a towel on the beach at Coney Island.

And so, in my mind's eye (oh, the good old mind's eye, such a steadfast companion through it all), I removed the towel, and then drew my son as I knew him to be. On his belly, one set of toes curled against his other set of toes, shoulder-shoulder, spine in a dip. His butt, high and diapered. Next came some lavishly painstaking and indulgent work with his face. Eyelashes and a half-shadowed nose, whorls of his ear and whirls of his hair, a squinched little tortellini of a mouth—all very romantic. Any parent gazing at their sleeping child understands.

Then. THEN. Then for the towel.

See . . . drawn with the towel removed, my poor kid was much too exposed on the beach (on the page). The UV index was 8, you know! And so I attempted to transcribe reality by drawing in the towel. Intuitive as it was physical, I followed the landmarks of his body that I'd already drawn in. I split my eye's time between the observed (Sonny) and the imagined (my paper). And as I drew the towel, I realized I was protecting him (Sonny on the paper) from the elements. The clearer and more rich the details of the towel became, the safer the baby on the page became. My son, literally in front of me, safe and sound and snoozing, slowly materialized *literarily* before me, locked into a legally binding drawing: safe and sound and snoozing.

In the hours after his death, my friend was laid out, in his living room, in Japan. He was in Smartwool socks, a Patagonia zip-up, and a mustard-yellow beanie. There was a blanket laid over him, chest to ankles, his arms on top of the blanket, hands resting at his sides. There were three separate ceremonies to lay him to rest. This was the first. He was physically there. I was not.

I watched through a livestream. The image was light-received by a phone's camera, then it was bouncing from satellite to satellite (looking down at clouds from above), to my computer through pixels, translating him back into light, which hit my eyes, which talked to my brain, where the image now lives. In my memory. Or, as I've been calling it in this essay, my mind's eye.

He looked comfortable.

There is no understanding that. There is no understanding a shocking and unexpected death. There is no understanding an accident. Or probably even joy, for that matter, which is what I had spent an accumulation of hours into days and weeks *hoping* (what a feeble word in this context) he'd been feeling in the moments before his death.

I saw without understanding. My friend, under a blanket. Simplified down now: he was form under textile.

It probably sounds ridiculous to you, bolstered by the framework of this essay, that in the wake of his death, when I was obsessively drawing blankets, I did not understand what I was drawing when I was drawing. That I honestly thought I was just drawing dishrags and bedsheets.

It might even seem like this image of him had been forgotten by me, only to resurface as I sat on the beach. Please believe me that this image, serrated, had been gouging me at dinnertimes. Jolting me out of half-sleep. Folding me over myself in public in a new and foreign country. And then, back home, folding me over myself in public in a new and foreign world.

How could I ever make it seem true to you, reader, that the image of him under that blanket is equal parts torturous and comforting? Torturous because it turns out his mortal form was the least important part of him, and it was all we had left. All we could hold on to for a few short days. Comforting because someone who loved him tucked him under that blanket. I've tried to think of a follow-up sentence here that would emphasize the gravity of that last statement, but there is none, so I'll just repeat it. Someone who loved him tucked him under that blanket.

Honestly, that's the third time I've mentioned that idea in just these few pages: There are no words. *There are no words.*

I wrote an entire novel about a woman who turns to drawing because there are no words.

This is a very difficult idea for me! I'm a writer. Writing (remember that aforementioned triangle?) is the cornerstone of how I understand my experiences here on this blue-green marble. But when I'm writing, I'm working from the outside in to get at that understanding. I take an experience and I ask, What is this *similar to*? And then, would you look at that, there's the metaphor I was looking for!

But drawing . . . drawing is that process in reverse. Every drawing is already a literal metaphor. Every drawing is already a thing represented as something else (e.g., That's not an apple, that's a drawing of an apple). So, when I'm drawing, what I'm doing is *first* constructing the metaphor, and then later—sometimes much later—upon introspection, upon inspection, upon understanding . . . I'm presented with a gift I'd wrapped without knowing what was inside. What does this drawing mean? Why have I been drawing my loved ones safe and sound under blankets? I look at my drawings and see *here, here's the thing I desperately want to understand about myself, about the world, about a precious memory that must, must, must live.*

So . . . why drawing? Why drawing over knitting or running a marathon? For me, drawing comes from the same place within me that kicking to the surface of the water comes from. I draw to get that precious gasp of air, to endure. I draw in a, yes, futile attempt to understand what has happened and what will be.

Memories, especially those seen through a cloud of pain, can be blurred or smeared, or the light within them degrades so that we can barely make out the landscape. Drawings, bless them, are painfully clear.

(For the record, I drafted *No Matter What* three more times after receiving the feedback mentioned at the beginning of this essay. The end result is something I'm extremely proud of. It is the polar opposite of *why drawing?* Now, the revelations these characters endure could *only* come from drawing.)

The world is terrifying and enormous and dangerous. (As my son slept, the ocean was twenty feet at our backs, restless and demanding and sipping itself closer to his toes with every passing second.) But! Good news! There is a place where the people I love are completely, entirely, inarguably safe. Bad news! That place doesn't exist in the you-can-go-there sense. Because that place is my mind's eye.

I draw my son on the beach and I, the one who loves him the most, tuck him in, forever, on that page. I draw that cloud through a plane window and my friend's likeness (translated through my injured heart) is an irreverent sunrise, burning with stars and incandescent calm. The moment is transcribed onto the page, never to be lost or altered by memory. I close my drawing pad and he is safe by my hands, remembered and unwaveringly loved. I've transcended technical skill. I, most humbly, will not be stymied by a lack of practical knowledge. I've found what I lost on that rooftop in Buenos Aires, counting leaves. It's understanding. As brief and sharp as it may be.

I'll have to search for it again, and soon, I know I will.

I'll reach for it again. I'll draw for it again.

Because, after all, he's just on the other side.

## Discover more charming rom-coms from Cara Bastone!

Available now!

**HEADLINE ETERNAL**

# Don't miss Cara Bastone's Love Lines series!

Available now!

## RAISING READERS
Books Build Bright Futures

Dear Reader,

We'd love your attention for one more page to tell you about the crisis in children's reading, and what we can all do.

Studies have shown that reading for fun is the **single biggest predictor of a child's future life chances** – more than family circumstance, parents' educational background or income. It improves academic results, mental health, wealth, communication skills, ambition and happiness.[1]

The number of children reading for fun is in rapid decline. Young people have a lot of competition for their time. In 2024, 1 in 10 children and young people in the UK aged 5 to 18 did not own a single book at home.[2]

Hachette works extensively with schools, libraries and literacy charities, but here are some ways we can all raise more readers:

- Reading to children for just 10 minutes a day makes a difference
- Don't give up if children aren't regular readers – there will be books for them!
- Visit bookshops and libraries to get recommendations
- Encourage them to listen to audiobooks
- Support school libraries
- Give books as gifts

There's a lot more information about how to encourage children to read on our website: **www.RaisingReaders.co.uk**

Thank you for reading.

hachette UK

---

[1] OECD, '21st-Century Readers: Developing Literacy Skills in a Digital World', 2021, https://www.oecd.org/en/publications/21st-century-readers_a83d84cb-en.html

[2] National Literacy Trust, 'Book Ownership in 2024', November 2024, https://literacytrust.org.uk/research-services/research-reports/book-ownership-in-2024

# FIND YOUR HEART'S DESIRE...

VISIT OUR WEBSITE: www.headlineeternal.com
FIND US ON FACEBOOK: facebook.com/eternalromance
CONNECT WITH US ON X: @eternal_books
FOLLOW US ON INSTAGRAM: @headlineeternal
EMAIL US: eternalromance@headline.co.uk